PENGUIN

KT-177-410

PERSUASION

with

A MEMOIR OF JANE AUSTEN

D. W. Harding is Emeritus Professor of Psychology in the University of London, having held the Chair of Psychology at Bedford College from 1945 to 1968. He was editor of the *British Journal of Psychology* from 1948 to 1954 and has written and edited several books, chiefly on the subject of psychology.

JANE AUSTEN
PERSUASION

WITH
A MEMOIR OF JANE AUSTEN
BY J. E. AUSTEN-LEIGH

EDITED
WITH AN INTRODUCTION BY
D. W. HARDING

PENGUIN BOOKS

Penguin Books Ltd, Harmondsworth, Middlesex, England
Penguin Books, 625 Madison Avenue, New York, New York 10022, U.S.A.
Penguin Books Australia Ltd, Ringwood, Victoria, Australia
Penguin Books Canada Ltd, 2801 John Street, Markham, Ontario, Canada L3R 1B4
Penguin Books (N.Z.) Ltd, 182–190 Wairau Road, Auckland 10, New Zealand

—

Persuasion first published 1818
A Memoir of Jane Austen first published 1870
Published in one volume in Penguin Books 1965
Reprinted 1968, 1970, 1971 (twice), 1972, 1973, 1974 (twice), 1975 (twice), 1976,
1977, 1978 (three times)

—

Introduction and notes copyright © D. W. Harding, 1965
All rights reserved

—

Made and printed in Great Britain
by Hazell Watson & Viney Ltd,
Aylesbury, Bucks
Set in Linotype Juliana

CONTENTS

INTRODUCTION

CHAWTON COTTAGE is one of the few places of literary
pilgrimage that have relevance to an appreciation of the writer
who lived there. At some little distance from the great house of
the rich brother who provided it, respectable but rather cramped,
with the small living room in which Jane Austen wrote – a room
shared by her sister Cassandra and her ailing mother and used
besides for receiving callers – the house speaks of the close pressure
of a social milieu, and heightens our wonder at the work that
emerged from it. The older idea that her novels simply offered
amusing entertainment for people like those she lived amongst
(and their successors down to our own time) has given way to the
recognition in her work of a much stronger dislike of the society
in which she seemed comfortably embedded, a dislike often implicit, often conveyed in passing and easily ignored, occasionally
intense and bitter. In 1940 I published an essay called 'Regulated
Hatred: an aspect of Jane Austen'; in 1964 a psychologist col-
league who had never heard of that essay mentioned that she had
recently tried in vain to recover the pleasure she took in the
novels as a girl. 'They used to seem so light and amusing, but
they're not like that at all. You know – she *hated* people.' Of
course this is too extreme. The urbanity, the charm, the wit and
lightness of touch, the good humour, are there as they always
were, but the other aspect which readers nowadays notice means
that for full enjoyment we have to appreciate a more complex
flavour.

The situation of being a poor relation was one that Jane Austen
could share with her sister and their widowed mother. The
situation of being the most brilliant, the most sensitive and penetrating member of her family, while she filled the roles of affectionate spinster aunt and of dutiful daughter to a hypochondriac
mother, was a situation she could share with no one. It is not
surprising, therefore, that variants of the Cinderella story, as well
as the psychologically allied story of the foundling princess,

7

should be prominent among the basic themes of her novels.

Anne Elliot, the heroine of *Persuasion*, her last novel, is the most mature and profound of Cinderellas. Earlier, in *Mansfield Park*, she had tried an out-and-out foundling princess and Cinderella in Fanny Price – all moral perfection, thoroughly oppressed, rather ailing, priggish, but finally vindicated and rewarded with the hero – and few people can stomach her. The theme is inevitably difficult to handle. For one thing the fantasy of being mysteriously superior to one's parentage is rather common ('I refused to believe', remarks T. S. Eliot's Lady Elizabeth, 'that my father could have been an ordinary earl! And I couldn't believe that my mother *was* my mother') and commonly unjustified. And the crushed dejection (masking resentment) of the self-cast Cinderellas of real life always provokes a sneaking sympathy for the ugly sisters. The novelist's difficulty with this theme is to secure a lively enough interest in the heroine during the early stages, when the reality of her dejection has to be enforced, and to retain interest and sympathy during the necessarily long period before the *bouleversement*. Fairy tale and pantomime can resort to caricaturing the heroine's oppressors. The serious novelist whose heroine must be unappreciated and neglected by a credible social world faces a harder problem.

It is solved in *Persuasion* partly by the dexterity of a practised writer, and partly through more mature understanding of the basic situation and the forms it may take. The vanity and shallow self-importance of Sir Walter Elliot and his eldest daughter, their heartless worldliness, accompanied by ill-judgement even in worldly things, are handled scathingly but with only a little caricature. The situation used to exemplify the clash between their values and Anne's – the problem of extravagance, debt and retrenchment – is more convincing to modern minds than the episode of the private theatricals in *Mansfield Park*. And the scales that were weighted too heavily against Fanny are here kept nearer level by the presence of Lady Russell, the influential friend, who not only sees Anne's worth (as Edmund did Fanny's) but is in many ways allied with her against the family and serves by her comments to indicate that people of good sense think as Anne does. Ill-health too is dealt with differently. Fanny's debility was

presented almost as morally superior to the rude health of her
companions. In *Persuasion*, which Jane Austen wrote when she
was dying of a malady that gradually sapped her strength (resting
on an arrangement of three chairs while her mother monopolized
the sofa in the living room), it is the heroine's patience that has
to be mustered to cope with the complaining hypochondria of her
younger sister. Poor health is now as little a recommendation as it
was in Miss De Bourgh in *Pride and Prejudice*. ('She looks sickly
and cross – Yes, she will do for him very well.')

Of even greater importance than these changes of treatment
is a more mature interpretation of the theme, one no longer
presenting the heroine as a passive sufferer of entirely unmerited
wrongs. Anne has brought her chief misfortune on herself
through a mistaken decision – to break her engagement with
Wentworth – to which she was persuaded by Lady Russell. Her
lapse from her own standard, in letting worldly prudence out-
weigh love and true esteem for personal qualities, is the error
which has also to be excused in her mother, who in marrying Sir
Walter was too much influenced by 'his good looks and his rank'.
We start then with a much more mature Cinderella, more
seriously tragic herself in having thrown away her own happiness,
more complex in her relation to the loved mother, who not only
made the same sort of mistake herself but now, brought back to
life in Lady Russell, shares the heroine's responsibility for her
disaster. Lady Russell is explicitly presented as the equivalent of a
greatly loved mother, more nearly ideal than any other living
mother that Jane Austen gives a heroine. In fairy tales the
baffling intermingling of the hateful and lovable attributes of all
mothers is simplified into a dichotomy between the ideal mother
– entirely lovable, dead and beyond the test of mature observation
– and the stepmother, living, entirely detestable and doing her
worst for the child. In the maturity of *Persuasion* Jane Austen
puts her heroine into relation with a lovable but not perfect
mother who, in doing her mistaken best for the girl, has caused
what seems an irremediable misfortune.

It is Wentworth's hurt feelings and his belief that Anne was
over-yielding in giving him up that create the barrier between
them when he comes back prosperous, seeking a wife and

attracted by the amiable, commonplace Musgrove girls. It is again
Lady Russell, perceptive of Anne's worth though not of his, who
provides a choric comment establishing the values. When Anne
tells her about the apparent attachment between him and Louisa,
'Lady Russell had only to listen composedly, and wish them
happy; but internally her heart revelled in angry pleasure, in
pleased contempt, that the man who at twenty-three had seemed
to understand somewhat of the value of an Anne Elliot, should,
eight years afterwards, be charmed by a Louisa Musgrove.'

In fact, by the time this comment is made, the emotional
barriers Wentworth had erected against Anne have been broken
down in a graded sequence of incidents, mingling observation and
action on his part, which Jane Austen manages with supremely
delicate skill: at first, his comment on Anne's altered looks, 'his
cold politeness, his ceremonious grace'; then his inquiry of the
others whether she never danced (while she is playing for them to
dance); later, his quite unceremoniously kind and understanding
act in relieving her of the troublesome child, 'his degree of feeling
and curiosity about her' when he is told of her having refused a
more recent proposal of marriage, his realizing her tiredness and
insisting on her going home in Admiral Croft's chaise ('a remainder of former sentiment,' Anne thinks, 'an impulse of pure,
though unacknowledged friendship'); finally, his noticing the
glance of admiration she receives from Mr Walter Elliot at Lyme,
followed quickly by the climax of the accident on the Cobb and
the instant partnership between him and Anne as the competent
and responsible people keeping their heads in a horrifying situation. From this point onward the tables are turned; Captain
Wentworth, in the full return of his early love, has to face the
anxieties of his apparent commitment to Louisa and his jealousy
at Mr Walter Elliot's wooing of Anne. Although suspense and
strong emotion are maintained to the last pages, the visit to Lyme
is the turning point at which the earlier sadness – wasted opportunity, regret, misunderstanding – has finally been modulated
with infinite skill into comedy.

It remains serious comedy. Captain Wentworth's release from
Louisa, it is true, has the arbitrariness of lighter comedy; it recalls
Edward Ferrars's release in *Sense and Sensibility*. The serious

problem lay in managing the psychological terms on which the lovers came together again. In the foreshortened ending of *Mansfield Park*, Fanny waits passively for Edmund to recognize her full value and transfer his wounded affections to her. Anne, who actively caused the breach with Wentworth, must take more than a passive part in its healing if she is to remain consistently more responsible than the simpler Cinderella. It is in this light that the cancelled chapter must be seen. J. E. Austen-Leigh (*Memoir*, Chapter II) describes her dissatisfaction with it; she had come with failing strength to the end of the novel and had little resilience left for rewriting; yet she felt that the chapter in which she brought the lovers together was so unsatisfactory that the effort must be made. What was wrong with it?

It is in the style of lighter comedy. In a rather artificially contrived incident Admiral Croft compels Captain Wentworth to give Anne a message which assumes that she is to marry Mr Elliot. This obliges her to tell Wentworth that she is not intending to marry Mr Elliot, and Wentworth does the rest. Thus only an external event forces her to accept even the small part she does play in clearing up the misunderstanding. She is nearly as passive as Fanny. In the revised chapters (22 and 23) her role is much more active. The problem for Jane Austen was how to give her an active part in promoting the reconciliation without the impossible breach of decorum involved in telling him of her love, in effect proposing to him. The same problem had been met in *Pride and Prejudice* by Elizabeth's refusal to assure Lady Catherine that she would *not* refuse Mr Darcy. In the revised chapters of *Persuasion* the solution lies in Anne's making an almost public avowal, easily overheard in the crowded room, of her ideals of unchanging love and her belief that women have the unenviable privilege 'of loving longest, when existence or when hope is gone.' She could not have spoken like this if she had accepted Mr Elliot, and it tells Captain Wentworth enough. Like Elizabeth Bennet, she had not deliberately spoken to convey a message to him, but by standing up for her standards and openly avowing them she had played her active part in bringing her lover back again. The chapter goes on to emphasize still more the active responsibility she feels she must take: Wentworth having smuggled his ardent

11

letter to her and gone, she has to make absolutely certain of giving him the word of encouragement he asks for. Her struggles to ensure this, in face of her friends' kind misunderstandings and ill-timed helpfulness, provide genial comedy, but none the less form part of the serious theme that distinguishes the revision from the cancelled chapter.

There is yet more of significance in the revision of the cancelled chapter, of significance for the central problem announced by the title of the novel – the rights and wrongs of Lady Russell's persuasion and of Anne's yielding. For all its general formulation the problem is embodied in the particular form created by the conflict between elderly prudence and the romantic love of two young people. The persuasion, or dissuasion, is exerted by an older person, disinterestedly concerned for the younger – but not in love; and the younger has to make up her mind. The novel was begun in 1815, and 150 years later the problem, in spite of an easier economic situation, is not unknown to girls of nineteen and their mothers.

In Jane Austen's time and in her social class, the ideal of marriage for personal love rather than for an establishment or a family alliance was in a transitional stage. The theme occurs in several of her novels, most centrally perhaps in *Mansfield Park* and *Persuasion*, and her attitude is consistent: marriage without love is wrong. In 1802 she herself suffered great agitation through accepting a proposal of marriage from a well-to-do man and then the next day withdrawing her acceptance. In *Mansfield Park* she expressed herself ironically on out-and-out worldliness in Mary's description of the Frasers:

'I look upon the Frasers to be about as unhappy as most other married people. And yet it was a most desirable match for Janet at the time. We were all delighted. She could not do otherwise than accept him, for he was rich, and she had nothing; but he turns out ill-tempered and *exigeant*; and wants a young woman, a beautiful young woman of five-and-twenty, to be as steady as himself ... Poor Janet has been sadly taken in; and yet there was nothing improper on her side; she did not run into the match inconsiderately, there was no want of foresight. She took three days to consider of his proposals; and during those three days asked the advice of everybody connected with her, whose opinion was worth having; and especially applied to my late dear aunt, whose knowledge of the world made her judgment very generally and deservedly looked up to by all the younger people of her acquaintance; and she was decidedly in favour of Mr Fraser. This seems as if nothing were a security for matrimonial comfort!'

But at the other extreme what of an engagement where there is love but poverty? She is no less clearsighted: 'Wait for his having a living!' exclaims Mrs Jennings in *Sense and Sensibility*,

'– aye, we all know how *that* will end; – they will wait a twelve-month, and finding no good comes of it, will set down upon a curacy of fifty pounds a year, with the interest of his two thousand pounds, and what little matter Mr Steele and Mr Pratt can give her. – Then they will have a child every year! and Lord help 'em! how poor they will be! – I must see what I can give them towards furnishing their house ...'

These are extremes. In *Persuasion*, on the other hand, the problem is posed without exaggeration or caricature and therefore in its most intractable form:

'Anne Elliot,' thinks Lady Russell, 'with all her claims of birth, beauty, and mind, to throw herself away at nineteen; involve herself at nineteen in an engagement with a young man, who had nothing but himself to recommend him, and no hopes of attaining affluence, but in the chances of a most uncertain profession, and no connexions to secure even his farther rise in that profession; would be, indeed, a throwing away, which she grieved to think of! Anne Elliot, so young; known to so few, to be snatched off by a stranger without alliance or fortune; or rather sunk by him into a state of most wearing, anxious, youth-killing dependance! It must not be, if by any fair interference of friendship, any representations from one who had almost a mother's love, and mother's right, it would be prevented.'

Some of the most interesting material in the revised chapters presents Jane Austen's attempt at an explicit answer to that problem, an enlargement and re-emphasis of what she had presented as Anne's opinion at the opening of the story. Here, however, in spite of some repetition (the extent of which she may possibly not have realized in this late revision), the answer is not without ambiguity. Once again, Anne is clear that she was right in yielding; it was a filial duty, and on that point there seems at first, as before, no question. Yet here she goes on immediately, in answer to Wentworth's question, to affirm that she would have renewed the engagement the following year if he had asked her when he returned to England 'with a few thousand pounds, and was posted into the Laconia'. His promotion to Captain, one profitable cruise in an old, worn-out sloop, and now a better posting, though it offered some promise would have been a weak answer to Lady Russell's full objections; and Jane Austen seems to imply that even a year's reflection and regret would have lessened the filial submissiveness of a girl like Anne. About Lady Russell's justification in the advice she gave there is a more decisive answer than that offered earlier. Then Anne did not blame her, though she felt now that she would never have given such advice herself. In the revised chapters the adverse judgement is strengthened:

'I am not saying she did not err in her advice. It was, perhaps, one of those cases in which advice is good or bad only as the event decides; and for myself, I certainly never should, in any circumstance of tolerable similarity, give such advice.'

Such an explicit and extended recurrence to the theme in her revised chapters brings out its importance to her conception of the novel.

This is not a problem that stands isolated, either in *Persuasion* or in her work as a whole; it is one outcome of the intense, highly organized pressures of a close-knit society. The functioning of individuals while they are hemmed in by others, all mutually controlled by the system of social forces, was one of her general preoccupations. The small country neighbourhood, with little travel, and no escape from the family by going to work in a large organization, precluded the individual from having the degree of anonymity we take for granted. He was, as Henry Tilney remarks in *Northanger Abbey*, 'surrounded by a neighbourhood of voluntary spies'. A characteristic feature, of which Jane Austen makes very frequent use, was the large party in the same drawing room, with the possibility of private conversations in an undertone, sometimes overheard, sometimes concealed by the conversation of others or the sound of the piano. Captain Wentworth and Anne manage to have their discussion of their broken engagement, and Lady Russell's part in it, during one of their short contacts at an evening party, 'each apparently occupied in admiring a fine display of green-house plants'. And Captain Wentworth listens contemptuously to Mary's remark after her snobbish sister has at last included him in her invitations :

'Only think of Elizabeth's including everybody !' whispered Mary very audibly. 'I do not wonder Captain Wentworth is delighted ! You see he cannot put the card out of his hand.'

Whether so much semi-privacy and overhearing were really part of the drawing-room society of the period, they provide a constantly recurring device in Jane Austen's novels, almost as usual as the soliloquy on which the theatre of the period still relied. She was presumably exaggerating something that really went on. And her exploitation of it is not only a technical device for narrative and comment but a means of conveying her characteristic sense of the compressed social milieu, the criss-cross of unspoken awareness that marks a group of people in close contact and makes privacy, especially within the family, a precarious luxury.

Although these are the conditions of all that happens, Jane Austen's focus of interest is the survival and development of the private individual within them. The pressure of social contact may be escaped for brief intervals, as for instance when the heroine goes to her own room for 'reflection' – the half hour or so that allows her, after an agitating experience, to analyse her state of mind and bring order into her feelings before returning to the drawing room and playing her usual role. It is a way of life in which the more sensitive person can experience great isolation. Actual loneliness has its place in *Mansfield Park* and *Persuasion*, highlighted by the episode in each when, during the course of a walk, the heroine is left sitting alone while the others wander off. She remains involved with them (as spectator or overhearer) but left out of account by them, a figure of the Cinderella who

15

turns novelist. Anne's detachment is presented again, within the framework of comedy, when she has to be confidante to both Mary and the Musgroves, sympathizing tactfully with the complaints of each about the others' household.

In such a society there are degrees of isolation. A high degree is created by the civil falsehood and polite evasion ('Emma denied none of it aloud and agreed to none of it in private') which break true social contact and leave the speaker in a position of tacit superiority but cut off from his hearers. So when Mary urges her sister to write home about the chance meeting with Mr Elliot, 'Anne avoided a direct reply, but it was just the circumstance which she considered as not merely unnecessary to be communicated, but as what ought to be suppressed.' And she deals similarly with the limitations of Admiral Croft, for whom she has real respect : 'Anne did not receive the perfect conviction which the Admiral meant to convey, but it would have been useless to press the enquiry farther. She, therefore satisfied herself with commonplace remarks, or quiet attention, and the Admiral had it all his own way.'

A second degree of social detachment, less complete, occurs when the heroine recognizes an obligation to try to communicate but, met by stupidity or stubbornness, feels exempt from farther effort and lets things take their course, as Anne does when she has failed to open Elizabeth's eyes to Mrs Clay's design to marry their father. When every man is surrounded by a neighbourhood of voluntary spies what should be told and what suppressed becomes a matter for careful thought; a mistake in that calculation – about Wickham's character – is a pivotal point of *Pride and Prejudice*, and in *Persuasion* a similar problem about Mr Elliot confronts Mrs Smith.

A third form of insulation in this close-pressing society, one implying less of superior detachment, is silently accepted reticence between equals. It creates the tension of confidence known to be withheld, but it remains social, since neither person breaks off the relation by resorting to deception or viewing the other clinically. In the much earlier *Sense and Sensibility* the withheld confidence, the 'reserve', although respected, is a source of some distress and mutual reproach for the sisters. In *Persuasion*, graver and much less effusive, there has been complete silence for several years between Anne and Lady Russell on the subject of the broken engagement: 'They knew not each other's opinion, either its constancy or its change, on the one leading point of Anne's conduct, for the subject was never alluded to.' The result is that Anne Elliot is presented as self-contained, controlled and with hidden power, in spite of her regrets and her real tenderness. She has the quiet maturity of a sensitive individual who is loyal to her own values without colliding needlessly and unprofitably with the social group she belongs to, or with people, like Lady Russell, to whom, in spite of seeing their limitations, she is deeply attached.

In so compact a civilized society, romantic love between individuals who freely choose each other for qualities not readily identified and categorized by those around them is a disruption. It seems to offer escape from that dependence on social support that discourages people from resisting the expectations of their immediate group. As Donne saw, the union of the two souls in love

Defects of loneliness controules.

Lovers assuage their loneliness without paying the price of full conformity. Whether the ideals of romantic love are expressed in an attachment, like Anne's for Wentworth, or in a refusal to marry for anything other than attachment, like her resistance to the match with Mr Elliot, they simultaneously express and support the individual's partial nonconformity, his selection from the values ruling around him. This aspect of romantic love relates it closely to Jane Austen's concern with the survival of the sensitive and penetrating individual in a society of conforming mediocrity.

Although the nucleus of the fable – Cinderella, the foundling princess – has its universal significance, there would be no novel unless it were embodied in a particular time and place, something realized more substantially than the sketchy never-never land of fairy tale and once-upon-a-time. In Jane Austen's society – as indeed in fairy tale – the girl who made an individual romantic choice might well have to defy the standards of class and social position. And in *Persuasion* the story is embedded in a study of snobbery, snobbery displayed amidst the sharply realized detail, social and physical, of life in country houses and Bath at the end of the Napoleonic wars. Jane Austen created the perfect starting point for her satire by giving Sir Walter Elliot a baronetcy, thus putting the family in a twilit region between the nobility and the gentry – still no more than gentry but distinguished among them by the hereditary title. His scorn for those beneath him and his anxious toadying to 'our cousins, the Dalrymples' who are of the nobility (Irish), provide a good deal of the astringent comedy of the book. By making him, moreover, financially embarrassed, she contrasts his pretensions, based on family and superficial elegance, with the solid security of the Musgroves, undistinguished landowners who look after their estates effectively, and of the families rising into social consequence on naval prize money. The querulous Mary, married into the Musgroves, carries on her struggle for precedence and proper attentions as a baronet's youngest daughter, and laments the impending disgrace of being connected, through her sister-in-law's marriage, with a family who actually farm. And Elizabeth, too, the eldest sister, has to come to terms with social dilution when she finally gives Captain Wentworth an invitation, realizing that in the conditions of Bath society a man of such distinguished bearing, whatever his forebears, will be an asset at her party. The standards that Anne has to resist are brought as close to her as possible by being shared in some degree even by Lady Russell, who 'had a value for rank and consequence, which blinded her a little to the faults of those who possessed them.'

Embodied and given life in the social realities of her own period, Jane Austen's satire still has currency in ours. The sense of the past which we need in reading it has two aspects, and the more familiar – the ability to enter into her social world and its outlook – counts for less than the other. The other is the ability to notice the people and the institutions of our own time on which her eye would have rested and her judgement been passed, and this means recognizing contemporary equivalents rather than seeking identities. We shall not look to Bath, then the last word in the contemporary, for parallels to Elizabeth Elliot's displaying,

18

as part of her own distinction, the latest in domestic architecture and fashionable décor for giving parties. And if we look around us for Sir Walter Elliot, 'prepared', on his departure from Kellynch Hall, 'with condescending bows for all the afflicted tenantry and cottagers who might have had a hint to shew themselves', we may not find him now in many landed baronets. But we may be reminded of the story Lord Woolton tells of Mr Gordon Selfridge, whose room at the store was always filled with flowers on his birthday, contributed, as he said, by 'those dear little girls' – meaning the sales assistants and clerks: 'When, one day, I remarked on his good fortune, he asked whether my staff in Lewis's paid such testimony to me, and when I replied, "Never even a daisy", this naive character replied, "You ought to give them a hint".' (Lord Woolton, *Memoirs*, London, 1959.)

At some points Sir Walter Elliot is touched with caricature. His considered twofold objection to the navy, for instance, as an occupation that may be 'the means of bringing persons of obscure birth into undue distinction' and one that also ruins the appearance has the exaggeration that places him with such figures as Mr Collins and Lady Catherine De Bourgh. But there is none of the mercy of caricature in the measured severity of the final summing up:

Captain Wentworth, with five-and-twenty thousand pounds, and as high in his profession as merit and activity could place him, was no longer nobody. He was now esteemed quite worthy to address the daughter of a foolish, spendthrift baronet, who had not had principle or sense enough to maintain himself in the situation in which Providence had placed him ...

And there is more than caricature in Elizabeth who 'felt her approach to the years of danger, and would have rejoiced to be certain of being properly solicited by baronet-blood within the next twelve-month or two.' Then she would be able to take up her father's favourite book, the Baronetage, 'with as much enjoyment as in her early youth; but now she liked it not. Always to be presented with the date of her own birth, and see no marriage follow but that of a youngest sister, made the book an evil; and more than once, when her father had left it open on the table near her, had she closed it with averted eyes, and pushed it away.' Although Elizabeth's conceit makes her ridiculous, in her relations with Mr Elliot and Mrs Clay for instance, she is not a figure of simple comedy. She is presented seriously, as a disappointed but cold-hearted and unlikeable young woman. Like Sir Walter, she is handled by Jane Austen with straightforward moral severity. When she faces the problem of entertaining the Musgroves on their unexpected visit to Bath :

Elizabeth was, for a short time, suffering a good deal. She felt that Mrs Musgrove and all her party ought to be asked to dine with them, but she could not bear to have the difference of style, the reduction of servants, which a dinner must betray, witnessed by those who had been always so inferior to the Elliots of Kellynch. It was a struggle between propriety and vanity; but vanity got the better, and then Elizabeth was happy again.

But the explicit moral comment is rare. Mainly the appraisal is implicit in the detail of setting and event: Elizabeth, once mistress of Kellynch Hall, exulting in the two drawing-rooms in Camden Place; the anxious renewal of acquaintance with the Dalrymples after the lapse occasioned by the accidental omission of a letter of condolence; the bustle and talking in Molland's, 'which must make all the little crowd in the shop understand that Lady Dalrymple was calling to convey Miss Elliot'.

A fable of profound human significance, embodied in people, time, place, and social setting acutely observed, vividly conveyed, justly appraised – but still *Persuasion* would not be the novel it is without that management of tone which was an essential part of Jane Austen's superb equipment, an integral characteristic of her writing at its best. The triumph in *Persuasion* is the harmonizing of several attitudes, which could have been distinct and even discordant, into a complex whole. Foremost among them is Anne's grave tone of regret in her reconsideration of the problems of personal relation which centred upon her yielding to Lady Russell; and later her gradual emergence from resignation to hope. With this goes the regretful clearsightedness with which she condemns the vanity of her family, an attitude consistent both with her filial obligations and with the author's ruthless contempt for Sir Walter and his other children. Contempt is not an

attitude Jane Austen shrank from; she gives it to Captain Wentworth, for instance, when he is the object of patronizing recognition by Anne's sisters. But in this novel it has to remain compatible with the good-humoured comedy found in the treatment
of Admiral Croft, where genuine respect for his kindness and
robust good sense is blended with amusement at his simplifications
and lack of subtlety in matters of love and marriage. Recovering
from his surprise at Captain Wentworth's not being to marry
Louisa Musgrove, he laments that the Captain 'must begin all
over again with somebody else. I think we must get him to
Bath. . . . Here are pretty girls enough, I am sure. It would be of
no use to go to Uppercross again, for that other Miss Musgrove, I
find, is bespoke by her cousin, the young parson'. The tone is of
good-humoured comedy. The robust simplifications are just exaggerated enough for every reader to be laughing a little at the
Admiral, and yet there is an after-taste, for on reflection one
notices that they exactly represent the level of personal and
romantic discrimination that Jane Austen has shown to be characteristic of the Musgroves.

Appreciative as she is of their warmhearted family feeling, and
sparing them the severity with which she treats the Elliots,
she remains a detached observer of the limitations of such people
as she represents in the Musgroves. One outcome of her detachment is the astringent handling of Mrs Musgrove's tearful laments
about her dead son, Richard, a passage that has been criticized by
people for whom Jane Austen's tough rationality in face of commonplace sentimentalism has been too much. Yet this passage is
one of fine discrimination as well as toughness. The 'large fat
sighings' of Mrs Musgrove are presented as ridiculous because
her upsurge of lamentation is for 'a thick-headed, unfeeling, unprofitable Dick Musgrove' who 'had been very little cared for at
any time by his family, though quite as much as he deserved;
seldom heard of, and scarcely at all regretted, when the intelligence of his death abroad had worked its way to Uppercross,
two years before.' The mother's lamentation now is sentimentalism. Even so, Captain Wentworth, who had once had the troublesome boy under his command, quickly controlled his scorn and
entered into conversation with Mrs Musgrove 'in a low voice,

about her son, doing it with so much sympathy and natural grace, as shewed the kindest consideration for all that was real and unabsurd in the parent's feelings'. The recognition that Captain Wentworth, more intelligent, more sensitive, and more mature than Mrs Musgrove, has the obligation of meeting her on whatever ground they genuinely share is balanced by the equally clear recognition that her emotion, though sincere, is based on delusions she has elaborated in a couple of days for the sake of having the emotion. The discriminations Jane Austen invites us to make allow her to claim our appreciation of the Musgroves' warm friendliness and delighted responsiveness to Captain Wentworth and at the same time to insist on our recognizing how commonplace and limited they are.

The mingling of tones is seen at its boldest in the climax, the accident on the Cobb, where elements of comedy are deliberately introduced into what is primarily a scene of shock and anxiety and family disaster. Some mis-readers have managed to ridicule the idea that a young woman could be seriously injured by slipping off a few steps, but in fact by impulsively jumping half a second before the reluctant Wentworth is ready to catch her Louisa launches herself on to her head on the stone quay and receives a severe concussion. There is nothing improbable about the seriousness of the accident or the consternation and terror of her friends. But although this gives the main note of the scene, the established character of her companions is used to bring in the overtones of comedy: Mary of course is hysterical and immobilizes her unfortunate husband, Henrietta faints and has to be supported by Anne and Captain Benwick, and Wentworth, desperate, is left with the real victim in his arms:

'Is there no one to help me?' were the first words which burst from Captain Wentworth, in a tone of despair, and as if all his own strength were gone.

The words are tragic but the tableau is comic, and after serious action has been taken and Benwick gone for a surgeon, the collapse of Mary and Henrietta is again used as a comic off-set to the real disaster:

As to the wretched party left behind, it could scarcely be said which of the three, who were completely rational, was suffering most, Captain Wentworth, Anne, or Charles, who, really a very affectionate brother, hung over Louisa with sobs of grief, and could only turn his eyes from one sister, to see the other in a state as insensible, or to witness the hysterical agitations of his wife, calling on him for help which he could not give.

And then, when the isolated group of friends has to be brought back into contact with the wider world, Jane Austen allows herself for a moment her characteristic note of banter :

By this time the report of the accident had spread among the workmen and boatmen about the Cobb, and many were collected near them, to be useful if wanted, at any rate, to enjoy the sight of a dead young lady, nay, two dead young ladies, for it proved twice as fine as the first report.

After this the high stress of the accident is eased off into the warmhearted care and generosity of the Harvilles, with the note of comedy sounding easily in their eager plans for somehow or other accommodating two or three more of the party in their tiny house.

For all its gravity and tenderness, *Persuasion* works within the convention of high comedy, like *Emma* and *Pride and Prejudice*. The inter-penetration of the various tones – severe satire, good-humoured comedy, appreciation of domestic affection, moral seriousness about personal relations and especially about love – is not merely a high development of skill in writing but reflects unity of conception and coherence of underlying values.

How far and in what ways *Persuasion* falls short of the novel Jane Austen would have written if she had been in full health can only be guessed at. It is not an unfinished novel, but by her standards it is short and there are hints towards the end of possible elaborations that were never carried out. It is about as long as the early *Northanger Abbey*, only about two thirds the length of *Sense and Sensibility* or *Pride and Prejudice*, and little more than half as long as *Mansfield Park* or *Emma*, the two novels which immediately preceded it.

The cancelled chapter indicates one way in which there might have been extensions. Had it stood, the novel would still have been complete, the outline unbroken, the story told, the characters and their pattern of interaction established. The revision brought not only the improvements that have already been discussed but substantial enlargement too, by the additional episode of the Musgroves' visit to Bath and the patterns of personal interchange which that allowed her to create. The Elliot snobbery, with Elizabeth's modified attitude to Captain Wentworth, is more fully exhibited, the good-natured confusion of a Musgrove gathering exemplified again, and Charles Musgrove's relations with his Elliot wife further illustrated. These enlargements repair no omission and correct no error of balance but, besides being entertaining in themselves, they enrich and strengthen the structure which has in essentials already been built. The same vitality and inventiveness, controlled within the main pattern, might presumably have amplified much of the latter part of the novel.

Possibly the revelation of Mr Elliot's character and past history is a problem that Jane Austen, given her earlier resources of physical energy, might have handled more enterprisingly (though Shakespeare found no better solution in *The Tempest*). But this is only one way in which the parts of the novel centring on Mr Elliot give an impression of something contemplated but not fully worked out. Though he is more villainous (a blacker villain than any other of Jane Austen's), his role is similar to Henry Crawford's in *Mansfield Park* : his charm is resisted by the morally perceptive Cinderella in spite of the attempted persuasion of her guardian figure, and the vanity of one of the Ugly Sisters allows him to lead her up the garden path. The two themes are given a much smaller part in this novel than in the earlier, and in particular Anne is not exposed to any persistent effort of persuasion from Lady Russell, who bides her time partly from caution and partly because Mr Elliot is still in mourning for his first wife. It may be that no more serious attempt at persuasion and no call for farther resistance by Anne would have formed part of a longer version, though it might well have done. What is much clearer, however, is that the tale of Mr Elliot's machinations is handled very cursorily and was never worked out in detail.

His main object was to prevent Sir Walter's remarriage and obviate the consequent threat to his own succession to the title. At the same time his attraction to Anne is shown as genuine, something quite other than the pretence with which he pays his attentions to her elder sister in order to gain admission to the household and keep an eye on the designing Mrs Clay. There are elements of conflict here. For although in her winding up of the loose threads Jane Austen suggests that as a son-in-law he would have had his best chance of keeping Sir Walter single, his marrying Anne would have so angered the deceived Elizabeth who controlled the household that his admission would have been on sufferance and his antagonism to Mrs Clay would have confirmed Elizabeth in keeping her there. In any case it is never clear what he could do to prevent Sir Walter's marrying her, beyond encouraging the snobbery that might oppose a 'degrading' connexion. Her chances are as prosperous as ever up to the last, and her throwing them up in order to become Mr Elliot's mistress (with the very slender chance of eventual marriage) is left exceedingly improbable.

That Jane Austen realized how poorly she had prepared for this last disentanglement is evident from two features of her revision of the cancelled chapter. One is the overseen meeting of Mrs Clay and Mr Elliot when he is supposed to be away from Bath, the first clear indication of anything between them (though a very subtle hint has been dropped earlier when Lady Dalrymple takes Miss Elliot home from the shop in Milsom-street). The second relevant feature of the revision is a little more puzzling – the repeated and carefully emphasized postponements of Anne's revelation to Lady Russell of Mr Elliot's deplorable character. She meant to tell her at once – and had she in fact done so it would have made no difference at all to the novel as it now stands. And yet the importance of the disclosure is stressed, and so is the fact of its being twice delayed, first by the Musgroves' arrival ('but Anne convinced herself that a day's delay of the intended communication could be of no consequence'), and then by her preoccupation with Captain Wentworth ('it became a matter of course the next morning, still to defer her explanatory visit ... and Mr Elliot's character, like the Sultaness Scheherazade's head, must live another day'). This has all the air of pre-paring us for some development in the story of Mr Elliot's scheming for which the continued ignorance of Lady Russell as well as of Sir Walter and Elizabeth was essential. Possibly she was feeling her way towards the sort of sub-plot she had used in Emma, the immediately preceding novel, where she had presented full-blown the modern detective story technique of giving the reader all the clues and still misleading him. Whatever she had in mind would have meant elaborating much more carefully Mr Elliot's part in the plot, and that evidently involved a greater enlargement or revision of the novel than she could feel was worth undertaking, especially as earlier chapters would also need revision if the extended sub-plot were to be fully integrated with the main theme.

We are left with a slight puzzle, of the fascinating kind that creative work not quite completed will always offer. Not that Persuasion is an unfinished novel, as Henry James's The Sense of the Past is, for instance, or The Last Tycoon of Scott Fitzgerald. After all, she had told the story that essentially interested her and told it with all the richness of social setting and personal relation that make it a self-sustaining complex structure. She rightly judged that in Persuasion she had, as she wrote to her favourite niece four months before she died, 'a something ready for Publi-cation'.

D.W.H.

Facsimile of the title page of the first edition of
Northanger Abbey and Persuasion (1818)

NORTHANGER ABBEY;

AND

PERSUASION.

BY THE AUTHOR OF " PRIDE AND PREJUDICE,"
" MANSFIELD-PARK," &C.

———

WITH A BIOGRAPHICAL NOTICE OF THE AUTHOR.

———

IN FOUR VOLUMES.

VOL. I.

———

LONDON:

JOHN MURRAY, ALBEMARLE-STREET.

1818.

BIOGRAPHICAL NOTICE OF
THE AUTHOR

[This note by Henry Austen, her brother, prefaced the posthumous publication of *Northanger Abbey* and *Persuasion* in 1818]

THE following pages are the production of a pen which has already contributed in no small degree to the entertainment of the public. And when the public, which has not been insensible to the merits of 'Sense and Sensibility', 'Pride and Prejudice', 'Mansfield Park', and 'Emma', shall be informed that the hand which guided that pen is now mouldering in the grave, perhaps a brief account of Jane Austen will be read with a kindlier sentiment than simple curiosity.

Short and easy will be the task of the mere biographer. A life of usefulness, literature, and religion, was not by any means a life of event. To those who lament their irreparable loss, it is consolatory to think that, as she never deserved disapprobation, so, in the circle of her family and friends, she never met reproof; that her wishes were not only reasonable, but gratified; and that to the little disappointments incidental to human life was never added, even for a moment, an abatement of good-will from any who knew her.

Jane Austen was born on the 16th of December, 1775, at Steventon, in the county of Hants. Her father was Rector of that parish upwards of forty years. There he resided, in the conscientious and unassisted discharge of his ministerial duties, until he was turned of seventy years. Then he retired with his wife, our authoress, and her sister, to Bath, for the remainder of his life, a period of about four years. Being not only a profound scholar, but possessing a most exquisite taste in every species of literature, it is not wonderful that his daughter Jane should, at a very early age, have become sensible to the charms of style, and enthusiastic in the cultivation of her own language. On the death of her father she removed, with her mother and sister, for a short time, to Southampton, and finally, in 1809, to the pleasant village of Chawton, in the same county. From this place she sent into the world those novels, which by many have been placed on the same shelf as the works of a D'Arblay and an Edgeworth. Some of these novels had been the gradual performances of her previous life. For though in composition she was equally rapid and correct, yet an invincible distrust of her own judgement induced her to withhold her works from the public, till time and many perusals had satisfied her that the charm of recent composition was dissolved. The natural constitution, the regular habits, the quiet and happy occupations of our authoress, seemed to promise a long succession of amusement to the public, and a gradual increase of reputation to herself. But the symptoms of a decay, deep and incurable, began to shew themselves in the commencement of 1816. Her decline was at first deceitfully slow; and until the spring of this present year, those who knew their happiness to be involved in her existence could not endure to despair. But in the month of May, 1817, it was found advisable that she should be moved to Winchester for the benefit of constant medical aid, which none even then dared to hope would be permanently beneficial. She supported, during two months, all the varying pain, irksomeness, and tedium, attendant on decaying nature, with more than resignation, with a truly elastic cheerfulness. She retained her faculties, her memory, her fancy, her temper, and her affections, warm, clear, and unimpaired, to the last. Neither her love of God, nor of her fellow creatures flagged for a moment. She made a point of receiving the sacrament before excessive bodily weakness might have rendered her perception unequal to her wishes. She wrote whilst she could hold a pen, and with a pencil when a pen was become too laborious. The day preceding her death she composed some stanzas replete with fancy and vigour. Her last voluntary speech conveyed thanks to her medical attendant; and to the final question asked of her, purporting to know her wants, she replied, 'I want nothing but death.'

She expired shortly after, on Friday the 18th of July, 1817, in the arms of her sister, who, as well as the relator of these events, feels too surely that they shall never look upon her like again.

Jane Austen was buried on the 24th of July, 1817, in the cathedral church of Winchester, which, in the whole catalogue of its mighty dead, does not contain the ashes of a brighter genius or a sincerer Christian.

Of personal attractions she possessed a considerable share. Her stature was that of true elegance. It could not have been increased without exceeding the middle height. Her carriage and deportment were quiet, yet graceful. Her features were separately good. Their assemblage produced an unrivalled expression of that cheerfulness, sensibility, and benevolence, which were her real characteristics. Her complexion was of the finest texture. It might with truth be said, that her eloquent blood spoke through her modest cheek. Her voice was extremely sweet. She delivered herself with fluency and precision. Indeed she was formed for elegant and rational society, excelling in conversation as much as in composition. In the present age it is hazardous to mention accomplishments. Our authoress would, probably, have been inferior to few in such acquirements, had she not been so superior to most in higher things. She had not only an excellent taste for drawing, but, in her earlier days, evinced great power of hand in the management of the pencil. Her own musical attainments she held very cheap. Twenty years ago they would have been thought more of, and twenty years hence many a parent will expect their daughters to be applauded for meaner performances. She was fond of dancing, and excelled in it. It remains now to add a few observations on that which her friends deemed more important, on those endowments which sweetened every hour of their lives.

If there be an opinion current in the world, that perfect placidity of temper is not reconcileable to the most lively imagination, and the keenest relish for wit, such an opinion will be rejected for ever by those who have had the happiness of knowing the authoress of the following works. Though the frailties, foibles, and follies of others could not escape her immediate detection, yet even on their vices did she never trust herself to comment with unkindness. The affectation of candour is not uncommon; but she had no affectation. Faultless herself, as nearly as human nature can be, she always sought, in the faults of others, something to excuse, to forgive or forget. Where extenuation was impossible, she had a sure refuge in silence. She never uttered either a hasty, a silly, or a severe expression. In short, her temper was as polished as her wit. Nor were her manners inferior to her temper. They were of the happiest kind. No one could be often in her company without feeling a strong desire of obtaining her friendship, and cherishing a hope of having obtained it. She was tranquil without reserve or stiffness; and communicative without intrusion or self-sufficiency. She became an authoress entirely from taste and inclination. Neither the hope of fame nor profit mixed with her early motives. Most of her works, as before observed, were composed many years previous to their publication. It was with extreme difficulty that her friends, whose partiality she suspected whilst she honoured their judgement, could prevail on her to publish her first work. Nay, so persuaded was she that its sale would not repay the expense of publication, that she actually made a reserve from her very moderate income to meet the expected loss. She could scarcely believe what she termed her great good fortune when 'Sense and Sensibility' produced a clear profit of about £150. Few so gifted were so truly unpretending. She regarded the above sum as a prodigious recompense for that which had cost her nothing. Her readers, perhaps, will wonder that such a work produced so little at a time when some authors have received more guineas than they have written lines. The works of our authoress, however, may live as long as those which have burst on the world with more éclat. But the public has not been unjust; and our authoress was far from thinking it so. Most gratifying to her was the applause which from time to time reached her ears from those who were competent to discriminate. Still, in spite of such applause, so much did she shrink from notoriety, that no accumulation of fame would have induced her, had she lived, to affix her name to any productions of her pen. In the bosom of her own family she talked of them freely, thankful for praise, open to remark, and submissive to criticism. But in public she turned away from any allusion to the character of an authoress. She read aloud with very great taste and effect. Her own works, probably, were never heard to so much advantage as from her own mouth; for she partook largely in all the best gifts of the comic muse. She was a warm and judicious admirer of landscape, both in nature and on canvass. At a very early age she was enamoured of Gilpin on the Picturesque; and she seldom changed her opinions either on books or men.

Her reading was very extensive in history and belles lettres; and her memory extremely tenacious. Her favourite moral writers were Johnson in prose, and Cowper in verse. It is difficult to say at what age she was not intimately acquainted with the merits and defects of the best essays and novels in the English language. Richardson's power of creating, and preserving the consistency of his characters, as particularly exemplified in 'Sir Charles Grandison', gratified the natural discrimination of her mind, whilst her taste secured her from the errors of his prolix style and tedious narrative. She did not rank any work of Fielding quite so high. Without the slightest affectation she recoiled from every thing gross. Neither nature, wit, nor humour, could make her amends for so very low a scale of morals.

Her power of inventing characters seems to have been intuitive, and almost unlimited. She drew from nature; but, whatever may have been surmised to the contrary, never from individuals.

The style of her familiar correspondence was in all respects the same as that of her novels. Every thing came finished from her pen; for on all subjects she had ideas as clear as her expressions were well chosen. It is not hazarding too much to say that she never dispatched a note or letter unworthy of publication.

One trait only remains to be touched on. It makes all others unimportant. She was thoroughly religious and devout; fearful of giving offence to God, and incapable of feeling it towards any fellow creature. On serious subjects she was well-instructed, both by reading and meditation, and her opinions accorded strictly with those of our Established Church.

London, Dec. 13, 1817.

POSTSCRIPT

Since concluding the above remarks, the writer of them has been put in possession of some extracts from the private correspondence of the authoress. They are few and short; but are submitted to the public without apology, as being more truly descriptive of her temper, taste, feelings, and principles than any thing which the pen of a biographer can produce.

The first extract is a playful defence of herself from a mock charge of having pilfered the manuscripts of a young relation.

'What should I do, my dearest E. with your manly, vigorous sketches, so full of life and spirit? How could I possibly join them on to a little bit of ivory, two inches wide, on which I work with a brush so fine as to produce little effect after much labour?'

The remaining extracts are from various parts of a letter written a few weeks before her death.

'My attendant is encouraging, and talks of making me quite well. I live chiefly on the sofa, but am allowed to walk from one room to the other. I have been out once in a sedan-chair, and am to repeat it, and be promoted to a wheel-chair as the weather serves. On this subject I will only say further that my dearest sister, my tender, watchful, indefatigable nurse, has not been made ill by her exertions. As to what I owe to her, and to the anxious affection of all my beloved family on this occasion, I can only cry over it, and pray to God to bless them more and more.'

She next touches with just and gentle animadversion on a subject of domestic disappointment. Of this the particulars do not concern the public. Yet in justice to her characteristic sweetness and resignation, the concluding observation of our authoress thereon must not be suppressed.

'But I am getting too near complaint. It has been the appointment of God, however secondary causes may have operated.'

The following and final extract will prove the facility with which she could correct every impatient thought, and turn from complaint to cheerfulness.

'You will find Captain — a very respectable, well-meaning man, without much manner, his wife and sister all good humour and obligingness, and I hope (since the fashion allows it) with rather longer petticoats than last year.'

London, Dec. 20, 1817.

CHAPTER 1

Sir Walter Elliot, of Kellynch-hall, in Somersetshire, was a man who, for his own amusement, never took up any book but the Baronetage; there he found occupation for an idle hour, and consolation in a distressed one; there his faculties were roused into admiration and respect, by contemplating the limited remnant of the earliest patents; there any unwelcome sensations, arising from domestic affairs, changed naturally into pity and contempt, as he turned over the almost endless creations of the last century — and there, if every other leaf were powerless, he could read his own history with an interest which never failed — this was the page at which the favourite volume always opened:

'ELLIOT OF KELLYNCH-HALL.

'Walter Elliot, born March 1, 1760, married, July 15, 1784, Elizabeth, daughter of James Stevenson, Esq. of South Park, in the county of Gloucester; by which lady (who died 1800) he has issue Elizabeth, born June 1, 1785; Anne, born August 9, 1787; a still-born son, Nov 5, 1789; Mary, born Nov. 20, 1791.'

Precisely such had the paragraph originally stood from the printer's hands; but Sir Walter had improved it by adding, for the information of himself and his family, these words, after the date of Mary's birth — 'married, Dec. 16, 1810, Charles, son and heir of Charles Musgrove, Esq. of Uppercross, in the county of Somerset,' — and by inserting most accurately the day of the month on which he had lost his wife.

Then followed the history and rise of the ancient and respectable family, in the usual terms: how it had been first settled in Cheshire; how mentioned in Dugdale — serving the office of High Sheriff, representing a borough in three successive parliaments, exertions of loyalty, and dignity of baronet, in the first year of Charles II., with all the Marys and Elizabeths they had married;

forming altogether two handsome duodecimo pages, and concluding with the arms and motto: 'Principal seat, Kellynch hall, in
the county of Somerset,' and Sir Walter's hand-writing again in
this finale:

'Heir presumptive, William Walter Elliot, Esq., great grandson
of the second Sir Walter.'

Vanity was the beginning and the end of Sir Walter Elliot's
character; vanity of person and of situation. He had been remarkably handsome in his youth; and, at fifty-four, was still a very
fine man. Few women could think more of their personal appearance than he did; nor could the valet of any new made
lord be more delighted with the place he held in society. He
considered the blessing of beauty as inferior only to the blessing of a baronetcy; and the Sir Walter Elliot, who united
these gifts, was the constant object of his warmest respect and
devotion.

His good looks and his rank had one fair claim on his attachment; since to them he must have owed a wife of very superior
character to any thing deserved by his own. Lady Elliot had been
an excellent woman, sensible and amiable; whose judgment and
conduct, if they might be pardoned the youthful infatuation
which made her Lady Elliot, had never required indulgence afterwards. – She had humoured, or softened, or concealed his failings,
and promoted his real respectability for seventeen years; and
though not the very happiest being in the world herself, had
found enough in her duties, her friends, and her children, to
attach her to life, and make it no matter of indifference to her
when she was called on to quit them. – Three girls, the two eldest
sixteen and fourteen, was an awful legacy for a mother to bequeath; an awful charge rather, to confide to the authority and
guidance of a conceited, silly father. She had, however, one very
intimate friend, a sensible, deserving woman, who had been
brought, by strong attachment to herself, to settle close by her, in
the village of Kellynch; and on her kindness and advice, Lady
Elliot mainly relied for the best help and maintenance of the good
principles and instruction which she had been anxiously giving
her daughters.

This friend, and Sir Walter, did *not* marry, whatever might have been anticipated on that head by their acquaintance. – Thirteen years had passed away since Lady Elliot's death, and they were still near neighbours and intimate friends; and one remained a widower, the other a widow.

That Lady Russell, of steady age and character, and extremely well provided for, should have no thought of a second marriage, needs no apology to the public, which is rather apt to be unreasonably discontented when a woman *does* marry again, than when she does *not*; but Sir Walter's continuing in singleness requires explanation. – Be it known then, that Sir Walter, like a good father, (having met with one or two private disappointments in very unreasonable applications) prided himself on remaining single for his dear daughters' [1] sake. For one daughter, his eldest, he would really have given up any thing, which he had not been very much tempted to do. Elizabeth had succeeded, at sixteen, to all that was possible, of her mother's rights and consequence; and being very handsome, and very like himself, her influence had always been great, and they had gone on together most happily. His two other children were of very inferior value. Mary had acquired a little artificial importance, by becoming Mrs Charles Musgrove; but Anne, with an elegance of mind and sweetness of character, which must have placed her high with any people of real understanding, was nobody with either father or sister : her word had no weight; her convenience was always to give way; – she was only Anne.

To Lady Russell, indeed, she was a most dear and highly valued god-daughter, favourite and friend. Lady Russell loved them all; but it was only in Anne that she could fancy the mother to revive again.

A few years before, Anne Elliot had been a very pretty girl, but her bloom had vanished early; and as even in its height, her father had found little to admire in her, (so totally different were her delicate features and mild dark eyes from his own); there could be nothing in them now that she was faded and thin, to excite his esteem. He had never indulged much hope, he had now none, of ever reading her name in any other page of his favourite work. All equality of alliance must rest with Elizabeth; for Mary had merely connected herself with an old country family of respectability and large fortune, and had therefore *given* all the honour, and received none: Elizabeth would, one day or other, marry suitably.

It sometimes happens, that a woman is handsomer at twenty-nine than she was ten years before; and, generally speaking, if there has been neither ill health nor anxiety, it is a time of life at which scarcely any charm is lost. It was so with Elizabeth; still the same handsome Miss Elliot that she had begun to be thirteen years ago; and Sir Walter might be excused, therefore, in forgetting her age, or, at least, be deemed only half a fool, for thinking himself and Elizabeth as blooming as ever, amidst the wreck of the good looks of every body else; for he could plainly see how old all the rest of his family and acquaintance were growing. Anne haggard, Mary coarse, every face in the neighbourhood worsting; and the rapid increase of the crow's foot about Lady Russell's temples had long been a distress to him.

Elizabeth did not quite equal her father in personal content-ment. Thirteen years had seen her mistress of Kellynch Hall, pre-siding and directing with a self-possession and decision which could never have given the idea of her being younger than she was. For thirteen years had she been doing the honours, and laying down the domestic law at home, and leading the way to the chaise and four, and walking immediately after Lady Russell out of all the drawing-rooms and dining-rooms in the country. Thirteen winters' revolving frosts had seen her opening every ball of credit which a scanty neighbourhood afforded; and thirteen springs shewn their blossoms, as she travelled up to London with her father, for a few weeks annual enjoyment of the great world. She had the remem-brance of all this; she had the consciousness of being nine-and-twenty, to give her some regrets and some apprehensions. She was fully satisfied of being still quite as handsome as ever; but she felt her approach to the years of danger, and would have rejoiced to be certain of being properly solicited by baronet-blood within the next twelvemonth or two. Then might she again take up the book of books with as much enjoyment as in her early youth; but now she liked it not. Always to be presented with the date of her own birth, and see no marriage follow but that of a youngest sister, made the book an evil; and more than once, when her father had left it open on the table near her, had she closed it, with averted eyes, and pushed it away.

She had had a disappointment, moreover, which that book, and especially the history of her own family, must ever present the remembrance of. The heir presumptive, the very William Walter Elliot, Esq. whose rights had been so generously supported by her father, had disapppointed her.

She had, while a very young girl, as soon as she had known him to be, in the event of her having no brother, the future baronet, meant to marry him; and her father had always meant that she should. He had not been known to them as a boy, but soon after Lady Elliot's death Sir Walter had sought the acquaintance, and though his overtures had not been met with any warmth, he had persevered in seeking it, making allowance for the modest drawing back of youth; and in one of their spring excursions to London, when Elizabeth was in her first bloom, Mr Elliot had been forced into the introduction.

He was at that time a very young man, just engaged in the study of the law; and Elizabeth found him extremely agreeable, and every plan in his favour was confirmed. He was invited to Kellynch Hall; he was talked of and expected all the rest of the year; but he never came. The following spring he was seen again in town, found equally agreeable, again encouraged, invited and expected, and again he did not come; and the next tidings were that he was married. Instead of pushing his fortune in the line marked out for the heir of the house of Elliot, he had purchased independence by uniting himself to a rich woman of inferior birth.

Sir Walter had resented it. As the head of the house, he felt that he ought to have been consulted, especially after taking the young man so publicly by the hand: 'For they must have been seen together,' he observed, 'once at Tattersal's, and twice in the lobby of the House of Commons.' His disapprobation was expressed, but apparently very little regarded. Mr Elliot had attempted no apology, and shewn himself as unsolicitous of being longer noticed by the family, as Sir Walter considered him unworthy of it: all acquaintance between them had ceased.

This very awkward history of Mr Elliot, was still, after an interval of several years, felt with anger by Elizabeth, who had liked the man for himself, and still more for being her father's heir, and whose strong family pride could see only in him, a proper match for Sir Walter Elliot's eldest daughter. There was not a baronet from A to Z, whom her feelings could have so willingly acknowledged as an equal. Yet so miserably had he conducted himself, that though she was at this present time, (the summer of 1814,) wearing black ribbons for his wife, she could not admit him to be worth thinking of again. The disgrace of his first marriage might, perhaps, as there was no reason to suppose it perpetuated by offspring, have been got over, had he not done worse; but he had, as by the accustomary intervention of kind friends they had been informed, spoken most disrespectfully of them all, most slightingly and contemptuously of the very blood he belonged to, and the honours which were hereafter to be his own. This could not be pardoned.

Such were Elizabeth Elliot's sentiments and sensations; such the cares to alloy, the agitations to vary, the sameness and the elegance, the prosperity and the nothingness, of her scene of life – such the feelings to give interest to a long, uneventful residence in one country circle, to fill the vacancies which there were no habits of utility abroad, no talents or accomplishments for home, to occupy.

But now, another occupation and solicitude of mind was beginning to be added to these. Her father was growing distressed for money. She knew, that when he now took up the Baronetage, it was to drive the heavy bills of his tradespeople, and the unwelcome hints of Mr Shepherd, his agent, from his thoughts. The Kellynch property was good, but not equal to Sir Walter's apprehension of the state required in its possessor. While Lady Elliot lived, there had been method, moderation, and economy, which had just kept him within his income; but with her had died all such right-mindedness, and from that period he had been constantly exceeding it. It had not been possible for him to spend less; he had done nothing but what Sir Walter Elliot was imperiously called on to do; but blameless as he was, he was not only growing dreadfully in debt, but was hearing of it so often, that it became vain to attempt concealing it longer, even partially, from his daughter. He had given her some hints of it the last spring in

40

town; he had gone so far even as to say, 'Can we retrench? does it occur to you that there is any one article in which we can retrench?' – and Elizabeth, to do her justice, had, in the first ardour of female alarm, set seriously to think what could be done, and had finally proposed these two branches of economy : to cut off some unnecessary charities, and to refrain from new-furnishing the drawing-room; to which expedients she afterwards added the happy thought of their taking no present down to Anne, as had been the usual yearly custom. But these measures, however good in themselves, were insufficient for the real extent of the evil, the whole of which Sir Walter found himself obliged to confess to her soon afterwards. Elizabeth had nothing to propose of deeper efficacy. She felt herself ill-used and unfortunate, as did her father; and they were neither of them able to devise any means of lessening their expenses without compromising their dignity, or relinquishing their comforts in a way not to be borne.

There was only a small part of his estate that Sir Walter could dispose of; but had every acre been alienable, it would have made no difference. He had condescended to mortgage as far as he had the power, but he would never condescend to sell. No; he would never disgrace his name so far. The Kellynch estate should be transmitted whole and entire, as he had received it.

Their two confidential friends, Mr Shepherd, who lived in the neighbouring market town, and Lady Russell, were called on to advise them; and both father and daughter seemed to expect that something should be struck out by one or the other to remove their embarrassments and reduce their expenditure, without involving the loss of any indulgence of taste or pride.

CHAPTER 2

MR SHEPHERD, a civil, cautious lawyer, who, whatever might be his hold or his views on Sir Walter, would rather have the *disagreeable* prompted by any body else, excused himself from offering the slightest hint, and only begged leave to recommend an implicit deference to the excellent judgment of Lady Russell, – from whose known good sense he fully expected to have just such resolute measures advised, as he meant to see finally adopted.

Lady Russell was most anxiously zealous on the subject, and gave it much serious consideration. She was a woman rather of sound than of quick abilities, whose difficulties in coming to any decision in this instance were great, from the opposition of two leading principles. She was of strict integrity herself, with a delicate sense of honour; but she was as desirous of saving Sir Walter's feelings, as solicitous for the credit of the family, as aristocratic in her ideas of what was due to them, as any body of sense and honesty could well be. She was a benevolent, charitable, good woman, and capable of strong attachments; most correct in her conduct, strict in her notions of decorum, and with manners that were held a standard of good-breeding. She had a cultivated mind, and was, generally speaking, rational and consistent – but she had prejudices on the side of ancestry; she had a value for rank and consequence, which blinded her a little to the faults of those who possessed them. Herself, the widow of only a knight, she gave the dignity of a baronet all its due; and Sir Walter, independent of his claims as an old acquaintance, an attentive neighbour, an obliging landlord, the husband of her very dear friend, the father of Anne and her sisters, was, as being Sir Walter, in her apprehension entitled to a great deal of compassion and consideration under his present difficulties.

They must retrench; that did not admit of a doubt. But she was very anxious to have it done with the least possible pain to him and Elizabeth. She drew up plans of economy, she made exact calculations, and she did, what nobody else thought of doing, she consulted Anne, who never seemed considered by the others as having any interest in the question. She consulted, and in a degree was influenced by her, in marking out the scheme of retrenchment, which was at last submitted to Sir Walter. Every emendation of Anne's had been on the side of honesty against importance. She wanted more vigorous measures, a more complete reformation, a quicker release from debt, a much higher tone of indifference for every thing but justice and equity.

'If we can persuade your father to all this,' said Lady Russell, looking over her paper, 'much may be done. If he will adopt these regulations, in seven years he will be clear; and I hope we may be able to convince him and Elizabeth, that Kellynch-hall has a respectability in itself, which cannot be affected by these reductions; and that the true dignity of Sir Walter Elliot will be very far from lessened in the eyes of sensible people, by his acting like a man of principle. What will he be doing, in fact, but what very many of our first families have done – or ought to do? – There will be nothing singular in his case; and it is singularity which often makes the worst part of our suffering, as it always does of our conduct. I have great hope of our prevailing. We must be serious and decided – for, after all, the person who has contracted debts must pay them; and though a great deal is due to the feelings of the gentleman, and the head of a house, like your father, there is still more due to the character of an honest man.'

This was the principle on which Anne wanted her father to be proceeding, his friends to be urging him. She considered it as an act of indispensable duty to clear away the claims of creditors, with all the expedition which the most comprehensive retrenchments could secure, and saw no dignity in any thing short of it. She wanted it to be prescribed, and felt as a duty. She rated Lady Russell's influence highly, and as to the severe degree of self-denial, which her own conscience prompted, she believed there might be little more difficulty in persuading them to a complete, than to half a reformation. Her knowledge of her father and Elizabeth, inclined her to think that the sacrifice of one pair of horses would be hardly less painful than of both, and soon, through the whole list of Lady Russell's too gentle reductions.

How Anne's more rigid requisitions might have been taken, is of little consequence. Lady Russell's had no success at all – could not be put up with – were not to be borne. 'What ! Every comfort of life knocked off ! Journeys, London, servants, horses, table, – contractions and restrictions every where. To live no longer with the decencies even of a private gentleman ! No, he would sooner quit Kellynch-hall at once, than remain in it on such disgraceful terms.'

'Quit Kellynch-hall.' The hint was immediately taken up by Mr Shepherd, whose interest was involved in the reality of Sir Walter's retrenching, and who was perfectly persuaded that nothing would be done without a change of abode. – 'Since the idea had been started in the very quarter which ought to dictate, he had no scruple,' he said, 'in confessing his judgment to be entirely on that side. It did not appear to him that Sir Walter could materially alter his style of living in a house which had such a character of hospitality and ancient dignity to support. – In any other place, Sir Walter might judge for himself; and would be looked up to, as regulating the modes of life, in whatever way he might choose to model his household.'

Sir Walter would quit Kellynch-hall; – and after a very few days more of doubt and indecision, the great question of whither he should go, was settled, and the first outline of this important change made out.

There had been three alternatives, London, Bath, or another house in the country. All Anne's wishes had been for the latter. A small house in their own neighbourhood, where they might still have Lady Russell's society, still be near Mary, and still have the pleasure of sometimes seeing the lawns and groves of Kellynch, was the object of her ambition. But the usual fate of Anne attended her, in having something very opposite from her inclination fixed on. She disliked Bath, and did not think it agreed with her – and Bath was to be her home.

Sir Walter had at first thought more of London, but Mr Shepherd felt that he could not be trusted in London, and had been skilful enough to dissuade him from it, and make Bath preferred. It was a much safer place for a gentleman in his predicament : – he might there be important at comparatively little expense. – Two material advantages of Bath over London had of course been given all their weight, its more convenient distance from Kellynch, only fifty miles, and Lady Russell's spending some part of every winter there; and to the very great satisfaction of Lady Russell, whose first views on the projected change had been for Bath, Sir Walter and Elizabeth were induced to believe that they should lose neither consequence nor enjoyment by settling there.

Lady Russell felt obliged to oppose her dear Anne's known wishes. It would be too much to expect Sir Walter to descend into a small house in his own neighbourhood. Anne herself would have found the mortifications of it more than she foresaw, and to Sir Walter's feelings they must have been dreadful. And with regard to Anne's dislike of Bath, she considered it as a prejudice and mistake, arising first from the circumstance of her having been three years at school there, after her mother's death, and, secondly, from her happening to be not in perfectly good spirits the only winter which she had afterwards spent there with herself.

Lady Russell was fond of Bath in short, and disposed to think it must suit them all; and as to her young friend's health, by passing all the warm months with her at Kellynch-lodge, every danger would be avoided; and it was, in fact, a change which must do both health and spirits good. Anne had been too little from home, too little seen. Her spirits were not high. A larger society would improve them. She wanted her to be more known.

The undesirableness of any other house in the same neighbourhood for Sir Walter, was certainly much strengthened by one part, and a very material part of the scheme, which had been happily engrafted on the beginning. He was not only to quit his home, but to see it in the hands of others; a trial of fortitude, which stronger heads than Sir Walter's have found too much. – Kellynch-hall was to be let. This, however, was a profound secret; not to be breathed beyond their own circle.

Sir Walter could not have borne the degradation of being known to design letting his house. – Mr Shepherd had once mentioned the word, 'advertise;' – but never dared approach it again; Sir Walter spurned the idea of its being offered in any manner; forbad the slightest hint being dropped of his having such an intention; and it was only on the supposition of his being spontaneously solicited by some most unexceptionable applicant, on his own terms, and as a great favour, that he would let it at all.

How quick come the reasons for approving what we like! — Lady Russell had another excellent one at hand, for being extremely glad that Sir Walter and his family were to remove from the country. Elizabeth had been lately forming an intimacy, which she wished to see interrupted. It was with a daughter of Mr Shepherd, who had returned, after an unprosperous marriage, to her father's house, with the additional burthen of two children. She was a clever young woman, who understood the art of pleasing; the art of pleasing, at least, at Kellynch-hall; and who had made herself so acceptable to Miss Elliot, as to have been already staying there more than once, in spite of all that Lady Russell, who thought it a friendship quite out of place, could hint of caution and reserve.

Lady Russell, indeed, had scarcely any influence with Elizabeth, and seemed to love her, rather because she would love her, than because Elizabeth deserved it. She had never received from her more than outward attention, nothing beyond the observances of complaisance; had never succeeded in any point which she wanted to carry, against previous inclination. She had been repeatedly very earnest in trying to get Anne included in the visit to London, sensibly open to all the injustice and all the discredit of the selfish arrangements which shut her out, and on many lesser occasions had endeavoured to give Elizabeth the advantage of her own better judgment and experience — but always in vain; Elizabeth would go her own way — and never had she pursued it in more decided opposition to Lady Russell, than in this selection of Mrs Clay; turning from the society of so deserving a sister to bestow her affection and confidence on one who ought to have been nothing to her but the object of distant civility.

From situation, Mrs Clay was, in Lady Russell's estimate, a very unequal, and in her character she believed a very dangerous companion — and a removal that would leave Mrs Clay behind, and bring a choice of more suitable intimates within Miss Elliot's reach, was therefore an object of first-rate importance.

CHAPTER 3

'I MUST take leave to observe, Sir Walter,' said Mr Shepherd one morning at Kellynch, as he laid down the newspaper, 'that the present juncture is much in our favour. This peace will be turning all our rich Navy Officers ashore. They will be all wanting a home. Could not be a better time, Sir Walter, for having a choice of tenants, very responsible tenants. Many a noble fortune has been made during the war. If a rich Admiral were to come in our way, Sir Walter –'

'He would be a very lucky man, Shepherd,' replied Sir Walter, 'that's all I have to remark. A prize indeed would Kellynch Hall be to him; rather the greatest prize of all, let him have taken ever so many before – hey, Shepherd?'

Mr Shepherd laughed, as he knew he must, at this wit, and then added,

'I presume to observe, Sir Walter, that, in the way of business, gentlemen of the navy are well to deal with. I have had a little knowledge of their methods of doing business, and I am free to confess that they have very liberal notions, and are as likely to make desirable tenants as any set of people one should meet with. Therefore, Sir Walter, what I would take leave to suggest is, that if in consequence of any rumours getting abroad of your intention – which must be contemplated as a possible thing, because we know how difficult it is to keep the actions and designs of one part of the world from the notice and curiosity of the other, – consequence has its tax – I, John Shepherd, might conceal any family-matters that I chose, for nobody would think it worth their while to observe me, but Sir Walter Elliot has eyes upon him which it may be very difficult to elude – and therefore, thus much I venture upon, that it will not greatly surprise me if, with all our caution, some rumour of the truth should get abroad – in the supposition of which, as I was going to observe, since applications will unquestionably follow, I should think any from our wealthy naval commanders particularly worth attending to – and beg leave to add, that two hours will bring me over at any time, to save you the trouble of replying.'

Sir Walter only nodded. But soon afterwards, rising and pacing the room, he observed sarcastically,

'There are few among the gentlemen of the navy, I imagine, who would not be surprised to find themselves in a house of this description.'

'They would look around them, no doubt, and bless their good fortune,' said Mrs Clay, for Mrs Clay was present; her father had driven her over, nothing being of so much use to Mrs Clay's health as a drive to Kellynch: 'but I quite agree with my father in thinking a sailor might be a very desirable tenant. I have known a good deal of the profession; and besides their liberality, they are so neat and careful in all their ways! These valuable pictures of yours, Sir Walter, if you chose to leave them, would be perfectly safe. Every thing in and about the house would be taken such excellent care of! the gardens and shrubberies would be kept in almost as high order as they are now. You need not be afraid, Miss Elliot, of your own sweet flower-garden's being neglected.'

'As to all that,' rejoined Sir Walter coolly, 'supposing I were induced to let my house, I have by no means made up my mind as to the privileges to be annexed to it. I am not particularly disposed to favour a tenant. The park would be open to him of course, and few navy officers, or men of any other description, can have had such a range; but what restrictions I might impose on the use of the pleasure-grounds, is another thing. I am not fond of the idea of my shrubberies being always approachable; and I should recommend Miss Elliot to be on her guard with respect to her flower-garden. I am very little disposed to grant a tenant of Kellynch Hall any extraordinary favour, I assure you, be he sailor or soldier.'

After a short pause, Mr Shepherd presumed to say,

'In all these cases, there are established usages which make every thing plain and easy between landlord and tenant. Your interest, Sir Walter, is in pretty safe hands. Depend upon me for taking care that no tenant has more than his just rights. I venture to hint, that Sir Walter Elliot cannot be half so jealous for his own, as John Shepherd will be for him.'

Here Anne spoke, –

'The navy, I think, who have done so much for us, have at least an equal claim with any other set of men, for all the comforts and all the privileges which any home can give. Sailors work hard enough for their comforts, we must all allow.'

'Very true, very true. What Miss Anne says, is very true,' was Mr Shepherd's rejoinder, and 'Oh ! certainly,' was his daughter's; but Sir Walter's remark was, soon afterwards –

'The profession has its utility, but I should be sorry to see any friend of mine belonging to it.'

'Indeed !' was the reply, and with a look of surprise.

'Yes; it is in two points offensive to me; I have two strong grounds of objection to it. First, as being the means of bringing persons of obscure birth into undue distinction, and raising men to honours which their fathers and grandfathers never dreamt of; and secondly, as it cuts up a man's youth and vigour most horribly; a sailor grows old sooner than any other man; I have observed it all my life. A man is in greater danger in the navy of being insulted by the rise of one whose father, his father might have disdained to speak to, and of becoming prematurely an object of disgust himself, than in any other line. One day last spring, in town, I was in company with two men, striking instances of what I am talking of, Lord St Ives, whose father we all know to have been a country curate, without bread to eat; I was to give place to Lord St Ives, and a certain Admiral Baldwin, the most deplorable looking personage you can imagine, his face the colour of mahogany, rough and rugged to the last degree, all lines and wrinkles, nine grey hairs of a side, and nothing but a dab of powder at top. – "In the name of heaven, who is that old fellow?" said I, to a friend of mine who was standing near, (Sir Basil Morley.) "Old fellow !" cried Sir Basil, "it is Admiral Baldwin. What do you take his age to be?" "Sixty," said I, "or perhaps sixty-two." "Forty," replied Sir Basil, "forty, and no more." Picture to yourselves my amazement; I shall not easily forget Admiral Baldwin. I never saw quite so wretched an example of what a sea-faring life can do; but to a degree, I know it is the same with them all : they are all knocked about, and exposed to every climate, and every weather, till they are not fit to be seen. It is a pity they are not knocked on the head at once, before they reach Admiral Baldwin's age.'

'Nay, Sir Walter,' cried Mrs Clay, 'this is being severe indeed. Have a little mercy on the poor men. We are not all born to be handsome. The sea is no beautifier, certainly; sailors do grow old betimes; I have often observed it; they soon lose the look of youth. But then, is not it the same with many other professions, perhaps most other? Soldiers, in active service, are not at all better off: and even in the quieter professions, there is a toil and a labour of the mind, if not of the body, which seldom leaves a man's looks to the natural effect of time. The lawyer plods, quite care-worn; the physician is up at all hours, and travelling in all weather; and even the clergyman —' she stopt a moment to consider what might do for the clergyman; – 'and even the clergyman, you know, is obliged to go into infected rooms, and expose his health and looks to all the injury of a poisonous atmosphere. In fact, as I have long been convinced, though every profession is necessary and honour-able in its turn, it is only the lot of those who are not obliged to follow any, who can live in a regular way, in the country, choosing their own hours, following their own pursuits, and living on their own property, without the torment of trying for more; it is only *their* lot, I say, to hold the blessings of health and a good appearance to the utmost: I know no other set of men but what lose something of their personableness when they cease to be quite young.'

It seemed as if Mr Shepherd, in this anxiety to bespeak Sir Walter's goodwill towards a naval officer as tenant, had been gifted with foresight; for the very first application for the house was from an Admiral Croft, with whom he shortly afterwards fell into company in attending the quarter sessions at Taunton; and indeed, he had received a hint of the admiral from a London correspondent. By the report which he hastened over to Kellynch to make, Admiral Croft was a native of Somersetshire, who having acquired a very handsome fortune, was wishing to settle in his own country, and had come down to Taunton in order to look at some advertised places in that immediate neighbourhood, which, however, had not suited him; that accidentally hearing – (it was just as he had foretold, Mr Shepherd observed, Sir Walter's concerns could not be kept a secret,) – accidentally hearing of the possibility of Kellynch Hall being to let, and understanding his (Mr Shepherd's) connection with the owner, he had introduced himself to him in order to make particular inquiries, and had, in the course of a pretty long conference, expressed as strong an inclination for the place as man who knew it only by description, could feel; and given Mr Shepherd, in his explicit account of himself, every proof of his being a most responsible, eligible tenant.

'And who is Admiral Croft?' was Sir Walter's cold suspicious inquiry.

Mr Shepherd answered for his being of a gentleman's family, and mentioned a place; and Anne, after the little pause which followed, added –

'He is rear admiral of the white.[2] He was in the Trafalgar action, and has been in the East Indies since; he has been stationed there, I believe, several years.'

'Then I take it for granted,' observed Sir Walter, 'that his face is about as orange as the cuffs and capes of my livery.'

Mr Shepherd hastened to assure him, that Admiral Croft was a very hale, hearty, well-looking man, a little weather-beaten, to be sure, but not much; and quite the gentleman in all his notions and behaviour; – not likely to make the smallest difficulty about terms; – only wanted a comfortable home, and to get into it as soon as possible; – knew he must pay for his convenience; – knew what rent a ready-furnished house of that consequence might fetch; – should not have been surprised if Sir Walter had asked more; – had inquired about the manor; – would be glad of the deputation,[3] certainly, but made no great point of it; – said he sometimes took out a gun, but never killed; – quite the gentleman.

Mr Shepherd was eloquent on the subject; pointing out all the circumstances of the admiral's family, which made him peculiarly desirable as a tenant. He was a married man, and without children; the very state to be wished for. A house was never taken good care of, Mr Shepherd observed, without a lady : he did not know, whether furniture might not be in danger of suffering as much where there was no lady, as where there were many children. A lady, without a family, was the very best preserver of furniture in the world. He had seen Mrs Croft, too; she was at Taunton with the admiral, and had been present almost all the time they were talking the matter over.

'And a very well-spoken, genteel, shrewd lady, she seemed to be,' continued he; 'asked more questions about the house, and terms, and taxes, than the admiral himself, and seemed more conversant with business. And moreover, Sir Walter, I found she was not quite unconnected in this country, any more than her husband; that is to say, she is sister to a gentleman who did live amongst us once; she told me so herself: sister to the gentleman who lived a few years back, at Monkford. Bless me! what was his name? At this moment I cannot recollect his name, though I have heard it so lately. Penelope, my dear, can you help me to the name of the gentleman who lived at Monkford – Mrs Croft's brother?'

But Mrs Clay was talking so eagerly with Miss Elliot, that she did not hear the appeal.

'I have no conception whom you can mean, Shepherd; I remember no gentleman resident at Monkford since the time of old Governor Trent.'

'Bless me! how very odd! I shall forget my own name soon, I suppose. A name that I am so very well acquainted with; knew the gentleman so well by sight; seen him a hundred times; came to consult me once, I remember, about a trespass of one of his neighbours; farmer's man breaking into his orchard – wall torn down – apples stolen – caught in the fact; and afterwards, contrary to my judgment, submitted to an amicable compromise. Very odd indeed!'

After waiting another moment –

'You mean Mr Wentworth, I suppose,' said Anne.

Mr Shepherd was all gratitude.

'Wentworth was the very name! Mr Wentworth was the very man. He had the curacy of Monkford, you know, Sir Walter, some time back, for two or three years. Came there about the year —5, I take it. You remember him, I am sure.'

'Wentworth? Oh! ay, – Mr Wentworth, the curate of Monkford. You misled me by the term *gentleman*. I thought you were speaking of some man of property: Mr Wentworth was nobody,

I remember; quite unconnected; nothing to do with the Strafford family. One wonders how the names of many of our nobility become so common.'

As Mr Shepherd perceived that this connexion of the Crofts did them no service with Sir Walter, he mentioned it no more; returning, with all his zeal, to dwell on the circumstances more indisputably in their favour; their age, and number, and fortune; the high idea they had formed of Kellynch Hall, and extreme solicitude for the advantage of renting it; making it appear as if they ranked nothing beyond the happiness of being the tenants of Sir Walter Elliot: an extraordinary taste, certainly, could they have been supposed in the secret of Sir Walter's estimate of the dues of a tenant.

It succeeded, however; and though Sir Walter must ever look with an evil eye on any one intending to inhabit that house, and think them infinitely too well off in being permitted to rent it on the highest terms, he was talked into allowing Mr Shepherd to proceed in the treaty, and authorising him to wait on Admiral Croft, who still remained at Taunton, and fix a day for the house being seen.

Sir Walter was not very wise; but still he had experience enough of the world to feel, that a more unobjectionable tenant, in all essentials, than Admiral Croft bid fair to be, could hardly offer. So far went his understanding; and his vanity supplied a little additional soothing, in the admiral's situation in life, which was just high enough, and not too high. 'I have let my house to Admiral Croft,' would sound extremely well; very much better than to any mere Mr —; a Mr (save, perhaps, some half dozen in the nation,) always needs a note of explanation. An admiral speaks his own consequence, and, at the same time, can never make a baronet look small. In all their dealings and intercourse, Sir Walter Elliot must ever have the precedence.

Nothing could be done without a reference to Elizabeth; but her inclination was growing so strong for a removal, that she was happy to have it fixed and expedited by a tenant at hand; and not a word to suspend decision was uttered by her.

Mr Shepherd was completely empowered to act; and no sooner had such an end been reached, than Anne, who had been a most attentive listener to the whole, left the room, to seek the comfort of cool air for her flushed cheeks; and as she walked along a favourite grove, said, with a gentle sigh, 'a few months more, and *he*, perhaps, may be walking here.'

CHAPTER 4

HE was not Mr Wentworth, the former curate of Monkford, however suspicious appearances may be, but a captain Frederick Wentworth, his brother, who being made commander in consequence of the action off St Domingo, and not immediately employed, had come into Somersetshire, in the summer of 1806; and having no parent living, found a home for half a year, at Monkford. He was, at that time, a remarkably fine young man, with a great deal of intelligence, spirit and brilliancy; and Anne an extremely pretty girl, with gentleness, modesty, taste, and feeling. – Half the sum of attraction, on either side, might have been enough, for he had nothing to do, and she had hardly any body to love; but the encounter of such lavish recommendations could not fail. They were gradually acquainted, and when acquainted, rapidly and deeply in love. It would be difficult to say which had seen highest perfection in the other, or which had been the happiest; she, in receiving his declarations and proposals, or he in having them accepted.

A short period of exquisite felicity followed, and but a short one. – Troubles soon arose. Sir Walter, on being applied to, without actually withholding his consent, or saying it should never be, gave it all the negative of great astonishment, great coldness, great silence, and a professed resolution of doing nothing for his daughter. He thought it a very degrading alliance; and Lady Russell, though with more tempered and pardonable pride, received it as a most unfortunate one.

Anne Elliot, with all her claims of birth, beauty, and mind, to throw herself away at nineteen; involve herself at nineteen in an engagement with a young man, who had nothing but himself to recommend him, and no hopes of attaining affluence, but in the chances of a most uncertain profession, and no connexions to secure even his farther rise in that profession; would be, indeed, a throwing away, which she grieved to think of! Anne Elliot, so young; known to so few, to be snatched off by a stranger without alliance or fortune; or rather sunk by him into a state of most wearing, anxious, youth-killing dependance! It must not be, if by any fair interference of friendship, any representations from one who had almost a mother's love, and mother's rights, it would be prevented.

Captain Wentworth had no fortune. He had been lucky in his profession, but spending freely, what had come freely, had realized nothing. But, he was confident that he should soon be rich; – full of life and ardour, he knew that he should soon have a ship, and soon be on a station that would lead to every thing he wanted. He had always been lucky; he knew he should be so still. – Such confidence, powerful in its own warmth, and bewitching in the wit which often expressed it, must have been enough for Anne; but Lady Russell saw it very differently. – His sanguine temper, and fearlessness of mind, operated very differently on her. She saw in it but an aggravation of the evil. It only added a dangerous character to himself. He was brilliant, he was headstrong. – Lady Russell had little taste for wit; and of any thing approaching to imprudence a horror. She deprecated the connexion in every light.

Such opposition, as these feelings produced, was more than Anne could combat. Young and gentle as she was, it might yet have been possible to withstand her father's ill-will, though unsoftened by one kind word or look on the part of her sister; – but Lady Russell, whom she had always loved and relied on, could not, with such steadiness of opinion, and such tenderness of manner, be continually advising her in vain. She was persuaded to believe the engagement a wrong thing – indiscreet, improper, hardly capable of success, and not deserving it. But it was not a merely selfish caution, under which she acted, in putting an end to it. Had she not imagined herself consulting his good, even more than her own, she could hardly have given him up. – The belief of being prudent, and self-denying principally for *his* advantage, was her chief consolation, under the misery of a parting – a final parting; and every consolation was required, for she had to encounter all the additional pain of opinions, on his side, totally unconvinced and unbending, and of his feeling himself ill-used by so forced a relinquishment. – He had left the country in consequence.

A few months had seen the beginning and the end of their

acquaintance; but, not with a few months ended Anne's share of suffering from it. Her attachment and regrets had, for a long time, clouded every enjoyment of youth; and an early loss of bloom and spirits had been their lasting effect.

More than seven years were gone since this little history of sorrowful interest had reached its close; and time had softened down much, perhaps nearly all of peculiar attachment to him, – but she had been too dependant on time alone; no aid had been given in change of place, (except in one visit to Bath soon after the rupture,) or in any novelty or enlargement of society. – No one had ever come within the Kellynch circle, who could bear a comparison with Frederick Wentworth, as he stood in her memory. No second attachment, the only thoroughly natural, happy, and sufficient cure, at her time of life, had been possible to the nice tone of her mind, the fastidiousness of her taste, in the small limits of the society around them. She had been solicited, when about two-and-twenty, to change her name, by the young man, who not long afterwards found a more willing mind in her younger sister; and Lady Russell had lamented her refusal; for Charles Musgrove was the eldest son of a man, whose landed property and general importance, were second, in that country, only to Sir Walter's, and of good character and appearance; and however Lady Russell might have asked yet for something more, while Anne was nineteen, she would have rejoiced to see her at twenty-two, so respectably removed from the partialities and injustice of her father's house, and settled so permanently near herself. But in this case, Anne had left nothing for advice to do; and though Lady Russell, as satisfied as ever with her own discretion, never wished the past undone, she began now to have the anxiety which borders on hopelessness for Anne's being tempted, by some man of talents and independence, to enter a state for which she held her to be peculiarly fitted by her warm affections and domestic habits.

They knew not each other's opinion, either its constancy or its change, on the one leading point of Anne's conduct, for the subject was never alluded to, – but Anne, at seven and twenty, thought very differently from what she had been made to think at nineteen. – She did not blame Lady Russell, she did not blame herself for having been guided by her; but she felt that were any young person, in similar circumstances, to apply to her for coun- sel, they would never receive any of such certain immediate wretchedness, such uncertain future good. – She was persuaded that under every disadvantage of disapprobation at home, and every anxiety attending his profession, all their probable fears, delays and disappointments, she should yet have been a happier woman in maintaining the engagement, than she had been in the sacrifice of it; and this, she fully believed, had the usual share, had even more than a usual share of all such solicitudes and suspense been theirs, without reference to the actual results of their case, which, as it happened, would have bestowed earlier prosperity than could be reasonably calculated on. All his sanguine expecta- tions, all his confidence had been justified. His genius and ardour had seemed to foresee and to command his prosperous path. He had, very soon after their engagement ceased, got employ; and all that he had told her would follow, had taken place. He had dis- tinguished himself, and early gained the other step in rank – and must now, by successive captures,[4] have made a handsome fortune. She had only navy lists and newspapers for her authority, but she could not doubt his being rich; – and, in favour of his constancy, she had no reason to believe him married.

How eloquent could Anne Elliot have been, – how eloquent, at least, were her wishes on the side of early warm attachment, and a cheerful confidence in futurity, against that over-anxious caution which seems to insult exertion and distrust Providence ! – She had been forced into prudence in her youth, she learned romance as she grew older – the natural sequel of an unnatural beginning.

With all these circumstances, recollections and feelings, she could not hear that Captain Wentworth's sister was likely to live at Kellynch, without a revival of former pain; and many a stroll and many a sigh were necessary to dispel the agitation of the idea. She often told herself it was folly, before she could harden her nerves sufficiently to feel the continual discussion of the Crofts and their business no evil. She was assisted, however, by that perfect indifference and apparent unconsciousness, among the only three of her own friends in the secret of the past, which seemed almost to deny any recollection of it. She could do justice to the superiority of Lady Russell's motives in this, over those of her father and Elizabeth; she could honour all the better feelings of her calmness – but the general air of oblivion among them was highly important, from whatever it sprung; and in the event of Admiral Croft's really taking Kellynch-hall, she rejoiced anew over the conviction which had always been most grateful to her, of the past being known to those three only among her connexions, by whom no syllable, she believed, would ever be whispered, and in the trust that among his, the brother only with whom he had been residing, had received any information of their short-lived engagement. – That brother had been long removed from the country – and being a sensible man, and, moreover, a single man at the time, she had a fond dependance on no human creature's having heard of it from him.

The sister, Mrs Croft, had then been out of England, accompanying her husband on a foreign station, and her own sister, Mary, had been at school while it all occurred – and never admitted by the pride of some, and the delicacy of others, to the smallest knowledge of it afterwards.

With these supports, she hoped that the acquaintance between herself and the Crofts, which, with Lady Russell still resident in Kellynch, and Mary fixed only three miles off, must be anticipated, need not involve any particular awkwardness.

CHAPTER 5

ON the morning appointed for Admiral and Mrs Croft's seeing Kellynch-hall, Anne found it most natural to take her almost daily walk to Lady Russell's, and keep out of the way till all was over; when she found it most natural to be sorry that she had missed the opportunity of seeing them.

This meeting of the two parties proved highly satisfactory, and decided the whole business at once. Each lady was previously well disposed for an agreement, and saw nothing, therefore, but good manners in the other; and, with regard to the gentlemen, there was such an hearty good humour, such an open, trusting liberality on the Admiral's side, as could not but influence Sir Walter, who had besides been flattered into his very best and most polished behaviour by Mr Shepherd's assurances of his being known, by report, to the Admiral, as a model of good breeding.

The house and grounds, and furniture, were approved, the Crofts were approved, terms, time, every thing, and every body, was right; and Mr Shepherd's clerks were set to work, without there having been a single preliminary difference to modify of all that 'This indenture sheweth.'

Sir Walter, without hesitation, declared the Admiral to be the best-looking sailor he had ever met with, and went so far as to say, that, if his own man might have had the arranging of his hair, he should not be ashamed of being seen with him any where; and the Admiral, with sympathetic cordiality, observed to his wife as they drove back through the Park, 'I thought we should soon come to a deal, my dear, in spite of what they told us at Taunton. The baronet will never set the Thames on fire, but there seems no harm in him : ' – reciprocal compliments, which would have been esteemed about equal.

The Crofts were to have possession at Michaelmas, and as Sir Walter proposed removing to Bath in the course of the preceding month, there was no time to be lost in making every dependant arrangement.

Lady Russell, convinced that Anne would not be allowed to be of any use, or any importance, in the choice of the house which they were going to secure, was very unwilling to have her hurried away so soon, and wanted to make it possible for her to stay behind, till she might convey her to Bath herself after Christmas; but having engagements of her own, which must take her from Kellynch for several weeks, she was unable to give the full invitation she wished; and Anne, though dreading the possible heats of September in all the white glare of Bath, and grieving to forego all the influence so sweet and so sad of the autumnal months in the country, did not think that, every thing considered, she wished to remain. It would be most right, and most wise, and, therefore, must involve least suffering, to go with the others.

Something occurred, however, to give her a different duty. Mary, often a little unwell, and always thinking a great deal of her own complaints, and always in the habit of claiming Anne when any thing was the matter, was indisposed; and foreseeing that she should not have a day's health all the autumn, entreated, or rather required her, for it was hardly entreaty, to come to Uppercross Cottage, and bear her company as long as she should want her, instead of going to Bath.

'I cannot possibly do without Anne,' was Mary's reasoning; and Elizabeth's reply was, 'Then I am sure Anne had better stay, for nobody will want her in Bath.'

To be claimed as a good, though in an improper style, is at least better than being rejected as no good at all; and Anne, glad to be thought of some use, glad to have any thing marked out as a duty, and certainly not sorry to have the scene of it in the country, and her own dear country, readily agreed to stay.

This invitation of Mary's removed all Lady Russell's difficulties, and it was consequently soon settled that Anne should not go to Bath till Lady Russell took her, and that all the intervening time should be divided between Uppercross Cottage and Kellynch-lodge.

So far all was perfectly right; but Lady Russell was almost startled by the wrong of one part of the Kellynch-hall plan, when it burst on her, which was, Mrs Clay's being engaged to go to Bath with Sir Walter and Elizabeth, as a most important and valuable assistant to the latter in all the business before her. Lady Russell was extremely sorry that such a measure should have been resorted to at all – wondered, grieved, and feared – and the affront it contained to Anne, in Mrs Clay's being of so much use, while Anne could be of none, was a very sore aggravation.

Anne herself was become hardened to such affronts; but she felt the imprudence of the arrangement quite as keenly as Lady Russell. With a great deal of quiet observation, and a knowledge, which she often wished less, of her father's character, she was sensible that results the most serious to his family from the intimacy were more than possible. She did not imagine that her father had at present an idea of the kind. Mrs Clay had freckles, and a projecting tooth, and a clumsy wrist, which he was continually making severe remarks upon, in her absence; but she was young, and certainly altogether well-looking, and possessed, in an acute mind and assiduous pleasing manners, infinitely more dangerous attractions than any merely personal might have been. Anne was so impressed by the degree of their danger, that she could not excuse herself from trying to make it perceptible to her sister. She had little hope of success; but Elizabeth, who in the event of such a reverse would be so much more to be pitied than herself, should never, she thought, have reason to reproach her for giving no warning.

She spoke, and seemed only to offend. Elizabeth could not conceive how such an absurd suspicion should occur to her; and indignantly answered for each party's perfectly knowing their situation.

'Mrs Clay,' she said warmly, 'never forgets who she is; and as I am rather better acquainted with her sentiments than you can be, I can assure you, that upon the subject of marriage they are particularly nice; and that she reprobates all inequality of condition and rank more strongly than most people. And as to my father, I really should not have thought that he, who has kept himself single so long for our sakes, need be suspected now. If Mrs Clay were a very beautiful woman, I grant you, it might be wrong to have her so much with me; not that any thing in the world, I am sure, would induce my father to make a degrading match; but he might be rendered unhappy. But poor Mrs Clay, who, with all her merits, can never have been reckoned tolerably pretty! I really think poor Mrs Clay may be staying here in perfect safety. One would imagine you had never heard my father speak of her personal misfortunes, though I know you must fifty times. That tooth of her's! and those freckles! Freckles do not disgust me so very much as they do him: I have known a face not materially disfigured by a few, but he abominates them. You must have heard him notice Mrs Clay's freckles.'

'There is hardly any personal defect,' replied Anne, 'which an agreeable manner might not gradually reconcile one to.'

'I think very differently,' answered Elizabeth, shortly; 'an agreeable manner may set off handsome features, but can never alter plain ones. However, at any rate, as I have a great deal more at stake on this point than any body else can have, I think it rather unnecessary in you to be advising me.'

Anne had done – glad that it was over, and not absolutely hopeless of doing good. Elizabeth, though resenting the suspicion, might yet be made observant by it.

The last office of the four carriage-horses was to draw Sir Walter, Miss Elliot, and Mrs Clay to Bath. The party drove off in very good spirits; Sir Walter prepared with condescending bows for all the afflicted tenantry and cottagers who might have had a hint to shew themselves: and Anne walked up at the same time, in a sort of desolate tranquillity, to the Lodge, where she was to spend the first week.

Her friend was not in better spirits than herself. Lady Russell felt this break-up of the family exceedingly. Their respectability was as dear to her as her own; and a daily intercourse had become precious by habit. It was painful to look upon their deserted grounds, and still worse to anticipate the new hands they were to fall into; and to escape the solitariness and the melancholy of so altered a village, and be out of the way when Admiral and Mrs Croft first arrived, she had determined to make her own absence from home begin when she must give up Anne. Accordingly their removal was made together, and Anne was set down at Uppercross Cottage, in the first stage of Lady Russell's journey.

Uppercross was a moderate-sized village, which a few years back had been completely in the old English style; containing only two houses superior in appearance to those of the yeomen and labourers, – the mansion of the 'squire, with its high walls, great gates, and old trees, substantial and unmodernized – and the compact, tight parsonage, enclosed in its own neat garden, with a vine and a pear-tree trained round its casements; but upon the marriage of the young 'squire, it had received the improvement of a farmhouse elevated into a cottage for his residence; and Uppercross Cottage, with its viranda, French windows, and other prettiness, was quite as likely to catch the traveller's eye, as the more consistent and considerable aspect and premises of the Great House, about a quarter of a mile farther on.

Here Anne had often been staying. She knew the ways of Uppercross as well as those of Kellynch. The two families were so continually meeting, so much in the habit of running in and out of each other's house at all hours, that it was rather a surprise to her to find Mary alone; but being alone, her being unwell and out of spirits, was almost a matter of course. Though better endowed than the elder sister, Mary had not Anne's understanding or temper. While well, and happy, and properly attended to, she had great good humour and excellent spirits; but any indisposition sunk her completely; she had no resources for solitude; and inheriting a considerable share of the Elliot self-importance, was very prone to add to every other distress that of fancying herself neglected and ill-used. In person, she was inferior to both sisters, and had, even in her bloom, only reached the dignity of being 'a fine girl.' She was now lying on the faded sofa of the pretty little drawing-room, the once elegant furniture of which had been gradually growing shabby, under the influence of four summers and two children; and, on Anne's appearing, greeted her with,

'So, you are come at last! I began to think I should never see you. I am so ill I can hardly speak. I have not seen a creature the whole morning!'

'I am sorry to find you unwell,' replied Anne. 'You sent me such a good account of yourself on Thursday!'

'Yes, I made the best of it; I always do; but I was very far from well at the time; and I do not think I ever was so ill in my life as I have been all this morning – very unfit to be left alone, I am sure. Suppose I were to be seized of a sudden in some dreadful way, and not able to ring the bell! So, Lady Russell would not get out. I do not think she has been in this house three times this summer.'

Anne said what was proper, and enquired after her husband. 'Oh! Charles is out shooting. I have not seen him since seven o'clock. He would go, though I told him how ill I was. He said he should not stay out long; but he has never come back, and now it is almost one. I assure you, I have not seen a soul this whole long morning.'

'You have had your little boys with you?'

'Yes, as long as I could bear their noise; but they are so unmanageable that they do me more harm than good. Little Charles does not mind a word I say, and Walter is growing quite as bad.'

'Well, you will soon be better now,' replied Anne, cheerfully. 'You know I always cure you when I come. How are your neighbours at the Great House?'

'I can give you no account of them. I have not seen one of them to-day, except Mr Musgrove, who just stopped and spoke through the window, but without getting off his horse; and though I told him how ill I was, not one of them have been near me. It did not happen to suit the Miss Musgroves, I suppose, and they never put themselves out of their way.'

'You will see them yet, perhaps, before the morning is gone. It is early.'

'I never want them, I assure you. They talk and laugh a great deal too much for me. O! Anne, I am so very unwell! It was quite unkind of you not to come on Thursday.'

'My dear Mary, recollect what a comfortable account you sent me of yourself! You wrote in the cheerfullest manner, and said you were perfectly well, and in no hurry for me; and that being the case, you must be aware that my wish would be to remain with Lady Russell to the last: and besides what I felt on her account, I have really been so busy, have had so much to do, that I could not very conveniently have left Kellynch sooner.'

'Dear me! what can *you* possibly have to do?'

'A great many things, I assure you. More than I can recollect in a moment: but I can tell you some. I have been making a duplicate of the catalogue of my father's books and pictures. I have been several times in the garden with Mackenzie, trying to understand, and make him understand, which of Elizabeth's plants are for Lady Russell. I have had all my own little concerns to arrange – books and music to divide, and all my trunks to re-pack, from not having understood in time what was intended as to the waggons. And one thing I have had to do, Mary, of a more trying nature; going to almost every house in the parish, as a sort of take-leave. I was told that they wished it. But all these things took up a great deal of time.'

'Oh! well;' – and after a moment's pause, 'But you have never asked me one word about our dinner at the Pooles yesterday.'

'Did you go then? I have made no enquiries, because I concluded you must have been obliged to give up the party.'

'Oh! yes, I went. I was very well yesterday; nothing at all the matter with me till this morning. It would have been strange if I had not gone.'

'I am very glad you were well enough, and I hope you had a pleasant party.'

'Nothing remarkable. One always knows beforehand what the dinner will be, and who will be there. And it is so very uncomfortable, not having a carriage of one's own. Mr and Mrs Musgrove took me, and we were so crowded! They are both so very large, and take up so much room! And Mr Musgrove always sits forward. So, there was I, crowded into the back seat with Henrietta and Louisa. And I think it very likely that my illness to-day may be owing to it.'

A little farther perseverance in patience, and forced cheerfulness on Anne's side, produced nearly a cure on Mary's. She could soon sit upright on the sofa, and began to hope she might be able to leave it by dinner-time. Then, forgetting to think of it, she was at the other end of the room, beautifying a nosegay; then, she ate her cold meat; and then she was well enough to propose a little walk.

'Where shall we go?' said she, when they were ready. 'I suppose you will not like to call at the Great House before they have been to see you?'

'I have not the smallest objection on that account,' replied Anne. 'I should never think of standing on such ceremony with people I know so well as Mrs and the Miss Musgroves.'

PERSUASION

'Oh! but they ought to call upon you as soon as possible. They ought to feel what is due to you as *my* sister. However, we may as well go and sit with them a little while, and when we have got that over, we can enjoy our walk.'

Anne had always thought such a style of intercourse highly imprudent; but she had ceased to endeavour to check it, from believing that, though there were on each side continual subjects of offence, neither family could now do without it. To the Great House accordingly they went, to sit the full half hour in the old-fashioned square parlour, with a small carpet and shining floor, to which the present daughters of the house were gradually giving the proper air of confusion by a grand piano forte and a harp, flower-stands and little tables placed in every direction. Oh! could the originals of the portraits against the wainscot, could the gentlemen in brown velvet and the ladies in blue satin have seen what was going on, have been conscious of such an overthrow of all order and neatness! The portraits themselves seemed to be staring in astonishment.

The Musgroves, like their houses, were in a state of alteration, perhaps of improvement. The father and mother were in the old English style, and the young people in the new. Mr and Mrs Musgrove were a very good sort of people; friendly and hospitable, not much educated, and not at all elegant. Their children had more modern minds and manners. There was a numerous family; but the only two grown up, excepting Charles, were Henrietta and Louisa, young ladies of nineteen and twenty, who had brought from a school at Exeter all the usual stock of accomplishments, and were now, like thousands of other young ladies, living to be fashionable, happy, and merry. Their dress had every advantage, their faces were rather pretty, their spirits extremely good, their manners unembarrassed and pleasant; they were of consequence at home, and favourites abroad. Anne always contemplated them as some of the happiest creatures of her acquaintance; but still, saved as we all are by some comfortable feeling of superiority from wishing for the possibility of exchange, she would not have given up her own more elegant and cultivated mind for all their enjoyments; and envied them nothing but that seemingly perfect good understanding and agreement together, that good-humoured

67

mutual affection, of which she had known so little herself with either of her sisters.

They were received with great cordiality. Nothing seemed amiss on the side of the Great House family, which was generally, as Anne very well knew, the least to blame. The half hour was chatted away pleasantly enough; and she was not at all surprised, at the end of it, to have their walking party joined by both the Miss Musgroves, at Mary's particular invitation.

CHAPTER 6

ANNE had not wanted this visit to Uppercross, to learn that a removal from one set of people to another, though at a distance of only three miles, will often include a total change of conversation, opinion, and idea. She had never been staying there before, without being struck by it, or without wishing that other Elliots could have her advantage in seeing how unknown, or unconsidered there, were the affairs which at Kellynch-hall were treated as of such general publicity and pervading interest; yet, with all this experience, she believed she must now submit to feel that another lesson, in the art of knowing our own nothingness beyond our own circle, was become necessary for her; – for certainly, coming as she did, with a heart full of the subject which had been completely occupying both houses in Kellynch for many weeks, she had expected rather more curiosity and sympathy than she found in the separate, but very similar remark of Mr and Mrs Musgrove – 'So, Miss Anne, Sir Walter and your sister are gone; and what part of Bath do you think they will settle in?' and this, without much waiting for an answer; – or in the young ladies' addition of, 'I hope *we* shall be in Bath in the winter; but remember, papa, if we do go, we must be in a good situation – none of your Queen-squares for us!' or in the anxious supplement from Mary, of 'Upon my word, I shall be pretty well off, when you are all gone away to be happy at Bath!'

She could only resolve to avoid such self-delusion in future, and think with heightened gratitude of the extraordinary blessing of having one such truly sympathising friend as Lady Russell.

The Mr Musgroves had their own game to guard, and to destroy; their own horses, dogs, and newspapers to engage them; and the females were fully occupied in all the other common subjects of house-keeping, neighbours, dress, dancing, and music. She acknowledged it to be very fitting, that every little social commonwealth should dictate its own matters of discourse; and hoped, ere long, to become a not unworthy member of the one she was now transplanted into. – With the prospect of spending at least two months at Uppercross, it was highly incumbent on her to clothe her imagination, her memory, and all her ideas in as much of Uppercross as possible.

She had no dread of these two months. Mary was not so repulsive and unsisterly as Elizabeth, nor so inaccessible to all influence of hers; neither was there any thing among the other component parts of the cottage inimical to comfort. – She was always on friendly terms with her brother-in-law; and in the children, who loved her nearly as well, and respected her a great deal more than their mother, she had an object of interest, amusement, and wholesome exertion.

Charles Musgrove was civil and agreeable; in sense and temper he was undoubtedly superior to his wife; but not of powers, or conversation, or grace, to make the past, as they were connected together, at all a dangerous contemplation; though, at the same time, Anne could believe, with Lady Russell, that a more equal match might have greatly improved him; and that a woman of real understanding might have given more consequence to his character, and more usefulness, rationality, and elegance to his habits and pursuits. As it was, he did nothing with much zeal, but sport; and his time was otherwise trifled away, without benefit from books, or any thing else. He had very good spirits, which never seemed much affected by his wife's occasional lowness; bore with her unreasonableness sometimes to Anne's admiration; and, upon the whole, though there was very often a little disagreement, (in which she had sometimes more share than she wished, being appealed to by both parties) they might pass for a happy couple. They were always perfectly agreed in the want of more money, and a strong inclination for a handsome present from his father; but here, as on most topics, he had the superiority, for while Mary thought it a great shame that such a present was not made, he always contended for his father's having many other uses for his money, and a right to spend it as he liked.

As to the management of their children, his theory was much better than his wife's, and his practice not so bad. – 'I could manage them very well, if it were not for Mary's interference,' – was what Anne often heard him say, and had a good deal of faith in; but when listening in turn to Mary's reproach of 'Charles spoils the children so that I cannot get them into any order,' – she never had the smallest temptation to say, 'Very true.'

One of the least agreeable circumstances of her residence there, was her being treated with too much confidence by all parties, and being too much in the secret of the complaints of each house. Known to have some influence with her sister, she was continually requested, or at least receiving hints to exert it, beyond what was practicable. 'I wish you could persuade Mary not to be always fancying herself ill,' was Charles's language; and, in an unhappy mood, thus spoke Mary; – 'I do believe if Charles were to see me dying, he would not think there was any thing the matter with me. I am sure, Anne, if you would, you might persuade him that I really am very ill – a great deal worse than I ever own.'

Mary's declaration was, 'I hate sending the children to the Great House, though their grandmamma is always wanting to see them, for she humours and indulges them to such a degree, and gives them so much trash and sweet things, that they are sure to come back sick and cross for the rest of the day.' – And Mrs Musgrove took the first opportunity of being alone with Anne, to say, 'Oh! Miss Anne, I cannot help wishing Mrs Charles had a little of your method with those children. They are quite different creatures with you! But to be sure, in general they are so spoilt! It is a pity you cannot put your sister in the way of managing them. They are as fine healthy children as ever were seen, poor little dears, without partiality; but Mrs Charles knows no more how they should be treated! – Bless me, how troublesome they are sometimes! – I assure you, Miss Anne, it prevents my wishing to see them at our house so often as I otherwise should. I believe Mrs Charles is not quite pleased with my not inviting them oftener; but you know it is very bad to have children with one, that one is obliged to be checking every moment: "don't do this, and don't do that;" – or that one can only keep in tolerable order by more cake than is good for them.'

She had this communication, moreover, from Mary. 'Mrs Musgrove thinks all her servants so steady, that it would be high treason to call it in question; but I am sure, without exaggeration, that her upper house-maid and laundry-maid, instead of being in their business, are gadding about the village, all day long. I meet them wherever I go; and I declare, I never go twice into my nursery without seeing something of them. If Jemima were not the trustiest, steadiest creature in the world, it would be enough to spoil her; for she tells me, they are always tempting her to take a walk with them.' And on Mrs Musgrove's side, it was, – 'I make a rule of never interfering in any of my daughter-in-law's concerns, for I know it would not do; but I shall tell *you*, Miss Anne, because you may be able to set things to rights, that I have no very good opinion of Mrs Charles's nursery-maid: I hear strange stories of her; she is always upon the gad: and from my own knowledge, I can declare, she is such a fine-dressing lady, that she is enough to ruin any servants she comes near. Mrs Charles quite swears by her, I know; but I just give you this hint, that you may be upon the watch; because, if you see any thing amiss, you need not be afraid of mentioning it.'

Again; it was Mary's complaint, that Mrs Musgrove was very apt not to give her the precedence that was her due, when they dined at the Great House with other families; and she did not see any reason why she was to be considered so much at home as to lose her place. And one day, when Anne was walking with only the Miss Musgroves, one of them, after talking of rank, people of rank, and jealousy of rank, said, 'I have no scruple of observing to *you*, how nonsensical some persons are about their place, be-cause, all the world knows how easy and indifferent you are about it: but I wish any body could give Mary a hint that it would be a great deal better if she were not so very tenacious; especially, if she would not be always putting herself forward to take place of mamma. Nobody doubts her right to have precedence of mamma, but it would be more becoming in her not to be always insisting on it. It is not that mamma cares about it the least in the world, but I know it is taken notice of by many persons.'

How was Anne to set all these matters to rights? She could do little more than listen patiently, soften every grievance, and excuse each to the other, give them all hints of the forbearance necessary between such near neighbours, and make those hints broadest which were meant for her sister's benefit.

In all other respects, her visit began and proceeded very well. Her own spirits improved by change of place and subject, by being removed three miles from Kellynch: Mary's ailments lessened by having a constant companion; and their daily intercourse with the other family, since there was neither superior affection, confidence, nor employment in the cottage, to be interrupted by it, was rather an advantage. It was certainly carried nearly as far as possible, for they met every morning, and hardly ever spent an evening asunder; but she believed they should not have done so well without the sight of Mr and Mrs Musgrove's respectable forms in the usual places, or without the talking, laughing, and singing of their daughters.

She played a great deal better than either of the Miss Musgroves; but having no voice, no knowledge of the harp, and no fond parents to sit by and fancy themselves delighted, her performance was little thought of, only out of civility, or to refresh the others, as she was well aware. She knew that when she played she was giving pleasure only to herself; but this was no new sensation: excepting one short period of her life, she had never, since the age of fourteen, never since the loss of her dear mother, known the happiness of being listened to, or encouraged by any just appreciation or real taste. In music she had been always used to feel alone in the world; and Mr and Mrs Musgrove's fond partiality for their own daughters' performance, and total indifference to any other person's, gave her much more pleasure for their sakes, than mortification for her own.

The party at the Great House was sometimes increased by other company. The neighbourhood was not large, but the Musgroves were visited by every body, and had more dinner parties, and more callers, more visitors by invitation and by chance, than any other family. They were more completely popular.

The girls were wild for dancing; and the evenings ended, occasionally, in an unpremeditated little ball. There was a family of cousins within a walk of Uppercross, in less affluent circumstances, who depended on the Musgroves for all their pleasures: they would come at any time, and help play at any thing, or dance any where; and Anne, very much preferring the office of musician to a more active post, played country dances to them by the hour together; a kindness which always recommended her musical powers to the notice of Mr and Mrs Musgrove more than any thing else, and often drew this compliment; – 'Well done, Miss Anne! very well done indeed! Lord bless me! how those little fingers of yours fly about!'

So passed the first three weeks. Michaelmas came; and now Anne's heart must be in Kellynch again. A beloved home made over to others; all the precious rooms and furniture, groves, and prospects, beginning to own other eyes and other limbs! She could not think of much else on the 29th of September; and she had this sympathetic touch in the evening, from Mary, who, on having occasion to note down the day of the month, exclaimed, 'Dear me! is not this the day the Crofts were to come to Kellynch? I am glad I did not think of it before. How low it makes me!'

The Crofts took possession with true naval alertness, and were to be visited. Mary deplored the necessity for herself. 'Nobody knew how much she should suffer. She should put it off as long as she could.' But was not easy till she had talked Charles into driving her over on an early day; and was in a very animated, comfortable state of imaginary agitation, when she came back. Anne had very sincerely rejoiced in there being no means of her going. She wished, however, to see the Crofts, and was glad to be within when the visit was returned. They came; the master of the house was not at home, but the two sisters were together; and as it chanced that Mrs Croft fell to the share of Anne, while the admiral sat by Mary, and made himself very agreeable by his good-humoured notice of her little boys, she was well able to watch for a likeness, and if it failed her in the features, to catch it in the voice, or the turn of sentiment and expression.

Mrs Croft, though neither tall nor fat, had a squareness, up-rightness, and vigour of form, which gave importance to her person. She had bright dark eyes, good teeth, and altogether an agreeable face; though her reddened and weather-beaten complexion, the consequence of her having been almost as much at sea as her husband, made her seem to have lived some years longer in the world than her real eight and thirty. Her manners were open, easy, and decided, like one who had no distrust of herself, and no doubts of what to do; without any approach to coarseness, however, or any want of good humour. Anne gave her credit, indeed, for feelings of great consideration towards herself, in all that related to Kellynch; and it pleased her : especially, as she had satisfied herself in the very first half minute, in the instant even of introduction, that there was not the smallest symptom of any knowledge or suspicion on Mrs Croft's side, to give a bias of any sort. She was quite easy on that head, and consequently full of strength and courage, till for a moment electrified by Mrs Croft's suddenly saying, –

'It was you, and not your sister, I find, that my brother had the pleasure of being acquainted with, when he was in this country.'

Anne hoped she had outlived the age of blushing; but the age of emotion she certainly had not.

'Perhaps you may not have heard that he is married,' added Mrs Croft.

She could now answer as she ought; and was happy to feel, when Mrs Croft's next words explained it to be Mr Wentworth of whom she spoke, that she had said nothing which might not do for either brother. She immediately felt how reasonable it was, that Mrs Croft should be thinking and speaking of Edward, and not of Frederick; and with shame at her own forgetfulness, applied herself to the knowledge of their former neighbour's present state, with proper interest.

The rest was all tranquillity; till just as they were moving, she heard the admiral say to Mary,

'We are expecting a brother of Mrs Croft's here soon; I dare say you know him by name.'

He was cut short by the eager attacks of the little boys, clinging to him like an old friend, and declaring he should not go; and being too much engrossed by proposals of carrying them away in his coat pocket, &c. to have another moment for finishing or recollecting what he had begun, Anne was left to persuade herself, as well as she could, that the same brother must still be in question. She could not, however, reach such a degree of certainty, as not to be anxious to hear whether any thing had been said on the subject at the other house, where the Crofts had previously been calling.

The folks of the Great House were to spend the evening of this

day at the Cottage; and it being now too late in the year for such
visits to be made on foot, the coach was beginning to be listened
for, when the youngest Miss Musgrove walked in. That she was
coming to apologize, and that they should have to spend the evening by themselves, was the first black idea; and Mary was quite
ready to be affronted, when Louisa made all right by saying, that
she only came on foot, to leave more room for the harp, which
was bringing in the carriage.

'And I will tell you our reason,' she added, 'and all about it. I
am come on to give you notice, that papa and mamma are out of
spirits this evening, especially mamma; she is thinking so much
of poor Richard! And we agreed it would be best to have the harp,
for it seems to amuse her more than the piano-forte. I will tell you
why she is out of spirits. When the Crofts called this morning,
(they called here afterwards, did not they?) they happened to say,
that her brother, Captain Wentworth, is just returned to England,
or paid off, or something, and is coming to see them almost
directly; and most unluckily it came into mamma's head, when
they were gone, that Wentworth, or something very like it, was
the name of poor Richard's captain, at one time, I do not know
when or where, but a great while before he died, poor fellow!
And upon looking over his letters and things, she found it was so;
and is perfectly sure that this must be the very man, and her
head is quite full of it, and of poor Richard! So we must all be as
merry as we can, that she may not be dwelling upon such gloomy
things.'

The real circumstances of this pathetic piece of family history
were, that the Musgroves had had the ill fortune of a very troublesome, hopeless son; and the good fortune to lose him before he
reached his twentieth year; that he had been sent to sea, because
he was stupid and unmanageable on shore; that he had been very
little cared for at any time by his family, though quite as much as
he deserved; seldom heard of, and scarcely at all regretted, when
the intelligence of his death abroad had worked its way to Uppercross, two years before.

He had, in fact, though his sisters were now doing all they
could for him, by calling him 'poor Richard,' been nothing better
than a thick-headed, unfeeling, unprofitable Dick Musgrove, who

had never done any thing to entitle himself to more than the abbreviation of his name, living or dead.

He had been several years at sea, and had, in the course of those removals to which all midshipmen are liable, and especially such midshipmen as every captain wishes to get rid of, been six months on board Captain Frederick Wentworth's frigate, the Laconia; and from the Laconia he had, under the influence of his captain, written the only two letters which his father and mother had ever received from him during the whole of his absence; that is to say, the only two disinterested letters; all the rest had been mere applications for money.

In each letter he had spoken well of his captain; but yet, so little were they in the habit of attending to such matters, so unobservant and incurious were they as to the names of men or ships, that it had made scarcely any impression at the time; and that Mrs Musgrove should have been suddenly struck, this very day, with a recollection of the name of Wentworth, as connected with her son, seemed one of those extraordinary bursts of mind which do sometimes occur.

She had gone to her letters, and found it all as she supposed; and the reperusal of these letters, after so long an interval, her poor son gone for ever, and all the strength of his faults forgotten, had affected her spirits exceedingly, and thrown her into greater grief for him than she had known on first hearing of his death. Mr Musgrove was, in a lesser degree, affected likewise; and when they reached the cottage, they were evidently in want, first, of being listened to anew on this subject, and afterwards, of all the relief which cheerful companions could give.

To hear them talking so much of Captain Wentworth, repeating his name so often, puzzling over past years, and at last ascertaining that it *might*, that it probably *would*, turn out to be the very same Captain Wentworth whom they recollected meeting, once or twice, after their coming back from Clifton; – a very fine young man; but they could not say whether it was seven or eight years ago, – was a new sort of trial to Anne's nerves. She found, however, that it was one to which she must enure herself. Since he actually was expected in the country, she must teach herself to be insensible on such points. And not only did it appear that

77

he was expected, and speedily, but the Musgroves, in their warm gratitude for the kindness he had shewn poor Dick, and very high respect for his character, stamped as it was by poor Dick's having been six months under his care, and mentioning him in strong, though not perfectly well spelt praise, as 'a fine dashing felow, only two perticular about the school-master,' [5] were bent on introducing themselves, and seeking his acquaintance, as soon as they could hear of his arrival.

The resolution of doing so helped to form the comfort of their evening.

CHAPTER 7

A VERY few days more, and Captain Wentworth was known to be at Kellynch, and Mr Musgrove had called on him, and come back warm in his praise, and he was engaged with the Crofts to dine at Uppercross, by the end of another week. It had been a great disappointment to Mr Musgrove, to find that no earlier day could be fixed, so impatient was he to shew his gratitude, by seeing Captain Wentworth under his own roof, and welcoming him to all that was strongest and best in his cellars. But a week must pass; only a week, in Anne's reckoning, and then, she supposed, they must meet; and soon she began to wish that she could feel secure even for a week.

Captain Wentworth made a very early return to Mr Musgrove's civility, and she was all but calling there in the same half hour! – She and Mary were actually setting forward for the great house, where, as she afterwards learnt, they must inevitably have found him, when they were stopped by the eldest boy's being at that moment brought home in consequence of a bad fall. The child's situation put the visit entirely aside, but she could not hear of her escape with indifference, even in the midst of the serious anxiety which they afterwards felt on his account.

His collar-bone was found to be dislocated, and such injury received in the back, as roused the most alarming ideas. It was an afternoon of distress, and Anne had every thing to do at once – the apothecary to send for – the father to have pursued and informed – the mother to support and keep from hysterics – the servants to control – the youngest child to banish, and the poor suffering one to attend and soothe; – besides sending, as soon as she recollected it, proper notice to the other house, which brought her an accession rather of frightened, enquiring companions, than of very useful assistants.

Her brother's return was the first comfort; he could take best care of his wife, and the second blessing was the arrival of the apothecary. Till he came and had examined the child, their apprehensions were the worse for being vague; – they suspected great injury, but knew not where; but now the collar-bone was soon replaced, and though Mr Robinson felt and felt, and rubbed, and looked grave, and spoke low words both to the father and the aunt, still they were all to hope the best, and to be able to part and eat their dinner in tolerable ease of mind; and then it was, just before they parted, that the two young aunts were able so far to digress from their nephew's state, as to give the information of Captain Wentworth's visit; – staying five minutes behind their father and mother, to endeavour to express how perfectly delighted they were with him, how much handsomer, how infinitely more agreeable they thought him than any individual among their male acquaintance, who had been at all a favourite before – how glad they had been to hear papa invite him to stay dinner – how sorry when he said it was quite out of his power – and how glad again, when he had promised in reply to papa and mamma's farther pressing invitations, to come and dine with them on the morrow, actually on the morrow ! – And he had promised it in so pleasant a manner, as if he felt all the motive of their attention just as he ought ! – And, in short, he had looked and said every thing with such exquisite grace, that they could assure them all, their heads were both turned by him ! – And off they ran, quite as full of glee as of love, and apparently more full of Captain Wentworth than of little Charles.

The same story and the same raptures were repeated, when the two girls came with their father, through the gloom of the evening, to make enquiries; and Mr Musgrove, no longer under the first uneasiness about his heir, could add his confirmation and praise, and hope there would be now no occasion for putting Captain Wentworth off, and only be sorry to think that the cottage party, probably, would not like to leave the little boy, to give him the meeting. – 'Oh, no ! as to leaving the little boy !' – both father and mother were in much too strong and recent alarm to bear the thought; and Anne, in the joy of the escape, could not help adding her warm protestations to theirs.

Charles Musgrove, indeed, afterwards shewed more of inclination; 'the child was going on so well – and he wished so much to be introduced to Captain Wentworth, that, perhaps, he might join them in the evening; he would not dine from home, but he might walk in for half an hour.' But in this he was eagerly opposed by his wife, with 'Oh, no! indeed, Charles, I cannot bear to have you go away. Only think, if any thing should happen!'

The child had a good night, and was going on well the next day. It must be a work of time to ascertain that no injury had been done to the spine, but Mr Robinson found nothing to increase alarm, and Charles Musgrove began consequently to feel no necessity for longer confinement. The child was to be kept in bed, and amused as quietly as possible; but what was there for a father to do? This was quite a female case, and it would be highly absurd in him, who could be of no use at home, to shut himself up. His father very much wished him to meet Captain Wentworth, and there being no sufficient reason against it, he ought to go; and it ended in his making a bold public declaration, when he came in from shooting, of his meaning to dress directly, and dine at the other house.

'Nothing can be going on better than the child,' said he, 'so I told my father just now that I would come, and he thought me quite right. Your sister being with you, my love, I have no scruple at all. You would not like to leave him yourself, but you see I can be of no use. Anne will send for me if any thing is the matter.'

Husbands and wives generally understand when opposition will be vain. Mary knew, from Charles's manner of speaking, that he was quite determined on going, and that it would be of no use to teaze him. She said nothing, therefore, till he was out of the room, but as soon as there was only Anne to hear,

'So! You and I are to be left to shift by ourselves, with this poor sick child – and not a creature coming near us all the evening! I knew how it would be. This is always my luck! If there is any thing disagreeable going on, men are always sure to get out of it, and Charles is as bad as any of them. Very unfeeling! I must say it is very unfeeling of him, to be running away from his poor little boy; talks of his being going on so well! How does he know that he is going on well, or that there may not be a sudden change half an hour hence? I did not think Charles would have been so unfeeling. So, here he is to go away and enjoy himself, and because I am the poor mother, I am not to be allowed to stir; – and yet, I am sure, I am more unfit than any body else to be about the child. My being the mother is the very reason why my feelings should not be tried. I am not at all equal to it. You saw how hysterical I was yesterday.'

'But that was only the effect of the suddenness of your alarm – of the shock. You will not be hysterical again. I dare say we shall have nothing to distress us. I perfectly understand Mr Robinson's directions, and have no fears; and indeed, Mary, I cannot wonder at your husband. Nursing does not belong to a man, it is not his province. A sick child is always the mother's property, her own feelings generally make it so.'

'I hope I am as fond of my child as any mother – but I do not know that I am of any more use in the sick-room than Charles, for I cannot be always scolding and teazing a poor child when it is ill; and you saw, this morning, that if I told him to keep quiet, he was sure to begin kicking about. I have not nerves for the sort of thing.'

'But, could you be comfortable yourself, to be spending the whole evening away from the poor boy?'

'Yes; you see his papa can, and why should not I? – Jemima is so careful! And she could send us word every hour how he was. I really think Charles might as well have told his father we would all come. I am not more alarmed about little Charles now than he is. I was dreadfully alarmed yesterday, but the case is very different to-day.'

'Well – if you do not think it too late to give notice for yourself, suppose you were to go, as well as your husband. Leave little Charles to my care. Mr and Mrs Musgrove cannot think it wrong, while I remain with him.'

'Are you serious?' cried Mary, her eyes brightening. 'Dear me! that's a very good thought, very good indeed. To be sure I may just as well go as not, for I am of no use at home – am I? and it only harasses me. You, who have not a mother's feelings, are a great deal the properest person. You can make little Charles do any thing; he always minds you at a word. It will be a great deal better than leaving him with only Jemima. Oh! I will certainly go; I am sure I ought if I can, quite as much as Charles, for they want me excessively to be acquainted with Captain Wentworth, and I know you do not mind being left alone. An excellent thought of yours, indeed, Anne! I will go and tell Charles, and get ready directly. You can send for us, you know, at a moment's notice, if any thing is the matter; but I dare say there will be nothing to alarm you. I should not go, you may be sure, if I did not feel quite at ease about my dear child.'

The next moment she was tapping at her husband's dressing-room door, and as Anne followed her up stairs, she was in time for the whole conversation, which began with Mary's saying, in a tone of great exultation,

'I mean to go with you, Charles, for I am of no more use at home than you are. If I were to shut myself up for ever with the child, I should not be able to persuade him to do any thing he did not like. Anne will stay; Anne undertakes to stay at home and take care of him. It is Anne's own proposal, and so I shall go with you, which will be a great deal better, for I have not dined at the other house since Tuesday.'

'This is very kind of Anne,' was her husband's answer, 'and I should be very glad to have you go; but it seems rather hard that she should be left at home by herself, to nurse our sick child.'

Anne was now at hand to take up her own cause, and the sincerity of her manner being soon sufficient to convince him, where conviction was at least very agreeable, he had no farther scruples as to her being left to dine alone, though he still wanted her to join them in the evening, when the child might be at rest for the night, and kindly urged her to let him come and fetch her; but she was quite unpersuadable; and this being the case, she had ere long the pleasure of seeing them set off together in high spirits. They were gone, she hoped, to be happy, however oddly constructed such happiness might seem; as for herself, she was left with as many sensations of comfort, as were, perhaps, ever likely to be hers. She knew herself to be of the first utility to the child; and what was it to her, if Frederick Wentworth were only half a mile distant, making himself agreeable to others!

She would have liked to know how he felt as to a meeting. Perhaps indifferent, if indifference could exist under such circumstances. He must be either indifferent or unwilling. Had he wished ever to see her again, he need not have waited till this time; he

would have done what she could not but believe that in his place
she should have done long ago, when events had been early giving
him the independence which alone had been wanting.

Her brother and sister came back delighted with their new
acquaintance, and their visit in general. There had been music,
singing, talking, laughing, all that was most agreeable; charming
manners in Captain Wentworth, no shyness or reserve; they
seemed all to know each other perfectly, and he was coming the
very next morning to shoot with Charles. He was to come to
breakfast, but not at the Cottage, though that had been proposed
at first; but then he had been pressed to come to the Great House
instead, and he seemed afraid of being in Mrs Charles Musgrove's
way, on account of the child; and therefore, somehow, they
hardly knew how, it ended in Charles's being to meet him to
breakfast at his father's.

Anne understood it. He wished to avoid seeing her. He had
enquired after her, she found, slightly, as might suit a former
slight acquaintance, seeming to acknowledge such as she had
acknowledged, actuated, perhaps, by the same view of escaping
introduction when they were to meet.

The morning hours of the Cottage were always later than those
of the other house; and on the morrow the difference was so great,
that Mary and Anne were not more than beginning breakfast
when Charles came in to say that they were just setting off, that
he was come for his dogs, that his sisters were following with
Captain Wentworth, his sisters meaning to visit Mary and the
child, and Captain Wentworth proposing also to wait on her for
a few minutes, if not inconvenient; and though Charles had
answered for the child's being in no such state as could make it
inconvenient, Captain Wentworth would not be satisfied without
his running on to give notice.

Mary, very much gratified by this attention, was delighted to
receive him; while a thousand feelings rushed on Anne, of which
this was the most consoling, that it would soon be over. And it
was soon over. In two minutes after Charles's preparation, the
others appeared; they were in the drawing-room. Her eye half
met Captain Wentworth's; a bow, a curtsey passed; she heard his
voice – he talked to Mary, said all that was right; said something

to the Miss Musgroves, enough to mark an easy footing: the room seemed full – full of persons and voices – but a few minutes ended it. Charles shewed himself at the window, all was ready, their visitor had bowed and was gone; the Miss Musgroves were gone too, suddenly resolving to walk to the end of the village with the sportsmen: the room was cleared, and Anne might finish her breakfast as she could.

'It is over! it is over!' she repeated to herself again, and again, in nervous gratitude. 'The worst is over!'

Mary talked, but she could not attend. She had seen him. They had met. They had been once more in the same room!

Soon, however, she began to reason with herself, and try to be feeling less. Eight years, almost eight years had passed, since all had been given up. How absurd to be resuming the agitation which such an interval had banished into distance and indistinctness! What might not eight years do? Events of every description, changes, alienations, removals, – all, all must be comprised in it; and oblivion of the past – how natural, how certain too! It included nearly a third part of her own life.

Alas! with all her reasonings, she found, that to retentive feelings eight years may be little more than nothing.

Now, how were his sentiments to be read? Was this like wishing to avoid her? And the next moment she was hating herself for the folly which asked the question.

On one other question, which perhaps her utmost wisdom might not have prevented, she was soon spared all suspense; for after the Miss Musgroves had returned and finished their visit at the Cottage, she had this spontaneous information from Mary:

'Captain Wentworth is not very gallant by you, Anne, though he was so attentive to me. Henrietta asked him what he thought of you, when they went away; and he said, 'You were so altered he should not have known you again.'

Mary had no feelings to make her respect her sister's in a common way; but she was perfectly unsuspicious of being inflicting any peculiar wound.

'Altered beyond his knowledge!' Anne fully submitted, in silent, deep mortification. Doubtless it was so; and she could take no revenge, for he was not altered, or not for the worse. She had already acknowledged it to herself, and she could not think differently, let him think of her as he would. No; the years which had destroyed her youth and bloom had only given him a more glowing, manly, open look, in no respect lessening his personal advantages. She had seen the same Frederick Wentworth.

'So altered that he should not have known her again!' These were words which could not but dwell with her. Yet she soon began to rejoice that she had heard them. They were of sobering tendency; they allayed agitation; they composed, and consequently must make her happier.

Frederick Wentworth had used such words, or something like them, but without an idea that they would be carried round to her. He had thought her wretchedly altered, and, in the first moment of appeal, had spoken as he felt. He had not forgiven Anne Elliot. She had used him ill; deserted and disappointed him; and worse, she had shewn a feebleness of character in doing so, which his own decided, confident temper could not endure. She had given him up to oblige others. It had been the effect of over-persuasion. It had been weakness and timidity.

He had been most warmly attached to her, and had never seen a woman since whom he thought her equal; but, except from some natural sensation of curiosity, he had no desire of meeting her again. Her power with him was gone for ever.

It was now his object to marry. He was rich, and being turned on shore, fully intended to settle as soon as he could be properly tempted; actually looking round, ready to fall in love with all the speed which a clear head and quick taste could allow. He had a heart for either of the Miss Musgroves, if they could catch it; a heart, in short, for any pleasing young woman who came in his way, excepting Anne Elliot. This was his only secret exception, when he said to his sister, in answer to her suppositions,

'Yes, here I am, Sophia, quite ready to make a foolish match. Any body between fifteen and thirty may have me for asking. A little beauty, and a few smiles, and a few compliments to the navy, and I am a lost man. Should not this be enough for a sailor, who has had no society among women to make him nice?'

He said it, she knew, to be contradicted. His bright, proud eye spoke the conviction that he was nice; and Anne Elliot was not out of his thoughts, when he more seriously described the woman he should wish to meet with. 'A strong mind, with sweetness of manner,' made the first and the last of the description.

'This is the woman I want, said he. Something a little inferior I shall of course put up with, but it must not be much. If I am a fool, I shall be a fool indeed, for I have thought on the subject more than most men.'

CHAPTER 8

FROM this time Captain Wentworth and Anne Elliot were repeatedly in the same circle. They were soon dining in company together at Mr Musgrove's, for the little boy's state could no longer supply his aunt with a pretence for absenting herself; and this was but the beginning of other dinings and other meetings.

Whether former feelings were to be renewed, must be brought to the proof; former times must undoubtedly be brought to the recollection of each; *they* could not but be reverted to; the year of their engagement could not but be named by him, in the little narratives or descriptions which conversation called forth. His profession qualified him, his disposition led him, to talk; and '*That* was in the year six;' '*That* happened before I went to sea in the year six,' occurred in the course of the first evening they spent together : and though his voice did not falter, and though she had no reason to suppose his eye wandering towards her while he spoke, Anne felt the utter impossibility, from her knowledge of his mind, that he could be unvisited by remembrance any more than herself. There must be the same immediate association of thought, though she was very far from conceiving it to be of equal pain.

They had no conversation together, no intercourse but what the commonest civility required. Once so much to each other ! Now nothing ! There *had* been a time, when of all the large party now filling the drawing-room at Uppercross, they would have found it most difficult to cease to speak to one another. With the exception, perhaps, of Admiral and Mrs Croft, who seemed particularly attached and happy, (Anne could allow no other exception even among the married couples) there could have been no two hearts so open, no tastes so similar, no feelings so in unison, no countenances so beloved. Now they were as strangers; nay, worse than strangers, for they could never become acquainted. It was a perpetual estrangement.

When he talked, she heard the same voice, and discerned the

same mind. There was a very general ignorance of all naval matters throughout the party; and he was very much questioned, and especially by the two Miss Musgroves, who seemed hardly to have any eyes but for him, as to the manner of living on board, daily regulations, food, hours, &c.; and their surprise at his accounts, at learning the degree of accommodation and arrangement which was practicable, drew from him some pleasant ridicule, which reminded Anne of the early days when she too had been ignorant, and she too had been accused of supposing sailors to be living on board without any thing to eat, or any cook to dress it if there were, or any servant to wait, or any knife and fork to use.

From thus listening and thinking, she was roused by a whisper of Mrs Musgrove's, who, overcome by fond regrets, could not help saying,

'Ah! Miss Anne, if it had pleased Heaven to spare my poor son, I dare say he would have been just such another by this time.'

Anne suppressed a smile, and listened kindly, while Mrs Musgrove relieved her heart a little more; and for a few minutes, therefore, could not keep pace with the conversation of the others. – When she could let her attention take its natural course again, she found the Miss Musgroves just fetching the navy-list, – (their own navy list, the first that had ever been at Uppercross); and sitting down together to pore over it, with the professed view of finding out the ships which Captain Wentworth had commanded.

'Your first was the Asp, I remember; we will look for the Asp.'

'You will not find her there. – Quite worn out and broken up. I was the last man who commanded her. – Hardly fit for service then. – Reported fit for home service for a year or two, – and so I was sent off to the West Indies.'

The girls looked all amazement.

'The admiralty,' he continued, 'entertain themselves now and then, with sending a few hundred men to sea, in a ship not fit to be employed. But they have a great many to provide for; and among the thousands that may just as well go to the bottom as not, it is impossible for them to distinguish the very set who may be least missed.'

'Phoo! phoo!' cried the admiral, 'what stuff these young fellows talk! Never was a better sloop than the Asp in her day. – For an old built sloop, you would not see her equal. Lucky fellow to get her! – He knows there must have been twenty better men than himself applying for her at the same time. Lucky fellow to get any thing so soon, with no more interest than his.'

'I felt my luck, admiral, I assure you;' replied Captain Wentworth, seriously. – 'I was as well satisfied with my appointment as you can desire. It was a great object with me, at that time, to be at sea, – a very great object. I wanted to be doing something.'

'To be sure you did. – What should a young fellow, like you, do ashore, for half a year together? – If a man has not a wife, he soon wants to be afloat again.'

'But, Captain Wentworth,' cried Louisa, 'how vexed you must have been when you came to the Asp, to see what an old thing they had given you.'

'I knew pretty well what she was, before that day;' said he, smiling. 'I had no more discoveries to make, than you would have as to the fashion and strength of any old pelisse, which you had seen lent about among half your acquaintance, ever since you could remember, and which at last, on some very wet day, is lent to yourself. – Ah! she was a dear old Asp to me. She did all that I wanted. I knew she would. – I knew that we should either go to the bottom together, or that she would be the making of me; and I never had two days of foul weather all the time I was at sea in her; and after taking privateers enough to be very entertaining, I had the good luck, in my passage home the next autumn, to fall in with the very French frigate I wanted. – I brought her into Plymouth; and here was another instance of luck. We had not been six hours in the Sound, when a gale came on, which lasted four days and nights, and which would have done for poor old Asp, in half the time; our touch with the Great Nation not having much improved our condition. Four-and-twenty hours later, and I should only have been a gallant Captain Wentworth, in a small paragraph at one corner of the newspapers; and being lost in only a sloop, nobody would have thought about me.'

Anne's shudderings were to herself alone: but the Miss Musgroves could be as open as they were sincere, in their exclamations of pity and horror.

'And so then, I suppose,' said Mrs Musgrove, in a low voice, as if thinking aloud, 'so then he went away to the Laconia, and there he met with our poor boy. – Charles, my dear,' (beckoning him to her), 'do ask Captain Wentworth where it was he first met with your poor brother. I always forget.'

'It was at Gibraltar, mother, I know. Dick had been left ill at Gibraltar, with a recommendation from his former captain to Captain Wentworth.'

'Oh ! – but, Charles, tell Captain Wentworth, he need not be afraid of mentioning poor Dick before me, for it would be rather a pleasure to hear him talked of, by such a good friend.'

Charles, being somewhat more mindful of the probabilities of the case, only nodded in reply, and walked away.

The girls were now hunting for the Laconia; and Captain Wentworth could not deny himself the pleasure of taking the precious volume into his own hands to save them the trouble, and once more read aloud the little statement of her name and rate and present non-commissioned class, observing over it, that she too had been one of the best friends man ever had.

'Ah ! those were pleasant days when I had the Laconia ! How fast I made money in her. – A friend of mine, and I, had such a lovely cruise together off the Western Islands. – Poor Harville, sister ! You know how much he wanted money – worse than myself. He had a wife. – Excellent fellow ! I shall never forget his happiness. He felt it all, so much for her sake. – I wished for him again the next summer, when I had still the same luck in the Mediterranean.'

'And I am sure, Sir,' said Mrs Musgrove, 'it was a lucky day for us, when you were put captain into that ship. We shall never forget what you did.'

Her feelings made her speak low; and Captain Wentworth, hearing only in part, and probably not having Dick Musgrove at all near his thoughts, looked rather in suspense, and as if waiting for more.

'My brother,' whispered one of the girls; 'mamma is thinking of poor Richard.'

'Poor dear fellow!' continued Mrs Musgrove; 'he was grown so steady, and such an excellent correspondent, while he was under your care! Ah! it would have been a happy thing, if he had never left you. I assure you, Captain Wentworth, we are very sorry he ever left you.'

There was a momentary expression in Captain Wentworth's face at this speech, a certain glance of his bright eye, and curl of his handsome mouth, which convinced Anne, that instead of sharing in Mrs Musgrove's kind wishes, as to her son, he had probably been at some pains to get rid of him; but it was too transient an indulgence of self-amusement to be detected by any who understood him less than herself; in another moment he was perfectly collected and serious; and almost instantly afterwards coming up to the sofa, on which she and Mrs Musgrove were sitting, took a place by the latter, and entered into conversation with her, in a low voice, about her son, doing it with so much sympathy and natural grace, as shewed the kindest consideration for all that was real and unabsurd in the parent's feelings.

They were actually on the same sofa, for Mrs Musgrove had most readily made room for him; – they were divided only by Mrs Musgrove. It was no insignificant barrier indeed. Mrs Musgrove was of a comfortable substantial size, infinitely more fitted by nature to express good cheer and good humour, than tenderness and sentiment; and while the agitations of Anne's slender form, and pensive face, may be considered as very completely screened, Captain Wentworth should be allowed some credit for the self-command with which he attended to her large fat sighings over the destiny of a son, whom alive nobody had cared for.

Personal size and mental sorrow have certainly no necessary proportions. A large bulky figure has as good a right to be in deep affliction, as the most graceful set of limbs in the world. But, fair or not fair, there are unbecoming conjunctions, which reason will patronize in vain, – which taste cannot tolerate, – which ridicule will seize.

The admiral, after taking two or three refreshing turns about the room with his hands behind him, being called to order by his wife, now came up to Captain Wentworth, and without taking any observation of what he might be interrupting, thinking only of his own thoughts, began with,

'If you had been a week later at Lisbon, last spring, Frederick, you would have been asked to give a passage to Lady Mary Grierson and her daughters.'

'Should I? I am glad I was not a week later then.'

The admiral abused him for his want of gallantry. He defended himself; though professing that he would never willingly admit any ladies on board a ship of his, excepting for a ball, or a visit, which a few hours might comprehend.

'But, if I know myself,' said he, 'this is from no want of gallantry towards them. It is rather from feeling how impossible it is, with all one's efforts, and all one's sacrifices, to make the accommodations on board, such as women ought to have. There can be no want of gallantry, admiral, in rating the claims of women to every personal comfort *high* – and this is what I do. I hate to hear of women on board, or to see them on board; and no ship, under my command, shall ever convey a family of ladies any where, if I can help it.'

This brought his sister upon him.

'Oh Frederick! – But I cannot believe it of you. – All idle refinement! – Women may be as comfortable on board, as in the best house in England. I believe I have lived as much on board as most women, and I know nothing superior to the accommodations of a man of war. I declare I have not a comfort or an indulgence about me, even at Kellynch-hall,' (with a kind bow to Anne) 'beyond what I always had in most of the ships I have lived in; and they have been five altogether.'

'Nothing to the purpose,' replied her brother. 'You were living with your husband: and were the only woman on board.'

'But you, yourself, brought Mrs Harville, her sister, her cousin, and the three children, round from Portsmouth to Plymouth. Where was this superfine, extraordinary sort of gallantry of yours, then?'

'All merged in my friendship, Sophia. I would assist any brother officer's wife that I could, and I would bring any thing of Harville's from the world's end, if he wanted it. But do not imagine that I did not feel it an evil in itself.'

'Depend upon it they were all perfectly comfortable.'

'I might not like them the better for that, perhaps. Such a number of women and children have no *right* to be comfortable on board.'

'My dear Frederick, you are talking quite idly. Pray, what would become of us poor sailors' wives, who often want to be conveyed to one port or another, after our husbands, if every body had your feelings?'

'My feelings, you see, did not prevent my taking Mrs Harville, and all her family, to Plymouth.'

'But I hate to hear you talking so, like a fine gentleman, and as if women were all fine ladies, instead of rational creatures. We none of us expect to be in smooth water all our days.'

'Ah! my dear,' said the admiral, 'when he has got a wife, he will sing a different tune. When he is married, if we have the good luck to live to another war, we shall see him do as you and I, and a great many others, have done. We shall have him very thankful to any body that will bring him his wife.'

'Ay, that we shall.'

'Now I have done,' cried Captain Wentworth – 'When once married people begin to attack me with, "Oh! you will think very differently, when you are married." I can only say, "No, I shall not;" and then they say again, "Yes, you will," and there is an end of it.'

He got up and moved away.

'What a great traveller you must have been, ma'am!' said Mrs Musgrove to Mrs Croft.

'Pretty well, ma'am, in the fifteen years of my marriage; though many women have done more. I have crossed the Atlantic four times, and have been once to the East Indies, and back again; and only once, besides being in different places about home – Cork, and Lisbon, and Gibraltar. But I never went beyond the Streights – and never was in the West Indies. We do not call Bermuda or Bahama, you know, the West Indies.'

Mrs Musgrove had not a word to say in dissent; she could not accuse herself of having ever called them any thing in the whole course of her life.

'And I do assure you, ma'am,' pursued Mrs Croft, 'that nothing can exceed the accommodations of a man of war; I speak, you know, of the higher rates. When you come to a frigate, of course, you are more confined – though any reasonable woman may be perfectly happy in one of them; and I can safely say, that the happiest part of my life has been spent on board a ship. While we were together, you know, there was nothing to be feared. Thank God! I have always been blessed with excellent health, and no climate disagrees with me. A little disordered always the first twenty-four hours of going to sea, but never knew what sickness was afterwards. The only time that I ever really suffered in body or mind, the only time that I ever fancied myself unwell, or had any ideas of danger, was the winter that I passed by myself at Deal, when the Admiral (*Captain* Croft then) was in the North Seas. I lived in perpetual fright at that time, and had all manner of imaginary complaints from not knowing what to do with my-self, or when I should hear from him next; but as long as we could be together, nothing ever ailed me, and I never met with the smallest inconvenience.'

'Ay, to be sure. – Yes, indeed, oh yes, I am quite of your opinion, Mrs Croft,' was Mrs Musgrove's hearty answer. 'There is nothing so bad as a separation. I am quite of your opinion. I know what it is, for Mr Musgrove always attends the assizes, and I am so glad when they are over, and he is safe back again.'

The evening ended with dancing. On its being proposed, Anne offered her services, as usual, and though her eyes would some-times fill with tears as she sat at the instrument, she was ex-tremely glad to be employed, and desired nothing in return but to be unobserved.

It was a merry, joyous party, and no one seemed in higher spirits than Captain Wentworth. She felt that he had every thing to elevate him, which general attention and deference, and espe-cially the attention of all the young women could do. The Miss Hayters, the females of the family of cousins already mentioned, were apparently admitted to the honour of being in love with him; and as for Henrietta and Louisa, they both seemed so entirely occupied by him, that nothing but the continued appearance of the most perfect good-will between themselves, could have made it credible that they were not decided rivals. If he were a little spoilt by such universal, such eager admiration, who could wonder?

These were some of the thoughts which occupied Anne, while her fingers were mechanically at work, proceeding for half an hour together, equally without error, and without consciousness. *Once* she felt that he was looking at herself – observing her altered features, perhaps, trying to trace in them the ruins of the face which had once charmed him; and *once* she knew that he must have spoken of her; – she was hardly aware of it, till she heard the answer; but then she was sure of his having asked his partner whether Miss Elliot never danced? The answer was, 'Oh! no, never; she has quite given up dancing. She had rather play. She is never tired of playing.' Once, too, he spoke to her. She had left the instrument on the dancing being over, and he had sat down to try to make out an air which he wished to give the Miss Musgroves an idea of. Unintentionally she returned to that part of the room; he saw her, and, instantly rising, said, with studied politeness,

'I beg your pardon, madam, this is your seat;' and though she immediately drew back with a decided negative, he was not to be induced to sit down again.

Anne did not wish for more of such looks and speeches. His cold politeness, his ceremonious grace, were worse than any thing.

CHAPTER 9

CAPTAIN WENTWORTH was come to Kellynch as to a home, to stay as long as he liked, being as thoroughly the object of the Admiral's fraternal kindness as of his wife's. He had intended, on first arriving, to proceed very soon into Shropshire, and visit the brother settled in that county, but the attractions of Uppercross induced him to put this off. There was so much of friendliness, and of flattery, and of every thing most bewitching in his reception there; the old were so hospitable, the young so agreeable, that he could not but resolve to remain where he was, and take all the charms and perfections of Edward's wife upon credit a little longer.

It was soon Uppercross with him almost every day. The Musgroves could hardly be more ready to invite than he to come, particularly in the morning, when he had no companion at home, for the Admiral and Mrs Croft were generally out of doors together, interesting themselves in their new possessions, their grass, and their sheep, and dawdling about in a way not endurable to a third person, or driving out in a gig, lately added to their establishment.

Hitherto there had been but one opinion of Captain Wentworth, among the Musgroves and their dependencies. It was unvarying, warm admiration every where. But this intimate footing was not more than established, when a certain Charles Hayter returned among them, to be a good deal disturbed by it, and to think Captain Wentworth very much in the way.

Charles Hayter was the eldest of all the cousins, and a very amiable, pleasing young man, between whom and Henrietta there had been a considerable appearance of attachment previous to Captain Wentworth's introduction. He was in orders, and having a curacy in the neighbourhood where residence was not required, lived at his father's house, only two miles from Uppercross. A short absence from home had left his fair one unguarded by his attentions at this critical period, and when he came back he had the pain of finding very altered manners, and of seeing Captain Wentworth.

Mrs Musgrove and Mrs Hayter were sisters. They had each had money, but their marriages had made a material difference in their degree of consequence. Mr Hayter had some property of his own, but it was insignificant compared with Mr Musgrove's; and while the Musgroves were in the first class of society in the country, the young Hayters would, from their parents' inferior, retired, and unpolished way of living, and their own defective education, have been hardly in any class at all, but for their connexion with Uppercross; this eldest son of course excepted, who had chosen to be a scholar and a gentleman, and who was very superior in cultivation and manners to all the rest.

The two families had always been on excellent terms, there being no pride on one side, and no envy on the other, and only such a consciousness of superiority in the Miss Musgroves, as made them pleased to improve their cousins. – Charles's attentions to Henrietta had been observed by her father and mother without any disapprobation. 'It would not be a great match for her; but if Henrietta liked him, – and Henrietta *did* seem to like him.'

Henrietta fully thought so herself, before Captain Wentworth came; but from that time Cousin Charles had been very much forgotten.

Which of the two sisters was preferred by Captain Wentworth was as yet quite doubtful, as far as Anne's observation reached. Henrietta was perhaps the prettiest, Louisa had the higher spirits; and she knew not *now*, whether the more gentle or the more lively character were most likely to attract him.

Mr and Mrs Musgrove, either from seeing little, or from an entire confidence in the discretion of both their daughters, and of all the young men who came near them, seemed to leave every thing to take its chance. There was not the smallest appearance of solicitude or remark about them, in the Mansion-house; but it was different at the Cottage: the young couple there were more disposed to speculate and wonder; and Captain Wentworth had not been above four or five times in the Miss Musgroves' company, and Charles Hayter had but just reappeared, when Anne had to listen to the opinions of her brother and sister, as to *which* was the one liked best. Charles gave it for Louisa, Mary for Henrietta, but quite agreeing that to have him marry either would be extremely delightful.

Charles 'had never seen a pleasanter man in his life; and from what he had once heard Captain Wentworth himself say, was very sure that he had not made less than twenty thousand pounds by the war. Here was a fortune at once; besides which, there would be the chance of what might be done in any future war; and he was sure Captain Wentworth was as likely a man to distinguish himself as any officer in the navy. Oh! it would be a capital match for either of his sisters.'

'Upon my word it would,' replied Mary. 'Dear me! If he should rise to any very great honours! If he should ever be made a Baronet! "Lady Wentworth" sounds very well. That would be a noble thing, indeed, for Henrietta! She would take place of me then, and Henrietta would not dislike that. Sir Frederick and Lady Wentworth! It would be but a new creation, however, and I never think much of your new creations.'

It suited Mary best to think Henrietta the one preferred on the very account of Charles Hayter, whose pretensions she wished to see put an end to. She looked down very decidedly upon the Hayters, and thought it would be quite a misfortune to have the existing connection between the families renewed – very sad for herself and her children.

'You know,' said she, 'I cannot think him at all a fit match for Henrietta; and considering the alliances which the Musgroves have made, she has no right to throw herself away. I do not think any young woman has a right to make a choice that may be disagreeable and inconvenient to the *principal* part of her family, and be giving bad connections to those who have not been used to them. And, pray, who is Charles Hayter? Nothing but a country curate. A most improper match for Miss Musgrove, of Uppercross.'

Her husband, however, would not agree with her here; for besides having a regard for his cousin, Charles Hayter was an eldest son, and he saw things as an eldest son himself.

'Now you are talking nonsense, Mary,' was therefore his answer. 'It would not be a *great* match for Henrietta, but Charles has a very fair chance, through the Spicers of getting something from the Bishop in the course of a year or two; and you will please to remember, that he is the eldest son; whenever my uncle dies, he steps into very pretty property. The estate at Winthrop is not less than two hundred and fifty acres, besides the farm near Taunton, which is some of the best land in the country. I grant you, that any of them but Charles would be a very shocking match for Henrietta, and indeed it could not be; he is the only one that could be possible; but he is a very good-natured, good sort of a fellow; and whenever Winthrop comes into his hands, he will make a different sort of place of it, and live in a very different sort of way; and with that property, he will never be a contemptible man. Good, freehold property. No, no; Henrietta might do worse than marry Charles Hayter; and if she has him, and Louisa can get Captain Wentworth, I shall be very well satisfied.'

'Charles may say what he pleases,' cried Mary to Anne, as soon as he was out of the room, 'but it would be shocking to have Henrietta marry Charles Hayter; a very bad thing for *her*, and still worse for *me*; and therefore it is very much to be wished that Captain Wentworth may soon put him quite out of her head, and I have very little doubt that he has. She took hardly any notice of Charles Hayter yesterday. I wish you had been there to see her behaviour. And as to Captain Wentworth's liking Louisa as well as Henrietta, it is nonsense to say so; for he certainly *does* like Henrietta a great deal the best. But Charles is so positive! I wish you had been with us yesterday, for then you might have decided between us; and I am sure you would have thought as I did, unless you had been determined to give it against me.'

A dinner at Mr Musgrove's had been the occasion, when all these things should have been seen by Anne; but she had staid at home, under the mixed plea of a head-ache of her own, and some return of indisposition in little Charles. She had thought only of avoiding Captain Wentworth; but an escape from being appealed to as umpire, was now added to the advantages of a quiet evening.

As to Captain Wentworth's views, she deemed it of more consequence that he should know his own mind, early enough not to be endangering the happiness of either sister, or impeaching his own honour, than that he should prefer Henrietta to Louisa, or Louisa to Henrietta. Either of them would, in all probability, make

him an affectionate, good-humoured wife. With regard to Charles
Hayter, she had delicacy which must be pained by any lightness
of conduct in a well-meaning young woman, and a heart to sym-
pathize in any of the sufferings it occasioned; but if Henrietta
found herself mistaken in the nature of her feelings, the alteration
could not be understood too soon.

Charles Hayter had met with much to disquiet and mortify him
in his cousin's behaviour. She had too old a regard for him to be so
wholly estranged, as might in two meetings extinguish every past
hope, and leave him nothing to do but to keep away from
Uppercross; but there was such a change as became very alarming,
when such a man as Captain Wentworth was to be regarded as
the probable cause. He had been absent only two Sundays; and
when they parted, had left her interested even to the height of his
wishes, in his prospect of soon quitting his present curacy, and
obtaining that of Uppercross instead. It had then seemed the
object nearest her heart, that Dr Shirley, the rector, who for more
than forty years had been zealously discharging all the duties of
his office, but was now growing too infirm for many of them,
should be quite fixed on engaging a curate; should make his curacy
quite as good as he could afford, and should give Charles Hayter
the promise of it. The advantage of his having to come only to
Uppercross, instead of going six miles another way; of his having,
in every respect, a better curacy; of his belonging to their dear Dr
Shirley, and of dear, good Dr Shirley's being relieved from the
duty which he could no longer get through without most injurious fatigue, had been a great deal, even to Louisa, but had
been almost every thing to Henrietta. When he came back, alas!
the zeal of the business was gone by. Louisa could not listen at all
to his account of a conversation which he had just held with Dr
Shirley : she was at window, looking out for Captain Wentworth;
and even Henrietta had at best only a divided attention to give,
and seemed to have forgotten all the former doubt and solicitude
of the negociation.

'Well, I am very glad indeed, but I always thought you would
have it; I always thought you sure. It did not appear to me that –
In short, you know, Dr Shirley *must* have a curate, and you had
secured his promise. Is he coming, Louisa?'

One morning, very soon after the dinner at the Musgroves, at which Anne had not been present, Captain Wentworth walked into the drawing-room at the Cottage, where were only herself and the little invalid Charles, who was lying on the sofa.

The surprise of finding himself almost alone with Anne Elliot, deprived his manners of their usual composure: he started, and could only say, 'I thought the Miss Musgroves had been here – Mrs Musgrove told me I should find them here,' before he walked to the window to recollect himself, and feel how he ought to behave.

'They are up stairs with my sister – they will be down in a few moment, I dare say,' – had been Anne's reply, in all the confusion that was natural; and if the child had not called her to come and do something for him, she would have been out of the room the next moment, and released Captain Wentworth as well as herself.

He continued at the window; and after calmly and politely saying, 'I hope the little boy is better,' was silent.

She was obliged to kneel down by the sofa, and remain there to satisfy her patient; and thus they continued a few minutes, when, to her very great satisfaction, she heard some other person crossing the little vestibule. She hoped, on turning her head, to see the master of the house; but it proved to be one much less calculated for making matters easy – Charles Hayter, probably not at all better pleased by the sight of Captain Wentworth, than Captain Wentworth had been by the sight of Anne.

She only attempted to say, 'How do you do? Will not you sit down? The others will be here presently.'

Captain Wentworth, however, came from his window, apparently not ill-disposed for conversation; but Charles Hayter soon put an end to his attempts, by seating himself near the table, and taking up the newspaper; and Captain Wentworth returned to his window.

Another minute brought another addition. The younger boy, a remarkable stout, forward child, of two years old, having got the door opened for him by some one without, made his determined appearance among them, and went straight to the sofa to see what was going on, and put in his claim to any thing good that might be giving away.

There being nothing to be eat, he could only have some play; and as his aunt would not let him teaze his sick brother, he began to fasten himself upon her, as she knelt, in such a way that, busy as she was about Charles, she could not shake him off. She spoke to him – ordered, intreated, and insisted in vain. Once she did contrive to push him away, but the boy had the greater pleasure in getting upon her back again directly.

'Walter,' said she, 'get down this moment. You are extremely troublesome. I am very angry with you.'

'Walter,' cried Charles Hayter, 'why do you not do as you are bid? Do not you hear your aunt speak? Come to me, Walter, come to cousin Charles.'

But not a bit did Walter stir.

In another moment, however, she found herself in the state of being released from him; some one was taking him from her, though he had bent down her head so much, that his little sturdy hands were unfastened from around her neck, and he was resolutely borne away, before she knew that Captain Wentworth had done it.

Her sensations on the discovery made her perfectly speechless. She could not even thank him. She could only hang over little Charles, with most disordered feelings. His kindness in stepping forward to her relief – the manner – the silence in which it had passed – the little particulars of the circumstance – with the conviction soon forced on her by the noise he was studiously making with the child, that he meant to avoid hearing her thanks, and rather sought to testify that her conversation was the last of his wants, produced such a confusion of varying, but very painful agitation, as she could not recover from, till enabled by the entrance of Mary and the Miss Musgroves to make over her little patient to their cares, and leave the room. She could not stay. It might have been an opportunity of watching the loves and jealousies of the four; they were now all together, but she could stay for none of it. It was evident that Charles Hayter was not well inclined towards Captain Wentworth. She had a strong impression of his having said, in a vext tone of voice, after Captain Wentworth's interference, 'You ought to have minded *me*, Walter; I told you not to teaze your aunt;' and could comprehend his regretting that Captain Wentworth should do what he ought to have done himself. But neither Charles Hayter's feelings, nor any body's feelings, could interest her, till she had a little better arranged her own. She was ashamed of herself, quite ashamed of being so nervous, so overcome by such a trifle; but so it was; and it required a long application of solitude and reflection to recover her.

CHAPTER 10

OTHER opportunities of making her observations could not fail
to occur. Anne had soon been in company with all the four together often enough to have an opinion, though too wise to
acknowledge as much at home, where she knew it would have
satisfied neither husband nor wife; for while she considered
Louisa to be rather the favourite, she could not but think, as far as
she might dare to judge from memory and experience, that Captain Wentworth was not in love with either. They were more in
love with him; yet there it was not love. It was a little fever of
admiration; but it might, probably must, end in love with some.
Charles Hayter seemed aware of being slighted, and yet Henrietta
had sometimes the air of being divided between them. Anne
longed for the power of representing to them all what they were
about, and of pointing out some of the evils they were exposing
themselves to. She did not attribute guile to any. It was the
highest satisfaction to her, to believe Captain Wentworth not in
the least aware of the pain he was occasioning. There was no
triumph, no pitiful triumph in his manner. He had, probably,
never heard, and never thought of any claims of Charles Hayter.
He was only wrong in accepting the attentions – (for accepting
must be the word) of two young women at once.

After a short struggle, however, Charles Hayter seemed to quit
the field. Three days had passed without his coming once to
Uppercross; a most decided change. He had even refused one
regular invitation to dinner; and having been found on the
occasion by Mr Musgrove with some large books before him, Mr
and Mrs Musgrove were sure all could not be right, and talked,
with grave faces, of his studying himself to death. It was Mary's
hope and belief, that he had received a positive dismissal from
Henrietta, and her husband lived under the constant dependance
of seeing him to-morrow. Anne could only feel that Charles
Hayter was wise.

One morning, about this time, Charles Musgrove and Captain

Wentworth being gone a shooting together, as the sisters in the cottage were sitting quietly at work, they were visited at the window by the sisters from the mansion-house.

It was a very fine November day, and the Miss Musgroves came through the little grounds, and stopped for no other purpose than to say, that they were going to take a *long* walk, and, therefore, concluded Mary could not like to go with them; and when Mary immediately replied, with some jealousy, at not being supposed a good walker, 'Oh, yes, I should like to join you very much, I am very fond of a long walk,' Anne felt persuaded, by the looks of the two girls, that it was precisely what they did not wish, and admired again the sort of necessity which the family-habits seemed to produce, of every thing being to be communicated, and every thing being to be done together, however undesired and inconvenient. She tried to dissuade Mary from going, but in vain; and that being the case, thought it best to accept the Miss Musgroves' much more cordial invitation to herself to go likewise, as she might be useful in turning back with her sister, and lessening the interference in any plan of their own.

'I cannot imagine why they should suppose I should not like a long walk!' said Mary, as she went up stairs. 'Every body is always supposing that I am not a good walker! And yet they would not have been pleased, if we had refused to join them. When people come in this manner on purpose to ask us, how can one say no?'

Just as they were setting off, the gentlemen returned. They had taken out a young dog, who had spoilt their sport, and sent them back early. Their time and strength, and spirits, were, therefore, exactly ready for this walk, and they entered into it with pleasure. Could Anne have foreseen such a junction, she would have staid at home; but, from some feelings of interest and curiosity, she fancied now that it was too late to retract, and the whole six set forward together in the direction chosen by the Miss Musgroves, who evidently considered the walk as under their guidance.

Anne's object was, not to be in the way of any body, and where the narrow paths across the fields made many separations necessary, to keep with her brother and sister. Her *pleasure* in the walk must arise from the exercise and the day, from the view of the last smiles of the year upon the tawny leaves and withered hedges, and from repeating to herself some few of the thousand poetical descriptions extant of autumn, that season of peculiar and inexhaustible influence on the mind of taste and tenderness, that season which has drawn from every poet, worthy of being read, some attempt at description, or some lines of feeling. She occupied her mind as much as possible in such like musings and quotations; but it was not possible, that when within reach of Captain Wentworth's conversation with either of the Miss Mus- groves, she should not try to hear it; yet she caught little very remarkable. It was mere lively chat, – such as any young persons, on an intimate footing, might fall into. He was more engaged with Louisa than with Henrietta. Louisa certainly put more for- ward for his notice than her sister. This distinction appeared to increase, and there was one speech of Louisa's which struck her. After one of the many praises of the day, which were continually bursting forth, Captain Wentworth added.

'What glorious weather for the Admiral and my sister! They meant to take a long drive this morning; perhaps we may hail them from some of these hills. They talked of coming into this side of the country. I wonder whereabouts they will upset to-day. Oh! it does happen very often, I assure you – but my sister makes nothing of it – she would as lieve be tossed out as not.'

'Ah! You make the most of it, I know,' cried Louisa, 'but if it were really so, I should do just the same in her place. If I loved a man, as she loves the Admiral, I would be always with him, nothing should ever separate us, and I would rather be overturned by him, than driven safely by anybody else.'

It was spoken with enthusiasm.

'Had you?' cried he, catching the same tone; 'I honour you!' And there was silence between them for a little while.

Anne could not immediately fall into a quotation again. The sweet scenes of autumn were for a while put by – unless some tender sonnet, fraught with the apt analogy of the declining year, with declining happiness, and the images of youth and hope, and spring, all gone together, blessed her memory. She roused herself to say, as they struck by order into another path,

'Is not this one of the ways to Winthrop?' But nobody heard, or, at least, nobody answered her.

Winthrop, however, or its environs – for young men are, sometimes, to be met with, strolling about near home, was their destination; and after another half mile of gradual ascent through large enclosures, where the ploughs at work, and the fresh-made path spoke the farmer, counteracting the sweets of poetical despondence, and meaning to have spring again, they gained the summit of the most considerable hill, which parted Uppercross and Winthrop, and soon commanded a full view of the latter, at the foot of the hill on the other side.

Winthrop, without beauty and without dignity, was stretched before them; an indifferent house, standing low, and hemmed in by the barns and buildings of a farm-yard.

Mary exclaimed, 'Bless me! here is Winthrop – I declare I had no idea! – well, now I think we had better turn back; I am excessively tired.'

Henrietta, conscious and ashamed, and seeing no cousin Charles walking along any path, or leaning against any gate, was ready to do as Mary wished; but 'No,' said Charles Musgrove, and 'No, no,' cried Louisa more eagerly, and taking her sister aside, seemed to be arguing the matter warmly.

Charles, in the meanwhile, was very decidedly declaring his resolution of calling on his aunt, now that he was so near; and very evidently, though more fearfully, trying to induce his wife to go too. But this was one of the points on which the lady shewed her strength, and when he recommended the advantage of resting herself a quarter of an hour at Winthrop, as she felt so tired, she resolutely answered, 'Oh! no, indeed! – walking up that hill again would do her more harm than any sitting down could do her good;' – and, in short, her look and manner declared, that go she would not.

After a little succession of these sort of debates and consultations, it was settled between Charles and his two sisters, that he, and Henrietta, should just run down for a few minutes, to see their aunt and cousins, while the rest of the party waited for them at the top of the hill. Louisa seemed the principal arranger of the plan; and, as she went a little way with them, down the hill, still talking to Henrietta, Mary took the opportunity of looking scorn-fully around her, and saying to Captain Wentworth,

'It is very unpleasant, having such connexions! But I assure you, I have never been in the house above twice in my life.'

She received no other answer, than an artificial, assenting smile, followed by a contemptuous glance, as he turned away, which Anne perfectly knew the meaning of.

The brow of the hill, where they remained, was a cheerful spot; Louisa returned, and Mary finding a comfortable seat for herself, on the step of a stile, was very well satisfied so long as the others all stood about her; but when Louisa drew Captain Wentworth away, to try for a gleaning of nuts in an adjoining hedge-row, and they were gone by degrees quite out of sight and sound, Mary was happy no longer; she quarrelled with her own seat, – was sure Louisa had got a much better somewhere, – and nothing could prevent her from going to look for a better also. She turned through the same gate, – but could not see them. – Anne found a nice seat for her, on a dry sunny bank, under the hedge-row, in which she had no doubt of their still being – in some spot or other. Mary sat down for a moment, but it would not do; she was sure Louisa had found a better seat somewhere else, and she would go on, till she overtook her.

Anne, really tired herself, was glad to sit down; and she very soon heard Captain Wentworth and Louisa in the hedge-row,[6] behind her, as if making their way back, along the rough, wild sort of channel, down the centre. They were speaking as they drew near. Louisa's voice was the first distinguished. She seemed to be in the middle of some eager speech. What Anne first heard was,

'And so, I made her go. I could not bear that she should be frightened from the visit by such nonsense. What! – would I be turned back from doing a thing that I had determined to do, and that I knew to be right, by the airs and interference of such a person? – or, of any person I may say. No, – I have no idea of being so easily persuaded. When I have made up my mind, I have made it. And Henrietta seemed entirely to have made up hers to call at Winthrop to-day – and yet, she was as near giving it up, out of nonsensical complaisance!'

'She would have turned back then, but for you?'

'She would indeed. I am almost ashamed to say it.'

'Happy for her, to have such a mind as yours at hand! – After the hints you gave just now, which did but confirm my own observations, the last time I was in company with him, I need not affect to have no comprehension of what is going on. I see that more than a mere dutiful morning-visit to your aunt was in question; – and woe betide him, and her too, when it comes to things of consequence, when they are placed in circumstances, requiring fortitude and strength of mind, if she have not resolution enough to resist idle interference in such a trifle as this. Your sister is an amiable creature; but *yours* is the character of decision and firmness, I see. If you value her conduct or happiness, infuse as much of your own spirit into her, as you can. But this, no doubt, you have been always doing. It is the worst evil of too yielding and indecisive a character, that no influence over it can be depended on. – You are never sure of a good impression being durable. Every body may sway it; let those who would be happy be firm. – Here is a nut,' said he, catching one down from an upper bough. 'To exemplify, – a beautiful glossy nut, which, blessed with original strength, has outlived all the storms of autumn. Not a puncture, not a weak spot any where. – This nut,' he continued, with playful solemnity, – 'while so many of its brethren have fallen and been trodden under foot, is still in possession of all the happiness that a hazel-nut can be supposed capable of.' Then, returning to his former earnest tone : 'My first wish for all, whom I am interested in, is that they should be firm. If Louisa Musgrove would be beautiful and happy in her November of life, she will cherish all her present powers of mind.'

He had done, – and was unanswered. It would have surprised Anne, if Louisa could have readily answered such a speech – words of such interest, spoken with such serious warmth! – she could imagine what Louisa was feeling. For herself – she feared to move, lest she should be seen. While she remained, a bush of low rambling holly protected her, and they were moving on. Before they were beyond her hearing, however, Louisa spoke again.

'Mary is good-natured enough in many respects,' said she; 'but she does sometimes provoke me excessively, by her nonsense and her pride; the Elliot pride. She has a great deal too much of the Elliot pride. – We do so wish that Charles had married Anne instead. – I suppose you know he wanted to marry Anne?'

After a moment's pause, Captain Wentworth said,

'Do you mean that she refused him?'

'Oh! yes, certainly.'

'When did that happen?'

'I do not exactly know, for Henrietta and I were at school at the time; but I believe about a year before he married Mary. I wish she had accepted him. We should all have liked her a great deal better; and papa and mamma always think it was her great friend Lady Russell's doing, that she did not. – They think Charles might not be learned and bookish enough to please Lady Russell, and that therefore, she persuaded Anne to refuse him.'

The sounds were retreating, and Anne distinguished no more. Her own emotions still kept her fixed. She had much to recover from, before she could move. The listener's proverbial fate was not absolutely hers; she had heard no evil of herself, – but she had heard a great deal of very painful import. She saw how her own character was considered by Captain Wentworth; and there had been just that degree of feeling and curiosity about her in his manner, which must give her extreme agitation.

As soon as she could, she went after Mary, and having found, and walked back with her to their former station, by the stile, felt some comfort in their whole party being immediately afterwards collected, and once more in motion together. Her spirits wanted the solitude and silence which only numbers could give.

Charles and Henrietta returned, bringing, as may be conjectured, Charles Hayter with them. The minutiæ of the business Anne could not attempt to understand; even Captain Wentworth did not seem admitted to perfect confidence here; but that there had been a withdrawing on the gentleman's side, and a relenting on the lady's, and that they were now very glad to be together again, did not admit a doubt. Henrietta looked a little ashamed, but very well pleased; – Charles Hayter exceedingly happy, and they were devoted to each other almost from the first instant of their all setting forward for Uppercross.

Every thing now marked out Louisa for Captain Wentworth;

nothing could be plainer; and where many divisions were necessary, or even where they were not, they walked side by side, nearly as much as the other two. In a long strip of meadow-land, where there was ample space for all, they were thus divided – forming three distinct parties; and to that party of the three which boasted least animation, and least complaisance, Anne necessarily belonged. She joined Charles and Mary, and was tired enough to be very glad of Charles's other arm; – but Charles, though in very good humour with her, was out of temper with his wife. Mary had shewn herself disobliging to him, and was now to reap the consequence, which consequence was his dropping her arm almost every moment, to cut off the heads of some nettles in the hedge with his switch; and when Mary began to complain of it, and lament her being ill-used, according to custom, in being on the hedge side, while Anne was never incommoded on the other, he dropped the arms of both to hunt after a weasel which he had a momentary glance of; and they could hardly get him along at all.

This long meadow bordered a lane, which their footpath, at the end of it, was to cross; and when the party had all reached the gate of exit, the carriage advancing in the same direction, which had been some time heard, was just coming up, and proved to be Admiral Croft's gig. – He and his wife had taken their intended drive, and were returning home. Upon hearing how long a walk the young people had engaged in, they kindly offered a seat to any lady who might be particularly tired; it would save her full a mile, and they were going through Uppercross. The invitation was general, and generally declined. The Miss Musgroves were not at all tired, and Mary was either offended, by not being asked before any of the others, or what Louisa called the Elliot pride could not endure to make a third in a one horse chaise.

The walking-party had crossed the lane, and were surmounting an opposite stile; and the admiral was putting his horse into motion again, when Captain Wentworth cleared the hedge in a moment to say something to his sister. – The something might be guessed by its effects.

'Miss Elliot, I am sure *you* are tired,' cried Mrs Croft. 'Do let us have the pleasure of taking you home. Here is excellent room for three, I assure you. If we were all like you, I believe we might sit four. – You must, indeed, you must.'

Anne was still in the lane; and though instinctively beginning to decline, she was not allowed to proceed. The admiral's kind urgency came in support of his wife's; they would not be refused; they compressed themselves into the smallest possible space to leave her a corner, and Captain Wentworth, without saying a word, turned to her, and quietly obliged her to be assisted into the carriage.

Yes, – he had done it. She was in the carriage, and felt that he had placed her there, that his will and his hands had done it, that she owed it to his perception of her fatigue, and his resolution to give her rest. She was very much affected by the view of his disposition towards her which all these things made apparent. This little circumstance seemed the completion of all that had gone before. She understood him. He could not forgive her, – but he could not be unfeeling. Though condemning her for the past, and considering it with high and unjust resentment, though perfectly careless of her, and though becoming attached to another, still he could not see her suffer, without the desire of giving her relief. It was a remainder of former sentiment; it was an impulse of pure, though unacknowledged friendship; it was a proof of his own warm and amiable heart, which she could not contemplate without emotions so compounded of pleasure and pain, that she knew not which prevailed.

Her answers to the kindness and the remarks of her companions were at first unconsciously given. They had travelled half their way along the rough lane, before she was quite awake to what they said. She then found them talking of 'Frederick.'

'He certainly means to have one or other of those two girls, Sophy,' said the admiral; – 'but there is no saying which. He has been running after them, too, long enough, one would think, to make up his mind. Ay, this comes of the peace. If it were war, now, he would have settled it long ago. – We sailors, Miss Elliot, cannot afford to make long courtships in time of war. How many days was it, my dear, between the first time of my seeing you, and our sitting down together in our lodgings at North Yarmouth?'

'We had better not talk about it, my dear,' replied Mrs Croft, pleasantly; 'for if Miss Elliot were to hear how soon we came to an understanding, she would never be persuaded that we could be happy together. I had known you by character, however, long before.'

'Well, and I had heard of you as a very pretty girl; and what were we to wait for besides? – I do not like having such things so long in hand. I wish Frederick would spread a little more canvas, and bring us home one of these young ladies to Kellynch. Then, there would always be company for them. – And very nice young ladies they both are; I hardly know one from the other.'

'Very good humoured, unaffected girls, indeed,' said Mrs Croft, in a tone of calmer praise, such as made Anne suspect that her keener powers might not consider either of them as quite worthy of her brother; 'and a very respectable family. One could not be connected with better people. – My dear admiral, that post ! – we shall certainly take that post.'

But by coolly giving the reins a better direction herself, they happily passed the danger; and by once afterwards judiciously putting out her hand, they neither fell into a rut, nor ran foul of a dung-cart; and Anne, with some amusement at their style of driving, which she imagined no bad representation of the general guidance of their affairs, found herself safely deposited by them at the cottage.

CHAPTER 11

THE time now approached for Lady Russell's return; the day was even fixed, and Anne, being engaged to join her as soon as she was resettled, was looking forward to an early removal to Kellynch, and beginning to think how her own comfort was likely to be affected by it.

It would place her in the same village with Captain Wentworth, within half a mile of him; they would have to frequent the same church, and there must be intercourse between the two families. This was against her; but, on the other hand, he spent so much of his time at Uppercross, that in removing thence she might be considered rather as leaving him behind, than as going towards him; and, upon the whole, she believed she must, on this interesting question, be the gainer, almost as certainly as in her change of domestic society, in leaving poor Mary for Lady Russell.

She wished it might be possible for her to avoid ever seeing Captain Wentworth at the hall; – those rooms had witnessed former meetings which would be brought too painfully before her; but she was yet more anxious for the possibility of Lady Russell and Captain Wentworth never meeting any where. They did not like each other, and no renewal of acquaintance now could do any good; and were Lady Russell to see them together, she might think that he had too much self-possession, and she too little.

These points formed her chief solicitude in anticipating her removal from Uppercross, where she felt she had been stationed quite long enough. Her usefulness to little Charles would always give some sweetness to the memory of her two months visit there, but he was gaining strength apace, and she had nothing else to stay for.

The conclusion of her visit, however, was diversified in a way which she had not at all imagined. Captain Wentworth, after being unseen and unheard of at Uppercross for two whole days, appeared again among them to justify himself by a relation of of what had kept him away.

A letter from his friend, Captain Harville, having found him out at last, had brought intelligence of Captain Harville's being settled with his family at Lyme for the winter; of their being therefore, quite unknowingly, within twenty miles of each other. Captain Harville had never been in good health since a severe wound which he received two years before, and Captain Wentworth's anxiety to see him had determined him to go immediately to Lyme. He had been there for four-and-twenty hours. His acquittal was complete, his friendship warmly honoured, a lively interest excited for his friend, and his description of the fine country about Lyme so feelingly attended to by the party, that an earnest desire to see Lyme themselves, and a project for going thither was the consequence.

The young people were all wild to see Lyme. Captain Wentworth talked of going there again himself; it was only seventeen miles from Uppercross; though November, the weather was by no means bad; and, in short, Louisa, who was the most eager of the eager, having formed the resolution to go, and besides the pleasure of doing as she liked, being now armed with the idea of merit in maintaining her own way, bore down all the wishes of her father and mother for putting it off till summer; and to Lyme they were to go – Charles, Mary, Anne, Henrietta, Louisa, and Captain Wentworth.

The first heedless scheme had been to go in the morning and return at night, but to this Mr Musgrove, for the sake of his horses, would not consent; and when it came to be rationally considered, a day in the middle of November would not leave much time for seeing a new place, after deducting seven hours, as the nature of the country required, for going and returning. They were consequently to stay the night there, and not to be expected back till the next day's dinner. This was felt to be a considerable amendment; and though they all met at the Great House at rather an early breakfast hour, and set off very punctually, it was so much past noon before the two carriages, Mr Musgrove's coach containing the four ladies, and Charles's curricle, in which he drove Captain Wentworth, were descending the long hill into Lyme, and entering upon the still steeper street of the town itself, that it was very evident they would not have

more than time for looking about them, before the light and
warmth of the day were gone.

After securing accommodations, and ordering a dinner at one
of the inns, the next thing to be done was unquestionably to
walk directly down to the sea. They were come too late in the
year for any amusement or variety which Lyme, as a public place,
might offer; the rooms were shut up, the lodgers almost all gone,
scarcely any family but of the residents left – and, as there is
nothing to admire in the buildings themselves, the remarkable
situation of the town, the principal street almost hurrying into the
water, the walk to the Cobb, skirting round the pleasant little
bay, which in the season is animated with bathing machines and
company, the Cobb itself, its old wonders and new improvements, with the very beautiful line of cliffs stretching out to the
east of the town, are what the stranger's eye will seek; and a
very strange stranger it must be, who does not see charms in the
immediate environs of Lyme, to make him wish to know it better.
The scenes in its neighbourhood, Charmouth, with its high
grounds and extensive sweeps of country, and still more its sweet
retired bay, backed by dark cliffs, where fragments of low rock
among the sands make it the happiest spot for watching the flow
of the tide, for sitting in unwearied contemplation; – the woody
varieties of the cheerful village of Up Lyme, and, above all,
Pinny, with its green chasms between romantic rocks, where the
scattered forest trees and orchards of luxuriant growth declare
that many a generation must have passed away since the first
partial falling of the cliff prepared the ground for such a state,
where a scene so wonderful and so lovely is exhibited, as may
more than equal any of the resembling scenes of the far-famed
Isle of Wight: these places must be visited, and visited again, to
make the worth of Lyme understood.

The party from Uppercross passing down by the now deserted
and melancholy looking rooms, and still descending, soon found
themselves on the sea shore, and lingering only, as all must linger
and gaze on a first return to the sea, who ever deserve to look on it
at all, proceeded towards the Cobb, equally their object in itself
and on Captain Wentworth's account; for in a small house, near
the foot of an old pier of unknown date, were the Harvilles

settled. Captain Wentworth turned in to call on his friend; the others walked on, and he was to join them on the Cobb.

They were by no means tired of wondering and admiring; and not even Louisa seemed to feel that they had parted with Captain Wentworth long, when they saw him coming after them, with three companions, all well known already by description to be Captain and Mrs Harville, and a Captain Benwick, who was staying with them.

Captain Benwick had some time ago been first lieutenant of the Laconia; and the account which Captain Wentworth had given of him, on his return from Lyme before; his warm praise of him as an excellent young man and an officer, whom he had always valued highly, which must have stamped him well in the esteem of every listener, had been followed by a little history of his private life, which rendered him perfectly interesting in the eyes of all the ladies. He had been engaged to Captain Harville's sister, and was now mourning her loss. They had been a year or two waiting for fortune and promotion. Fortune came, his prize-money as lieutenant being great, – promotion, too, came at *last*; but Fanny Harville did not live to know it. She had died the preceding summer, while he was at sea. Captain Wentworth believed it impossible for man to be more attached to woman than poor Benwick had been to Fanny Harville, or to be more deeply afflicted under the dreadful change. He considered his disposition as of the sort which must suffer heavily, uniting very strong feelings with quiet, serious, and retiring manners, and a decided taste for reading, and sedentary pursuits. To finish the interest of the story, the friendship between him and the Harvilles seemed, if possible, augmented by the event which closed all their views of alliance, and Captain Benwick was now living with them entirely. Captain Harville had taken his present house for half a year, his taste, and his health, and his fortune all directing him to a residence unexpensive, and by the sea; and the grandeur of the country, and the retirement of Lyme in the winter, appeared exactly adapted to Captain Benwick's state of mind. The sympathy and good-will excited towards Captain Benwick was very great.

'And yet,' said Anne to herself, as they now moved forward to meet the party, 'he has not, perhaps, a more sorrowing heart than

I have. I cannot believe his prospects so blighted for ever. He is younger than I am; younger in feeling, if not in fact; younger as a man. He will rally again, and be happy with another.'

They all met, and were introduced. Captain Harville was a tall, dark man, with a sensible, benevolent countenance; a little lame; and from strong features, and want of health, looking much older than Captain Wentworth. Captain Benwick looked and was the youngest of the three, and, compared with either of them, a little man. He had a pleasing face and a melancholy air, just as he ought to have, and drew back from conversation.

Captain Harville, though not equalling Captain Wentworth in manners, was a perfect gentleman, unaffected, warm, and obliging. Mrs Harville, a degree less polished than her husband, seemed however to have the same good feelings; and nothing could be more pleasant than their desire of considering the whole party as friends of their own, because the friends of Captain Wentworth, or more kindly hospitable than their entreaties for their all promising to dine with them. The dinner, already ordered at the inn, was at last, though unwillingly, accepted as an excuse; but they seemed almost hurt that Captain Wentworth should have brought any such party to Lyme, without considering it as a thing of course that they should dine with them.

There was so much attachment to Captain Wentworth in all this, and such a bewitching charm in a degree of hospitality so uncommon, so unlike the usual style of give-and-take invitations, and dinners of formality and display, that Anne felt her spirits not likely to be benefited by an increasing acquaintance among his brother-officers. 'These would have been all my friends,' was her thought; and she had to struggle against a great tendency to lowness.

On quitting the Cobb, they all went indoors with their new friends, and found rooms so small as none but those who invite from the heart could think capable of accommodating so many. Anne had a moment's astonishment on the subject herself; but it was soon lost in the pleasanter feelings which sprang from the sight of all the ingenious contrivances and nice arrangements of Captain Harville, to turn the actual space to the best possible account, to supply the deficiencies of lodging-house furniture, and defend the windows and doors against the winter storms to be expected. The varieties in the fitting-up of the rooms, where the common necessaries provided by the owner, in the common indifferent plight, were contrasted with some few articles of a rare species of wood, excellently worked up, and with something curious and valuable from all the distant countries Captain Harville had visited, were more than amusing to Anne: connected as it all was with his profession, the fruit of its labours, the effect of its influence on his habits, the picture of repose and domestic happiness it presented, made it to her a something more, or less, than gratification.

Captain Harville was no reader; but he had contrived excellent accommodations, and fashioned very pretty shelves, for a tolerable collection of well-bound volumes, the property of Captain Benwick. His lameness prevented him from taking much exercise; but a mind of usefulness and ingenuity seemed to furnish him with constant employment within. He drew, he varnished, he carpentered, he glued; he made toys for the children, he fashioned new netting-needles and pins with improvements; and if every thing else was done, sat down to his large fishing-net at one corner of the room.

Anne thought she left great happiness behind her when they quitted the house; and Louisa, by whom she found herself walking, burst forth into raptures of admiration and delight on the character of the navy – their friendliness, their brotherliness, their openness, their uprightness; protesting that she was convinced of sailors having more worth and warmth than any other set of men in England; that they only knew how to live, and they only deserved to be respected and loved.

They went back to dress and dine; and so well had the scheme answered already, that nothing was found amiss; though its being 'so entirely out of season,' and the 'no-thorough-fare of Lyme,' and the 'no expectation of company,' had brought many apologies from the heads of the inn.

Anne found herself by this time growing so much more hardened to being in Captain Wentworth's company than she had at first imagined could ever be, that the sitting down to the same table with him now, and the interchange of the common civilities attending on it – (they never got beyond) was become a mere nothing.

The nights were too dark for the ladies to meet again till the morrow, but Captain Harville had promised them a visit in the evening; and he came, bringing his friend also, which was more than had been expected, it having been agreed that Captain Benwick had all the appearance of being oppressed by the presence of so many strangers. He ventured among them again, however, though his spirits certainly did not seem fit for the mirth of the party in general.

While Captains Wentworth and Harville led the talk on one side of the room, and, by recurring to former days, supplied anecdotes in abundance to occupy and entertain the others, it fell to Anne's lot to be placed rather apart with Captain Benwick; and a very good impulse of her nature obliged her to begin an acquaintance with him. He was shy, and disposed to abstraction; but the engaging mildness of her countenance, and gentleness of her manners, soon had their effect; and Anne was well repaid the first trouble of exertion. He was evidently a young man of considerable taste in reading, though principally in poetry; and besides the persuasion of having given him at least an evening's indulgence in the discussion of subjects, which his usual companions had probably no concern in, she had the hope of being of real use to him in some suggestions as to the duty and benefit of struggling against affliction, which had naturally grown out of their conversation. For, though shy, he did not seem reserved; it had rather the appearance of feelings glad to burst their usual restraints; and having talked of poetry, the richness of the present age, and gone through a brief comparison of opinion as to the first-rate poets, trying to ascertain whether *Marmion* or *The Lady of the Lake* were to be preferred, and how ranked the *Giaour* and *The Bride of Abydos*; and moreover, how the *Giaour* was to be pronounced, he shewed himself so intimately acquainted with all the tenderest songs of the one poet, and all the impassioned descriptions of hopeless agony of the other; he repeated, with such tremulous feeling, the various lines which imaged a broken heart, or a mind destroyed by wretchedness, and looked so entirely as if he meant to be understood, that she ventured to hope he did not always read only poetry; and to say, that she thought it was the misfortune of poetry, to be seldom safely enjoyed by those who enjoyed it completely; and that the strong feelings which alone could estimate it truly, were the very feelings which ought to taste it but sparingly.

His looks shewing him not pained, but pleased with this allusion to his situation, she was emboldened to go on; and feeling in herself the right of seniority of mind, she ventured to recommend a larger allowance of prose in his daily study; and on being requested to particularize, mentioned such works of our best moralists, such collections of the finest letters, such memoirs of characters of worth and suffering, as occurred to her at the moment as calculated to rouse and fortify the mind by the highest precepts, and the strongest examples of moral and religious endurances.

Captain Benwick listened attentively, and seemed grateful for the interest implied; and though with a shake of the head, and sighs which declared his little faith in the efficacy of any books on grief like his, noted down the names of those she recommended, and promised to procure and read them.

When the evening was over, Anne could not but be amused at the idea of her coming to Lyme, to preach patience and resignation to a young man whom she had never seen before; nor could she help fearing, on more serious reflection, that, like many other great moralists and preachers, she had been eloquent on a point in which her own conduct would ill bear examination.

CHAPTER 12

ANNE and Henrietta, finding themselves the earliest of the party the next morning, agreed to stroll down to the sea before breakfast. – They went to the sands, to watch the flowing of the tide, which a fine south-easterly breeze was bringing in with all the grandeur which so flat a shore admitted. They praised the morning; gloried in the sea; sympathized in the delight of the fresh-feeling breeze – and were silent; till Henrietta suddenly began again, with,

'Oh! yes, – I am quite convinced that, with very few exceptions, the sea-air always does good. There can be no doubt of its having been of the greatest service to Dr Shirley, after his illness, last spring twelvemonth. He declares himself, that coming to Lyme for a month, did him more good than all the medicine he took; and, that being by the sea, always makes him feel young again. Now, I cannot help thinking it a pity that he does not live entirely by the sea. I do think he had better leave Uppercross entirely, and fix at Lyme. – Do not you, Anne? – Do not you agree with me, that it is the best thing he could do, both for himself and Mrs Shirley? – She has cousins here, you know, and many acquaintance, which would make it cheerful for her, – and I am sure she would be glad to get to a place where she could have medical attendance at hand, in case of his having another seizure. Indeed I think it quite melancholy to have such excellent people as Dr and Mrs Shirley, who have been doing good all their lives, wearing out their last days in a place like Uppercross, where, excepting our family, they seem shut out from all the world. I wish his friends would propose it to him. I really think they ought. And, as to procuring a dispensation,[7] there could be no difficulty at his time of life, and with his character. My only doubt is, whether any thing could persuade him to leave his parish. He is so very strict and scrupulous in his notions; over-scrupulous, I must say. Do not you think, Anne, it is being over-scrupulous? Do not you think it is quite a mistaken point of conscience, when a

clergyman sacrifices his health for the sake of duties, which may
be just as well performed by another person? – And at Lyme too,
– only seventeen miles off, – he would be near enough to hear, if
people thought there was any thing to complain of.'

Anne smiled more than once to herself during this speech, and
entered into the subject, as ready to do good by entering into the
feelings of a young lady as of a young man, – though here it was
good of a lower standard, for what could be offered but general
acquiescence? – She said all that was reasonable and proper on
the business; felt the claims of Dr Shirley to repose, as she ought;
saw how very desirable it was that he should have some active,
respectable young man, as a resident curate, and was even courteous enough to hint at the advantage of such resident curate's
being married.

'I wish,' said Henrietta, very well pleased with her companion,
'I wish Lady Russell lived at Uppercross, and were intimate with
Dr Shirley. I have always heard of Lady Russell, as a woman of
the greatest influence with every body! I always look upon her
as able to persuade a person to any thing! I am afraid of her, as
I have told you before, quite afraid of her, because she is so very
clever; but I respect her amazingly, and wish we had such a neighbour at Uppercross.'

Anne was amused by Henrietta's manner of being grateful,
and amused also, that the course of events and the new interests
of Henrietta's views should have placed her friend at all in favour
with any of the Musgrove family; she had only time, however,
for a general answer, and a wish that such another woman were at
Uppercross, before all subjects suddenly ceased, on seeing Louisa
and Captain Wentworth coming towards them. They came also
for a stroll till breakfast was likely to be ready; but Louisa recollecting, immediately afterwards, that she had something to procure at a shop, invited them all to go back with her into the town.
They were all at her disposal.

When they came to the steps, leading upwards from the beach,
a gentleman at the same moment preparing to come down, politely
drew back, and stopped to give them way. They ascended and
passed him; and as they passed, Anne's face caught his eye, and
he looked at her with a degree of earnest admiration, which she

could not be insensible of. She was looking remarkably well; her very regular, very pretty features, having the bloom and freshness of youth restored by the fine wind which had been blowing on her complexion, and by the animation of eye which it had also produced. It was evident that the gentleman, (completely a gentleman in manner) admired her exceedingly. Captain Wentworth looked round at her instantly in a way which shewed his noticing of it. He gave her a momentary glance, – a glance of brightness, which seemed to say, 'That man is struck with you, – and even I, at this moment, see something like Anne Elliot again.'

After attending Louisa through her business, and loitering about a little longer, they returned to the inn; and Anne in passing afterwards quickly from her own chamber to their dining-room, had nearly run against the very same gentleman, as he came out of an adjoining apartment. She had before conjectured him to be a stranger like themselves, and determined that a well-looking groom, who was strolling about near the two inns as they came back, should be his servant. Both master and man being in mourning assisted the idea. It was now proved that he belonged to the same inn as themselves; and this second meeting, short as it was, also proved again by the gentleman's looks, that he thought hers very lovely, and by the readiness and propriety of his apologies, that he was a man of exceedingly good manners. He seemed about thirty, and, though not handsome, had an agreeable person. Anne felt that she should like to know who he was.

They had nearly done breakfast, when the sound of a carriage, (almost the first they had heard since entering Lyme) drew half the party to the window. 'It was a gentleman's carriage – a curricle – but only coming round from the stable-yard to the front door – Somebody must be going away. – It was driven by a servant in mourning.'

The word curricle made Charles Musgrove jump up, that he might compare it with his own, the servant in mourning roused Anne's curiosity, and the whole six were collected to look, by the time the owner of the curricle was to be seen issuing from the door amidst the bows and civilities of the household, and taking his seat, to drive off.

'Ah!' cried Captain Wentworth, instantly, and with half a glance at Anne; 'it is the very man we passed.'

The Miss Musgroves agreed to it; and having all kindly watched him as far up the hill as they could, they returned to the breakfast-table. The waiter came into the room soon afterwards.

'Pray,' said Captain Wentworth, immediately, 'can you tell us the name of the gentleman who is just gone away?'

'Yes, Sir, a Mr Elliot; a gentleman of large fortune, – came in last night from Sidmouth, – dare say you heard the carriage, Sir, while you were at dinner; and going on now for Crewkherne, in his way to Bath and London.'

'Elliot!' – Many had looked on each other, and many had repeated the name, before all this had been got through, even by the smart rapidity of a waiter.

'Bless me!' cried Mary; 'it must be our cousin; – it must be our Mr Elliot, it must, indeed! – Charles, Anne, must not it? In mourning, you see, just as our Mr Elliot must be. How very extraordinary! In the very same inn with us! Anne, must not it be our Mr Elliot; my father's next heir? Pray Sir,' (turning to the waiter), 'did not you hear, – did not his servant say whether he belonged to the Kellynch family?'

'No, ma'am, – he did not mention no particular family; but he said his master was a very rich gentleman, and would be a baronight some day.'

'There! you see!' cried Mary, in an ecstasy, 'Just as I said! Heir to Sir Walter Elliot! – I was sure that would come out, if it was so. Depend upon it, that is a circumstance which his servants take care to publish wherever he goes. But, Anne, only conceive how extraordinary! I wish I had looked at him more. I wish we had been aware in time, who it was, that he might have been introduced to us. What a pity that we should not have been introduced to each other! – Do you think he had the Elliot countenance? I hardly looked at him, I was looking at the horses; but I think he had something of the Elliot countenance. I wonder the arms did not strike me! Oh! – the great-coat was hanging over the panel, and hid the arms; so it did, otherwise, I am sure, I should have observed them, and the livery too; if the servant had not been in mourning, one should have known him by the livery.'

'Putting all these very extraordinary circumstances together,' said Captain Wentworth, 'we must consider it to be the arrangement of Providence, that you should not be introduced to your cousin.'

When she could command Mary's attention, Anne quietly tried to convince her that their father and Mr Elliot had not, for many years, been on such terms as to make the power of attempting an introduction at all desirable.

At the same time, however, it was a secret gratification to herself to have seen her cousin, and to know that the future owner of Kellynch was undoubtedly a gentleman, and had an air of good sense. She would not, upon any account, mention her having met with him the second time; luckily Mary did not much attend to their having passed close by him in their early walk, but she would have felt quite ill-used by Anne's having actually run against him in the passage, and received his very polite excuses, while she had never been near him at all; no, that cousinly little interview must remain a perfect secret.

'Of course,' said Mary, 'you will mention our seeing Mr Elliot, the next time you write to Bath. I think my father certainly ought to hear of it; do mention all about him.'

Anne avoided a direct reply, but it was just the circumstance which she considered as not merely unnecessary to be communicated, but as what ought to be suppressed. The offence which had been given her father, many years back, she knew; Elizabeth's particular share in it she suspected; and that Mr Elliot's idea always produced irritation in both, was beyond a doubt. Mary never wrote to Bath herself; all the toil of keeping up a slow and unsatisfactory correspondence with Elizabeth fell on Anne.

Breakfast had not been long over, when they were joined by Captain and Mrs Harville, and Captain Benwick, with whom they had appointed to take their last walk about Lyme. They ought to be setting off for Uppercross by one, and in the meanwhile were to be all together, and out of doors as long as they could.

Anne found Captain Benwick getting near her, as soon as they were all fairly in the street. Their conversation, the preceding evening, did not disincline him to seek her again; and they walked together some time, talking as before of Mr Scott and Lord Byron, and still as unable, as before, and as unable as any other two readers, to think exactly alike of the merits of either, till something occasioned an almost general change amongst their party, and instead of Captain Benwick, she had Captain Harville by her side.

'Miss Elliot,' said he, speaking rather low, 'you have done a good deed in making that poor fellow talk so much. I wish he could have such company oftener. It is bad for him, I know, to be shut up as he is; but what can we do? we cannot part.'

'No,' said Anne, 'that I can easily believe to be impossible; but in time, perhaps – we know what time does in every case of affliction, and you must remember, Captain Harville, that your friend may yet be called a young mourner – Only last summer, I understand.'

'Ay, true enough,' (with a deep sigh) 'only June.'

'And not known to him, perhaps, so soon.'

'Not till the first week in August, when he came home from the Cape, – just made into the Grappler. I was at Plymouth, dreading to hear of him; he sent in letters, but the Grappler was under orders for Portsmouth. There the news must follow him, but who was to tell it? not I. I would as soon have been run up to the yard-arm. Nobody could do it, but that good fellow, (pointing to Captain Wentworth.) The Laconia had come into Plymouth the week before; no danger of her being sent to sea again. He stood his chance for the rest – wrote up for leave of absence, but without waiting the return, travelled night and day till he got to Portsmouth, rowed off to the Grappler that instant, and never left the poor fellow for a week; that's what he did, and nobody else could have saved poor James. You may think, Miss Elliot, whether he is dear to us!'

Anne did think on the question with perfect decision, and said as much in reply as her own feelings could accomplish, or as his seemed able to bear, for he was too much affected to renew the subject – and when he spoke again, it was of something totally different.

Mrs Harville's giving it as her opinion that her husband would have quite walking enough by the time he reached home, determined the direction of all the party in what was to be their last walk; they would accompany them to their door, and then return and set off themselves. By all their calculations there was just time for this; but as they drew near the Cobb, there was such a general wish to walk along it once more, all were so inclined, and Louisa soon grew so determined, that the difference of a quarter of an hour, it was found, would be no difference at all, so with all the kind leave-taking, and all the kind interchange of invitations and promises which may be imagined, they parted from Captain and Mrs Harville at their own door, and still accompanied by Captain Benwick, who seemed to cling to them to the last, proceeded to make the proper adieus to the Cobb.

Anne found Captain Benwick again drawing near her. Lord Byron's 'dark blue seas' could not fail of being brought forward by their present view, and she gladly gave him all her attention as long as attention was possible. It was soon drawn per force another way.

There was too much wind to make the high part of the new Cobb pleasant for the ladies, and they agreed to get down the steps to the lower, and all were contented to pass quietly and carefully down the steep flight, excepting Louisa; she must be jumped down them by Captain Wentworth. In all their walks, he had had to jump her from the stiles; the sensation was delightful to her. The hardness of the pavement for her feet, made him less willing upon the present occasion; he did it, however; she was safely down, and instantly, to shew her enjoyment, ran up the steps to be jumped down again. He advised her against it, thought the jar too great; but no, he reasoned and talked in vain; she smiled and said, 'I am determined I will:' he put out his hands; she was too precipitate by half a second, she fell on the pavement on the Lower Cobb, and was taken up lifeless!

There was no wound, no blood, no visible bruise; but her eyes were closed, she breathed not, her face was like death. – The horror of that moment to all who stood around!

Captain Wentworth, who had caught her up, knelt with her in his arms, looking on her with a face as pallid as her own, in an agony of silence. 'She is dead! she is dead!' screamed Mary, catching hold of her husband, and contributing with his own horror to make him immoveable; and in another moment, Henrietta, sinking under the conviction, lost her senses too, and would have fallen on the steps, but for Captain Benwick and Anne, who caught and supported her between them.

'Is there no one to help me?' were the first words which burst from Captain Wentworth, in a tone of despair, and as if all his own strength were gone.

'Go to him, go to him,' cried Anne, 'for heaven's sake go to him. I can support her myself. Leave me, and go to him. Rub her hands, rub her temples; here are salts, – take them, take them.'

Captain Benwick obeyed, and Charles at the same moment, disengaging himself from his wife, they were both with him; and Louisa was raised up and supported more firmly between them, and every thing was done that Anne had prompted, but in vain; while Captain Wentworth, staggering against the wall for his support, exclaimed in the bitterest agony,

'Oh God! her father and mother!'

' A surgeon!' said Anne.

He caught the word; it seemed to rouse him at once, and saying only 'True, true, a surgeon this instant,' was darting away, when Anne eagerly suggested,

'Captain Benwick, would not it be better for Captain Benwick? He knows where a surgeon is to be found.'

Every one capable of thinking felt the advantage of the idea, and in a moment (it was all done in rapid moments) Captain Benwick had resigned the poor corpse-like figure entirely to the brother's care, and was off for the town with the utmost rapidity.

As to the wretched party left behind, it could scarcely be said which of the three, who were completely rational, was suffering most, Captain Wentworth, Anne, or Charles, who, really a very affectionate brother, hung over Louisa with sobs of grief, and could only turn his eyes from one sister, to see the other in a state as insensible, or to witness the hysterical agitations of his wife, calling on him for help which he could not give.

Anne, attending with all the strength and zeal, and thought, which instinct supplied, to Henrietta, still tried, at intervals, to suggest comfort to the others, tried to quiet Mary, to animate

PERSUASION

Charles, to assuage the feelings of Captain Wentworth. Both seemed to look to her for directions.

'Anne, Anne,' cried Charles, 'what is to be done next? What, in heaven's name, is to be done next?'

Captain Wentworth's eyes were also turned towards her.

'Had not she better be carried to the inn? Yes, I am sure, carry her gently to the inn.'

'Yes, yes, to the inn,' repeated Captain Wentworth, comparatively collected, and eager to be doing something. 'I will carry her myself. Musgrove, take care of the others.'

By this time the report of the accident had spread among the workmen and boatmen about the Cobb, and many were collected near them, to be useful if wanted, at any rate, to enjoy the sight of a dead young lady, nay, two dead young ladies, for it proved twice as fine as the first report. To some of the best-looking of these good people Henrietta was consigned, for, though partially revived, she was quite helpless; and in this manner, Anne walking by her side, and Charles attending to his wife, they set forward, treading back with feelings unutterable, the ground, which so lately, so very lately, and so light of heart, they had passed along.

They were not off the Cobb, before the Harvilles met them. Captain Benwick had been seen flying by their house, with a countenance which shewed something to be wrong; and they had set off immediately, informed and directed, as they passed, towards the spot. Shocked as Captain Harville was, he brought senses and nerves that could be instantly useful; and a look between him and his wife decided what was to be done. She must be taken to their house – all must go to their house – and await the surgeon's arrival there. They would not listen to scruples : he was obeyed; they were all beneath his roof; and while Louisa, under Mrs Harville's direction, was conveyed up stairs, and given possession of her own bed, assistance, cordials, restoratives were supplied by her husband to all who needed them.

Louisa had once opened her eyes, but soon closed them again, without apparent consciousness. This had been a proof of life, however, of service to her sister; and Henrietta, though perfectly incapable of being in the same room with Louisa, was kept, by

131

the agitation of hope and fear, from a return of her own insensibility. Mary, too, was growing calmer.

The surgeon was with them almost before it had seemed possible. They were sick with horror while he examined; but he was not hopeless. The head had received a severe contusion, but he had seen greater injuries recovered from: he was by no means hopeless; he spoke cheerfully.

That he did not regard it as a desperate case – that he did not say a few hours must end it – was at first felt, beyond the hope of most; and the ecstasy of such a reprieve, the rejoicing, deep and silent, after a few fervent ejaculations of gratitude to Heaven had been offered, may be conceived.

The tone, the look, with which 'Thank God!' was uttered by Captain Wentworth, Anne was sure could never be forgotten by her; nor the sight of them afterwards, as he sat near a table, leaning over it with folded arms, and face concealed, as if overpowered by the various feelings of his soul, and trying by prayer and reflection to calm them.

Louisa's limbs had escaped. There was no injury but to the head.

It now became necessary for the party to consider what was best to be done, as to their general situation. They were now able to speak to each other, and consult. That Louisa must remain where she was, however distressing to her friends to be involving the Harvilles in such trouble, did not admit a doubt. Her removal was impossible. The Harvilles silenced all scruples; and, as much as they could, all gratitude. They had looked forward and arranged every thing, before the others began to reflect. Captain Benwick must give up his room to them, and get a bed elsewhere – and the whole was settled. They were only concerned that the house could accommodate no more; and yet perhaps by 'putting the children away in the maids' room, or swinging a cot somewhere,' they could hardly bear to think of not finding room for two or three besides, supposing they might wish to stay; though, with regard to any attendance on Miss Musgrove, there need not be the least uneasiness in leaving her to Mrs Harville's care entirely. Mrs Harville was a very experienced nurse; and her nursery-maid, who had lived with her long and gone about with her every where, was just such another. Between those two, she could want no possible attendance by day or night. And all this was said with a truth and sincerity of feeling irresistible.

Charles, Henrietta, and Captain Wentworth were the three in consultation, and for a little while it was only an interchange of perplexity and terror. 'Uppercross, – the necessity of some one's going to Uppercross, – the news to be conveyed – how it could be broken to Mr and Mrs Musgrove – the lateness of the morning, – an hour already gone since they ought to have been off, – the impossibility of being in tolerable time.' At first, they were capable of nothing more to the purpose than such exclamations; but, after a while, Captain Wentworth, exerting himself, said,

'We must be decided, and without the loss of another minute. Every minute is valuable. Some must resolve on being off for Uppercross instantly. Musgrove, either you or I must go.'

Charles agreed; but declared his resolution of not going away. He would be as little incumbrance as possible to Captain and Mrs Harville; but as to leaving his sister in such a state, he neither ought, nor would. So far it was decided; and Henrietta at first declared the same. She, however, was soon persuaded to think differently. The usefulness of her staying ! – She, who had not been able to remain in Louisa's room, or to look at her, without sufferings which made her worse than helpless ! She was forced to acknowledge that she could do no good; yet was still unwilling to be away, till touched by the thought of her father and mother, she gave it up; she consented, she was anxious to be at home.

The plan had reached this point, when Anne, coming quietly down from Louisa's room, could not but hear what followed, for the parlour door was open.

'Then it is settled, Musgrove,' cried Captain Wentworth, 'that you stay, and that I take care of your sister home. But as to the rest; – as to the others; – If one stays to assist Mrs Harville, I think it need be only one. – Mrs Charles Musgrove will, of course, wish to get back to her children; but, if Anne will stay, no one so proper, so capable as Anne !'

She paused a moment to recover from the emotion of hearing herself so spoken of. The other two warmly agreed to what he said, and she then appeared.

'You will stay, I am sure; you will stay and nurse her;' cried he, turning to her and speaking with a glow, and yet a gentleness, which seemed almost restoring the past. – She coloured deeply; and he recollected himself, and moved away. – She expressed herself most willing, ready, happy to remain. 'It was what she had been thinking of, and wishing to be allowed to do. – A bed on the floor in Louisa's room would be sufficient for her, if Mrs Harville would but think so.'

One thing more, and all seemed arranged. Though it was rather desirable that Mr and Mrs Musgrove should be previously alarmed by some share of delay; yet the time required by the Uppercross horses to take them back, would be a dreadful extension of suspense; and Captain Wentworth proposed, and Charles Musgrove agreed, that it would be much better for him to take a chaise from the inn, and leave Mr Musgrove's carriage and horses to be sent home the next morning early, when there would be the farther advantage of sending an account of Louisa's night.

Captain Wentworth now hurried off to get every thing ready on his part, and to be soon followed by the two ladies. When the plan was made known to Mary, however, there was an end of all peace in it. She was so wretched, and so vehement, complained so much of injustice in being expected to go away, instead of Anne; – Anne, who was nothing to Louisa, while she was her sister, and had the best right to stay in Henrietta's stead! Why was not she to be as useful as Anne? And to go home without Charles, too – without her husband! No, it was too unkind! And, in short, she said more than her husband could long withstand; and as none of the others could oppose when he gave way, there was no help for it: the change of Mary for Anne was inevitable.

Anne had never submitted more reluctantly to the jealous and ill-judging claims of Mary; but so it must be, and they set off for the town, Charles taking care of his sister, and Captain Benwick attending to her. She gave a moment's recollection, as they hurried along, to the little circumstances which the same spots had witnessed earlier in the morning. There she had listened to Henrietta's schemes for Dr Shirley's leaving Uppercross; farther on, she had first seen Mr Elliot; a moment seemed all that could now be given to any one but Louisa, or those who were wrapt up in her welfare.

Captain Benwick was most considerately attentive to her; and, united as they all seemed by the distress of the day, she felt an increasing degree of good-will towards him, and a pleasure even in thinking that it might, perhaps, be the occasion of continuing their acquaintance.

Captain Wentworth was on the watch for them, and a chaise and four in waiting, stationed for their convenience in the lowest part of the street; but his evident surprise and vexation, at the substitution of one sister for the other – the change of his countenance – the astonishment – the expressions begun and suppressed, with which Charles was listened to, made but a mortifying reception of Anne; or must at least convince her that she was valued only as she could be useful to Louisa.

She endeavoured to be composed, and to be just. Without emulating the feelings of an Emma towards her Henry,[8] she would have attended on Louisa with a zeal above the common claims of regard, for his sake; and she hoped he would not long be so unjust as to suppose she would shrink unnecessarily from the office of a friend.

In the meantime she was in the carriage. He had handed them both in, and placed himself between them; and in this manner, under these circumstances full of astonishment and emotion to Anne, she quitted Lyme. How the long stage would pass; how it was to affect their manners; what was to be their sort of intercourse, she could not foresee. It was all quite natural, however. He was devoted to Henrietta; always turning towards her; and when he spoke at all, always with the view of supporting her hopes and raising her spirits. In general, his voice and manner were studiously calm. To spare Henrietta from agitation seemed the governing principle. Once only, when she had been grieving over the last ill-judged, ill-fated walk to the Cobb, bitterly lamenting that it ever had been thought of, he burst forth, as if wholly overcome –

'Don't talk of it, don't talk of it,' he cried. 'Oh God! that I had not given way to her at the fatal moment! Had I done as I ought! But so eager and so resolute! Dear, sweet Louisa!'

Anne wondered whether it ever occurred to him now, to question the justness of his own previous opinion as to the universal felicity and advantage of firmness of character; and whether it might not strike him, that, like all other qualities of the mind, it should have its proportions and limits. She thought it could scarcely escape him to feel, that a persuadable temper might sometimes be as much in favour of happiness, as a very resolute character.

They got on fast. Anne was astonished to recognise the same hills and the same objects so soon. Their actual speed, heightened by some dread of the conclusion, made the road appear but half as long as on the day before. It was growing quite dusk, however, before they were in the neighbourhood of Uppercross, and there had been total silence among them for some time, Henrietta leaning back in the corner, with a shawl over her face, giving the hope of her having cried herself to sleep; when, as they were going up their last hill, Anne found herself all at once addressed by Captain Wentworth. In a low, cautious voice, he said,

'I have been considering what we had best do. She must not appear at first. She could not stand it. I have been thinking whether you had not better remain in the carriage with her, while I go in and break it to Mr and Mrs Musgrove. Do you think this a good plan?'

She did: he was satisfied, and said no more. But the remembrance of the appeal remained a pleasure to her – as a proof of friendship, and of deference for her judgment, a great pleasure; and when it became a sort of parting proof, its value did not lessen.

When the distressing communication at Uppercross was over, and he had seen the father and mother quite as composed as could be hoped, and the daughter all the better for being with them, he announced his intention of returning in the same carriage to Lyme; and when the horses were baited, he was off.

[*In the original edition the first volume ended here.*]

CHAPTER 13

THE remainder of Anne's time at Uppercross, comprehending only two days, was spent entirely at the mansion-house, and she had the satisfaction of knowing herself extremely useful there, both as an immediate companion, and as assisting in all those arrangements for the future, which, in Mr and Mrs Musgrove's distressed state of spirits, would have been difficulties.

They had an early account from Lyme the next morning. Louisa was much the same. No symptoms worse than before had appeared. Charles came a few hours afterwards, to bring a later and more particular account. He was tolerably cheerful. A speedy cure must not be hoped, but every thing was going on as well as the nature of the case admitted. In speaking of the Harvilles, he seemed unable to satisfy his own sense of their kindness, especially of Mrs Harville's exertions as a nurse. 'She really left nothing for Mary to do. He and Mary had been persuaded to go early to their inn last night. Mary had been hysterical again this morning. When he came away, she was going to walk out with Captain Benwick, which, he hoped, would do her good. He almost wished she had been prevailed on to come home the day before; but the truth was, that Mrs Harville left nothing for any body to do.'

Charles was to return to Lyme the same afternoon, and his father had at first half a mind to go with him, but the ladies could not consent. It would be going only to multiply trouble to the others, and increase his own distress; and a much better scheme followed and was acted upon. A chaise was sent for from Crewkherne, and Charles conveyed back a far more useful person in the old nursery-maid of the family, one who having brought up all the children, and seen the very last, the lingering and long-petted master Harry, sent to school after his brothers, was now living in her deserted nursery to mend stockings, and dress all the blains and bruises she could get near her, and who, consequently, was only too happy in being allowed to go and help nurse dear

137

Miss Louisa. Vague wishes of getting Sarah thither, had occurred before to Mrs Musgrove and Henrietta; but without Anne, it would hardly have been resolved on, and found practicable so soon.

They were indebted, the next day, to Charles Hayter for all the minute knowledge of Louisa, which it was so essential to obtain every twenty-four hours. He made it his business to go to Lyme, and his account was still encouraging. The intervals of sense and consciousness were believed to be stronger. Every report agreed in Captain Wentworth's appearing fixed in Lyme.

Anne was to leave them on the morrow, an event which they all dreaded. 'What should they do without her? They were wretched comforters for one another!' And so much was said in this way, that Anne thought she could not do better than impart among them the general inclination to which she was privy, and persuade them all to go to Lyme at once. She had little difficulty; it was soon determined that they would go, go to-morrow, fix themselves at the inn, or get into lodgings, as it suited, and there remain till dear Louisa could be moved. They must be taking off some trouble from the good people she was with; they might at least relieve Mrs Harville from the care of her own children; and in short they were so happy in the decision, that Anne was delighted with what she had done, and felt that she could not spend her last morning at Uppercross better than in assisting their preparations, and sending them off at an early hour, though her being left to the solitary range of the house was the consequence.

She was the last, excepting the little boys at the cottage, she was the very last, the only remaining one of all that had filled and animated both houses, of all that had given Uppercross its cheerful character. A few days had made a change indeed!

If Louisa recovered, it would all be well again. More than former happiness would be restored. There could not be a doubt, to her mind there was none, of what would follow her recovery. A few months hence, and the room now so deserted, occupied but by her silent, pensive self, might be filled again with all that was happy and gay, all that was glowing and bright in prosperous love, all that was most unlike Anne Elliot!

An hour's complete leisure for such reflections as these, on a dark November day, a small thick rain almost blotting out the very few objects ever to be discerned from the windows, was enough to make the sound of Lady Russell's carriage exceedingly welcome; and yet, though desirous to be gone, she could not quit the mansion-house, or look an adieu to the cottage, with its black, dripping, and comfortless veranda, or even notice through the misty glasses the last humble tenements of the village, without a saddened heart. – Scenes had passed in Uppercross, which made it precious. It stood the record of many sensations of pain, once severe, but now softened; and of some instances of relenting feeling, some breathings of friendship and reconciliation, which could never be looked for again, and which could never cease to be dear. She left it all behind her; all but the recollection that such things had been.

Anne had never entered Kellynch since her quitting Lady Russell's house, in September. It had not been necessary, and the few occasions of its being possible for her to go to the hall she had contrived to evade and escape from. Her first return, was to resume her place in the modern and elegant apartments of the lodge, and to gladden the eyes of its mistress.

There was some anxiety mixed with Lady Russell's joy in meeting her. She knew who had been frequenting Uppercross. But happily, either Anne was improved in plumpness and looks, or Lady Russell fancied her so; and Anne, in receiving her compliments on the occasion, had the amusement of connecting them with the silent admiration of her cousin, and of hoping that she was to be blessed with a second spring of youth and beauty.

When they came to converse, she was soon sensible of some mental change. The subjects of which her heart had been full on leaving Kellynch, and which she had felt slighted, and been compelled to smother among the Musgroves, were now become but of secondary interest. She had lately lost sight even of her father and sister and Bath. Their concerns had been sunk under those of Uppercross, and when Lady Russell reverted to their former hopes and fears, and spoke her satisfaction in the house in Camden-place, which had been taken, and her regret that Mrs Clay should still be with them, Anne would have been ashamed to have it known, how much more she was thinking of Lyme, and Louisa

Musgrove, and all her acquaintance there; how much more interesting to her was the home and the friendship of the Harvilles
and Captain Benwick, than her own father's house in Camden-
place, or her own sister's intimacy with Mrs Clay. She was
actually forced to exert herself, to meet Lady Russell with any
thing like the appearance of equal solicitude, on topics which had
by nature the first claim on her.

There was a little awkwardness at first in their discourse on
another subject. They must speak of the accident at Lyme. Lady
Russell had not been arrived five minutes the day before, when a
full account of the whole had burst on her; but still it must be
talked of, she must make enquiries, she must regret the imprudence, lament the result, and Captain Wentworth's name must
be mentioned by both. Anne was conscious of not doing it so
well as Lady Russell. She could not speak the name, and look
straight forward to Lady Russell's eye, till she had adopted the
expedient of telling her briefly what she thought of the attachment between him and Louisa. When this was told, his name distressed her no longer.

Lady Russell had only to listen composedly, and wish them
happy; but internally her heart revelled in angry pleasure, in
pleased contempt, that the man who at twenty-three had seemed
to understand somewhat of the value of an Anne Elliot, should,
eight years afterwards, be charmed by a Louisa Musgrove.

The first three or four days passed most quietly, with no circumstance to mark them excepting the receipt of a note or two
from Lyme, which found their way to Anne, she could not tell
how, and brought a rather improving account of Louisa. At the
end of that period, Lady Russell's politeness could repose no
longer, and the fainter self-threatenings of the past, became in a
decided tone, 'I must call on Mrs Croft; I really must call upon
her soon. Anne, have you courage to go with me, and pay a visit
in that house? It will be some trial to us both.'

Anne did not shrink from it; on the contrary, she truly felt as
she said, in observing,

'I think you are very likely to suffer the most of the two; your
feelings are less reconciled to the change than mine. By remaining in the neighbourhood, I am become inured to it.'

She could have said more on the subject; for she had in fact so high an opinion of the Crofts, and considered her father so very fortunate in his tenants, felt the parish to be so sure of a good example, and the poor of the best attention and relief, that however sorry and ashamed for the necessity of the removal, she could not but in conscience feel that they were gone who deserved not to stay, and that Kellynch-hall had passed into better hands than its owners'. These convictions must unquestionably have their own pain, and severe was its kind; but they precluded that pain which Lady Russell would suffer in entering the house again, and returning through the well-known apartments.

In such moments Anne had no power of saying to herself, 'These rooms ought to belong only to us. Oh, how fallen in their destination! How unworthily occupied! An ancient family to be so driven away! Strangers filling their place!' No, except when she thought of her mother, and remembered where she had been used to sit and preside, she had no sigh of that description to heave.

Mrs Croft always met her with a kindness which gave her the pleasure of fancying herself a favourite; and on the present occasion, receiving her in that house, there was particular attention.

The sad accident at Lyme was soon the prevailing topic; and on comparing their latest accounts of the invalid, it appeared that each lady dated her intelligence from the same hour of yester morn, that Captain Wentworth had been in Kellynch yesterday – (the first time since the accident) had brought Anne the last note, which she had not been able to trace the exact steps of, had staid a few hours and then returned again to Lyme – and without any present intention of quitting it any more. – He had enquired after her, she found, particularly; – had expressed his hope of Miss Elliot's not being the worse for her exertions, and had spoken of those exertions as great. – This was handsome, – and gave her more pleasure than almost any thing else could have done.

As to the sad catastrophe itself, it could be canvassed only in one style by a couple of steady, sensible women, whose judgments had to work on ascertained events; and it was perfectly decided that it had been the consequence of much thoughtlessness and much imprudence; that its effects were most alarming, and that it was frightful to think, how long Miss Musgrove's recovery might yet be doubtful, and how liable she would still remain to suffer from the concussion hereafter! – The Admiral wound it all up summarily by exclaiming,

'Ay, a very bad business indeed. – A new sort of way this, for a young fellow to be making love, by breaking his mistress's head! – is not it, Miss Elliot? – This is breaking a head and giving a plaister truly!'

Admiral Croft's manners were not quite of the tone to suit Lady Russell, but they delighted Anne. His goodness of heart and simplicity of character were irresistible.

'Now, this must be very bad for you,' said he, suddenly rousing from a little reverie, 'to be coming and finding us here. – I had not recollected it before, I declare, – but it must be very bad. – But now, do not stand upon ceremony. – Get up and go over all the rooms in the house if you like it.'

'Another time, Sir, I thank you, not now.'

'Well, whenever it suits you. – You can slip in from the shrubbery at any time. And there you will find we keep our umbrellas, hanging up by that door. A good place, is not it? But' (checking himself) 'you will not think it a good place, for yours were always kept in the butler's room. Ay, so it always is, I believe. One man's ways may be as good as another's, but we all like our own best. And so you must judge for yourself, whether it would be better for you to go about the house or not.'

Anne, finding she might decline it, did so, very gratefully.

'We have made very few changes either!' continued the Admiral, after thinking a moment. 'Very few. – We told you about the laundry-door, at Uppercross. That has been a very great improvement. The wonder was, how any family upon earth could bear with the inconvenience of its opening as it did, so long! – You will tell Sir Walter what we have done, and that Mr Shepherd thinks it the greatest improvement the house ever had. Indeed, I must do ourselves the justice to say, that the few alterations we have made have been all very much for the better. My wife should have the credit of them, however. I have done very little besides sending away some of the large looking-glasses from my dressing-room, which was your father's. A very good man, and very much the gentleman I am sure – but I should think, Miss Elliot' (looking with serious reflection) 'I should think he must be rather a dressy man for his time of life. – Such a number of looking-glasses! oh Lord! there was no getting away from oneself. So I got Sophy to lend me a hand, and we soon shifted their quarters; and now I am quite snug, with my little shaving glass in one corner, and another great thing that I never go near.'

Anne, amused in spite of herself, was rather distressed for an answer, and the Admiral, fearing he might not have been civil enough, took up the subject again, to say,

'The next time you write to your good father, Miss Elliot, pray give him my compliments and Mrs Croft's, and say that we are settled here quite to our liking, and have no fault at all to find with the place. The breakfast-room chimney smokes a little, I grant you, but it is only when the wind is due north and blows hard, which may not happen three times a winter. And take it altogether, now that we have been into most of the houses here-abouts and can judge, there is not one that we like better than this. Pray say so, with my compliments. He will be glad to hear it.'

Lady Russell and Mrs Croft were very well pleased with each other; but the acquaintance which this visit began, was fated not to proceed far at present; for when it was returned, the Crofts announced themselves to be going away for a few weeks, to visit their connexions in the north of the county, and probably might not be at home again before Lady Russell would be removing to Bath.

So ended all danger to Anne of meeting Captain Wentworth at Kellynch-hall, or of seeing him in company with her friend. Every thing was safe enough, and she smiled over the many anxious feelings she had wasted on the subject.

CHAPTER 14

THOUGH Charles and Mary had remained at Lyme much longer after Mr and Mrs Musgrove's going, than Anne conceived they could have been at all wanted, they were yet the first of the family to be at home again, and as soon as possible after their return to Uppercross, they drove over to the lodge. – They had left Louisa beginning to sit up; but her head, though clear, was exceedingly weak, and her nerves susceptible to the highest extreme of tenderness; and though she might be pronounced to be altogether doing very well, it was still impossible to say when she might be able to bear the removal home; and her father and mother, who must return in time to receive their younger children for the Christmas holidays, had hardly a hope of being allowed to bring her with them.

They had been all in lodgings together. Mrs Musgrove had got Mrs Harville's children away as much as she could, every possible supply from Uppercross had been furnished, to lighten the inconvenience to the Harvilles, while the Harvilles had been wanting them to come to dinner every day; and in short, it seemed to have been only a struggle on each side as to which should be most disinterested and hospitable.

Mary had had her evils; but upon the whole, as was evident by her staying so long, she had found more to enjoy than to suffer. – Charles Hayter had been at Lyme oftener than suited her, and when they dined with the Harvilles there had been only a maid-servant to wait, and at first, Mrs Harville had always given Mrs Musgrove precedence; but then, she had received so very handsome an apology from her on finding out whose daughter she was, and there had been so much going on every day, there had been so many walks between their lodgings and the Harvilles, and she had got books from the library and changed them so often, that the balance had certainly been much in favour of Lyme. She had been taken to Charmouth too, and she had bathed, and she had gone to church, and there were a great many more people to look at in the church at Lyme than at Uppercross, – and all this, joined to the sense of being so very useful, had made really an agreeable fortnight.

Anne enquired after Captain Benwick. Mary's face was clouded directly. Charles laughed.

'Oh! Captain Benwick is very well, I believe, but he is a very odd young man. I do not know what he would be at. We asked him to come home with us for a day or two; Charles undertook to give him some shooting, and he seemed quite delighted, and for my part, I thought it was all settled; when behold! on Tuesday night, he made a very awkward sort of excuse; "he never shot" and he had "been quite misunderstood," – and he had promised this and he had promised that, and the end of it was, I found, that he did not mean to come. I suppose he was afraid of finding it dull; but upon my word I should have thought we were lively enough at the Cottage for such a heart-broken man as Captain Benwick.'

Charles laughed again and said, 'Now Mary, you know very well how it really was. – It was all your doing,' (turning to Anne.) 'He fancied that if he went with us, he should find you close by; he fancied every body to be living in Uppercross; and when he discovered that Lady Russell lived three miles off, his heart failed him, and he had not courage to come. That is the fact, upon my honour. Mary knows it is.'

But Mary did not give into it very graciously; whether from not considering Captain Benwick entitled by birth and situation to be in love with an Elliot, or from not wanting to believe Anne a greater attraction to Uppercross than herself, must be left to be guessed. Anne's good-will, however, was not to be lessened by what she heard. She boldly acknowledged herself flattered, and continued her enquiries.

'Oh! he talks of you,' cried Charles, 'in such terms,' – Mary interrupted him. 'I declare, Charles, I never heard him mention Anne twice all the time I was there. I declare, Anne, he never talks of you at all.'

'No,' admitted Charles, 'I do not know that he ever does, in a general way – but however, it is a very clear thing that he admires you exceedingly. – His head is full of some books that he is reading upon your recommendation, and he wants to talk to you about them; he has found out something or other in one of them which he thinks – Oh! I cannot pretend to remember it, but it was something very fine – I overheard him telling Henrietta all about it – and then "Miss Elliot" was spoken of in the highest terms! – Now Mary, I declare it was so, I heard it myself, and you were in the other room. – "Elegance, sweetness, beauty," Oh! there was no end of Miss Elliot's charms.'

'And I am sure,' cried Mary warmly, 'it was very little to his credit, if he did. Miss Harville only died last June. Such a heart is very little worth having; is it, Lady Russell? I am sure you will agree with me.'

'I must see Captain Benwick before I decide,' said Lady Russell, smiling.

'And that you are very likely to do very soon, I can tell you, ma'am,' said Charles. 'Though he had not nerves for coming away with us and setting off again afterwards to pay a formal visit here, he will make his way over to Kellynch one day by himself, you may depend on it. I told him the distance and the road, and I told him of the church's being so very well worth seeing, for as he has a taste for those sort of things, I thought that would be a good excuse, and he listened with all his understanding and soul; and I am sure from his manner that you will have him calling here soon. So, I give you notice, Lady Russell.'

'Any acquaintance of Anne's will always be welcome to me,' was Lady Russell's kind answer.

'Oh! as to being Anne's acquaintance,' said Mary, 'I think he is rather my acquaintance, for I have been seeing him every day this last fortnight.'

'Well, as your joint acquaintance, then, I shall be very happy to see Captain Benwick.'

'You will not find any thing very agreeable in him, I assure you, ma'am. He is one of the dullest young men that ever lived. He has walked with me, sometimes, from one end of the sands to the other, without saying a word. He is not at all a well-bred young man. I am sure you will not like him.'

'There we differ, Mary,' said Anne. 'I think Lady Russell would like him. I think she would be so much pleased with his mind, that she would very soon see no deficiency in his manner.'

'So do I, Anne,' said Charles. 'I am sure Lady Russell would like him. He is just Lady Russell's sort. Give him a book, and he will read all day long.'

'Yes, that he will!' exclaimed Mary, tauntingly. 'He will sit poring over his book, and not know when a person speaks to him, or when one drops one's scissors, or any thing that happens. Do you think Lady Russell would like that?'

Lady Russell could not help laughing. 'Upon my word,' said she, 'I should not have supposed that my opinion of any one could have admitted of such difference of conjecture, steady and matter of fact as I may call myself. I have really a curiosity to see the person who can give occasion to such directly opposite notions. I wish he may be induced to call here. And when he does, Mary, you may depend upon hearing my opinion; but I am determined not to judge him before-hand.'

'You will not like him, I will answer for it.'

Lady Russell began talking of something else. Mary spoke with animation of their meeting with, or rather missing, Mr Elliot so extraordinarily.

'He is a man,' said Lady Russell, 'whom I have no wish to see. His declining to be on cordial terms with the head of his family, has left a very strong impression in his disfavour with me.'

This decision checked Mary's eagerness, and stopped her short in the midst of the Elliot countenance.

With regard to Captain Wentworth, though Anne hazarded no enquiries, there was voluntary communication sufficient. His spirits had been greatly recovering lately, as might be expected. As Louisa improved, he had improved; and he was now quite a different creature from what he had been the first week. He had not seen Louisa; and was so extremely fearful of any ill consequence to her from an interview, that he did not press for it at all; and, on the contrary, seemed to have a plan of going away for a week or ten days, till her head were stronger. He had talked of going down to Plymouth for a week, and wanted to persuade Captain Benwick to go with him; but, as Charles maintained to the last, Captain Benwick seemed much more disposed to ride over to Kellynch.

There can be no doubt that Lady Russell and Anne were both occasionally thinking of Captain Benwick, from this time. Lady Russell could not hear the door-bell without feeling that it might be his herald; nor could Anne return from any stroll of solitary indulgence in her father's grounds, or any visit of charity in the village, without wondering whether she might see him or hear of him. Captain Benwick came not, however. He was either less disposed for it than Charles had imagined, or he was too shy; and after giving him a week's indulgence, Lady Russell determined him to be unworthy of the interest which he had been beginning to excite.

The Musgroves came back to receive their happy boys and girls from school, bringing with them Mrs Harville's little children, to improve the noise of Uppercross, and lessen that of Lyme. Henrietta remained with Louisa; but all the rest of the family were again in their usual quarters.

Lady Russell and Anne paid their compliments to them once, when Anne could not but feel that Uppercross was already quite alive again. Though neither Henrietta, nor Louisa, nor Charles Hayter, nor Captain Wentworth were there, the room presented as strong a contrast as could be wished, to the last state she had seen it in.

Immediately surrounding Mrs Musgrove were the little Harvilles, whom she was sedulously guarding from the tyranny of the two children from the Cottage, expressly arrived to amuse them. On one side was a table, occupied by some chattering girls, cutting up silk and gold paper; and on the other were tressels and trays, bending under the weight of brawn and cold pies, where riotous boys were holding high revel; the whole completed by a roaring Christmas fire, which seemed determined to be heard, in spite of all the noise of the others. Charles and Mary also came in, of course, during their visit; and Mr Musgrove made a point of paying his respects to Lady Russell, and sat down close to her for ten minutes, talking with a very raised voice, but, from the clamour of the children on his knees, generally in vain. It was a fine family-piece.

Anne, judging from her own temperament, would have deemed such a domestic hurricane a bad restorative of the nerves, which Louisa's illness must have so greatly shaken; but Mrs Musgrove, who got Anne near her on purpose to thank her most cordially, again and again, for all her attentions to them, concluded a short recapitulation of what she had suffered herself, by observing, with a happy glance round the room, that after all she had gone through, nothing was so likely to do her good as a little quiet cheerfulness at home.

Louisa was now recovering apace. Her mother could even think of her being able to join their party at home, before her brothers and sisters went to school again. The Harvilles had promised to come with her and stay at Uppercross, whenever she returned. Captain Wentworth was gone, for the present, to see his brother in Shropshire.

'I hope I shall remember, in future,' said Lady Russell, as soon as they were reseated in the carriage, 'not to call at Uppercross in the Christmas holidays.'

Every body has their taste in noises as well as in other matters; and sounds are quite innoxious, or most distressing, by their sort rather than their quantity. When Lady Russell, not long afterwards, was entering Bath on a wet afternoon, and driving through the long course of streets from the Old Bridge to Camden-place, amidst the dash of other carriages, the heavy rumble of carts and drays, the bawling of newsmen, muffin-men and milkmen, and the ceaseless clink of pattens, she made no complaint. No, these were noises which belonged to the winter pleasures; her spirits rose under their influence; and, like Mrs Musgrove, she was feeling, though not saying, that, after being long in the country, nothing could be so good for her as a little quiet cheerfulness.

Anne did not share these feelings. She persisted in a very determined, though very silent, disinclination for Bath; caught the first dim view of the extensive buildings, smoking in rain, without any wish of seeing them better; felt their progress through the streets to be, however disagreeable, yet too rapid; for who would be glad to see her when she arrived? And looked back, with fond regret, to the bustles of Uppercross and the seclusion of Kellynch.

Elizabeth's last letter had communicated a piece of news of some interest. Mr Elliot was in Bath. He had called in Camden-place; had called a second time, a third; had been pointedly attentive: if Elizabeth and her father did not deceive themselves, had been taking as much pains to seek the acquaintance, and proclaim the value of the connection, as he had formerly taken pains to shew neglect. This was very wonderful, if it were true; and Lady Russell was in a state of very agreeable curiosity and perplexity about Mr Elliot, already recanting the sentiment she had so lately expressed to Mary, of his being 'a man whom she had no wish to see.' She had a great wish to see him. If he really sought to reconcile himself like a dutiful branch, he must be for-given for having dismembered himself from the paternal tree.

Anne was not animated to an equal pitch by the circumstance; but she felt that she would rather see Mr Elliot again than not, which was more than she could say for many other persons in Bath.

She was put down in Camden-place; and Lady Russell then drove to her own lodgings, in Rivers-street.

CHAPTER 15

SIR WALTER had taken a very good house in Camden-place, a lofty, dignified situation, such as becomes a man of consequence; and both he and Elizabeth were settled there, much to their satisfaction.

Anne entered it with a sinking heart, anticipating an imprisonment of many months, and anxiously saying to herself, 'Oh! when shall I leave you again?' A degree of unexpected cordiality, however, in the welcome she received, did her good. Her father and sister were glad to see her, for the sake of shewing her the house and furniture, and met her with kindness. Her making a fourth, when they sat down to dinner, was noticed as an advantage.

Mrs Clay was very pleasant, and very smiling; but her courtesies and smiles were more a matter of course. Anne had always felt that she would pretend what was proper on her arrival; but the complaisance of the others was unlooked for. They were evidently in excellent spirits, and she was soon to listen to the causes. They had no inclination to listen to her. After laying out for some compliments of being deeply regretted in their old neighbourhood, which Anne could not pay, they had only a few faint enquiries to make, before the talk must be all their own. Uppercross excited no interest, Kellynch very little, it was all Bath.

They had the pleasure of assuring her that Bath more than answered their expectations in every respect. Their house was undoubtedly the best in Camden-place; their drawing-rooms had many decided advantages over all the others which they had either seen or heard of; and the superiority was not less in the style of the fitting-up, or the taste of the furniture. Their acquaintance was exceedingly sought after. Every body was wanting to visit them. They had drawn back from many introductions, and still were perpetually having cards left by people of whom they knew nothing.

Here were funds of enjoyment! Could Anne wonder that her father and sister were happy? She might not wonder, but she must sigh that her father should feel no degradation in his change; should see nothing to regret in the duties and dignity of the resident land-holder; should find so much to be vain of in the littlenesses of a town; and she must sigh, and smile, and wonder too, as Elizabeth threw open the folding-doors, and walked with exultation from one drawing-room to the other, boasting of their space, at the possibility of that woman, who had been mistress of Kellynch Hall, finding extent to be proud of between two walls, perhaps thirty feet asunder.

But this was not all which they had to make them happy. They had Mr Elliot, too. Anne had a great deal to hear of Mr Elliot. He was not only pardoned, they were delighted with him. He had been in Bath about a fortnight; (he had passed through Bath in November, in his way to London, when the intelligence of Sir Walter's being settled there had of course reached him, though only twenty-four hours in the place, but he had not been able to avail himself of it): but he had now been a fortnight in Bath, and his first object, on arriving, had been to leave his card in Camden-place, following it up by such assiduous endeavours to meet, and, when they did meet, by such great openness of conduct, such readiness to apologize for the past, such solicitude to be received as a relation again, that their former good understanding was completely re-established.

They had not a fault to find in him. He had explained away all the appearance of neglect on his own side. It had originated in misapprehension entirely. He had never had an idea of throwing himself off; he had feared that he was thrown off, but knew not why; and delicacy had kept him silent. Upon the hint of having spoken disrespectfully or carelessly of the family, and the family honours, he was quite indignant. He, who had ever boasted of being an Elliot, and whose feelings, as to connection, were only too strict to suit the unfeudal tone of the present day! He was astonished, indeed! But his character and general conduct must refute it. He could refer Sir Walter to all who knew him; and, certainly, the pains he had been taking on this, the first opportunity of reconciliation, to be restored to the footing of a relation and heir-presumptive, was a strong proof of his opinions on the subject.

The circumstances of his marriage too were found to admit of much extenuation. This was an article not to be entered on by himself; but a very intimate friend of his, a Colonel Wallis, a highly respectable man, perfectly the gentleman, (and not an ill-looking man, Sir Walter added) who was living in very good style in Marlborough Buildings, and had, at his own particular request, been admitted to their acquaintance through Mr Elliot, had mentioned one or two things relative to the marriage, which made a material difference in the discredit of it.

Colonel Wallis had known Mr Elliot long, had been well acquainted also with his wife, had perfectly understood the whole story. She was certainly not a woman of family, but well educated, accomplished, rich, and excessively in love with his friend. There had been the charm. She had sought him. Without that attraction, not all her money would have tempted Elliot, and Sir Walter was, moreover, assured of her having been a very fine woman. Here was a great deal to soften the business. A very fine woman, with a large fortune, in love with him! Sir Walter seemed to admit it as complete apology, and though Elizabeth could not see the circumstance in quite so favourable a light, she allowed it be a great extenuation.

Mr Elliott had called repeatedly, had dined with them once, evidently delighted by the distinction of being asked, for they gave no dinners in general; delighted, in short, by every proof of cousinly notice, and placing his whole happiness in being on intimate terms in Camden-place.

Anne listened, but without quite understanding it. Allowances, large allowances, she knew, must be made for the ideas of those who spoke. She heard it all under embellishment. All that sounded extravagant or irrational in the progress of the reconciliation might have no origin but in the language of the relators. Still, however, she had the sensation of there being something more than immediately appeared, in Mr Elliot's wishing, after an interval of so many years, to be well received by them. In a worldly view, he had nothing to gain by being on terms with Sir Walter, nothing to risk by a state of variance. In all probability

he was already the richer of the two, and the Kellynch estate
would as surely be his hereafter as the title. A sensible man! and
he had looked like a *very* sensible man, why should it be an object
to him? She could only offer one solution; it was, perhaps, for
Elizabeth's sake. There might really have been a liking formerly,
though convenience and accident had drawn him a different way,
and now that he could afford to please himself, he might mean
to pay his addresses to her. Elizabeth was certainly very handsome, with well-bred, elegant manners, and her character might
never have been penetrated by Mr Elliot, knowing her but in
public, and when very young himself. How her temper and understanding might bear the investigation of his present keener time
of life was another concern, and rather a fearful one. Most
earnestly did she wish that he might not be too nice, or too observant, if Elizabeth were his object; and that Elizabeth was disposed to believe herself so, and that her friend Mrs Clay was
encouraging the idea, seemed apparent by a glance or two between
them, while Mr Elliot's frequent visits were talked of.

Anne mentioned the glimpses she had had of him at Lyme, but
without being much attended to. 'Oh! yes, perhaps, it had been
Mr Elliot. They did not know. It might be him, perhaps.' They
could not listen to her description of him. They were describing
him themselves; Sir Walter especially. He did justice to his very
gentlemanlike appearance, his air of elegance and fashion, his
good shaped face, his sensible eye, but, at the same time, 'must
lament his being very much under-hung, a defect which time
seemed to have increased; nor could he pretend to say that ten
years had not altered almost every feature for the worse. Mr
Elliot appeared to think that he (Sir Walter) was looking exactly
as he had done when they last parted;' but Sir Walter had 'not
been able to return the compliment entirely, which had embarrassed him. He did not mean to complain, however. Mr Elliot
was better to look at than most men, and he had no objection to
being seen with him any where.'

Mr Elliot, and his friends in Marlborough Buildings, were talked
of the whole evening. 'Colonel Wallis had been so impatient to
be introduced to them! and Mr Elliot so anxious that he should!'
And there was a Mrs Wallis, at present only known to them by

description, as she was in daily expectation of her confinement; but Mr Elliot spoke of her as 'a most charming woman, quite worthy of being known in Camden-place,' and as soon as she recovered, they were to be acquainted. Sir Walter thought much of Mrs Wallis; she was said to be an excessively pretty woman, beautiful. 'He longed to see her. He hoped she might make some amends for the many very plain faces he was continually passing in the streets. The worst of Bath was, the number of its plain women. He did not mean to say that there were no pretty women, but the number of the plain was out of all proportion. He had frequently observed, as he walked, that one handsome face would be followed by thirty, or five and thirty frights; and once, as he had stood in a shop in Bond-street he had counted eighty-seven women go by, one after another, without there being a tolerable face among them. It had been a frosty morning, to be sure, a sharp frost, which hardly one woman in a thousand could stand the test of. But still, there certainly were a dreadful multitude of ugly women in Bath; and as for the men! they were infinitely worse. Such scare-crows as the streets were full of! It was evident how little the women were used to the sight of any thing tolerable, by the effect which a man of decent appearance produced. He had never walked any where arm in arm with Colonel Wallis, (who was a fine military figure, though sandy-haired) without observing that every woman's eye was upon him; every woman's eye was sure to be upon Colonel Wallis.' Modest Sir Walter! He was not allowed to escape, however. His daughter and Mrs Clay united in hinting that Colonel Wallis's companion might have as good a figure as Colonel Wallis, and certainly was not sandy-haired.

'How is Mary looking?' said Sir Walter, in the height of his good humour. 'The last time I saw her, she had a red nose, but I hope that may not happen every day.'

'Oh! no, that must have been quite accidental. In general she has been in very good health, and very good looks since Michaelmas.'

'If I thought it would not tempt her to go out in sharp winds, and grow coarse, I would send her a new hat and pelisse.'

Anne was considering whether she should venture to suggest

that a gown, or a cap, would not be liable to any such misuse,
when a knock at the door suspended every thing. 'A knock at the
door ! and so late ! It was ten o'clock. Could it be Mr Elliot? They
knew he was to dine in Lansdown Crescent. It was possible that
he might stop in his way home, to ask them how they did. They
could think of no one else. Mrs Clay decidedly thought it Mr
Elliot's knock.' Mrs Clay was right. With all the state which a
butler and foot-boy could give, Mr Elliot was ushered into the
room.

It was the same, the very same man, with no difference but of
dress. Anne drew a little back, while the others received his
compliments, and her sister his apologies for calling at so unusual
an hour, but 'he could not be so near without wishing to know
that neither she nor her friend had taken cold the day before,
&c. &c.' which was all as politely done, and as politely taken as
possible, but her part must follow then. Sir Walter talked of his
youngest daughter; 'Mr Elliot must give him leave to present
him to his youngest daughter' – (there was no occasion for remembering Mary) and Anne, smiling and blushing, very becom-
ingly shewed to Mr Elliot the pretty features which he had by no
means forgotten, and instantly saw, with amusement at his little
start of surprise, that he had not been at all aware of who she
was. He looked completely astonished, but not more astonished
than pleased; his eyes brightened, and with the most perfect
alacrity he welcomed the relationship, alluded to the past, and
entreated to be received as an acquaintance already. He was quite
as good-looking as he had appeared at Lyme, his countenance
improved by speaking, and his manners were so exactly what they
ought to be, so polished, so easy, so particularly agreeable, that
she could compare them in excellence to only one person's manners. They were not the same, but they were, perhaps, equally
good.

He sat down with them, and improved their conversation very
much. There could be no doubt of his being a sensible man. Ten
minutes were enough to certify that. His tone, his expressions,
his choice of subject, his knowing where to stop, – it was all the
operation of a sensible, discerning mind. As soon as he could, he
began to talk to her of Lyme, wanting to compare opinions

respecting the place, but especially wanting to speak of the circumstance of their happening to be guests in the same inn at the same time, to give his own route, understand something of hers, and regret that he should have lost such an opportunity of paying his respects to her. She gave him a short account of her party, and business at Lyme. His regret increased as he listened. He had spent his whole solitary evening in the room adjoining theirs; had heard voices – mirth continually; thought they must be a most delightful set of people – longed to be with them; but certainly without the smallest suspicion of his possessing the shadow of a right to introduce himself. If he had but asked who the party were ! The name of Musgrove would have told him enough. 'Well, it would serve to cure him of an absurd practice of never asking a question at an inn, which he had adopted, when quite a young man, on the principle of its being very ungenteel to be curious.

'The notions of a young man of one or two and twenty,' said he, 'as to what is necessary in manners to make him quite the thing, are more absurd, I believe, than those of any other set of beings in the world. The folly of the means they often employ is only to be equalled by the folly of what they have in view.'

But he must not be addressing his reflections to Anne alone; he knew it; he was soon diffused again among the others, and it was only at intervals that he could return to Lyme.

His enquiries, however, produced at length an account of the scene she had been engaged in there, soon after his leaving the place. Having alluded to 'an accident,' he must hear the whole. When he questioned, Sir Walter and Elizabeth began to question also; but the difference in their manner of doing it could not be unfelt. She could only compare Mr Elliot to Lady Russell, in the wish of really comprehending what had passed, and in the degree of concern for what she must have suffered in witnessing it.

He staid an hour with them. The elegant little clock on the mantel-piece had struck 'eleven with its silver sounds,' and the watchman was beginning to be heard at a distance telling the same tale, before Mr Elliot or any of them seemed to feel that he had been there long.

Anne could not have supposed it possible that her first evening in Camden-place could have passed so well !

CHAPTER 16

THERE was one point which Anne, on returning to her family, would have been more thankful to ascertain, even than Mr Elliot's being in love with Elizabeth, which was, her father's not being in love with Mrs Clay; and she was very far from easy about it, when she had been at home a few hours. On going down to breakfast the next morning, she found there had just been a decent pretence on the lady's side of meaning to leave them. She could imagine Mrs Clay to have said, that 'now Miss Anne was come, she could not suppose herself at all wanted;' for Elizabeth was replying, in a sort of whisper, 'That must not be any reason, indeed. I assure you I feel it none. She is nothing to me, compared with you;' and she was in full time to hear her father say, 'My dear Madam, this must not be. As yet, you have seen nothing of Bath. You have been here only to be useful. You must not run away from us now. You must stay to be acquainted with Mrs Wallis, the beautiful Mrs Wallis. To your fine mind, I well know the sight of beauty is a real gratification.'

He spoke and looked so much in earnest, that Anne was not surprised to see Mrs Clay stealing a glance at Elizabeth and herself. Her countenance, perhaps, might express some watchfulness; but the praise of the fine mind did not appear to excite a thought in her sister. The lady could not but yield to such joint entreaties, and promise to stay.

In the course of the same morning, Anne and her father chancing to be alone together, he began to compliment her on her improved looks; he thought her 'less thin in her person, in her cheeks; her skin, her complexion, greatly improved – clearer, fresher. Had she been using any thing in particular !' 'No, nothing.' 'Merely Gowland,' [9] he supposed. 'No, nothing at all.' 'Ha ! he was surprised at that;' and added, 'Certainly you cannot do better than continue as you are; you cannot be better than well; or I should recommend Gowland, the constant use of Gowland, during the spring months. Mrs Clay has been using it at my recommendation, and you see what it has done for her. You see how it has carried away her freckles.'

If Elizabeth could but have heard this! Such personal praise might have struck her, especially as it did not appear to Anne that the freckles were at all lessened. But every thing must take its chance. The evil of the marriage would be much diminished, if Elizabeth were also to marry. As for herself, she might always command a home with Lady Russell.

Lady Russell's composed mind and polite manners were put to some trial on this point, in her intercourse in Camden-place. The sight of Mrs Clay in such favour, and of Anne so overlooked, was a perpetual provocation to her there; and vexed her as much when she was away, as a person in Bath who drinks the water, gets all the new publications, and has a very large acquaintance, has time to be vexed.

As Mr Elliot became known to her, she grew more charitable, or more indifferent, towards the others. His manners were an immediate recommendation; and on conversing with him she found the solid so fully supporting the superficial, that she was at first, as she told Anne, almost ready to exclaim, 'Can this be Mr Elliot?' and could not seriously picture to herself a more agreeable or estimable man. Every thing united in him; good understanding, correct opinions, knowledge of the world, and a warm heart. He had strong feelings of family-attachment and family-honour, without pride or weakness; he lived with the liberality of a man of fortune, without display; he judged for himself in every thing essential, without defying public opinion in any point of worldly decorum. He was steady, observant, moderate, candid; never run away with by spirits or by selfishness, which fancied itself strong feeling; and yet, with a sensibility to what was amiable and lovely, and a value for all the felicities of domestic life, which characters of fancied enthusiasm and violent agitation seldom really possess. She was sure that he had not been happy in marriage. Colonel Wallis said it, and Lady Russell saw it; but it had been no unhappiness to sour his mind, nor (she began pretty soon to suspect) to prevent his thinking of a second choice. Her satisfaction in Mr Elliot outweighed all the plague of Mrs Clay.

It was now some years since Anne had begun to learn that she and her excellent friend could sometimes think differently; and it did not surprise her, therefore, that Lady Russell should see nothing suspicious or inconsistent, nothing to require more motives than appeared, in Mr Elliot's great desire of a reconciliation. In Lady Russell's view, it was perfectly natural that Mr Elliot, at a mature time of life, should feel it a most desirable object, and what would very generally recommend him, among all sensible people, to be on good terms with the head of his family; the simplest process in the world of time upon a head naturally clear, and only erring in the heyday of youth. Anne presumed, however, still to smile about it; and at last to mention 'Elizabeth.' Lady Russell listened, and looked, and made only this cautious reply: 'Elizabeth! Very well. Time will explain.'

It was a reference to the future, which Anne, after a little observation, felt she must submit to. She could determine nothing at present. In that house Elizabeth must be first; and she was in the habit of such general observance as 'Miss Elliot,' that any particularity of attention seemed almost impossible. Mr Elliot, too, it must be remembered, had not been a widower seven months. A little delay on his side might be very excusable. In fact, Anne could never see the crape round his hat, without fearing that she was the inexcusable one, in attributing to him such imaginations; for though his marriage had not been very happy, still it had existed so many years that she could not comprehend a very rapid recovery from the awful impression of its being dissolved.

However it might end, he was without any question their pleasantest acquaintance in Bath; she saw nobody equal to him; and it was a great indulgence now and then to talk to him about Lyme, which he seemed to have as lively a wish to see again, and to see more of, as herself. They went through the particulars of their first meeting a great many times. He gave her to understand that he had looked at her with some earnestness. She knew it well; and she remembered another person's look also.

They did not always think alike. His value for rank and connexion she perceived to be greater than hers. It was not merely complaisance, it must be a liking to the cause, which made him enter warmly into her father and sister's solicitudes on a subject which she thought unworthy to excite them. The Bath paper one morning announced the arrival of the Dowager Viscountess Dalrymple, and her daughter, the Honourable Miss Carteret; and all the comfort of No. —, Camden-place, was swept away for many days; for the Dalrymples (in Anne's opinion, most unfortunately) were cousins of the Elliots; and the agony was, how to introduce themselves properly.

Anne had never seen her father and sister before in contact with nobility, and she must acknowledge herself disappointed. She had hoped better things from their high ideas of their own situation in life, and was reduced to form a wish which she had never foreseen – a wish that they had more pride; for 'our cousins Lady Dalrymple and Miss Carteret;' 'our cousins, the Dalrymples,' sounded in her ears all day long.

Sir Walter had once been in company with the late Viscount, but had never seen any of the rest of the family, and the difficulties of the case arose from there having been a suspension of all intercourse by letters of ceremony, ever since the death of that said late Viscount, when, in consequence of a dangerous illness of Sir Walter's at the same time, there had been an unlucky omission at Kellynch. No letter of condolence had been sent to Ireland. The neglect had been visited on the head of the sinner, for when poor Lady Elliot died herself, no letter of condolence was received at Kellynch, and, consequently, there was but too much reason to apprehend that the Dalrymples considered the relationship as closed. How to have this anxious business set to rights, and be admitted as cousins again, was the question; and it was a question which, in a more rational manner, neither Lady Russell nor Mr Elliot thought unimportant. 'Family connexions were always worth preserving, good company always worth seeking; Lady Dalrymple had taken a house, for three months, in Laura-place, and would be living in style. She had been at Bath the year before, and Lady Russell had heard her spoken of as a charming woman. It was very desirable that the connexion should be renewed, if it could be done, without any compromise of propriety on the side of the Elliots.'

Sir Walter, however, would choose his own means, and at last wrote a very fine letter of ample explanation, regret and entreaty, to his right honourable cousin. Neither Lady Russell nor Mr Elliot could admire the letter; but it did all that was wanted, in bringing three lines of scrawl from the Dowager Viscountess. 'She was very much honoured, and should be happy in their acquaintance.' The toils of the business were over, the sweets began. They visited in Laura-place, they had the cards of Dowager Viscountess Dalrymple, and the Hon. Miss Carteret, to be arranged wherever they might be most visible; and 'Our cousins in Laura-place,' – 'Our cousin, Lady Dalrymple and Miss Carteret,' were talked of to every body.

Anne was ashamed. Had Lady Dalrymple and her daughter even been very agreeable, she would still have been ashamed of the agitation they created, but they were nothing. There was no superiority of manner, accomplishment, or understanding. Lady Dalrymple had acquired the name of 'a charming woman,' because she had a smile and a civil answer for every body. Miss Carteret, with still less to say, was so plain and so awkward, that she would never have been tolerated in Camden-place but for her birth.

Lady Russell confessed that she had expected something better; but yet 'it was an acquaintance worth having,' and when Anne ventured to speak her opinion of them to Mr Elliot, he agreed to their being nothing in themselves, but still maintained that as a family connexion, as good company, as those who would collect good company around them, they had their value. Anne smiled and said,

'My idea of good company, Mr Elliot, is the company of clever, well-informed people, who have a great deal of conversation; that is what I call good company.'

'You are mistaken,' said he gently, 'that is not good company, that is the best. Good company requires only birth, education and manners, and with regard to education is not very nice. Birth and good manners are essential; but a little learning is by no means a dangerous thing in good company, on the contrary, it will do very well. My cousin, Anne, shakes her head. She is not satisfied. She is fastidious. My dear cousin, (sitting down by her) you have a better right to be fastidious than almost any other woman I know; but will it answer? Will it make you happy? Will it not be wiser to accept the society of these good ladies in Laura-place, and enjoy all the advantages of the connexion as far as possible? You may depend upon it, that they will move in the first set in Bath this winter, and as rank is rank, your being known to be related to them will have its use in fixing your family (our family let me say) in that degree of consideration which we must all wish for.'

'Yes,' sighed Anne, 'we shall, indeed, be known to be related to them!' – then recollecting herself, and not wishing to be answered, she added, 'I certainly do think there has been by far too much trouble taken to procure the acquaintance. I suppose (smiling) I have more pride than any of you; but I confess it does vex me, that we should be so solicitous to have the relationship acknowledged, which we may be very sure is a matter of perfect indifference to them.'

'Pardon me, dear cousin, you are unjust to your own claims. In London, perhaps, in your present quiet style of living, it might be as you say: but in Bath, Sir Walter Elliot and his family will always be worth knowing, always acceptable as acquaintance.'

'Well,' said Anne, 'I certainly am proud, too proud to enjoy a welcome which depends so entirely upon place.'

'I love your indignation,' said he; 'it is very natural. But here you are in Bath, and the object is to be established here with all the credit and dignity which ought to belong to Sir Walter Elliot. You talk of being proud, I am called proud I know, and I shall not wish to believe myself otherwise, for our pride, if investigated, would have the same object, I have no doubt, though the kind may seem a little different. In one point, I am sure, my dear cousin, (he continued, speaking lower, though there was no one else in the room) in one point, I am sure, we must feel alike. We must feel that every addition to your father's society, among his equals or superiors, may be of use in diverting his thoughts from those who are beneath him.'

He looked, as he spoke, to the seat which Mrs Clay had been lately occupying, a sufficient explanation of what he particularly meant; and though Anne could not believe in their having the same sort of pride, she was pleased with him for not liking Mrs Clay; and her conscience admitted that his wishing to promote her father's getting great acquaintance, was more than excusable in the view of defeating her.

CHAPTER 17

WHILE Sir Walter and Elizabeth were assiduously pushing their good fortune in Laura-place, Anne was renewing an acquaintance of a very different description.

She had called on her former governess, and had heard from her of there being an old school-fellow in Bath, who had the two strong claims on her attention, of past kindness and present suffering. Miss Hamilton, now Mrs Smith, had shewn her kindness in one of those periods of her life when it had been most valuable. Anne had gone unhappy to school, grieving for the loss of a mother whom she had dearly loved, feeling her separation from home, and suffering as a girl of fourteen, of strong sensibility and not high spirits, must suffer at such a time; and Miss Hamilton, three years older than herself, but still from the want of near relations and a settled home, remaining another year at school, had been useful and good to her in a way which had considerably lessened her misery, and could never be remembered with indifference.

Miss Hamilton had left school, had married not long afterwards, was said to have married a man of fortune, and this was all that Anne had known of her, till now that their governess's account brought her situation forward in a more decided but very different form.

She was a widow, and poor. Her husband had been extravagant; and at his death, about two years before, had left his affairs dreadfully involved. She had had difficulties of every sort to contend with, and in addition to these distresses, had been afflicted with a severe rheumatic fever, which finally settling in her legs, had made her for the present a cripple. She had come to Bath on that account, and was now in lodgings near the hot-baths, living in a very humble way, unable even to afford herself the comfort of a servant, and of course almost excluded from society.

Their mutual friend answered for the satisfaction which a visit from Miss Elliot would give Mrs Smith, and Anne therefore lost no time in going. She mentioned nothing of what she had heard, or what she intended, at home. It would excite no proper interest there. She only consulted Lady Russell, who entered thoroughly into her sentiments, and was most happy to convey her as near to Mrs Smith's lodgings in Westgate-buildings, as Anne chose to be taken.

The visit was paid, their acquaintance re-established, their interest in each other more than re-kindled. The first ten minutes had its awkwardness and its emotion. Twelve years were gone since they had parted, and each presented a somewhat different person from what the other had imagined. Twelve years had changed Anne from the blooming, silent, unformed girl of fifteen, to the elegant little woman of seven and twenty, with every beauty excepting bloom, and with manners as consciously right as they were invariably gentle; and twelve years had transformed the fine-looking, well-grown Miss Hamilton, in all the glow of health and confidence of superiority, into a poor, infirm, helpless widow, receiving the visit of her former protegée as a favour; but all that was uncomfortable in the meeting had soon passed away, and left only the interesting charm of remembering former partialities and talking over old times.

Anne found in Mrs Smith the good sense and agreeable manners which she had almost ventured to depend on, and a disposition to converse and be cheerful beyond her expectation. Neither the dissipations of the past – and she had lived very much in the world, nor the restrictions of the present; neither sickness nor sorrow seemed to have closed her heart or ruined her spirits.

In the course of a second visit she talked with great openness, and Anne's astonishment increased. She could scarcely imagine a more cheerless situation in itself than Mrs Smith's. She had been very fond of her husband, – she had buried him. She had been used to affluence, – it was gone. She had no child to connect her with life and happiness again, no relations to assist in the arrangement of perplexed affairs, no health to make all the rest supportable. Her accommodations were limited to a noisy parlour, and a dark bed-room behind, with no possibility of moving from one to the other without assistance, which there was only one servant in the house to afford, and she never quitted the house but to be conveyed into the warm bath. – Yet, in spite of all this, Anne had reason to believe that she had moments only of languor and depression, to hours of occupation and enjoyment. How could it be? – She watched – observed – reflected – and finally determined that this was not a case of fortitude or of resignation only. – A submissive spirit might be patient, a strong understanding would supply resolution, but here was something more: here was that elasticity of mind, that disposition to be comforted, that power of turning readily from evil to good, and of finding employment which carried her out of herself, which was from Nature alone. It was the choicest gift of Heaven; and Anne viewed her friend as one of those instances in which, by a merciful appointment, it seems designed to counterbalance almost every other want.

There had been a time, Mrs Smith told her, when her spirits had nearly failed. She could not call herself an invalid now, compared with her state on first reaching Bath. Then, she had indeed been a pitiable object – for she had caught cold on the journey, and had hardly taken possession of her lodgings, before she was again confined to her bed, and suffering under severe and constant pain; and all this among strangers – with the absolute necessity of having a regular nurse, and finances at that moment particularly unfit to meet any extraordinary expense. She had weathered it however, and could truly say that it had done her good. It had increased her comforts by making her feel herself to be in good hands. She had seen too much of the world, to expect sudden or disinterested attachment any where, but her illness had proved to her that her landlady had a character to preserve, and would not use her ill; and she had been particularly fortunate in her nurse, as a sister of her landlady, a nurse by profession, and who had always a home in that house when unemployed, chanced to be at liberty just in time to attend her. – 'And she,' said Mrs Smith, 'besides nursing me most admirably, has really proved an invaluable acquaintance. – As soon as I could use my hands, she taught me to knit, which has been a great amusement; and she put me in the way of making these little thread-cases, pin-cushions and card-racks, which you always find me so busy about, and which supply me with the means of doing a little good to one or two very poor families in this neighbourhood. She has a large acquaintance, of course professionally, among those who can afford to buy, and she disposes of my merchandize. She always takes the right time for applying. Every body's heart is open, you know, when they have recently escaped from severe pain, or are recovering the blessing of health, and nurse Rooke thoroughly understands when to speak. She is a shrewd, intelligent, sensible woman. Hers is a line for seeing human nature; and she has a fund of good sense and observation which, as a companion, make her infinitely superior to thousands of those who having only received "the best education in the world," know nothing worth attending to. Call it gossip if you will; but when nurse Rooke has half an hour's leisure to bestow on me, she is sure to have something to relate that is entertaining and profitable, something that makes one know one's species better. One likes to hear what is going on, to be *au fait* as to the newest modes of being trifling and silly. To me, who live so much alone, her conversation I assure you is a treat.'

Anne, far from wishing to cavil at the pleasure, replied, 'I can easily believe it. Women of that class have great opportunities, and if they are intelligent may be well worth listening to. Such varieties of human nature as they are in the habit of witnessing! And it is not merely in its follies, that they are well read; for they see it occasionally under every circumstance that can be most interesting or affecting. What instances must pass before them of ardent, disinterested, self-denying attachment, of heroism, fortitude, patience, resignation – of all the conflicts and all the sacrifices that ennoble us most. A sick chamber may often furnish the worth of volumes.'

'Yes,' said Mrs Smith more doubtingly, 'sometimes it may, though I fear its lessons are not often in the elevated style you describe. Here and there, human nature may be great in times of trial, but generally speaking it is its weakness and not its strength that appears in a sick chamber; it is selfishness and impatience rather than generosity and fortitude, that one hears of. There is so little real friendship in the world! – and unfortunately' (speaking low and tremulously) 'there are so many who forget to think seriously till it is almost too late.'

Anne saw the misery of such feelings. The husband had not

been what he ought, and the wife had been led among that part
of mankind which made her think worse of the world, than she
hoped it deserved. It was but a passing emotion however with
Mrs Smith, she shook it off, and soon added in a different tone,

'I do not suppose the situation my friend Mrs Rooke is in at
present, will furnish much either to interest or edify me. – She
is only nursing Mrs Wallis of Marlborough-buildings – a mere
pretty, silly, expensive, fashionable woman, I believe – and of
course will have nothing to report but of lace and finery. – I
mean to make my profit of Mrs Wallis, however. She has plenty
of money, and I intend she shall buy all the high-priced things I
have in hand now.'

Anne had called several times on her friend, before the existence of such a person was known in Camden-place. At last, it
became necessary to speak of her. – Sir Walter, Elizabeth and Mrs
Clay returned one morning from Laura-place, with a sudden invitation from Lady Dalrymple for the same evening, and Anne
was already engaged, to spend that evening in Westgate-buildings.
She was not sorry for the excuse. They were only asked, she was
sure, because Lady Dalrymple being kept at home by a bad cold,
was glad to make use of the relationship which had been so
pressed on her, –and she declined on her own account with great
alacrity – 'She was engaged to spend the evening with an old
schoolfellow.' They were not much interested in any thing relative to Anne, but still there were questions enough asked, to make
it understood what this old schoolfellow was; and Elizabeth was
disdainful, and Sir Walter severe.

'Westgate-buildings!' said he; 'and who is Miss Anne Elliot
to be visiting in Westgate-buildings? – A Mrs Smith. A widow
Mrs Smith, – and who was her husband? One of the five thousand
Mr Smiths whose names are to be met with every where. And
what is her attraction? That she is old and sickly.–Upon my word,
Miss Anne Elliot, you have the most extraordinary taste! Every
thing that revolts other people, low company, paltry rooms, foul
air, disgusting associations are inviting to you. But surely, you
may put off this old lady till to-morrow. She is not so near her
end, I presume, but that she may hope to see another day. What
is her age? Forty?'

'No, Sir, she is not one and thirty; but I do not think I can put off my engagement, because it is the only evening for some time which will at once suit her and myself. – She goes into the warm bath to-morrow, and for the rest of the week you know we are engaged.'

'But what does Lady Russell think of this acquaintance?' asked Elizabeth.

'She sees nothing to blame in it,' replied Anne; 'on the contrary, she approves it; and has generally taken me, when I have called on Mrs Smith.'

'Westgate-buildings must have been rather surprised by the appearance of a carriage drawn up near its pavement!' observed Sir Walter. – 'Sir Henry Russell's widow, indeed, has no honours to distinguish her arms; but still, it is a handsome equipage, and no doubt is well known to convey a Miss Elliot. – A widow Mrs Smith, lodging in Westgate-buildings! – A poor widow, barely able to live, between thirty and forty – a mere Mrs Smith, an every day Mrs Smith, of all people and all names in the world, to be the chosen friend of Miss Anne Elliot, and to be preferred by her, to her own family connections among the nobility of England and Ireland! Mrs Smith, such a name!'

Mrs Clay, who had been present while all this passed, now thought it advisable to leave the room, and Anne could have said much and did long to say a little, in defence of *her* friend's not very dissimilar claims to theirs, but her sense of personal respect to her father prevented her. She made no reply. She left it to himself to recollect, that Mrs Smith was not the only widow in Bath between thirty and forty, with little to live on, and no sirname of dignity.

Anne kept her appointment; the others kept theirs, and of course she heard the next morning that they had had a delightful evening. – She had been the only one of the set absent; for Sir Walter and Elizabeth had not only been quite at her ladyship's service themselves, but had actually been happy to be employed by her in collecting others, and had been at the trouble of inviting both Lady Russell and Mr Elliot; and Mr Elliot had made a point of leaving Colonel Wallis early, and Lady Russell had fresh arranged all her evening engagements in order to wait on her. Ann had the whole history of all that such an evening could supply, from Lady Russell. To her, its greatest interest must be, in having been very much talked of between her friend and Mr Elliot, in having been wished for, regretted, and at the same time honoured for staying away in such a cause. – Her kind, compassionate visits to this old schoolfellow, sick and reduced, seemed to have quite delighted Mr Elliot. He thought her a most extraordinary young woman; in her temper, manners, mind, a model of female excellence. He could meet even Lady Russell in a discussion of her merits; and Anne could not be given to understand so much by her friend, could not know herself to be so highly rated by a sensible man, without many of those agreeable sensations which her friend meant to create.

Lady Russell was now perfectly decided in her opinion of Mr Elliot. She was as much convinced of his meaning to gain Anne in time, as of his deserving her; and was beginning to calculate the number of weeks which would free him from all the remaining restraints of widowhood, and leave him at liberty to exert his most open powers of pleasing. She would not speak to Anne with half the certainty she felt on the subject, she would venture on little more than hints of what might be hereafter, of a possible attachment on his side, of the desirableness of the alliance, supposing such attachment to be real, and returned. Anne heard her, and made no violent exclamations. She only smiled, blushed, and gently shook her head.

'I am no match-maker, as you well know,' said Lady Russell, 'being much too well aware of the uncertainty of all human events and calculations. I only mean that if Mr Elliot should some time hence pay his addresses to you, and if you should be disposed to accept him, I think there would be every possibility of your being happy together. A most suitable connection every body must consider it – but I think it might be a very happy one.

'Mr Elliot is an exceedingly agreeable man, and in many respects I think highly of him,' said Anne; 'but we should not suit.'

Lady Russell let this pass, and only said in rejoinder, 'I own that to be able to regard you as the future mistress of Kellynch, the future Lady Elliot – to look forward and see you occupying your dear mother's place, succeeding to all her rights, and all her popularity, as well as to all her virtues, would be the highest possible gratification to me. – You are your mother's self in countenance and disposition; and if I might be allowed to fancy you such as she was, in situation, and name, and home, presiding and blessing in the same spot, and only superior to her in being more highly valued! My dearest Anne, it would give me more delight than is often felt at my time of life!'

Anne was obliged to turn away, to rise, to walk to a distant table, and, leaning there in pretended employment, try to subdue the feelings this picture excited. For a few moments her imagination and her heart were bewitched. The idea of becoming what her mother had been; of having the precious name of 'Lady Elliot' first revived in herself; of being restored to Kellynch, calling it her home again, her home for ever, was a charm which she could not immediately resist. Lady Russell said not another word, willing to leave the matter to its own operation; and believing that, could Mr Elliot at that moment with propriety have spoken for himself! – She believed, in short, what Anne did not believe. The same image of Mr Elliot speaking for himself, brought Anne to composure again. The charm of Kellynch and of 'Lady Elliot' all faded away. She never could accept him. And it was not only that her feelings were still adverse to any man save one; her judgment, on a serious consideration of the possibilities of such a case, was against Mr Elliot.

Though they had now been acquainted a month, she could not be satisfied that she really knew his character. That he was a sensible man, an agreeable man, – that he talked well, professed good opinions, seemed to judge properly and as a man of principle, – this was all clear enough. He certainly knew what was right, nor could she fix on any one article of moral duty evidently transgressed; but yet she would have been afraid to answer for his conduct. She distrusted the past, if not the present. The names which occasionally dropt of former associates, the allusions to former practices and pursuits, suggested suspicions not favourable of what he had been. She saw that there had been bad habits; that Sunday-travelling had been a common thing; that there had been a period of his life (and probably not a short one) when he had been, at least, careless on all serious matters; and, though he might now think very differently, who could answer for the true sentiments of a clever, cautious man, grown old enough to appreciate a fair character? How could it ever be ascertained that his mind was truly cleansed?

Mr Elliot was rational, discreet, polished, – but he was not open. There was never any burst of feeling, any warmth of indignation or delight, at the evil or good of others. This, to Anne, was a decided imperfection. Her early impressions were incurable. She prized the frank, the open-hearted, the eager character beyond all others. Warmth and enthusiasm did captivate her still. She felt that she could so much more depend upon the sincerity of those who sometimes looked or said a careless or a hasty thing, than of those whose presence of mind never varied, whose tongue never slipped.

Mr Elliot was too generally agreeable. Various as were the tempers in her father's house, he pleased them all. He endured too well, – stood too well with everybody. He had spoken to her with some degree of openness of Mrs Clay; had appeared completely to see what Mrs Clay was about, and to hold her in contempt; and yet Mrs Clay found him as agreeable as anybody.

Lady Russell saw either less or more than her young friend, for she saw nothing to excite distrust. She could not imagine a man more exactly what he ought to be than Mr Elliot; nor did she ever enjoy a sweeter feeling than the hope of seeing him receive the hand of her beloved Anne in Kellynch church, in the course of the following autumn.

CHAPTER 18

It was the beginning of February; and Anne, having been a month in Bath, was growing very eager for news from Uppercross and Lyme. She wanted to hear much more than Mary communicated. It was three weeks since she had heard at all. She only knew that Henrietta was at home again; and that Louisa, though considered to be recovering fast, was still at Lyme; and she was thinking of them all very intently one evening, when a thicker letter than usual from Mary was delivered to her, and, to quicken the pleasure and surprise, with Admiral and Mrs Croft's compliments.

The Crofts must be in Bath! A circumstance to interest her. They were people whom her heart turned to very naturally.

'What is this?' cried Sir Walter. 'The Crofts arrived in Bath? The Crofts who rent Kellynch? What have they brought you?'

'A letter from Uppercross Cottage, Sir.'

'Oh! those letters are convenient passports. They secure an introduction. I should have visited Admiral Croft, however, at any rate. I know what is due to my tenant.'

Anne could listen no longer; she could not even have told how the poor Admiral's complexion escaped; her letter engrossed her. It had been begun several days back.

'February 1st, ——.

'My dear Anne,

'I make no apology for my silence, because I know how little people think of letters in such a place as Bath. You must be a great deal too happy to care for Uppercross, which, as you well know, affords little to write about. We have had a very dull Christmas; Mr and Mrs Musgrove have not had one dinner-party all the holidays. I do not reckon the Hayters as any body. The holidays, however, are over at last: I believe no children ever had such long ones. I am sure I had not. The house was cleared yesterday, except of the little Harvilles; but you will be surprised to hear they have never gone home. Mrs Harville must be an odd mother to part with them so long. I do not understand it. They are not at all nice children, in my opinion; but Mrs Musgrove seems to like them quite as well, if not better, than her grand-children. What dreadful weather we have had! It may not be felt in Bath, with your nice pavements; but in the country it is of some consequence. I have not had a creature call on me since the second week in January, except Charles Hayter, who has been calling much oftener than was welcome. Between ourselves, I think it a great pity Henrietta did not remain at Lyme as long as Louisa; it would have kept her a little out of his way. The carriage is gone to-day, to bring Louisa and the Harvilles to-morrow. We are not asked to dine with them, however, till the day after, Mrs Musgrove is so afraid of her being fatigued by the journey, which is not very likely, considering the care that will be taken of her; and it would be much more convenient to me to dine there to-morrow. I am glad you find Mr Elliot so agreeable, and wish I could be acquainted with him too; but I have my usual luck, I am always out of the way when any thing desirable is going on; always the last of my family to be noticed. What an immense time Mrs Clay has been staying with Elizabeth! Does she never mean to go away? But perhaps if she were to leave the room vacant we might not be invited. Let me know what you think of this. I do not expect my children to be asked, you know. I can leave them at the Great House very well, for a month or six weeks. I have this moment heard that the Crofts are going to Bath almost immediately; they think the admiral gouty. Charles heard it quite by chance: they have not had the civility to give me any notice, or offer to take any thing. I do not think they improve at all as neighbours. We see nothing of them, and this is really an instance of gross inattention. Charles joins me in love, and every thing proper. Yours, affectionately,

'Mary M——.'

'I am sorry to say that I am very far from well; and Jemima has just told me that the butcher says there is a bad sore-throat very much about. I dare say I shall catch it; and my sore-throats, you know, are always worse than anybody's.'

So ended the first part, which had been afterwards put into an envelop, containing nearly as much more.

'I kept my letter open, that I might send you word how Louisa bore her journey, and now I am extremely glad I did, having a great deal to add. In the first place, I had a note from Mrs Croft yesterday, offering to convey any thing to you; a very kind, friendly note indeed, addressed to me, just as it ought; I shall therefore be able to make my letter as long as I like. The admiral does not seem very ill, and I sincerely hope Bath will do him all the good he wants. I shall be truly glad to have them back again. Our neighbourhood cannot spare such a pleasant family. But now for Louisa. I have something to communicate that will astonish you not a little. She and the Harvilles came on Tuesday very safely, and in the evening we went to ask her how she did, when we were rather surprised not to find Captain Benwick of the party, for he had been invited as well as the Harvilles; and what do you think was the reason? Neither more nor less than his being in love with Louisa, and not choosing to venture to Uppercross till he had had an answer from Mr Musgrove; for it was all settled between him and her before she came away, and he had written to her father by Captain Harville. True, upon my honour. Are not you astonished? I shall be surprised at least if you ever received a hint of it, for I never did. Mrs Musgrove protests solemnly that she knew nothing of the matter. We are all very well pleased, however; for though it is not equal to her marrying Captain Wentworth, it is infinitely better than Charles Hayter; and Mr Musgrove has written his consent, and Captain Benwick is expected to-day. Mrs Harville says her husband feels a good deal on his poor sister's account; but, however, Louisa is a great favourite with both. Indeed Mrs Harville and I quite agree that we love her the better for having nursed her. Charles wonders what Captain Wentworth will say; but if you remember, I never thought him attached to Louisa; I never could see any thing of it. And this is the end, you see, of Captain Benwick's being supposed to be an admirer of yours. How Charles could take such a thing into his head was always incomprehensible to me. I hope he will be more agreeable now. Certainly not a great match for Louisa Musgrove; but a million times better than marrying among the Hayters.'

Mary need not have feared her sister's being in any degree prepared for the news. She had never in her life been more astonished. Captain Benwick and Louisa Musgrove! It was almost too wonderful for belief; and it was with the greatest effort that she could remain in the room, preserve an air of calmness, and answer the common questions of the moment. Happily for her, they were not many. Sir Walter wanted to know whether the Crofts travelled with four horses, and whether they were likely to be situated in such a part of Bath as it might suit Miss Elliot and himself to visit in; but had little curiosity beyond.

'How is Mary?' said Elizabeth; and without waiting for an answer, 'And pray what brings the Crofts to Bath?'

'They come on the Admiral's account. He is thought to be gouty.'

'Gout and decrepitude !' said Sir Walter. 'Poor old gentleman.'

'Have they any acquaintance here?' asked Elizabeth.

'I do not know; but I can hardly suppose that, at Admiral Croft's time of life, and in his profession, he should not have many acquaintance in such a place as this.'

'I suspect,' said Sir Walter coolly, 'that Admiral Croft will be best known in Bath as the renter of Kellynch-hall. Elizabeth, may we venture to present him and his wife in Laura-place?'

'Oh ! no, I think not. Situated as we are with Lady Dalrymple, cousins, we ought to be very careful not to embarrass her with acquaintance she might not approve. If we were not related, it would not signify; but as cousins, she would feel scrupulous as to any proposal of ours. We had better leave the Crofts to find their own level. There are several odd-looking men walking about here, who, I am told, are sailors. The Crofts will associate with them !'

This was Sir Walter and Elizabeth's share of interest in the letter; when Mrs Clay had paid her tribute of more decent attention, in an enquiry after Mrs Charles Musgrove, and her fine little boys, Anne was at liberty.

In her own room she tried to comprehend it. Well might Charles wonder how Captain Wentworth would feel ! Perhaps he had quitted the field, had given Louisa up, had ceased to love, had found he did not love her. She could not endure the idea of treachery or levity, or any thing akin to ill-usage between him and his friend. She could not endure that such a friendship as theirs should be severed unfairly.

Captain Benwick and Louisa Musgrove ! The high-spirited, joyous, talking Louisa Musgrove, and the dejected, thinking, feeling, reading Captain Benwick, seemed each of them every thing that would not suit the other. Their minds most dissimilar ! Where could have been the attraction? The answer soon presented itself. It had been in situation. They had been thrown together several weeks; they had been living in the same small family party; since Henrietta's coming away, they must have been depending almost entirely on each other, and Louisa, just recovering from illness, had been in an interesting state, and

Captain Benwick was not inconsolable. That was a point which Anne had not been able to avoid suspecting before; and instead of drawing the same conclusion as Mary, from the present course of events, they served only to confirm the idea of his having felt some dawning of tenderness toward herself. She did not mean, however, to derive much more from it to gratify her vanity, than Mary might have allowed. She was persuaded that any tolerably pleasing young woman who had listened and seemed to feel for him, would have received the same compliment. He had an affectionate heart. He must love somebody.

She saw no reason against their being happy. Louisa had fine naval fervour to begin with, and they would soon grow more alike. He would gain cheerfulness, and she would learn to be an enthusiast for Scott and Lord Byron; nay, that was probably learnt already; of course they had fallen in love over poetry. The idea of Louisa Musgrove turned into a person of literary taste, and sentimental reflection, was amusing, but she had no doubt of its being so. The day at Lyme, the fall from the Cobb, might influence her health, her nerves, her courage, her character to the end of her life, as thoroughly as it appeared to have influenced her fate.

The conclusion of the whole was, that if the woman who had been sensible of Captain Wentworth's merits could be allowed to prefer another man, there was nothing in the engagement to excite lasting wonder; and if Captain Wentworth lost no friend by it, certainly nothing to be regretted. No, it was not regret which made Anne's heart beat in spite of herself, and brought the colour into her cheeks when she thought of Captain Wentworth unshackled and free. She had some feelings which she was ashamed to investigate. They were too much like joy, senseless joy!

She longed to see the Crofts, but when the meeting took place, it was evident that no rumour of the news had yet reached them. The visit of ceremony was paid and returned, and Louisa Musgrove was mentioned, and Captain Benwick too, without even half a smile.

The Crofts had placed themselves in lodgings in Gay-street, perfectly to Sir Walter's satisfaction. He was not at all ashamed of the acquaintance, and did, in fact, think and talk a great deal

more about the Admiral, than the Admiral ever thought or
talked about him.

The Crofts knew quite as many people in Bath as they wished
for, and considered their intercourse with the Elliots as a mere
matter of form, and not in the least likely to afford them any
pleasure. They brought with them their country habit of being
almost always together. He was ordered to walk, to keep off the
gout, and Mrs Croft seemed to go shares with him in every thing,
and to walk for her life, to do him good. Anne saw them wherever
she went. Lady Russell took her out in her carriage almost every
morning, and she never failed to think of them, and never failed
to see them. Knowing their feelings as she did, it was a most
attractive picture of happiness to her. She always watched them
as long as she could; delighted to fancy she understood what they
might be talking of, as they walked along in happy independence,
or equally delighted to see the Admiral's hearty shake of the
hand when he encountered an old friend, and observe their eagerness of conversation when occasionally forming into a little knot
of the navy, Mrs Croft looking as intelligent and keen as any of
the officers around her.

Anne was too much engaged with Lady Russell to be often
walking herself, but it so happened that one morning, about a
week or ten days after the Crofts' arrival, it suited her best to
leave her friend, or her friend's carriage, in the lower part of the
town, and return alone to Camden-place; and in walking up
Milsom-street, she had the good fortune to meet with the Admiral.
He was standing by himself, at a printshop window, with his
hands behind him, in earnest contemplation of some print, and she
not only might have passed him unseen, but was obliged to
touch as well as address him before she could catch his notice.
When he did perceive and acknowledge her, however, it was
done with all his usual frankness and good humour. 'Ha! is it
you? Thank you, thank you. This is treating me like a friend.
Here I am, you see, staring at a picture. I can never get by this
shop without stopping. But what a thing here is, by way of a
boat. Do look at it. Did you ever see the like? What queer fellows
your fine painters must be, to think that any body would venture
their lives in such a shapeless old cockleshell as that. And yet,

here are two gentlemen stuck up in it mightily at their ease, and looking about them at the rocks and mountains, as if they were not to be upset the next moment, which they certainly must be. I wonder where that boat was built!' (laughing heartily) 'I would not venture over a horsepond in it. Well,' (turning away) 'now, where are you bound? Can I go any where for you, or with you? Can I be of any use?'

'None, I thank you, unless you will give me the pleasure of your company the little way our road lies together. I am going home.'

'That I will, with all my heart, and farther too. Yes, yes, we will have a snug walk together; and I have something to tell you as we go along. There, take my arm; that's right: I do not feel comfortable if I have not a woman there. Lord! what a boat it is!' taking a last look at the picture, as they began to be in motion.

'Did you say that you had something to tell me, sir?'

'Yes, I have. Presently. But here comes a friend, Captain Brigden; I shall only say, "How d'ye do," as we pass, however. I shall not stop. "How d'ye do." Brigden stares to see anybody with me but my wife. She, poor soul, is tied by the leg. She has a blister on one of her heels, as large as a three shilling piece.[10] If you look across the street, you will see Admiral Brand coming down and his brother. Shabby fellows, both of them! I am glad they are not on this side of the way. Sophy cannot bear them. They played me a pitiful trick once – got away some of my best men. I will tell you the whole story another time. There comes old Sir Archibald Drew and his grandson. Look, he sees us; he kisses his hand to you; he takes you for my wife. Ah! the peace has come too soon for that younker. Poor old Sir Archibald! How do you like Bath, Miss Elliot? It suits us very well. We are always meeting with some old friend or other; the streets full of them every morning; sure to have plenty of chat; and then we get away from them all, and shut ourselves into our lodgings, and draw in our chairs, and are as snug as if we were at Kellynch, ay, or as we used to be even at North Yarmouth and Deal. We do not like our lodgings here the worse, I can tell you, for putting us in mind of those we first had at North Yarmouth. The wind blows through one of the cupboards just in the same way.'

When they were got a little farther, Anne ventured to press again for what he had to communicate. She had hoped, when clear of Milsom-street, to have her curiosity gratified; but she was still obliged to wait, for the Admiral had made up his mind not to begin, till they had gained the greater space and quiet of Belmont, and as she was not really Mrs Croft, she must let him have his own way. As soon as they were fairly ascending Belmont, he began,

'Well, now you shall hear something that will surprise you. But first of all, you must tell me the name of the young lady I am going to talk about. That young lady, you know, that we have all been so concerned for. The Miss Musgrove, that all this has been happening to. Her christian name – I always forget her christian name.'

Anne had been ashamed to appear to comprehend so soon as she really did; but now she could safely suggest the name of 'Louisa.'

'Ay, ay, Miss Louisa Musgrove, that is the name. I wish young ladies had not such a number of fine christian names. I should never be out, if they were all Sophys, or something of that sort. Well, this Miss Louisa, we all thought, you know, was to marry Frederick. He was courting her week after week. The only wonder was, what they could be waiting for, till the business at Lyme came; then, indeed, it was clear enough that they must wait till her brain was set to right. But even then, there was something odd in their way of going on. Instead of staying at Lyme, he went off to Plymouth, and then he went off to see Edward. When we came back from Minehead, he was gone down to Edward's, and there he has been ever since. We have seen nothing of him since November. Even Sophy could not understand it. But now, the matter has taken the strangest turn of all; for this young lady, this same Miss Musgrove, instead of being to marry Frederick, is to marry James Benwick. You know James Benwick. '

'A little. I am a little acquainted with Captain Benwick.'

'Well, she is to marry him. Nay, most likely they are married already, for I do not know what they should wait for.'

'I thought Captain Benwick a very pleasing young man,' said Anne, 'and I understand that he bears an excellent character.'

'Oh! yes, yes, there is not a word to be said against James

Benwick. He is only a commander, it is true, made last summer, and these are bad times for getting on, but he has not another fault that I know of. An excellent, good-hearted fellow, I assure you, a very active, zealous officer too, which is more than you would think for, perhaps, for that soft sort of manner does not do him justice.'

'Indeed you are mistaken there, sir. I should never augur want of spirit from Captain Benwick's manners. I thought them particularly pleasing, and I will answer for it they would generally please.'

'Well, well, ladies are the best judges; but James Benwick is rather too piano for me, and though very likely it is all our partiality, Sophy and I cannot help thinking Frederick's manners better than his. There is something about Frederick more to our taste.'

Anne was caught. She had only meant to oppose the too-common idea of spirit and gentleness being incompatible with each other, not at all to represent Captain Benwick's manners as the very best that could possibly be, and, after a little hesitation, she was beginning to say, 'I was not entering into any comparison of the two friends,' but the Admiral interrupted her with,

'And the thing is certainly true. It is not a mere bit of gossip. We have it from Frederick himself. His sister had a letter from him yesterday, in which he tells us of it, and he had just had it in a letter from Harville, written upon the spot, from Uppercross. I fancy they are all at Uppercross.'

This was an opportunity which Anne could not resist; she said, therefore, 'I hope, Admiral, I hope there is nothing in the style of Captain Wentworth's letter to make you and Mrs Croft particularly uneasy. It did certainly seem, last autumn, as if there were an attachment between him and Louisa Musgrove; but I hope it may be understood to have worn out on each side equally, and without violence. I hope his letter does not breathe the spirit of an ill-used man.'

'Not at all, not at all; there is not an oath or a murmur from beginning to end.'

Anne looked down to hide her smile.

'No, no; Frederick is not a man to whine and complain; he has too much spirit for that. If the girl likes another man better, it is very fit she should have him.'

'Certainly. But what I mean is, that I hope there is nothing in Captain Wentworth's manner of writing to make you suppose he thinks himself ill-used by his friend, which might appear, you know, without its being absolutely said. I should be very sorry that such a friendship as has subsisted between him and Captain Benwick should be destroyed, or even wounded, by a circumstance of this sort.'

'Yes, yes, I understand you. But there is nothing at all of that nature in the letter. He does not give the least fling at Benwick; does not so much as say, "I wonder at it, I have a reason of my own for wondering at it." No, you would not guess, from his way of writing, that he had ever thought of this Miss (what's her name?) for himself. He very handsomely hopes they will be happy together, and there is nothing very unforgiving in that, I think.'

Anne did not receive the perfect conviction which the Admiral meant to convey, but it would have been useless to press the enquiry farther. She, therefore, satisfied herself with common-place remarks, or quiet attention, and the Admiral had it all his own way.

'Poor Frederick!' said he at last. 'Now he must begin all over again with somebody else. I think we must get him to Bath. Sophy must write, and beg him to come to Bath. Here are pretty girls enough, I am sure. It would be of no use to go to Uppercross again, for that other Miss Musgrove, I find, is bespoke by her cousin, the young parson. Do not you think, Miss Elliot, we had better try to get him to Bath?'

CHAPTER 19

WHILE Admiral Croft was taking this walk with Anne, and expressing his wish of getting Captain Wentworth to Bath, Captain Wentworth was already on his way thither. Before Mrs Croft had written, he was arrived; and the very next time Anne walked out, she saw him.

Mr Elliot was attending his two cousins and Mrs Clay. They were in Milsom-street. It began to rain, not much, but enough to make shelter desirable for women, and quite enough to make it very desirable for Miss Elliot to have the advantage of being conveyed home in Lady Dalrymple's carriage, which was seen waiting at a little distance; she, Anne, and Mrs Clay, therefore, turned into Molland's,[11] while Mr Elliot stepped to Lady Dalrymple, to request her assistance. He soon joined them again, successful, of course; Lady Dalrymple would be most happy to take them home, and would call for them in a few minutes.

Her ladyship's carriage was a barouche, and did not hold more than four with any comfort. Miss Carteret was with her mother; consequently it was not reasonable to expect accommodation for all the three Camden-place ladies. There could be no doubt as to Miss Elliot. Whoever suffered inconvenience, she must suffer none, but it occupied a little time to settle the point of civility between the other two. The rain was a mere trifle, and Anne was most sincere in preferring a walk with Mr Elliot. But the rain was also a mere trifle to Mrs Clay; she would hardly allow it even to drop at all, and her boots were so thick! much thicker than Miss Anne's; and, in short, her civility rendered her quite as anxious to be left to walk with Mr Elliot, as Anne could be, and it was discussed between them with a generosity so polite and so determined, that the others were obliged to settle it for them; Miss Elliot maintaining that Mrs Clay had a little cold already, and Mr Elliot deciding on appeal, that his cousin Anne's boots were rather the thickest.

PERSUASION

It was fixed accordingly that Mrs Clay should be of the party in the carriage; and they had just reached this point when Anne, as she sat near the window, descried, most decidedly and distinctly, Captain Wentworth walking down the street.

Her start was perceptible only to herself; but she instantly felt that she was the greatest simpleton in the world, the most unaccountable and absurd! For a few minutes she saw nothing before her. It was all confusion. She was lost; and when she had scolded back her senses, she found the others still waiting for the carriage, and Mr Elliot (always obliging) just setting off for Union-street on a commission of Mrs Clay's.

She now felt a great inclination to go to the outer door; she wanted to see if it rained. Why was she to suspect herself of another motive? Captain Wentworth must be out of sight. She left her seat, she would go, one half of her should not be always so much wiser than the other half, or always suspecting the other of being worse than it was. She would see if it rained. She was sent back, however, in a moment by the entrance of Captain Wentworth himself, among a party of gentlemen and ladies, evidently his acquaintance, and whom he must have joined a little below Milsom-street. He was more obviously struck and confused by the sight of her, than she had ever observed before; he looked quite red. For the first time, since their renewed acquaintance, she felt that she was betraying the least sensibility of the two. She had the advantage of him, in the preparation of the last few moments. All the overpowering, blinding, bewildering, first effects of strong surprise were over with her. Still, however, she had enough to feel! It was agitation, pain, pleasure, a something between delight and misery.

He spoke to her, and then turned away. The character of his manner was embarrassment. She could not have called it either cold or friendly, or any thing so certainly as embarrassed.

After a short interval, however, he came towards her and spoke again. Mutual enquiries on common subjects passed; neither of them, probably, much the wiser for what they heard, and Anne continuing fully sensible of his being less at ease than formerly. They had, by dint of being so very much together, got to speak to each other with a considerable portion of apparent indifference

185

and calmness; but he could not do it now. Time had changed him, or Louisa had changed him. There was consciousness of some sort or other. He looked very well, not as if he had been suffering in health or spirits, and he talked of Uppercross, of the Musgroves, nay, even of Louisa, and had even a momentary look of his own arch significance as he named her; but yet it was Captain Wentworth not comfortable, not easy, not able to feign that he was.

It did not surprise, but it grieved Anne to observe that Elizabeth would not know him. She saw that he saw Elizabeth, that Elizabeth saw him, that there was complete internal recognition on each side; she was convinced that he was ready to be acknowledged as an acquaintance, expecting it, and she had the pain of seeing her sister turn away with unalterable coldness.

Lady Dalrymple's carriage, for which Miss Elliot was growing very impatient, now drew up; the servant came in to announce it. It was beginning to rain again, and altogether there was a delay, and a bustle, and a talking, which must make all the little crowd in the shop understand that Lady Dalrymple was calling to convey Miss Elliot. At last Miss Elliot and her friend, unattended but by the servant, (for there was no cousin returned) were walking off; and Captain Wentworth, watching them, turned again to Anne, and by manner, rather than words, was offering his services to her.

'I am much obliged to you,' was her answer, 'but I am not going with them. The carriage would not accommodate so many. I walk. I prefer walking.'

'But it rains.'

'Oh! very little. Nothing that I regard.'

After a moment's pause he said, 'Though I came only yesterday, I have equipped myself properly for Bath already, you see,' (pointing to a new umbrella) 'I wish you would make use of it, if you are determined to walk; though, I think, it would be more prudent to let me get you a chair.'

She was very much obliged to him, but declined it all, repeating her conviction, that the rain would come to nothing at present, and adding, 'I am only waiting for Mr Elliot. He will be here in a moment, I am sure.'

She had hardly spoken the words, when Mr Elliot walked in. Captain Wentworth recollected him perfectly. There was no difference between him and the man who had stood on the steps at Lyme, admiring Anne as she passed, except in the air and look and manner of the privileged relation and friend. He came in with eagerness, appeared to see and think only of her, apologised for his stay, was grieved to have kept her waiting, and anxious to get her away without further loss of time, and before the rain increased; and in another moment they walked off together, her arm under his, a gentle and embarrassed glance, and a 'good morning to you,' being all that she had time for, as she passed away.

As soon as they were out of sight, the ladies of Captain Wentworth's party began talking of them.

'Mr Elliot does not dislike his cousin, I fancy?'

'Oh! no, that is clear enough. One can guess what will happen there. He is always with them; half lives in the family, I believe. What a very good-looking man!'

'Yes, and Miss Atkinson, who dined with him once at the Wallises, says he is the most agreeable man she ever was in company with.'

'She is pretty, I think; Anne Elliot; very pretty, when one comes to look at her. It is not the fashion to say so, but I confess I admire her more than her sister.'

'Oh! so do I.'

'And so do I. No comparison. But the men are all wild after Miss Elliot. Anne is too delicate for them.'

Anne would have been particularly obliged to her cousin, if he would have walked by her side all the way to Camden-place, without saying a word. She had never found it so difficult to listen to him, though nothing could exceed his solicitude and care, and though his subjects were principally such as were wont to be always interesting – praise, warm, just, and discriminating, of Lady Russell, and insinuations highly rational against Mrs Clay. But just now she could think only of Captain Wentworth. She could not understand his present feelings, whether he were really suffering much from disappointment or not; and till that point were settled, she could not be quite herself.

She hoped to be wise and reasonable in time; but alas! alas! she must confess to herself that she was not wise yet.

Another circumstance very essential for her to know, was how long he meant to be in Bath; he had not mentioned it, or she could not recollect it. He might be only passing through. But it was more probable that he should be come to stay. In that case, so liable as every body was to meet every body in Bath, Lady Russell would in all likelihood see him somewhere. – Would she recollect him? How would it all be?

She had already been obliged to tell Lady Russell that Louisa Musgrove was to marry Captain Benwick. It had cost her something to encounter Lady Russell's surprise; and now, if she were by any chance to be thrown into company with Captain Wentworth, her imperfect knowledge of the matter might add another shade of prejudice against him.

The following morning Anne was out with her friend, and for the first hour, in an incessant and fearful sort of watch for him in vain; but at last, in returning down Pulteney-street, she distinguished him on the right hand pavement at such a distance as to have him in view the greater part of the street. There were many other men about him, many groups walking the same way, but there was no mistaking him. She looked instinctively at Lady Russell; but not from any mad idea of her recognising him so soon as she did herself. No, it was not to be supposed that Lady Russell would perceive him till they were nearly opposite. She looked at her however, from time to time, anxiously; and when the moment approached which must point him out, though not daring to look again (for her own countenance she knew was unfit to be seen), she was yet perfectly conscious of Lady Russell's eyes being turned exactly in the direction for him, of her being in short intently observing him. She could thoroughly comprehend the sort of fascination he must possess over Lady Russell's mind, the difficulty it must be for her to withdraw her eyes, the astonishment she must be feeling that eight or nine years should have passed over him, and in foreign climes and in active service too, without robbing him of one personal grace!

At last, Lady Russell drew back her head. – 'Now, how would she speak of him?'

'You will wonder,' said she, 'what has been fixing my eye so long; but I was looking after some window-curtains, which Lady Alicia and Mrs Frankland were telling me of last night. They described the drawing-room window-curtains of one of the houses on this side of the way, and this part of the street, as being the handsomest and best hung of any in Bath, but could not recollect the exact number, and I have been trying to find out which it could be; but I confess I can see no curtains hereabouts that answer their description.'

Anne sighed and blushed and smiled, in pity and disdain,[12] either at her friend or herself. – The part which provoked her most, was that in all this waste of foresight and caution, she should have lost the right moment for seeing whether he saw them.

A day or two passed without producing any thing. – The theatre or the rooms, where he was most likely to be, were not fashionable enough for the Elliots, whose evening amusements were solely in the elegant stupidity of private parties, in which they were getting more and more engaged; and Anne, wearied of such a state of stagnation, sick of knowing nothing, and fancying herself stronger because her strength was not tried, was quite impatient for the concert evening. It was a concert for the benefit of a person patronised by Lady Dalrymple. Of course they must attend. It was really expected to be a good one, and Captain Wentworth was very fond of music. If she could only have a few minutes conversation with him again, she fancied she should be satisfied; and as to the power of addressing him she felt all over courage if the opportunity occurred. Elizabeth had turned from him, Lady Russell overlooked him; her nerves were strengthened by these circumstances; she felt that she owed him attention.

She had once partly promised Mrs Smith to spend the evening with her; but in a short hurried call she excused herself and put it off, with the more decided promise of a longer visit on the morrow. Mrs Smith gave a most good-humoured acquiescence.

'By all means,' said she; 'only tell me all about it, when you do come. Who is your party?'

Anne named them all. Mrs Smith made no reply; but when she was leaving her, said, and with an expression half serious, half arch, 'Well, I heartily wish your concert may answer; and do not fail me to-morrow if you can come; for I begin to have a foreboding that I may not have many more visits from you.'

Anne was startled and confused, but after standing in a moment's suspense, was obliged, and not sorry to be obliged, to hurry away.

CHAPTER 20

SIR WALTER, his two daughters, and Mrs Clay, were the earliest of all their party, at the rooms in the evening; and as Lady Dalrymple must be waited for, they took their station by one of the fires in the octagon room. But hardly were they settled, when the door opened again, and Captain Wentworth walked in alone. Anne was the nearest to him, and making yet a little advance, she instantly spoke. He was preparing only to bow and pass on, but her gentle 'How do you do?' brought him out of the straight line to stand near her, and make enquiries in return, in spite of the formidable father and sister in the back ground. Their being in the back ground was a support to Anne; she knew nothing of their looks, and felt equal to everything which she believed right to be done.

While they were speaking, a whispering between her father and Elizabeth caught her ear. She could not distinguish, but she must guess the subject; and on Captain Wentworth's making a distant bow, she comprehended that her father had judged so well as to give him that simple acknowledgment of acquaintance, and she was just in time by a side glance to see a slight curtsey from Elizabeth herself. This, though late and reluctant and ungracious, was yet better than nothing, and her spirits improved.

After talking however of the weather and Bath and the concert, their conversation began to flag, and so little was said at last, that she was expecting him to go every moment; but he did not; he seemed in no hurry to leave her; and presently with renewed spirit, with a little smile, a little glow, he said,

'I have hardly seen you since our day at Lyme. I am afraid you must have suffered from the shock, and the more from its not overpowering you at the time.'

She assured him that she had not.

'It was a frightful hour,' said he, 'a frightful day!' and he passed his hand across his eyes, as if the remembrance were still too painful; but in a moment half smiling again, added, 'The day has produced some effects however – has had some consequences which must be considered as the very reverse of frightful. – When you had the presence of mind to suggest that Benwick would be the properest person to fetch a surgeon, you could have little idea of his being eventually one of those most concerned in her recovery.'

'Certainly I could have none. But it appears – I should hope it would be a very happy match. There are on both sides good principles and good temper.'

'Yes,' said he, looking not exactly forward – 'but there I think ends the resemblance. With all my soul I wish them happy, and rejoice over every circumstance in favour of it. They have no difficulties to contend with at home, no opposition, no caprice, no delays. – The Musgroves are behaving like themselves, most honourably and kindly, only anxious with true parental hearts to promote their daughter's comfort. All this is much, very much in favour of their happiness; more than perhaps –'

He stopped. A sudden recollection seemed to occur, and to give him some taste of that emotion which was reddening Anne's cheeks and fixing her eyes on the ground. – After clearing his throat, however, he proceeded thus,

'I confess that I do think there is a disparity, too great a disparity, and in a point no less essential than mind. – I regard Louisa Musgrove as a very amiable, sweet-tempered girl, and not deficient in understanding; but Benwick is something more. He is a clever man, a reading man – and I confess that I do consider his attaching himself to her, with some surprise. Had it been the effect of gratitude, had he learnt to love her, because he believed her to be preferring him, it would have been another thing. But I have no reason to suppose it so. It seems, on the contrary, to have been a perfectly spontaneous, untaught feeling on his side, and this surprises me. A man like him, in his situation! With a heart pierced, wounded, almost broken! Fanny Harville was a very superior creature; and his attachment to her was indeed attachment. A man does not recover from such a devotion of the heart to such a woman! – He ought not – he does not.'

Either from the consciousness, however, that his friend had recovered, or from other consciousness, he went no farther; and

Anne, who, in spite of the agitated voice in which the latter part had been uttered, and in spite of all the various noises of the room, the almost ceaseless slam of the door, and ceaseless buzz of persons walking through, had distinguished every word, was struck, gratified, confused, and beginning to breathe very quick, and feel an hundred things in a moment. It was impossible for her to enter on such a subject; and yet, after a pause, feeling the necessity of speaking, and having not the smallest wish for a total change, she only deviated so far as to say,

'You were a good while at Lyme, I think?'

'About a fortnight. I could not leave it till Louisa's doing well was quite ascertained. I had been too deeply concerned in the mischief to be soon at peace. It had been my doing – solely mine. She would not have been obstinate if I had not been weak. The country round Lyme is very fine. I walked and rode a great deal; and the more I saw, the more I found to admire.'

'I should very much like to see Lyme again,' said Anne.

'Indeed! I should not have supposed that you could have found any thing in Lyme to inspire such a feeling. The horror and distress you were involved in – the stretch of mind, the wear of spirits! – I should have thought your last impressions of Lyme must have been strong disgust.'

'The last few hours were certainly very painful,' replied Anne: 'but when pain is over, the remembrance of it often becomes a pleasure. One does not love a place the less for having suffered in it, unless it has been all suffering, nothing but suffering – which was by no means the case at Lyme. We were only in anxiety and distress during the last two hours; and, previously, there had been a great deal of enjoyment. So much novelty and beauty! I have travelled so little, that every fresh place would be interesting to me – but there is real beauty at Lyme: and in short' (with a faint blush at some recollections) 'altogether my impressions of the place are very agreeable.'

As she ceased, the entrance door opened again, and the very party appeared for whom they were waiting. 'Lady Dalrymple, Lady Dalrymple,' was the rejoicing sound; and with all the eagerness compatible with anxious elegance, Sir Walter and his two ladies stepped forward to meet her. Lady Dalrymple and Miss

Carteret, escorted by Mr Elliot and Colonel Wallis, who had happened to arrive nearly at the same instant, advanced into the room. The others joined them, and it was a group in which Anne found herself also necessarily included. She was divided from Captain Wentworth. Their interesting, almost too interesting conversation must be broken up for a time; but slight was the penance compared with the happiness which brought it on! She had learnt, in the last ten minutes, more of his feelings towards Louisa, more of all his feelings, than she dared to think of! and she gave herself up to the demands of the party, to the needful civilities of the moment, with exquisite, though agitated sensations. She was in good humour with all. She had received ideas which disposed her to be courteous and kind to all, and to pity every one, as being less happy than herself.

The delightful emotions were a little subdued, when, on stepping back from the group, to be joined again by Captain Wentworth, she saw that he was gone. She was just in time to see him turn into the concert room. He was gone – he had disappeared: she felt a moment's regret. But 'they should meet again. He would look for her – he would find her out long before the evening were over – and at present, perhaps, it was as well to be asunder. She was in need of a little interval for recollection.'

Upon Lady Russell's appearance soon afterwards, the whole party was collected, and all that remained, was to marshal themselves, and proceed into the concert room; and be of all the consequence in their power, draw as many eyes, excite as many whispers, and disturb as many people as they could.

Very, very happy were both Elizabeth and Anne Elliot as they walked in. Elizabeth, arm in arm with Miss Carteret, and looking on the broad back of the dowager Viscountess Dalrymple before her, had nothing to wish for which did not seem within her reach; and Anne – but it would be an insult to the nature of Anne's felicity, to draw any comparison between it and her sister's; the origin of one all selfish vanity, of the other all generous attachment.

Anne saw nothing, thought nothing of the brilliancy of the room. Her happiness was from within. Her eyes were bright, and her cheeks glowed, – but she knew nothing about it. She was thinking only of the last half hour, and as they passed to their seats, her mind took a hasty range over it. His choice of subjects, his expressions, and still more his manner and look, had been such as she could see in only one light. His opinion of Louisa Musgrove's inferiority, an opinion which he had seemed solicitous to give, his wonder at Captain Benwick, his feelings as to a first, strong attachment, – sentences begun which he could not finish – his half averted eyes, and more than half expressive glance, – all, all declared that he had a heart returning to her at least; that anger, resentment, avoidance, were no more; and that they were succeeded, not merely by friendship and regard, but by the tenderness of the past; yes, some share of the tenderness of the past. She could not contemplate the change as implying less. – He must love her.

These were thoughts, with their attendant visions, which occupied and flurried her too much to leave her any power of observation; and she passed along the room without having a glimpse of him, without even trying to discern him. When their places were determined on, and they were all properly arranged, she looked round to see if he should happen to be in the same part of the room, but he was not, her eye could not reach him; and the concert being just opening, she must consent for a time to be happy in an humbler way.

The party was divided, and disposed of on two contiguous benches: Anne was among those on the foremost, and Mr Elliot had manœuvred so well, with the assistance of his friend Colonel Wallis, as to have a seat by her. Miss Elliot, surrounded by her cousins, and the principal object of Colonel Wallis's gallantry, was quite contented.

Anne's mind was in a most favourable state for the entertainment of the evening: it was just occupation enough: she had feelings for the tender, spirits for the gay, attention for the scientific, and patience for the wearisome; and had never liked a concert better, at least during the first act. Towards the close of it, in the interval succeeding an Italian song, she explained the words of the song to Mr Elliot. – They had a concert bill between them.

'This,' said she, 'is nearly the sense, or rather the meaning of the words, for certainly the sense of an Italian love-song must not be talked of, – but it is as nearly the meaning as I can give; for I do not pretend to understand the language. I am a very poor Italian scholar.'

'Yes, yes, I see you are. I see you know nothing of the matter. You have only knowledge enough of the language, to translate at sight these inverted, transposed, curtailed Italian lines, into clear, comprehensible, elegant English. You need not say anything more of your ignorance. – Here is complete proof.'

'I will not oppose such kind politeness; but I should be sorry to be examined by a real proficient.'

'I have not had the pleasure of visiting in Camden-place so long,' replied he, 'without knowing something of Miss Anne Elliot; and I do regard her as one who is too modest, for the world in general to be aware of half her accomplishments, and too highly accomplished for modesty to be natural in any other woman.'

'For shame! for shame! – this is too much flattery. I forget what we are to have next,' turning to the bill.

'Perhaps,' said Mr Elliot, speaking low, 'I have had a longer acquaintance with your character than you are aware of.'

'Indeed! – How so? You can have been acquainted with it only since I came to Bath, excepting as you might hear me previously spoken of in my own family.'

'I knew you by report long before you came to Bath. I had heard you described by those who knew you intimately. I have been acquainted with you by character many years. Your person, your disposition, accomplishments, manner – they were all present to me.'

Mr Elliot was not disappointed in the interest he hoped to raise. No one can withstand the charm of such a mystery. To have been described long ago to a recent acquaintance, by nameless people, is irresistible; and Anne was all curiosity. She wondered, and questioned him eagerly – but in vain. He delighted in being asked, but he would not tell.

'No, no – some time or other perhaps, but not now. He would mention no names now; but such, he could assure her, had been the fact. He had many years ago received such a description of

Miss Anne Elliot, as had inspired him with the highest idea of her merit, and excited the warmest curiosity to know her.'

Anne could think of no one so likely to have spoken with partiality of her many years ago, as the Mr Wentworth, of Monkford, Captain Wentworth's brother. He might have been in Mr Elliot's company, but she had not courage to ask the question.

'The name of Anne Elliot,' said he, 'has long had an interesting sound to me. Very long has it possessed a charm over my fancy; and, if I dared, I would breathe my wishes that the name might never change.'

Such she believed were his words; but scarcely had she received their sound, than her attention was caught by other sounds immediately behind her, which rendered every thing else trivial. Her father and Lady Dalrymple were speaking.

'A well-looking man,' said Sir Walter, 'a very well-looking man.'

'A very fine young man indeed!' said Lady Dalrymple. 'More air than one often sees in Bath. – Irish, I dare say.'

'No, I just know his name. A bowing acquaintance. Wentworth – Captain Wentworth of the navy. His sister married my tenant in Somersetshire, – the Croft, who rents Kellynch.'

Before Sir Walter had reached this point, Anne's eyes had caught the right direction, and distinguished Captain Wentworth, standing among a cluster of men at a little distance. As her eyes fell on him, his seemed to be withdrawn from her. It had that appearance. It seemed as if she had been one moment too late; and as long as she dared observe, he did not look again: but the performance was re-commencing, and she was forced to seem to restore her attention to the orchestra, and look straight forward.

When she could give another glance, he had moved away. He could not have come nearer to her if he would; she was so surrounded and shut in : but she would rather have caught his eye.

Mr Elliot's speech too distressed her. She had no longer any inclination to talk to him. She wished him not so near her.

The first act was over. Now she hoped for some beneficial change; and, after a period of nothing-saying amongst the party, some of them did decide on going in quest of tea. Anne was one of the few who did not choose to move. She remained in her seat, and so did Lady Russell; but she had the pleasure of getting rid of Mr Elliot; and she did not mean, whatever she might feel on Lady Russell's account, to shrink from conversation with Captain Wentworth, if he gave her the opportunity. She was persuaded by Lady Russell's countenance that she had seen him.

He did not come however. Anne sometimes fancied she discerned him at a distance, but he never came. The anxious interval wore away unproductively. The others returned, the room filled again, benches were reclaimed and re-possessed, and another hour of pleasure or of penance was to be set out, another hour of music was to give delight or the gapes, as real or affected taste for it prevailed. To Anne, it chiefly wore the prospect of an hour of agitation. She could not quit that room in peace without seeing Captain Wentworth once more, without the interchange of one friendly look.

In re-settling themselves, there were now many changes, the result of which was favourable for her. Colonel Wallis declined sitting down again, and Mr Elliot was invited by Elizabeth and Miss Carteret, in a manner not to be refused, to sit between them; and by some other removals, and a little scheming of her own, Anne was enabled to place herself much nearer the end of the bench than she had been before, much more within reach of a passer-by. She could not do so, without comparing herself with Miss Larolles,[13] the inimitable Miss Larolles, – but still she did it, and not with much happier effect; though by what seemed prosperity in the shape of an early abdication in her next neighbours, she found herself at the very end of the bench before the concert closed.

Such was her situation, with a vacant space at hand, when Captain Wentworth was again in sight. She saw him not far off. He saw her too; yet he looked grave, and and seemed irresolute, and only by very slow degrees came at last near enough to speak to her. She felt that something must be the matter. The change was indubitable. The difference between his present air and what it had been in the octagon room was strikingly great. – Why was it? She thought of her father – of Lady Russell. Could there have been any unpleasant glances? He began by speaking of the concert, gravely; more like the Captain Wentworth of Uppercross; owned himself disappointed, had expected better singing; and, in short, must confess that he should not be sorry when it was over. Anne replied, and spoke in defence of the performance so well, and yet in allowance for his feelings, so pleasantly, that his countenance improved, and he replied again with almost a smile. They talked for a few minutes more; the improvement held; he even looked down towards the bench, as if he saw a place on it well worth occupying; when, at that moment, a touch on her shoulder obliged Anne to turn round. – It came from Mr Elliot. He begged her pardon, but she must be applied to, to explain Italian again. Miss Carteret was very anxious to have a general idea of what was next to be sung. Anne could not refuse; but never had she sacrificed to politeness with a more suffering spirit.

A few minutes, though as few as possible, were inevtably consumed; and when her own mistress again, when able to turn and look as she had done before, she found herself accosted by Captain Wentworth, in a reserved yet hurried sort of farewell. 'He must wish her good night. He was going – he should get home as fast as he could.'

'Is not this song worth staying for?' said Anne, suddenly struck by an idea which made her yet more anxious to be encouraging.

'No!' he replied impressively, 'there is nothing worth my staying for;' and he was gone directly.

Jealousy of Mr Elliot! It was the only intelligible motive. Captain Wentworth jealous of her affection! Could she have believed it a week ago – three hours ago! For a moment the gratification was exquisite. But alas! there were very different thoughts to succeed. How was such jealousy to be quieted? How was the truth to reach him? How, in all the peculiar disadvantages of their respective situations, would he ever learn her real sentiments? It was misery to think of Mr Elliot's attentions. – Their evil was incalculable.

CHAPTER 21

ANNE recollected with pleasure the next morning her promise of going to Mrs Smith; meaning that it should engage her from home at the time when Mr Elliot would be most likely to call; for to avoid Mr Elliot was almost a first object.

She felt a great deal of good will towards him. In spite of the mischief of his attentions, she owed him gratitude and regard, perhaps compassion. She could not help thinking much of the extraordinary circumstances attending their acquaintance; of the right which he seemed to have to interest her, by every thing in situation, by his own sentiments, by his early prepossession. It was altogether very extraordinary. – Flattering, but painful. There was much to regret. How she might have felt, had there been no Captain Wentworth in the case, was not worth enquiry; for there was a Captain Wentworth: and be the conclusion of the present suspense good or bad, her affection would be his for ever. Their union, she believed, could not divide her more from other men, than their final separation.

Prettier musings of high-wrought love and eternal constancy, could never have passed along the streets of Bath, than Anne was sporting with from Camden-place to Westgate-buildings. It was almost enough to spread purification and perfume all the way.

She was sure of a pleasant reception; and her friend seemed this morning particularly obliged to her for coming, seemed hardly to have expected her, though it had been an appointment.

An account of the concert was immediately claimed; and Anne's recollections of the concert were quite happy enough to animate her features, and make her rejoice to talk of it. All that she could tell, she told most gladly; but the all was little for one who had been there, and unsatisfactory for such an enquirer as Mrs Smith, who had already heard, through the short cut of a laundress and a waiter, rather more of the general success and produce of the evening than Anne could relate; and who now asked in vain for several particulars of the company. Every body of any consequence or notoriety in Bath was well known by name to Mrs Smith.

'The little Durands were there, I conclude,' said she, 'with their mouth open to catch the music; like unfledged sparrows ready to be fed. They never miss a concert.'

'Yes. I did not see them myself, but I heard Mr Elliot say they were in the room.'

'The Ibbotsons – were they there? and the two new beauties, with the tall Irish officer, who is talked of for one of them.'

'I do not know. – I do not think they were.'

'Old Lady Mary Maclean? I need not ask after her. She never misses, I know; and you must have seen her. She must have been in your own circle, for as you went with Lady Dalrymple, you were in the seats of grandeur; round the orchestra, of course.'

'No, that was what I dreaded. It would have been very unpleasant to me in every respect. But happily Lady Dalrymple always chooses to be farther off; and we were exceedingly well placed – that is for hearing; I must not say for seeing, because I appear to have seen very little.'

'Oh! you saw enough for your own amusement. – I can understand. There is a sort of domestic enjoyment to be known even in a crowd, and this you had. You were a large party in yourselves, and you wanted nothing beyond.'

'But I ought to have looked about me more,' said Anne, conscious while she spoke, that there had in fact been no want of looking about; that the object only had been deficient.

'No, no – you were better employed. You need not tell me that you had a pleasant evening. I see it in your eye. I perfectly see how the hours passed – that you had always something agreeable to listen to. In the intervals of the concert, it was conversation.'

Anne half smiled and said, 'Do you see that in my eye?'

'Yes, I do. Your countenance perfectly informs me that you were in company last night with the person, whom you think the most agreeable in the world, the person who interests you at this present time, more than all the rest of the world put together.'

A blush overspread Anne's cheeks. She could say nothing.

'And such being the case,' continued Mrs Smith, after a short pause, 'I hope you believe that I do know how to value your kindness in coming to me this morning. It is really very good of you to come and sit with me, when you must have so many pleasanter demands upon your time.'

Anne heard nothing of this. She was still in the astonishment and confusion excited by her friend's penetration, unable to imagine how any report of Captain Wentworth could have reached her. After another short silence –

'Pray,' said Mrs Smith, 'is Mr Elliot aware of your acquaintance with me? Does he know that I am in Bath?'

'Mr Elliot!' repeated Anne, looking up surprised. A moment's reflection shewed her the mistake she had been under. She caught it instantaneously; and, recovering courage with the feeling of safety, soon added, more composedly, 'are you acquainted with Mr Elliot?'

'I have been a good deal acquainted with him,' replied Mrs Smith, gravely, 'but it seems worn out now. It is a great while since we met.'

'I was not at all aware of this. You never mentioned it before. Had I known it, I would have had the pleasure of talking to him about you.'

'To confess the truth,' said Mrs Smith, assuming her usual air of cheerfulness, 'that is exactly the pleasure I want you to have. I want you to talk about me to Mr Elliot. I want your interest with him. He can be of essential service to me; and if you would have the goodness, my dear Miss Elliot, to make it an object to yourself, of course it is done.'

'I should be extremely happy – I hope you cannot doubt my willingness to be of even the slightest use to you,' replied Anne; 'but I suspect that you are considering me as having a higher claim on Mr Elliot – a greater right to influence him, than is really the case. I am sure you have, somehow or other, imbibed such a notion. You must consider me only as Mr Elliot's relation. If in that light, if there is any thing which you suppose his cousin might fairly ask of him, I beg you would not hesitate to employ me.'

Mrs Smith gave her a penetrating glance, and then, smiling, said,

'I have been a little premature, I perceive. I beg your pardon. I ought to have waited for official information. But now, my dear Miss Elliot, as an old friend, do give me a hint as to when I may speak. Next week? To be sure by next week I may be allowed to think it all settled, and build my own selfish schemes on Mr Elliot's good fortune.'

'No,' replied Anne, 'nor next week, nor next, nor next. I assure you that nothing of the sort you are thinking of will be settled any week. I am not going to marry Mr Elliot. I should like to know why you imagine I am.'

Mrs Smith looked at her again, looked earnestly, smiled, shook her head, and exclaimed,

'Now, how I do wish I understood you! How I do wish I knew what you were at! I have a great idea that you do not design to be cruel, when the right moment comes. Till it does come, you know, we women never mean to have any body. It is a thing of course among us, that every man is refused – till he offers. But why should you be cruel? Let me plead for my – present friend I cannot call him – but for my former friend. Where can you look for a more suitable match? Where could you expect a more gentle-manlike, agreeable man? Let me recommend Mr Elliot. I am sure you hear nothing but good of him from Colonel Wallis; and who can know him better than Colonel Wallis?'

'My dear Mrs Smith, Mr Elliot's wife has not been dead much above half a year. He ought not to be supposed to be paying his addresses to any one.'

'Oh! if these are your only objections,' cried Mrs Smith, archly, 'Mr Elliot is safe, and I shall give myself no more trouble about him. Do not forget me when you are married, that's all. Let him know me to be a friend of yours, and then he will think little of the trouble required, which it is very natural for him now, with so many affairs and engagements of his own, to avoid and get rid of as he can – very natural, perhaps. Ninety-nine out of a hun-dred would do the same. Of course, he cannot be aware of the im-portance to me. Well, my dear Miss Elliot, I hope and trust you will be very happy. Mr Elliot has sense to understand the value of such a woman. Your peace will not be shipwrecked as mine has been. You are safe in all worldly matters, and safe in his char-acter. He will not be led astray, he will not be misled by others to his ruin.'

'No,' said Anne, 'I can readily believe all that of my cousin. He seems to have a calm, decided temper, not at all open to dangerous impressions. I consider him with great respect. I have no reason, from any thing that has fallen within my observation, to do otherwise. But I have not known him long; and he is not a man, I think, to be known intimately soon. Will not this manner of speaking of him, Mrs Smith, convince you that he is nothing to me? Surely, this must be calm enough. And, upon my word, he is nothing to me. Should he ever propose to me (which I have very little reason to imagine he has any thought of doing), I shall not accept him. I assure you I shall not. I assure you Mr Elliot had not the share which you have been supposing, in whatever pleasure the concert of last night might afford : – not Mr Elliot; it is not Mr Elliot that –'

She stopped, regretting with a deep blush that she had implied so much; but less would hardly have been sufficient. Mrs Smith would hardly have believed so soon in Mr Elliot's failure, but from the perception of there being a somebody else. As it was, she instantly submitted, and with all the semblance of seeing nothing beyond; and Anne, eager to escape farther notice, was impatient to know why Mrs Smith should have fancied she was to marry Mr Elliot, where she could have received the idea, or from whom she could have heard it.

'Do tell me how it first came into your head.'

'It first came into my head,' replied Mrs Smith, 'upon finding how much you were together, and feeling it to be the most probable thing in the world to be wished for by everybody belonging to either of you; and you may depend upon it that all your acquaintance have disposed of you in the same way. But I never heard it spoken of till two days ago.'

'And has it indeed been spoken of?'

'Did you observe the woman who opened the door to you, when you called yesterday?'

'No. Was not it Mrs Speed, as usual, or the maid? I observed no one in particular.'

'It was my friend, Mrs Rooke – Nurse Rooke, who, by the by, had a great curiosity to see you, and was delighted to be in the way to let you in. She came away from Marlborough-buildings

only on Sunday; and she it was who told me you were to marry
Mr Elliot. She had had it from Mrs Wallis herself, which did not
seem bad authority. She sat an hour with me on Monday evening, and gave me the whole history.'

'The whole history!' repeated Anne, laughing. 'She could not
make a very long history, I think, of one such little article of unfounded news.'

Mrs Smith said nothing.

'But,' continued Anne, presently, 'though there is no truth in
my having this claim on Mr Elliot, I should be extremely happy
to be of use to you, in any way that I could. Shall I mention to
him your being in Bath? Shall I take any message?'

'No; I thank you: no, certainly not. In the warmth of the
moment, and under a mistaken impression, I might, perhaps,
have endeavoured to interest you in some circumstances. But not
now: no, I thank you, I have nothing to trouble you with.'

'I think you spoke of having known Mr Elliot many years?'

'I did.'

'Not before he married, I suppose?'

'Yes; he was not married when I knew him first.'

'And – were you much acquainted?'

'Intimately.'

'Indeed! Then do tell me what he was at that time of life. I
have a great curiosity to know what Mr Elliot was as a very
young man. Was he at all such as he appears now?'

'I have not seen Mr Elliot these three years,' was Mrs Smith's
answer, given so gravely that it was impossible to pursue the
subject farther; and Anne felt that she had gained nothing but an
increase of curiosity. They were both silent – Mrs Smith very
thoughtful. At last,

'I beg your pardon, my dear Miss Elliot,' she cried, in her
natural tone of cordiality, 'I beg your pardon for the short
answers I have been giving you, but I have been uncertain what
I ought to do. I have been doubting and considering as to what I
ought to tell you. There were many things to be taken into the
account. One hates to be officious, to be giving bad impressions,
making mischief. Even the smooth surface of family-union seems
worth preserving, though there may be nothing durable be-

neath. However, I have determined; I think I am right; I think you ought to be made acquainted with Mr Elliot's real character. Though I fully believe that, at present, you have not the smallest intention of accepting him, there is no saying what may happen. You might, some time or other, be differently affected towards him. Hear the truth, therefore, now, while you are unprejudiced. Mr Elliot is a man without heart or conscience; a designing, wary, cold-blooded being, who thinks only of himself; who, for his own interest or ease, would be guilty of any cruelty, or any treachery, that could be perpetrated without risk of his general character. He has no feeling for others. Those whom he has been the chief cause of leading into ruin, he can neglect and desert without the smallest compunction. He is totally beyond the reach of any sentiment of justice or compassion. Oh! he is black at heart, hollow and black!'

Anne's astonished air, and exclamation of wonder, made her pause, and in a calmer manner she added,

'My expressions startle you. You must allow for an injured, angry woman. But I will try to command myself. I will not abuse him. I will only tell you what I have found him. Facts shall speak. He was the intimate friend of my dear husband, who trusted and loved him, and thought him as good as himself. The intimacy had been formed before our marriage. I found them most intimate friends; and I, too, became excessively pleased with Mr Elliot, and entertained the highest opinion of him. At nineteen, you know, one does not think very seriously, but Mr Elliot appeared to me quite as good as others, and much more agreeable than most others, and we were almost always together. We were principally in town, living in very good style. He was then the inferior in circumstances, he was then the poor one; he had chambers in the Temple, and it was as much as he could do to support the appearance of a gentleman. He had always a home with us whenever he chose it; he was always welcome; he was like a brother. My poor Charles, who had the finest, most generous spirit in the world, would have divided his last farthing with him; and I know that his purse was open to him; I know that he often assisted him.'

'This must have been about that very period of Mr Elliot's

life,' said Anne, 'which has always excited my particular curiosity. It must have been about the same time that he became known to my father and sister. I never knew him myself, I only heard of him, but there was a something in his conduct then with regard to my father and sister, and afterwards in the circumstances of his marriage, which I never could quite reconcile with present times. It seemed to announce a different sort of man.'

'I know it all, I know it all,' cried Mrs Smith. 'He had been introduced to Sir Walter and your sister before I was acquainted with him, but I heard him speak of them for ever. I know he was invited and encouraged, and I know he did not choose to go. I can satisfy you, perhaps, on points which you would little expect; and as to his marriage, I knew all about it at the time. I was privy to all the fors and againsts, I was the friend to whom he confided his hopes and plans, and though I did not know his wife previously, (her inferior situation in society, indeed, rendered that impossible) yet I knew her all her life afterwards, or, at least, till within the last two years of her life, and can answer any question you wish to put.'

'Nay,' said Anne, 'I have no particular enquiry to make about her. I have always understood they were not a happy couple. But I should like to know why, at that time of his life, he should slight my father's acquaintance as he did. My father was certainly disposed to take very kind and proper notice of him. Why did Mr Elliot draw back?'

'Mr Elliot,' replied Mrs Smith, 'at that period of his life, had one object in view – to make his fortune, and by a rather quicker process than the law. He was determined to make it by marriage. He was determined, at least, not to mar it by an imprudent marriage; and I know it was his belief, (whether justly or not, of course I cannot decide) that your father and sister, in their civilities and invitations, were designing a match between the heir and the young lady; and it was impossible that such a match should have answered his ideas of wealth and independence. That was his motive for drawing back, I can assure you. He told me the whole story. He had no concealments with me. It was curious, that having just left you behind me in Bath, my first and principal acquaintance on marrying, should be your cousin; and that, through him, I should be continually hearing of your father and sister. He described one Miss Elliot, and I thought very affectionately of the other.'

'Perhaps,' cried Anne, struck by a sudden idea, 'you sometimes spoke of me to Mr Elliot?'

'To be sure I did, very often. I used to boast of my own Anne Elliot, and vouch for your being a very different creature from –'

She checked herself just in time.

'This accounts for something which Mr Elliot said last night,' cried Anne. 'This explains it. I found he had been used to hear of me. I could not comprehend how. What wild imaginations one forms, where dear self is concerned! How sure to be mistaken! But I beg your pardon; I have interrupted you. Mr Elliot married, then, completely for money? The circumstance, probably, which first opened your eyes to his character.'

Mrs Smith hesitated a little here. 'Oh! those things are too common. When one lives in the world, a man or woman's marrying for money is too common to strike one as it ought. I was very young, and associated only with the young, and we were a thoughtless, gay set, without any strict rules of conduct. We lived for enjoyment. I think differently now; time and sickness, and sorrow, have given me other notions; but, at that period, I must own I saw nothing reprehensible in what Mr Elliot was doing. "To do the best for himself," passed as a duty.'

'But was not she a very low woman?'

'Yes; which I objected to, but he would not regard. Money, money, was all that he wanted. Her father was a grazier, her grandfather had been a butcher, but that was all nothing. She was a fine woman, had had a decent education, was brought forward by some cousins, thrown by chance into Mr Elliot's company, and fell in love with him; and not a difficulty or a scruple was there on his side, with respect to her birth. All his caution was spent in being secured of the real amount of her fortune, before he committed himself. Depend upon it, whatever esteem Mr Elliot may have for his own situation in life now, as a young man he had not the smallest value for it. His chance of the Kellynch estate was something, but all the honour of the family he held as cheap as dirt. I have often heard him declare, that if

baronetcies were saleable, any body should have his for fifty
pounds, arms and motto, name and livery included; but I will not
pretend to repeat half that I used to hear him say on that subject.
It would not be fair. And yet you ought to have proof; for what
is all this but assertion? and you shall have proof.'

'Indeed, my dear Mrs Smith, I want none,' cried Anne. 'You
have asserted nothing contradictory to what Mr Elliot appeared to
be some years ago. This is all in confirmation, rather, of what we
used to hear and believe. I am more curious to know why he
should be so different now?'

'But for my satisfaction; if you will have the goodness to ring
for Mary — stay, I am sure you will have the still greater goodness of going yourself into my bed-room, and bringing me the
small inlaid box which you will find on the upper shelf of the
closet.'

Anne, seeing her friend to be earnestly bent on it, did as she
was desired. The box was brought and placed before her, and
Mrs Smith, sighing over it as she unlocked it, said,

'This is full of papers belonging to him, to my husband, a
small portion only of what I had to look over when I lost him.
The letter I am looking for, was one written by Mr Elliot to him
before our marriage, and happened to be saved; why, one can
hardly imagine. But he was careless and immethodical, like other
men, about those things; and when I came to examine his papers,
I found it with others still more trivial from different people
scattered here and there, while many letters and memorandums
of real importance had been destroyed. Here it is. I would not
burn it, because being even then very little satisfied with Mr
Elliot, I was determined to preserve every document of former
intimacy. I have now another motive for being glad that I can
produce it.'

This was the letter, directed to 'Charles Smith, Esq. Tunbridge
Wells,' and dated from London, as far back as July, 1803.

'Dear Smith,

'I have received yours. Your kindness almost overpowers me. I
wish nature had made such hearts as yours more common, but I
have lived three and twenty years in the world, and have seen none

like it. At present, believe me, I have no need of your services, being in cash again. Give me joy: I have got rid of Sir Walter and Miss. They are gone back to Kellynch, and almost made me swear to visit them this summer, but my first visit to Kellynch will be with a surveyor, to tell me how to bring it with best advantage to the hammer. The baronet, nevertheless, is not unlikely to marry again; he is quite fool enough. If he does, however, they will leave me in peace, which may be a decent equivalent for the reversion. He is worse than last year.

'I wish I had any name but Elliot. I am sick of it. The name of Walter I can drop, thank God! and I desire you will never insult me with my second W. again, meaning, for the rest of my life, to be only yours truly,

'Wm. Elliot.'

Such a letter could not be read without putting Anne in a glow; and Mrs Smith, observing the high colour in her face, said,

'The language, I know, is highly disrespectful. Though I have forgot the exact terms, I have a perfect impression of the general meaning. But it shews you the man. Mark his professions to my poor husband. Can any thing be stronger?'

Anne could not immediately get over the shock and mortification of finding such words applied to her father. She was obliged to recollect that her seeing the letter was a violation of the laws of honour, that no one ought to be judged or to be known by such testimonies, that no private correspondence could bear the eye of others, before she could recover calmness enough to return the letter which she had been meditating over, and say,

'Thank you. This is full proof undoubtedly, proof of every thing you were saying. But why be acquainted with us now?'

'I can explain this too,' cried Mrs Smith, smiling.

'Can you really?'

'Yes. I have shewn you Mr Elliot, as he was a dozen years ago, and I will shew him as he is now. I cannot produce written proof again, but I can give as authentic oral testimony as you can desire, of what he is now wanting, and what he is now doing. He is no hypocrite now. He truly wants to marry you. His present attentions to your family are very sincere, quite from the heart. I will give you my authority; his friend Colonel Wallis.'

'Colonel Wallis! you are acquainted with him?'

'No. It does not come to me in quite so direct a line as that; it takes a bend or two, but nothing of consequence. The stream is as good as at first; the little rubbish it collects in the turnings, is easily moved away. Mr Elliot talks unreservedly to Colonel Wallis of his views on you – which said Colonel Wallis I imagine to be in himself a sensible, careful, discerning sort of character; but Colonel Wallis has a very pretty silly wife, to whom he tells things which he had better not, and he repeats it all to her. She, in the overflowing spirits of her recovery, repeats it all to her nurse; and the nurse, knowing my acquaintance with you, very naturally brings it all to me. On Monday evening my good friend Mrs Rooke let me thus much into the secrets of Marlborough-buildings. When I talked of a whole history there-fore, you see, I was not romancing so much as you supposed.'

'My dear Mrs Smith, your authority is deficient. This will not do. Mr Elliot's having any views on me will not in the least account for the efforts he made towards a reconciliation with my father. That was all prior to my coming to Bath. I found them on the most friendly terms when I arrived.'

'I know you did; I know it all perfectly, but' –

'Indeed, Mrs Smith, we must not expect to get real information in such a line. Facts or opinions which are to pass through the hands of so many, to be misconceived by folly in one, and ignor-ance in another, can hardly have much truth left.'

'Only give me a hearing. You will soon be able to judge of the general credit due, by listening to some particulars which you can yourself immediately contradict or confirm. Nobody supposes that you were his first inducement. He had seen you indeed, before he came to Bath, and admired you, but without knowing it to be you. So says my historian at least. Is this true? Did he see you last summer or autumn, "somewhere down in the west," to use her own words, without knowing it to be you?'

'He certainly did. So far it is very true. At Lyme; I happened to be at Lyme.'

'Well,' continued Mrs Smith triumphantly, 'grant my friend the credit due to the establishment of the first point asserted. He saw you then at Lyme, and liked you so well as to be exceedingly pleased to meet with you again in Camden-place, as Miss Anne Elliot, and from that moment, I have no doubt, had a double motive in his visits there. But there was another, and an earlier; which I will now explain. If there is any thing in my story which you know to be either false or improbable, stop me. My account states, that your sister's friend, the lady now staying with you, whom I have heard you mention, came to Bath with Miss Elliot and Sir Walter as long ago as September, (in short when they first came themselves) and has been staying there ever since; that she is a clever, insinuating, handsome woman, poor and plausible, and altogether such in situation and manner, as to give a general idea among Sir Walter's acquaintance, of her meaning to be Lady Elliot, and as general a surprise that Miss Elliot should be apparently blind to the danger.'

Here Mrs Smith paused a moment; but Anne had not a word to say, and she continued,

'This was the light in which it appeared to those who knew the family, long before your return to it; and Colonel Wallis had his eye upon your father enough to be sensible of it, though he did not then visit in Camden-place; but his regard for Mr Elliot gave him an interest in watching all that was going on there, and when Mr Elliot came to Bath for a day or two, as he happened to do a little before Christmas, Colonel Wallis made him acquainted with the appearance of things, and the reports beginning to prevail. – Now you are to understand that time had worked a very material change in Mr Elliot's opinions as to the value of a baronetcy. Upon all points of blood and connexion, he is a completely altered man. Having long had as much money as he could spend, nothing to wish for on the side of avarice or indulgence, he has been gradually learning to pin his happiness upon the consequence he is heir to. I thought it coming on, before our acquaintance ceased, but it is now a confirmed feeling. He cannot bear the idea of not being Sir William. You may guess therefore that the news he heard from his friend, could not be very agreeable, and you may guess what it produced; the resolution of coming back to Bath as soon as possible, and of fixing himself here for a time, with the view of renewing his former acquaintance and recovering such a footing in the family, as might give him the means of ascertaining the degree of his danger, and of circumventing the lady if he found it material. This was agreed upon between the two friends, as the only thing to be done; and Colonel Wallis was to assist in every way that he could. He was to be introduced, and Mrs Wallis was to be introduced, and every body was to be introduced. Mr Elliot came back accordingly; and on application was forgiven, as you know, and re-admitted into the family; and there it was his constant object, and his only object (till your arrival added another motive) to watch Sir Walter and Mrs Clay. He omitted no opportunity of being with them, threw himself in their way, called at all hours – but I need not be particular on this subject. You can imagine what an artful man would do; and with this guide, perhaps, may recollect what you have seen him do.'

'Yes,' said Anne, 'you tell me nothing which does not accord with what I have known, or could imagine. There is always something offensive in the details of cunning. The manœuvres of selfishness and duplicity must ever be revolting, but I have heard nothing which really surprises me. I know those who would be shocked by such a representation of Mr Elliot, who would have difficulty in believing it; but I have never been satisfied. I have always wanted some other motive for his conduct than appeared. – I should like to know his present opinion, as to the probability of the event he has been in dread of; whether he considers the danger to be lessening or not.'

'Lessening, I understand,' replied Mrs Smith. 'He thinks Mrs Clay afraid of him, aware that he sees through her, and not daring to proceed as she might do in his absence. But since he must be absent some time or other, I do not perceive how he can ever be secure, while she holds her present influence. Mrs Wallis has an amusing idea, as nurse tells me, that it is to be put into the marriage articles when you and Mr Elliot marry, that your father is not to marry Mrs Clay. A scheme, worthy of Mrs Wallis's understanding, by all accounts; but my sensible nurse Rooke sees the absurdity of it. – "Why, to be sure, ma'am," said she, "it would not prevent his marrying any body else." And indeed, to own the truth, I do not think nurse in her heart is a very strenuous opposer of Sir Walter's making a second match. She must be allowed to be a favourer of matrimony you know, and (since self will intrude) who can say that she may not have some flying visions of attending the next Lady Elliot, through Mrs Wallis's recommendation?'

'I am very glad to know all this,' said Anne, after a little thoughtfulness. 'It will be more painful to me in some respects to be in company with him, but I shall know better what to do. My line of conduct will be more direct. Mr Elliot is evidently a disingenuous, artificial, worldly man, who has never had any better principle to guide him than selfishness.'

But Mr Elliot was not yet done with. Mrs Smith had been carried away from her first direction, and Anne had forgotten, in the interest of her own family concerns, how much had been originally implied against him; but her attention was now called to the explanation of those first hints, and she listened to a recital which, if it did not perfectly justify the unqualified bitterness of Mrs Smith, proved him to have been very unfeeling in his conduct towards her, very deficient both in justice and compassion.

She learned that (the intimacy between them continuing unimpaired by Mr Elliot's marriage) they had been as before always together, and Mr Elliot had led his friend into expenses much beyond his fortune. Mrs Smith did not want to take blame to herself, and was most tender of throwing any on her husband; but Anne could collect that their income had never been equal to their style of living, and that from the first, there had been a great deal of general and joint extravagance. From his wife's account of him, she could discern Mr Smith to have been a man of warm feelings, easy temper, careless habits, and not strong understanding, much more amiable than his friend, and very unlike him – led by him, and probably despised by him. Mr Elliot, raised by his marriage to great affluence, and disposed to every gratification of pleasure and vanity which could be commanded without involving himself, (for with all his self-indulgence he had become a prudent man) and beginning to be rich, just as his friend ought to have found himself to be poor, seemed to have had no concern at all for that friend's probable finances, but, on the contrary, had been prompting and encouraging expenses, which could end only in ruin. And the Smiths accordingly had been ruined.

The husband had died just in time to be spared the full knowledge of it. They had previously known embarrassments enough to try the friendship of their friends, and to prove that Mr Elliot's had better not be tried; but it was not till his death that the wretched state of his affairs was fully known. With a confidence in Mr Elliot's regard, more creditable to his feelings than his judgment, Mr Smith had appointed him the executor of his will; but Mr Elliot would not act, and the difficulties and distresses which this refusal had heaped on her, in addition to the inevitable sufferings of her situation, had been such as could not be related without anguish of spirit, or listened to without corresponding indignation.

Anne was shewn some letters of his on the occasion, answers to urgent applications from Mrs Smith, which all breathed the same stern resolution of not engaging in a fruitless trouble, and, under a cold civility, the same hard-hearted indifference to any of the evils it might bring on her. It was a dreadful picture of ingratitude and inhumanity; and Anne felt at some moments, that no flagrant open crime could have been worse. She had a great deal to listen to; all the particulars of past sad scenes, all the minutiæ of distress upon distress, which in former conversations had been merely hinted at, were dwelt on now with a natural indulgence. Anne could perfectly comprehend the exquisite relief, and was only the more inclined to wonder at the composure of her friend's usual state of mind.

There was one circumstance in the history of her grievances of particular irritation. She had good reason to believe that some property of her husband in the West Indies, which had been for many years under a sort of sequestration for the payment of its own incumbrances, might be recoverable by proper measures; and this property, though not large, would be enough to make her comparatively rich. But there was nobody to stir in it. Mr Elliot would do nothing, and she could do nothing herself, equally disabled from personal exertion by her state of bodily weakness, and from employing others by her want of money. She had no natural connexions to assist her even with their counsel, and she could not afford to purchase the assistance of the law. This was a cruel aggravation of actually streightened means. To feel that she ought to be in better circumstances, that a little trouble in the right place might do it, and to fear that delay might be even weakening her claims, was hard to bear!

It was on this point that she had hoped to engage Anne's good offices with Mr Elliot. She had previously, in the anticipation of their marriage, been very apprehensive of losing her friend by it; but on being assured that he could have made no attempt of that nature, since he did not even know her to be in Bath, it immediately occurred, that something might be done in her favour by the influence of the woman he loved, and she had been hastily preparing to interest Anne's feelings, as far as the observances due to Mr Elliot's character would allow, when Anne's refutation of the supposed engagement changed the face of every thing, and while it took from her the new-formed hope of succeeding in the object of her first anxiety, left her at least the comfort of telling the whole story her own way.

After listening to this full description of Mr Elliot, Anne could not but express some surprise at Mrs Smith's having spoken of him so favourably in the beginning of their conversation. 'She had seemed to recommend and praise him!'

'My dear,' was Mrs Smith's reply, 'there was nothing else to be done. I considered your marrying him as certain, though he might not yet have made the offer, and I could no more speak the truth of him, than if he had been your husband. My heart bled for you, as I talked of happiness. And yet, he is sensible, he is agreeable, and with such a woman as you, it was not absolutely hopeless. He was very unkind to his first wife. They were wretched together. But she was too ignorant and giddy for respect, and he had never loved her. I was willing to hope that you must fare better.'

Anne could just acknowledge within herself such a possibility of having been induced to marry him, as made her shudder at the idea of the misery which must have followed. It was just possible that she might have been persuaded by Lady Russell! And under such a supposition, which would have been most miserable, when time had disclosed all, too late?

It was very desirable that Lady Russell should be no longer deceived; and one of the concluding arrangements of this important conference, which carried them through the greater part of the morning, was, that Anne had full liberty to communicate to her friend every thing relative to Mrs Smith, in which his conduct was involved.

CHAPTER 22

ANNE went home to think over all that she had heard. In one point, her feelings were relieved by this knowledge of Mr Elliot. There was no longer any thing of tenderness due to him. He stood, as opposed to Captain Wentworth, in all his own unwelcome obtrusiveness; and the evil of his attentions last night, the irremediable mischief he might have done, was considered with sensations unqualified, unperplexed. – Pity for him was all over. But this was the only point of relief. In every other respect, in looking around her, or penetrating forward, she saw more to distrust and to apprehend. She was concerned for the disappointment and pain Lady Russell would be feeling, for the mortifications which must be hanging over her father and sister, and had all the distress of foreseeing many evils, without knowing how to avert any one of them. – She was most thankful for her own knowledge of him. She had never considered herself as entitled to reward for not slighting an old friend like Mrs Smith, but here was a reward indeed springing from it! – Mrs Smith had been able to tell her what no one else could have done. Could the knowledge have been extended through her family! – But this was a vain idea. She must talk to Lady Russell, tell her, consult with her, and having done her best, wait the event with as much composure as possible; and after all, her greatest want of composure would be in that quarter of the mind which could not be opened to Lady Russell, in that flow of anxieties and fears which must be all to herself.

She found, on reaching home, that she had, as she intended, escaped seeing Mr Elliot; that he had called and paid them a long morning visit; but hardly had she congratulated herself, and felt safe till to-morrow, when she heard that he was coming again in the evening.

'I had not the smallest intention of asking him,' said Elizabeth, with affected carelessness, 'but he gave so many hints; so Mrs Clay says, at least.'

'Indeed I do say it. I never saw any body in my life spell harder for an invitation. Poor man! I was really in pain for him; for your hard-hearted sister, Miss Anne, seems bent on cruelty.'

'Oh!' cried Elizabeth, 'I have been rather too much used to the game to be soon overcome by a gentleman's hints. However, when I found how excessively he was regretting that he should miss my father this morning, I gave way immediately, for I would never really omit an opportunity of bringing him and Sir Walter together. They appear to so much advantage in company with each other! Each behaving so pleasantly! Mr Elliot looking up with so much respect!'

'Quite delightful!' cried Mrs Clay, not daring, however, to turn her eyes towards Anne. 'Exactly like father and son! Dear Miss Elliot, may I not say father and son?'

'Oh! I lay no embargo on any body's words. If you will have such ideas! But, upon my word, I am scarcely sensible of his attentions being beyond those of other men.'

'My dear Miss Elliot!' exclaimed Mrs Clay, lifting up her hands and eyes, and sinking all the rest of her astonishment in a convenient silence.

'Well, my dear Penelope, you need not be so alarmed about him. I did invite him, you know. I sent him away with smiles. When I found he was really going to his friends at Thornberry-park for the whole day to-morrow, I had compassion on him.'

Anne admired the good acting of the friend, in being able to shew such pleasure as she did, in the expectation, and in the actual arrival of the very person whose presence must really be interfering with her prime object. It was impossible but that Mrs Clay must hate the sight of Mr Elliot; and yet she could assume a most obliging, placid look, and appear quite satisfied with the curtailed license of devoting herself only half as much to Sir Walter as she would have done otherwise.

To Anne herself it was most distressing to see Mr Elliot enter the room; and quite painful to have him approach and speak to her. She had been used before to feel that he could not be always quite sincere, but now she saw insincerity in every thing. His attentive deference to her father, contrasted with his former language, was odious; and when she thought of his cruel conduct towards Mrs Smith, she could hardly bear the sight of his present smiles and mildness, or the sound of his artificial good sentiments. She meant to avoid any such alteration of manners as might provoke a remonstrance on his side. It was a great object with her to escape all enquiry or eclat; but it was her intention to be as decidedly cool to him as might be compatible with their relationship, and to retrace, as quietly as she could, the few steps of unnecessary intimacy she had been gradually led along. She was accordingly more guarded, and more cool, than she had been the night before.

He wanted to animate her curiosity again as to how and where he could have heard her formerly praised; wanted very much to be gratified by more solicitation; but the charm was broken: he found that the heat and animation of a public room were necessary to kindle his modest cousin's vanity; he found, at least, that it was not to be done now, by any of those attempts which he could hazard among the too-commanding claims of the others. He little surmised that it was a subject acting now exactly against his interest, bringing immediately into her thoughts all those parts of his conduct which were least excusable.

She had some satisfaction in finding that he was really going out of Bath the next morning, going early, and that he would be gone the greater part of two days. He was invited again to Camden-place the very evening of his return; but from Thursday to Saturday evening his absence was certain. It was bad enough that a Mrs Clay should be always before her; but that a deeper hypocrite should be added to their party, seemed the destruction of every thing like peace and comfort. It was so humiliating to reflect on the constant deception practised on her father and Elizabeth; to consider the various sources of mortfication preparing for them! Mrs Clay's selfishness was not so complicate nor so revolting as his; and Anne would have compounded for the marriage at once, with all its evils, to be clear of Mr Elliot's subtleties, in endeavouring to prevent it.

On Friday morning she meant to go very early to Lady Russell, and accomplish the necessary communication; and she would have gone directly after breakfast but that Mrs Clay was also going out on some obliging purpose of saving her sister trouble, which determined her to wait till she might be safe from such a companion. She saw Mrs Clay fairly off, therefore, before she began to talk of spending the morning in Rivers-street.

'Very well,' said Elizabeth, 'I have nothing to send but my love. Oh! you may as well take back that tiresome book she would lend me, and pretend I have read it through. I really cannot be plaguing myself for ever with all the new poems and states of the nation that come out. Lady Russell quite bores one with her new publications. You need not tell her so, but I thought her dress hideous the other night. I used to think she had some taste in dress, but I was ashamed of her at the concert. Something so formal and *arrangé* in her air! and she sits so upright! My best love, of course.'

'And mine,' added Sir Walter. 'Kindest regards. And you may say, that I mean to call upon her soon. Make a civil message. But I shall only leave my card. Morning visits are never fair by women at her time of life, who make themselves up so little. If she would only wear rouge, she would not be afraid of being seen; but last time I called, I observed the blinds were let down immediately.'

While her father spoke, there was a knock at the door. Who could it be? Anne, remembering the preconcerted visits, at all hours, of Mr Elliot, would have expected him, but for his known engagement seven miles off. After the usual period of suspense, the usual sounds of approach were heard, and 'Mr and Mrs Charles Musgrove' were ushered into the room.

Surprise was the strongest emotion raised by their appearance; but Anne was really glad to see them; and the others were not so sorry but that they could put on a decent air of welcome; and as soon as it became clear that these, their nearest relations, were not arrived with any views of accommodation in that house, Sir Walter and Elizabeth were able to rise in cordiality, and do the honours of it very well. They were come to Bath for a few days with Mrs Musgrove, and were at the White Hart. So much was pretty soon understood; but till Sir Walter and Elizabeth were walking Mary into the other drawing-room, and regaling themselves with her admiration, Anne could not draw upon Charles's brain for a regular history of their coming, or an explanation of some smiling hints of particular business, which had been ostentatiously dropped by Mary, as well as of some apparent confusion as to whom their party consisted of.

She then found that is consisted of Mrs Musgrove, Henrietta, and Captain Harville, beside their two selves. He gave her a very plain, intelligible account of the whole; a narration in which she saw a great deal of most characteristic proceeding. The scheme had received its first impulse by Captain Harville's wanting to come to Bath on business. He had begun to talk of it a week ago; and by way of doing something, as shooting was over, Charles had proposed coming with him, and Mrs Harville had seemed to like the idea of it very much, as an advantage to her husband; but Mary could not bear to be left, and had made herself so unhappy about it that, for a day or two, every thing seemed to be in suspense, or at an end. But then, it had been taken up by his father and mother. His mother had some old friends in Bath, whom she wanted to see; it was thought a good opportunity for Henrietta to come and buy wedding-clothes for herself and her sister; and, in short, it ended in being his mother's party, that every thing might be comfortable and easy to Captain Harville; and he and Mary were included in it, by way of general convenience. They had arrived late the night before. Mrs Harville, her children, and Captain Benwick, remained with Mr Musgrove and Louisa at Uppercross.

Anne's only surprise was, that affairs should be in forwardness enough for Henrietta's wedding-clothes to be talked of: she had imagined such difficulties of fortune to exist there as must prevent the marriage from being near at hand; but she learned from Charles that, very recently, (since Mary's last letter to herself) Charles Hayter had been applied to by a friend to hold a living for a youth who could not possibly claim it under many years; and that, on the strength of his present income, with almost a certainty of something more permanent long before the term in question, the two families had consented to the young people's wishes, and that their marriage was likely to take place in a few months, quite as soon as Louisa's. 'And a very good living it was,' Charles added, 'only five-and-twenty miles from Uppercross, and in a very fine country – fine part of Dorsetshire.

In the centre of some of the best preserves in the kingdom, surrounded by three great proprietors, each more careful and jealous than the other; and to two of the three, at least, Charles Hayter might get a special recommendation. Not that he will value it as he ought,' he observed, 'Charles is too cool about sporting. That's the worst of him.'

'I am extremely glad, indeed,' cried Anne, 'particularly glad that this should happen: and that of two sisters, who both deserve equally well, and who have always been such good friends, the pleasant prospects of one should not be dimming those of the other – that they should be so equal in their prosperity and comfort. I hope your father and mother are quite happy with regard to both.'

'Oh! yes. My father would be well pleased if the gentlemen were richer, but he has no other fault to find. Money, you know, coming down with money – two daughters at once – it cannot be a very agreeable operation, and it streightens him as to many things. However, I do not mean to say they have not a right to it. It is very fit they should have daughters' shares; and I am sure he has always been a very kind, liberal father to me. Mary does not above half like Henrietta's match. She never did, you know. But she does not do him justice, nor think enough about Winthrop. I cannot make her attend to the value of the property. It is a very fair match, as times go; and I have liked Charles Hayter all my life, and I shall not leave off now.'

'Such excellent parents as Mr and Mrs Musgrove,' exclaimed Anne, 'should be happy in their children's marriages. They do every thing to confer happiness, I am sure. What a blessing to young people to be in such hands! Your father and mother seem so totally free from all those ambitious feelings which have led to so much misconduct and misery, both in young and old! I hope you think Louisa perfectly recovered now?'

He answered rather hesitatingly, 'Yes, I believe I do – very much recovered; but she is altered: there is no running or jumping about, no laughing or dancing; it is quite different. If one happens only to shut the door a little hard, she starts and wriggles like a young dab chick in the water; and Benwick sits at her elbow, reading verses, or whispering to her, all day long.'

Anne could not help laughing. 'That cannot be much to your taste, I know,' said she; 'but I do believe him to be an excellent young man.'

'To be sure he is. Nobody doubts it; and I hope you do not think I am so illiberal as to want every man to have the same objects and pleasures as myself. I have a great value for Benwick; and when one can but get him to talk, he has plenty to say. His reading has done him no harm, for he has fought as well as read. He is a brave fellow. I got more acquainted with him last Monday than ever I did before. We had a famous set-to at rat-hunting all the morning, in my father's great barns; and he played his part so well, that I have liked him the better ever since.'

Here they were interrupted by the absolute necessity of Charles's following the others to admire mirrors and china; but Anne had heard enough to understand the present state of Uppercross, and rejoice in its happiness; and though she sighed as she rejoiced, her sigh had none of the ill-will of envy in it. She would certainly have risen to their blessings if she could, but she did not want to lessen theirs.

The visit passed off altogether in high good humour. Mary was in excellent spirits, enjoying the gaiety and the change; and so well satisfied with the journey in her mother-in-law's carriage with four horses, and with her own complete independence of Camden-place, that she was exactly in a temper to admire every thing as she ought, and enter most readily into all the superiorities of the house, as they were detailed to her. She had no demands on her father or sister, and her consequence was just enough increased by their handsome drawing-rooms.

Elizabeth was, for a short time, suffering a good deal. She felt that Mrs Musgrove and all her party ought to be asked to dine with them, but she could not bear to have the difference of style, the reduction of servants, which a dinner must betray, witnessed by those who had been always so inferior to the Elliots of Kellynch. It was a struggle between propriety and vanity; but vanity got the better, and then Elizabeth was happy again. These were her internal persuasions. – 'Old fashioned notions – country hospitality – we do not profess to give dinners – few people in Bath do – Lady Alicia never does; did not even ask her own sister's family, though they were here a month: and I dare say it would be very inconvenient to Mrs Musgrove – put her quite out of her way. I am sure she would rather not come – she cannot feel easy with us. I will ask them all for an evening; that will be much better – that will be a novelty and a treat. They have not seen two such drawing rooms before. They will be delighted to come to-morrow evening. It shall be a regular party – small, but most elegant.' And this satisfied Elizabeth: and when the invitation was given to the two present, and promised for the absent, Mary was as completely satisfied. She was particularly asked to meet Mr Elliot, and be introduced to Lady Dalrymple and Miss Carteret, who were fortunately already engaged to come; and she could not have received a more gratifying attention. Miss Elliot was to have the honour of calling on Mrs Musgrove in the course of the morning, and Anne walked off with Charles and Mary, to go and see her and Henrietta directly.

Her plan of sitting with Lady Russell must give way for the present. They all three called in Rivers-street for a couple of minutes; but Anne convinced herself that a day's delay of the intended communication could be of no consequence, and hastened forward to the White Hart, to see again the friends and companions of the last autumn, with an eagerness of good will which many associations contributed to form.

They found Mrs Musgrove and her daughter within, and by themselves, and Anne had the kindest welcome from each. Henrietta was exactly in that state of recently-improved views, of fresh-formed happiness, which made her full of regard and interest for every body she had ever liked before at all; and Mrs Musgrove's real affection had been won by her usefulness when they were in distress. It was a heartiness, and a warmth, and a sincerity which Anne delighted in the more, from the sad want of such blessings at home. She was intreated to give them as much of her time as possible, invited for every day and all day long, or rather claimed as a part of the family; and in return, she naturally fell into all her wonted ways of attention and assistance, and on Charles's leaving them together, was listening to Mrs Musgrove's history of Louisa, and to Henrietta's of herself, giving opinions on business, and recommendations to shops; with intervals of every help which Mary required, from altering her ribbon to settling her accounts, from finding her keys, and assorting her trinkets, to trying to convince her that she was not ill used by any body; which Mary, well amused as she generally was in her station, at a window overlooking the entrance to the pump-room, could not but have her moments of imagining.

A morning of thorough confusion was to be expected. A large party in an hotel ensured a quick-changing, unsettled scene. One five minutes brought a note, the next a parcel, and Anne had not been there half an hour, when their dining-room, spacious as it was, seemed more than half filled: a party of steady old friends were seated round Mrs Musgrove, and Charles came back with Captains Harville and Wentworth. The appearance of the latter could not be more than the surprise of the moment. It was impossible for her to have forgotten to feel, that this arrival of their common friends must be soon bringing them together again. Their last meeting had been most important in opening his feelings; she had derived from it a delightful conviction; but she feared from his looks, that the same unfortunate persuasion, which had hastened him away from the concert room, still governed. He did not seem to want to be near enough for conversation.

She tried to be calm, and leave things to take their course; and tried to dwell much on this argument of rational dependance – 'Surely, if there be constant attachment on each side, our hearts must understand each other ere long. We are not boy and girl, to be captiously irritable, misled by every moment's inadvertence, and wantonly playing with our own happiness.' And yet, a few minutes afterwards, she felt as if their being in company with each other, under their present circumstances, could only be exposing them to inadvertencies and misconstructions of the most mischievous kind.

'Anne,' cried Mary, still at her window, 'there is Mrs Clay, I am sure, standing under the colonnade, and a gentleman with her. I saw them turn the corner from Bath-street just now. They seem deep in talk. Who is it? – Come, and tell me. Good heavens! I recollect. – It is Mr Elliot himself.'

'No,' cried Anne quickly, 'it cannot be Mr Elliot, I assure you.

He was to leave Bath at nine this morning, and does not come back till to-morrow.'

As she spoke, she felt that Captain Wentworth was looking at her; the consciousness of which vexed and embarrassed her, and made her regret that she had said so much, simple as it was.

Mary, resenting that she should be supposed not to know her own cousin, began talking very warmly about the family features, and protesting still more positively that it was Mr Elliot, calling again upon Anne to come and look herself; but Anne did not mean to stir, and tried to be cool and unconcerned. Her distress returned, however, on perceiving smiles and intelligent glances pass between two or three of the lady visitors, as if they believed themselves quite in the secret. It was evident that the report concerning her had spread; and a short pause succeeded, which seemed to ensure that it would now spread farther.

'Do come, Anne,' cried Mary, 'come and look yourself. You will be too late, if you do not make haste. They are parting, they are shaking hands. He is turning away. Not know Mr Elliot, indeed ! – You seem to have forgot all about Lyme.'

To pacify Mary, and perhaps screen her own embarrassment, Anne did move quietly to the window. She was just in time to ascertain that it really was Mr Elliot (which she had never believed), before he disappeared on one side, as Mrs Clay walked quickly off on the other; and checking the surprise which she could not but feel at such an appearance of friendly conference between two persons of totally opposite interests, she calmly said, 'Yes, it is Mr Elliot certainly. He has changed his hour of going, I suppose, that is all – or I may be mistaken; I might not attend;' and walked back to her chair, recomposed, and with the comfortable hope of having acquitted herself well.

The visitors took their leave; and Charles, having civilly seen them off, and then made a face at them, and abused them for coming, began with –

'Well, mother, I have done something for you that you will like. I have been to the theatre, and secured a box for to-morrow night. A'n't I a good boy? I know you love a play; and there is room for us all. It holds nine. I have engaged Captain Wentworth. Anne will not be sorry to join us, I am sure. We all like a play. Have not I done well, mother?'

Mrs Musgrove was good humouredly beginning to express her perfect readiness for the play, if Henrietta and all the others liked it, when Mary eagerly interrupted her by exclaiming,

'Good heavens, Charles! how can you think of such a thing? Take a box for to-morrow night! Have you forgot that we are engaged to Camden-place to-morrow night? and that we were most particularly asked on purpose to meet Lady Dalrymple and her daughter, and Mr Elliot – all the principal family connexions – on purpose to be introduced to them? How can you be so forgetful?'

'Phoo! phoo!' replied Charles, 'what's an evening party? Never worth remembering. Your father might have asked us to dinner, I think, if he had wanted to see us. You may do as you like, but I shall go to the play.'

'Oh! Charles, I declare it will be too abominable if you do! when you promised to go.'

'No, I did not promise. I only smirked and bowed, and said the word "happy." There was no promise.'

'But you must go, Charles. It would be unpardonable to fail. We were asked on purpose to be introduced. There was always such a great connexion between the Dalrymples and ourselves. Nothing ever happened on either side that was not announced immediately. We are quite near relations, you know: and Mr Elliot too, whom you ought so particularly to be acquainted with! Every attention is due to Mr Elliot. Consider, my father's heir – the future representative of the family.'

'Don't talk to me about heirs and representatives,' cried Charles. 'I am not one of those who neglect the reigning power to bow to the rising sun. If I would not go for the sake of your father, I should think it scandalous to go for the sake of his heir. What is Mr Elliot to me?'

The careless expression was life to Anne, who saw that Captain Wentworth was all attention, looking and listening with his whole soul; and that the last words brought his enquiring eyes from Charles to herself.

Charles and Mary still talked on in the same style; he, half serious and half jesting, maintaining the scheme for the play; and she, invariably serious, most warmly opposing it, and not omitting to make it known, that however determined to go to Camden-place herself, she should not think herself very well used, if they went to the play without her. Mrs Musgrove interposed.

'We had better put it off. Charles, you had much better go back, and change the box for Tuesday. It would be a pity to be divided, and we should be losing Miss Anne too, if there is a party at her father's; and I am sure neither Henrietta nor I should care at all for the play, if Miss Anne could not be with us.'

Anne felt truly obliged to her for such kindness; and quite as much so, moreover, for the opportunity it gave her of decidedly saying –

'If it depended only on my inclination, ma'am, the party at home (excepting on Mary's account) would not be the smallest impediment. I have no pleasure in the sort of meeting, and should be too happy to change it for a play, and with you. But, it had better not be attempted, perhaps.'

She had spoken it; but she trembled when it was done, conscious that her words were listened to, and daring not even to try to observe their effect.

It was soon generally agreed that Tuesday should be the day, Charles only reserving the advantage of still teasing his wife, by persisting that he would go to the play to-morrow, if nobody else would.

Captain Wentworth left his seat, and walked to the fire-place; probably for the sake of walking away from it soon afterwards, and taking a station, with less bare-faced design, by Anne.

'You have not been long enough in Bath,' said he, 'to enjoy the evening parties of the place.'

'Oh! no. The usual character of them has nothing for me. I am no card-player.'

'You were not formerly, I know. You did not use to like cards; but time makes many changes.'

'I am not yet so much changed,' cried Anne, and stopped, fearing she hardly knew what misconstruction. After waiting a few moments he said – and as if it were the result of immediate feel-ing – 'It is a period, indeed! Eight years and a hálf is a period!'

Whether he would have proceeded farther was left to Anne's imagination to ponder over in a calmer hour; for while still hear-ing the sounds he had uttered, she was startled to other subjects by Henrietta, eager to make use of the present leisure for getting out, and calling on her companions to lose no time, lest some-body else should come in.

They were obliged to move. Anne talked of being perfectly ready, and tried to look it; but she felt that could Henrietta have known the regret and reluctance of her heart in quitting that chair, in preparing to quit the room, she would have found, in all her own sensations for her cousin, in the very security of his affection, wherewith to pity her.

Their preparations, however, were stopped short. Alarming sounds were heard; other visitors approached, and the door was thrown open for Sir Walter and Miss Elliot, whose entrance seemed to give a general chill. Anne felt an instant oppression, and, wherever she looked, saw symptoms of the same. The com-fort, the freedom, the gaiety of the room was over, hushed into cold composure, determined silence, or insipid talk, to meet the heartless elegance of her father and sister. How mortifying to feel that it was so!

Her jealous eye was satisfied in one particular. Captain Went-worth was acknowledged again by each, by Elizabeth more graciously than before. She even addressed him once, and looked at him more than once. Elizabeth was, in fact, revolving a great measure. The sequel explained it. After the waste of a few minutes in saying the proper nothings, she began to give the invitation which was to comprise all the remaining dues of the Musgroves. 'To-morrow evening, to meet a few friends, no formal party.' It was all said very gracefully, and the cards with which she had provided herself, the 'Miss Elliot at home,' were laid on the table, with a courteous, comprehensive smile to all; and one smile and one card more decidedly for Captain Wentworth. The truth was, that Elizabeth had been long enough in Bath, to under-stand the importance of a man of such an air and appearance as his. The past was nothing. The present was that Captain Wentworth would move about well in her drawing-room. The card was pointedly given, and Sir Walter and Elizabeth arose and disappeared.

The interruption had been short, though severe; and ease and animation returned to most of those they left, as the door shut them out, but not to Anne. She could think only of the invitation she had with such astonishment witnessed; and of the manner in which it had been received, a manner of doubtful meaning, of surprise rather than gratification, of polite acknowledgment rather than acceptance. She knew him; she saw disdain in his eye, and could not venture to believe that he had determined to accept such an offering, as atonement for all the insolence of the past. Her spirits sank. He held the card in his hand after they were gone, as if deeply considering it.

'Only think of Elizabeth's including every body !' whispered Mary very audibly. 'I do not wonder Captain Wentworth is delighted ! You see he cannot put the card out of his hand.'

Anne caught his eye, saw his cheeks glow, and his mouth form itself into a momentary expression of contempt, and turned away, that she might neither see nor hear more to vex her.

The party separated. The gentlemen had their own pursuits, the ladies proceeded on their own business, and they met no more while Anne belonged to them. She was earnestly begged to return and dine, and give them all the rest of the day; but her spirits had been so long exerted, that at present she felt unequal to more, and fit only for home, where she might be sure of being as silent as she chose.

Promising to be with them the whole of the following morning, therefore, she closed the fatigues of the present, by a toilsome walk to Camden-place, there to spend the evening chiefly in listening to the busy arrangements of Elizabeth and Mrs Clay for the morrow's party, the frequent enumeration of the persons invited, and the continually improving detail of all the embellishments which were to make it the most completely elegant of its kind in Bath, while harassing herself in secret with the never-ending question, of whether Captain Wentworth would come or not? They were reckoning him as certain, but, with her, it was a gnawing solicitude never appeased for five minutes together. She generally thought he would come, because she generally thought he ought; but it was a case which she could not so shape into any positive act of duty or discretion, as inevitably to defy the suggestions of very opposite feelings.

She only roused herself from the broodings of this restless agitation, to let Mrs Clay know that she had been seen with Mr Elliot three hours after his being supposed to be out of Bath; for having watched in vain for some intimation of the interview from the lady herself, she determined to mention it; and it seemed to her that there was guilt in Mrs Clay's face as she listened. It was transient, cleared away in an instant, but Anne could imagine she read there the consciousness of having, by some complication of mutual trick, or some overbearing authority of his, been obliged to attend (perhaps for half an hour) to his lectures and restrictions on her designs on Sir Walter. She exclaimed, however, with a very tolerable imitation of nature,

'Oh dear! very true. Only think, Miss Elliot, to my great surprise I met with Mr Elliot in Bath-street! I was never more astonished. He turned back and walked with me to the Pump-yard. He had been prevented setting off for Thornberry, but I really forget by what – for I was in a hurry, and could not much attend, and I can only answer for his being determined not to be delayed in his return. He wanted to know how early he might be admitted to-morrow. He was full of "to-morrow;" and it is very evident that I have been full of it too ever since I entered the house, and learnt the extension of your plan, and all that had happened, or my seeing him could never have gone so entirely out of my head.'

CHAPTER 23

ONE day only had passed since Anne's conversation with Mrs Smith; but a keener interest had succeeded, and she was now so little touched by Mr Elliot's conduct, except by its effects in one quarter, that it became a matter of course the next morning, still to defer her explanatory visit in Rivers-street. She had promised to be with the Musgroves from breakfast to dinner. Her faith was plighted, and Mr Elliot's character, like the Sultaness Scheherazade's head, must live another day.

She could not keep her appointment punctually, however; the weather was unfavourable, and she had grieved over the rain on her friends' account, and felt it very much on her own, before she was able to attempt the walk. When she reached the White Hart, and made her way to the proper apartment, she found herself neither arriving quite in time, nor the first to arrive. The party before her were Mrs Musgrove, talking to Mrs Croft, and Captain Harville to Captain Wentworth, and she immediately heard that Mary and Henrietta, too impatient to wait, had gone out the moment it had cleared, but would be back again soon, and that the strictest injunctions had been left with Mrs Musgrove, to keep her there till they returned. She had only to submit, sit down, be outwardly composed, and feel herself plunged at once in all the agitations which she had merely laid her account of tasting a little before the morning closed. There was no delay, no waste of time. She was deep in the happiness of such misery, or the misery of such happiness, instantly. Two minutes after her entering the room, Captain Wentworth said,

'We will write the letter we were talking of, Harville, now, if you will give me materials.'

Materials were all at hand, on a separate table; he went to it, and nearly turning his back on them all, was engrossed by writing.

Mrs Musgrove was giving Mrs Croft the history of her eldest daughter's engagement, and just in that inconvenient tone of voice which was perfectly audible while it pretended to be a whisper. Anne felt that she did not belong to the conversation, and yet, as Captain Harville seemed thoughtful and not disposed to talk, she could not avoid hearing many undesirable particulars, such as 'how Mr Musgrove and my brother Hayter had met again and again to talk it over; what my brother Hayter had said one day, and what Mr Musgrove had proposed the next, and what had occurred to my sister Hayter, and what the young people had wished, and what I said at first I never could consent to, but was afterwards persuaded to think might do very well,' and a great deal in the same style of open-hearted communication – Minutiæ which, even with every advantage of taste and delicacy which good Mrs Musgrove could not give, could be properly interesting only to the principals. Mrs Croft was attending with great good humour, and whenever she spoke at all, it was very sensibly. Anne hoped the gentlemen might each be too much self-occupied to hear.

'And so, ma'am, all these things considered,' said Mrs Musgrove in her powerful whisper, 'though we could have wished it different, yet altogether we did not think it fair to stand out any longer; for Charles Hayter was quite wild about it, and Henrietta was pretty near as bad; and so we thought they had better marry at once, and make the best of it, as many others have done before them. At any rate, said I, it will be better than a long engagement.'

'That is precisely what I was going to observe,' cried Mrs Croft. 'I would rather have young people settle on a small income at once, and have to struggle with a few difficulties together, than be involved in a long engagement. I always think that no mutual –'

'Oh! dear Mrs Croft,' cried Mrs Musgrove, unable to let her finish her speech, 'there is nothing I so abominate for young people as a long engagement. It is what I always protested against for my children. It is all very well, I used to say, for young people to be engaged, if there is a certainty of their being able to marry in six months, or even in twelve, but a long engagement!'

'Yes, dear ma'am,' said Mrs Croft, 'or an uncertain engagement; an engagement which may be long. To begin without knowing that at such a time there will be the means of marrying,

I hold to be very unsafe and unwise, and what, I think, all parents should prevent as far as they can.'

Anne found an unexpected interest here. She felt its application to herself, felt it in a nervous thrill all over her, and at the same moment that her eyes instinctively glanced towards the distant table, Captain Wentworth's pen ceased to move, his head was raised, pausing, listening, and he turned round the next instant to give a look – one quick, conscious look at her.

The two ladies continued to talk, to re-urge the same admitted truths, and enforce them with such examples of the ill effect of a contrary practice, as had fallen within their observation, but Anne heard nothing distinctly; it was only a buzz of words in her ear, her mind was in confusion.

Captain Harville, who had in truth been hearing none of it, now left his seat, and moved to a window; and Anne seeming to watch him, though it was from thorough absence of mind, became gradually sensible that he was inviting her to join him where he stood. He looked at her with a smile, and a little motion of the head, which expressed, 'Come to me, I have something to say;' and the unaffected, easy kindness of manner which denoted the feelings of an older acquaintance than he really was, strongly enforced the invitation. She roused herself and went to him. The window at which he stood, was at the other end of the room from where the two ladies were sitting, and though nearer to Captain Wentworth's table, not very near. As she joined him, Captain Harville's countenance reassumed the serious, thoughtful expression which seemed its natural character.

'Look here,' said he, unfolding a parcel in his hand, and displaying a small miniature painting, 'do you know who that is?'

'Certainly, Captain Benwick.'

'Yes, and you may guess who it is for. But (in a deep tone) it was not done for her. Miss Elliot, do you remember our walking together at Lyme, and grieving for him? I little thought then – but no matter. This was drawn at the Cape. He met with a clever young German artist at the Cape, and in compliance with a promise to my poor sister, sat to him, and was bringing it home for her. And I have now the charge of getting it properly set for another! It was a commission to me! But who else was there to employ? I hope I can allow for him. I am not sorry, indeed, to make it over to another. He undertakes it – (looking towards Captain Wentworth) he is writing about it now.' And with a quivering lip he wound up the whole by adding, 'Poor Fanny! she would not have forgotten him so soon!'

'No,' replied Anne, in a low feeling voice. 'That I can easily believe.'

'It was not in her nature. She doated on him.'

'It would not be the nature of any woman who truly loved.'

Captain Harville smiled, as much as to say, 'Do you claim that for your sex?' and she answered the question, smiling also, 'Yes. We certainly do not forget you, so soon as you forget us. It is, perhaps, our fate rather than our merit. We cannot help ourselves. We live at home, quiet, confined, and our feelings prey upon us. You are forced on exertion. You have always a profession, pursuits, business of some sort or other, to take you back into the world immediately, and continual occupation and change soon weaken impressions.'

'Granting your assertion that the world does all this so soon for men, (which, however, I do not think I shall grant) it does not apply to Benwick. He has not been forced upon any exertion. The peace turned him on shore at the very moment, and he has been living with us, in our little family-circle, ever since.'

'True,' said Anne, 'very true; I did not recollect; but what shall we say now, Captain Harville? If the change be not from outward circumstances, it must be from within; it must be nature, man's nature, which has done the business for Captain Benwick.'

'No, no, it is not man's nature. I will not allow it to be more man's nature than woman's to be inconstant and forget those they do love, or have loved. I believe the reverse. I believe in a true analogy between our bodily frames and our mental; and that as our bodies are the strongest, so are our feelings; capable of bearing most rough usage, and riding out the heaviest weather.'

'Your feelings may be the strongest,' replied Anne, 'but the same spirit of analogy will authorise me to assert that ours are the most tender. Man is more robust than woman, but he is not longer-lived; which exactly explains my view of the nature of their attachments. Nay, it would be too hard upon you, if it were otherwise. You have difficulties, and privations, and dangers enough to struggle with. You are always labouring and toiling, exposed to every risk and hardship. Your home, country, friends, all quitted. Neither time, nor health, nor life, to be called your own. It would be too hard indeed' (with a faltering voice) 'if woman's feelings were to be added to all this.'

'We shall never agree upon this question' – Captain Harville was beginning to say, when a slight noise called their attention to Captain Wentworth's hitherto perfectly quiet division of the room. It was nothing more than that his pen had fallen down, but Anne was startled at finding him nearer than she supposed, and half inclined to suspect that the pen had only fallen, because he had been occupied by them, striving to catch sounds, which yet she did not think he could have caught.

'Have you finished your letter?' said Captain Harville.

'Not quite, a few lines more. I shall have done in five minutes.'

'There is no hurry on my side. I am only ready whenever you are. – I am in very good anchorage here,' (smiling at Anne) 'well supplied, and want for nothing. – No hurry for a signal at all. – Well, Miss Elliot,' (lowering his voice) 'as I was saying, we shall never agree I suppose upon this point. No man and woman would, probably. But let me observe that all histories are against you, all stories, prose and verse. If I had such a memory as Benwick, I could bring you fifty quotations in a moment on my side the argument, and I do not think I ever opened a book in my life which had not something to say upon woman's inconstancy. Songs and proverbs, all talk of woman's fickleness. But perhaps you will say, these were all written by men.'

'Perhaps I shall. – Yes, yes, if you please, no reference to examples in books. Men have had every advantage of us in telling their own story. Education has been theirs in so much higher a degree; the pen has been in their hands. I will not allow books to prove any thing.'

'But how shall we prove any thing?'

'We never shall. We never can expect to prove any thing upon such a point. It is a difference of opinion which does not admit of proof. We each begin probably with a little bias towards our own sex, and upon that bias build every circumstance in favour of it which has occurred within our own circle; many of which circumstances (perhaps those very cases which strike us the most) may be precisely such as cannot be brought forward without betraying a confidence, or in some respect saying what should not be said.'

'Ah!' cried Captain Harville, in a tone of strong feeling, 'if I could but make you comprehend what a man suffers when he takes a last look at his wife and children, and watches the boat that he has sent them off in, as long as it is in sight, and then turns away and says, "God knows whether we ever meet again!" And then, if I could convey to you the glow of his soul when he does see them again; when, coming back after a twelvemonth's absence perhaps, and obliged to put into another port, he calculates how soon it be possible to get them there, pretending to deceive himself, and saying, "They cannot be here till such a day," but all the while hoping for them twelve hours sooner, and seeing them arrive at last, as if Heaven had given them wings, by many hours sooner still! If I could explain to you all this, and all that a man can bear and do, and glories to do for the sake of these treasures of his existence! I speak, you know, only of such men as have hearts!' pressing his own with emotion.

'Oh!' cried Anne eagerly, 'I hope I do justice to all that is felt by you, and by those who resemble you. God forbid that I should undervalue the warm and faithful feelings of any of my fellow-creatures. I should deserve utter contempt if I dared to suppose that true attachment and constancy were known only by woman. No, I believe you capable of every thing great and good in your married lives. I believe you equal to every important exertion, and to every domestic forbearance, so long as – if I may be allowed the expression, so long as you have an object. I mean, while the woman you love lives, and lives for you. All the privilege I claim for my own sex (it is not a very enviable one, you need not covet it) is that of loving longest, when existence or when hope is gone.'

She could not immediately have uttered another sentence; her heart was too full, her breath too much oppressed.

'You are a good soul,' cried Captain Harville, putting his hand on her arm quite affectionately. 'There is no quarrelling with you. – And when I think of Benwick, my tongue is tied.'

Their attention was called towards the others. – Mrs Croft was taking leave.

'Here, Frederick, you and I part company, I believe,' said she. 'I am going home, and you have an engagement with your friend. – To-night we may have the pleasure of all meeting again, at your party,' (turning to Anne.) 'We had your sister's card yesterday, and I understood Frederick had a card too, though I did not see it – and you are disengaged, Frederick, are you not, as well as ourselves?'

Captain Wentworth was folding up a letter in great haste, and either could not or would not answer fully.

'Yes,' said he, 'very true; here we separate, but Harville and I shall soon be after you, that is, Harville, if you are ready, I am in half a minute. I know you will not be sorry to be off. I shall be at your service in half a minute.'

Mrs Croft left them, and Captain Wentworth, having sealed his letter with great rapidity, was indeed ready, and had even a hurried, agitated air, which shewed impatience to be gone. Anne knew not how to understand it. She had the kindest 'Good morning, God bless you,' from Captain Harville, but from him not a word, nor a look. He had passed out of the room without a look!

She had only time, however, to move closer to the table where he had been writing, when footsteps were heard returning; the door opened; it was himself. He begged their pardon, but he had forgotten his gloves, and instantly crossing the room to the writing table, and standing with his back towards Mrs Musgrove, he drew out a letter from under the scattered paper, placed it before Anne with eyes of glowing entreaty fixed on her for a moment, and hastily collecting his gloves, was again out of the room, almost before Mrs Musgrove was aware of his being in it – the work of an instant!

The revolution which one instant had made in Anne, was almost beyond expression. The letter, with a direction hardly legible, to 'Miss A. E. –.' was evidently the one which he had been folding so hastily. While supposed to be writing only to Captain Benwick, he had been also addressing her! On the contents of that letter depended all which this world could do for her! Any thing was possible, any thing might be defied rather than suspense. Mrs Musgrove had little arrangements of her own at her own table; to their protection she must trust, and sinking into the chair which he had occupied, succeeding to the very spot where he had leaned and written, her eyes devoured the following words:

'I can listen no longer in silence. I must speak to you by such means as are within my reach. You pierce my soul. I am half agony, half hope. Tell me not that I am too late, that such precious feelings are gone for ever. I offer myself to you again with a heart even more your own, than when you almost broke it eight years and a half ago. Dare not say that man forgets sooner than woman, that his love has an earlier death. I have loved none but you. Unjust I may have been, weak and resentful I have been, but never inconstant. You alone have brought me to Bath. For you alone I think and plan. – Have you not seen this? Can you fail to have understood my wishes? – I had not waited even these ten days, could I have read your feelings, as I think you must have penetrated mine. I can hardly write. I am every instant hearing something which overpowers me. You sink your voice, but I can distinguish the tones of that voice, when they would be lost on others. – Too good, too excellent creature! You do us justice indeed. You do believe that there is true attachment and constancy among men. Believe it to be most fervent, most undeviating in

'F. W.

'I must go, uncertain of my fate; but I shall return hither, or follow your party, as soon as possible. A word, a look will be enough to decide whether I enter your father's house this evening or never.'

Such a letter was not to be soon recovered from. Half an hour's solitude and reflection might have tranquillized her; but the ten minutes only, which now passed before she was interrupted, with all the restraints of her situation, could do nothing towards tranquillity. Every moment rather brought fresh agitation. It was an overpowering happiness. And before she was beyond the first stage of full sensation, Charles, Mary, and Henrietta all came in.

The absolute necessity of seeming like herself produced then an immediate struggle; but after a while she could do no more. She began not to understand a word they said, and was obliged to plead indisposition and excuse herself. They could then see that she looked very ill – were shocked and concerned – and would not stir without her for the world. This was dreadful! Would they only have gone away, and left her in the quiet possession of that room, it would have been her cure; but to have them all standing or waiting around her was distracting, and, in desperation, she said she would go home.

'By all means, my dear,' cried Mrs Musgrove, 'go home directly and take care of yourself, that you may be fit for the evening. I wish Sarah was here to doctor you, but I am no doctor myself. Charles, ring and order a chair. She must not walk.'

But the chair would never do. Worse than all! To lose the possibility of speaking two words to Captain Wentworth in the course of her quiet, solitary progress up the town (and she felt almost certain of meeting him) could not be borne. The chair was earnestly protested against; and Mrs Musgrove, who thought only of one sort of illness, having assured herself, with some anxiety, that there had been no fall in the case; that Anne had not, at any time lately, slipped down, and got a blow on her head; that she was perfectly convinced of having had no fall, could part with her cheerfully, and depend on finding her better at night.

Anxious to omit no possible precaution, Anne struggled, and said,

'I am afraid, ma'am, that it is not perfectly understood. Pray be so good as to mention to the other gentlemen that we hope to see your whole party this evening. I am afraid there has been some mistake; and I wish you particularly to assure Captain Harville, and Captain Wentworth, that we hope to see them both.'

'Oh! my dear, it is quite understood, I give you my word. Captain Harville has no thought but of going.'

'Do you think so? But I am afraid; and I should be so very sorry! Will you promise me to mention it, when you see them again? You will see them both again this morning, I dare say. Do promise me.'

'To be sure I will, if you wish it. Charles, if you see Captain Harville any where, remember to give Miss Anne's message. But indeed, my dear, you need not be uneasy. Captain Harville holds himself quite engaged, I'll answer for it; and Captain Wentworth the same, I dare say.'

Anne could do no more; but her heart prophesied some mischance, to damp the perfection of her felicity. It could not be very lasting, however. Even if he did not come to Camden-place himself, it would be in her power to send an intelligible sentence by Captain Harville.

Another momentary vexation occurred. Charles, in his real concern and good-nature, would go home with her; there was no preventing him. This was almost cruel! But she could not be long ungrateful; he was sacrificing an engagement at a gunsmith's to be of use to her; and she set off with him, with no feeling but gratitude apparent.

They were in Union-street, when a quicker step behind, a something of familiar sound, gave her two moments preparation for the sight of Captain Wentworth. He joined them; but, as if irresolute whether to join or to pass on, said nothing – only looked. Anne could command herself enough to receive that look, and not repulsively. The cheeks which had been pale now glowed, and the movements which had hesitated were decided. He walked by her side. Presently, struck by a sudden thought, Charles said,

'Captain Wentworth, which way are you going? only to Gay-street, or farther up the town?'

'I hardly know,' replied Captain Wentworth, surprised.

'Are you going as high as Belmont? Are you going near Camden-place? Because if you are, I shall have no scruple in asking you to take my place, and give Anne your arm to her father's door. She is rather done for this morning, and must not go so far without help. And I ought to be at that fellow's in the market-place. He promised me the sight of a capital gun he is just going to send off; said he would keep it unpacked to the last possible moment, that I might see it; and if I do not turn back now, I have no chance. By his description, a good deal like the second-sized double-barrel of mine, which you shot with one day, round Winthrop.'

There could not be an objection. There could be only a most proper alacrity, a most obliging compliance for public view; and smiles reined in and spirits dancing in private rapture. In half a minute, Charles was at the bottom of Union-street again, and the other two proceeding together; and soon words enough had passed between them to decide their direction towards the comparatively quiet and retired gravel-walk, where the power of conversation would make the present hour a blessing indeed; and prepare it for all the immortality [14] which the happiest recollections of their own future lives could bestow. There they exchanged again those feelings and those promises which had once before seemed to secure every thing, but which had been followed by so many, many years of division and estrangement. There they returned again into the past, more exquisitely happy, perhaps, in their re-union, than when it had been first projected; more tender, more tried, more fixed in a knowledge of each other's character, truth, and attachment; more equal to act, more justified in acting. And there, as they slowly paced the gradual ascent, heedless of every group around them, seeing neither sauntering politicians, bustling house-keepers, flirting girls, nor nursery-maids and children, they could indulge in those retrospections and acknowledgments, and especially in those explanations of what had directly preceded the present moment, which were so poignant and so ceaseless in interest. All the little variations of the last week were gone through; and of yesterday and to-day there could scarcely be an end.

She had not mistaken him. Jealousy of Mr Elliot had been the retarding weight, the doubt, the torment. That had begun to operate in the very hour of first meeting her in Bath; that had returned, after a short suspension, to ruin the concert; and that had influenced him in every thing he had said and done, or omitted to say and do, in the last four-and-twenty hours. It had been gradually yielding to the better hopes which her looks, or words, or actions occasionally encouraged; it had been vanquished at last by those sentiments and those tones which had reached him while she talked with Captain Harville; and under the irresistible governance of which he had seized a sheet of paper, and poured out his feelings.

Of what he had then written, nothing was to be retracted or qualified. He persisted in having loved none but her. She had never been supplanted. He never even believed himself to see her equal. Thus much indeed he was obliged to acknowledge – that he had been constant unconsciously, nay unintentionally; that he had meant to forget her, and believed it to be done. He had imagined himself indifferent, when he had only been angry; and he had been unjust to her merits, because he had been a sufferer from them. Her character was now fixed on his mind as perfection itself, maintaining the loveliest medium of fortitude and gentleness; but he was obliged to acknowledge that only at Uppercross had he learnt to do her justice, and only at Lyme had he begun to understand himself.

At Lyme, he had received lessons of more than one sort. The passing admiration of Mr Elliot had at least roused him, and the scenes on the Cobb, and at Captain Harville's, had fixed her superiority.

In his preceding attempts to attach himself to Louisa Musgrove (the attempts of angry pride), he protested that he had for ever felt it to be impossible; that he had not cared, could not care for Louisa; though, till that day, till the leisure for reflection which followed it, he had not understood the perfect excellence of the mind with which Louisa's could so ill bear a comparison; or the perfect, unrivalled hold it possessed over his own. There, he had learnt to distinguish between the steadiness of principle and the obstinacy of self-will, between the darings of heedlessness and the resolution of a collected mind. There, he had seen every thing to exalt in his estimation the woman he had lost, and there begun to deplore the pride, the folly, the madness of resentment, which had kept him from trying to regain her when thrown in his way.

From that period his penance had become severe. He had no sooner been free from the horror and remorse attending the first few days of Louisa's accident, no sooner begun to feel himself alive again, than he had begun to feel himself, though alive, not at liberty.

'I found,' said he, 'that I was considered by Harville an engaged man! That neither Harville nor his wife entertained a doubt of our mutual attachment. I was startled and shocked. To a degree, I could contradict this instantly; but, when I began to reflect that others might have felt the same – her own family, nay, perhaps herself, I was no longer at my own disposal I was hers in honour if she wished it. I had been unguarded. I had not thought seriously on this subject before. I had not considered that my excessive intimacy must have its danger of ill consequence in many ways; and that I had no right to be trying whether I could attach myself to either of the girls, at the risk of raising even an unpleasant report, were there no other ill effects. I had been grossly wrong, and must abide the consequences.'

He found too late, in short, that he had entangled himself; and that precisely as he became fully satisfied of his not caring for Louisa at all, he must regard himself as bound to her, if her sentiments for him were what the Harvilles supposed. It determined him to leave Lyme, and await her complete recovery elsewhere. He would gladly weaken, by any fair means, whatever feelings or speculations concerning him might exist; and he went, therefore, to his brother's, meaning after a while to return to Kellynch, and act as circumstances might require.

'I was six weeks with Edward,' said he, 'and saw him happy. I could have no other pleasure. I deserved none. He enquired after you very particularly; asked even if you were personally altered, little suspecting that to my eye you could never alter.'

Anne smiled, and let it pass. It was too pleasing a blunder for a reproach. It is something for a woman to be assured, in her eight-and-twentieth year, that she has not lost one charm of earlier youth : but the value of such homage was inexpressibly increased to Anne, by comparing it with former words, and feeling it to be the result, not the cause of a revival of his warm attachment.

He had remained in Shropshire, lamenting the blindness of his own pride, and the blunders of his own calculations, till at once released from Louisa by the astonishing and felicitous intelligence of her engagement with Benwick.

'Here,' said he, 'ended the worst of my state; for now I could at least put myself in the way of happiness, I could exert myself, I could do something. But to be waiting so long in inaction, and waiting only for evil, had been dreadful. Within the first five minutes I said, "I will be at Bath on Wednesday," and I was. Was it unpardonable to think it worth my while to come? and to

245

arrive with some degree of hope? You were single. It was possible that you might retain the feelings of the past, as I did; and one encouragement happened to be mine. I could never doubt that you would be loved and sought by others, but I knew to a certainty that you had refused one man at least, of better pretensions than myself : and I could not help often saying, Was this for me?'

Their first meeting in Milsom-street afforded much to be said, but the concert still more. That evening seemed to be made up of exquisite moments. The moment of her stepping forward in the octagon-room to speak to him, the moment of Mr Elliot's appearing and tearing her away, and one or two subsequent moments, marked by returning hope or increasing despondence, were dwelt on with energy.

'To see you,' cried he, 'in the midst of those who could not be my well-wishers, to see your cousin close by you, conversing and smiling, and feel all the horrible eligibilities and proprieties of the match ! To consider it as the certain wish of every being who could hope to influence you ! Even, if your own feelings were reluctant or indifferent, to consider what powerful supports would be his ! Was it not enough to make the fool of me which I appeared? How could I look on without agony? Was not the very sight of the friend who sat behind you, was not the recollection of what had been, the knowledge of her influence, the indelible, immoveable impression of what persuasion had once done – was it not all against me?'

'You should have distinguished,' replied Anne. 'You should not have suspected me now; the case so different, and my age so different. If I was wrong in yielding to persuasion once, remember that it was to persuasion exerted on the side of safety, not of risk. When I yielded, I thought it was to duty; but no duty could be called in aid here. In marrying a man indifferent to me, all risk would have been incurred, and all duty violated.'

'Perhaps I ought to have reasoned thus,' he replied, 'but I could not. I could not derive benefit from the late knowledge I had acquired of your character. I could not bring it into play : it was overwhelmed, buried, lost in those earlier feelings which I had been smarting under year after year. I could think of you only as one who had yielded, who had given me up, who had been in-

fluenced by any one rather than by me. I saw you with the very
person who had guided you in that year of misery. I had no
reason to believe her of less authority now. – The force of habit
was to be added.'

'I should have thought,' said Anne, 'that my manner to yourself might have spared you much or all of this.'

'No, no !' your manner might be only the ease which your engagement to another man would give. I left you in this belief; and
yet – I was determined to see you again. My spirits rallied with
the morning, and I felt that I had still a motive for remaining
here.'

At last Anne was at home again, and happier than any one in
that house could have conceived. All the surprise and suspense,
and every other painful part of the morning dissipated by this
conversation, she re-entered the house so happy as to be obliged to
find an alloy in some momentary apprehensions of its being impossible to last. An interval of meditation, serious and grateful,
was the best corrective of every thing dangerous in such high-
wrought felicity; and she went to her room, and grew steadfast
and fearless in the thankfulness of her enjoyment.

The evening came, the drawing-rooms were lighted up, the
company assembled. It was but a card-party, it was but a mixture
of those who had never met before, and those who met too often –
a common-place business, too numerous for intimacy, too small
for variety; but Anne had never found an evening shorter. Glowing and lovely in sensibility and happiness, and more generally
admired than she thought about or cared for, she had cheerful or
forbearing feelings for every creature around her. Mr Elliot was
there; she avoided, but she could pity him. The Wallises; she had
amusement in understanding them. Lady Dalrymple and Miss
Carteret; they would soon be innoxious cousins to her. She cared
not for Mrs Clay, and had nothing to blush for in the public
manners of her father and sister. With the Musgroves, there was
the happy chat of perfect ease; with Captain Harville, the kind-
hearted intercourse of brother and sister; with Lady Russell,
attempts at conversation, which a delicious consciousness cut
short; with Admiral and Mrs Croft, every thing of peculiar cordiality and fervent interest, which the same consciousness sought

to conceal; – and with Captain Wentworth, some moments of communication continually occurring, and always the hope of more, and always the knowledge of his being there!

It was in one of these short meetings, each apparently occupied in admiring a fine display of green-house plants, that she said –

'I have been thinking over the past, and trying impartially to judge of the right and wrong, I mean with regard to myself; and I must believe that I was right, much as I suffered from it, that I was perfectly right in being guided by the friend whom you will love better than you do now. To me, she was in the place of a parent. Do not mistake me, however. I am not saying that she did not err in her advice. It was, perhaps, one of those cases in which advice is good or bad only as the event decides; and for my-self, I certainly never should, in any circumstance of tolerable similarity, give such advice. But I mean, that I was right in sub-mitting to her, and that if I had done otherwise, I should have suffered more in continuing the engagement than I did even in giving it up, because I should have suffered in my conscience. I have now, as far as such a sentiment is allowable in human nature, nothing to reproach myself with; and if I mistake not, a strong sense of duty is no bad part of a woman's portion.'

He looked at her, looked at Lady Russell, and looking again at her, replied, as if in cool deliberation,

'Not yet. But there are hopes of her being forgiven in time. I trust to being in charity with her soon. But I too have been thinking over the past, and a question has suggested itself, whether there may not have been one person more my enemy even than that lady? My own self. Tell me if, when I returned to England in the year eight, with a few thousand pounds, and was posted into the Laconia,[15] if I had then written to you, would you have answered my letter? would you, in short, have re-newed the engagement then?'

'Would I!' was all her answer; but the accent was decisive enough.

'Good God!' he cried, 'you would! It is not that I did not think of it, or desire it, as what could alone crown all my other success. But I was proud, too proud to ask again. I did not understand you. I shut my eyes, and would not understand you, or do you justice.

This is a recollection which ought to make me forgive every one sooner than myself. Six years of separation and suffering might have been spared. It is a sort of pain, too, which is new to me. I have been used to the gratification of believing myself to earn every blessing that I enjoyed. I have valued myself on honourable toils and just rewards. Like other great men under reverses,' he added with a smile, 'I must endeavour to subdue my mind to my fortune. I must learn to brook being happier than I deserve.'

CHAPTER 24

WHO can be in doubt of what followed? When any two young people take it into their heads to marry, they are pretty sure by perseverance to carry their point, be they ever so poor, or ever so imprudent, or ever so little likely to be necessary to each other's ultimate comfort. This may be bad morality to conclude with, but I believe it to be truth; and if such parties succeed, how should a Captain Wentworth and an Anne Elliot, with the advantage of maturity of mind, consciousness of right, and one independent fortune between them, fail of bearing down every opposition? They might in fact have borne down a great deal more than they met with, for there was little to distress them beyond the want of graciousness and warmth. – Sir Walter made no objection, and Elizabeth did nothing worse than look cold and unconcerned. Captain Wentworth, with five-and-twenty thousand pounds, and as high in his profession as merit and activity could place him,[16] was no longer nobody. He was now esteemed quite worthy to address the daughter of a foolish spendthrift baronet, who had not had principle or sense enough to maintain himself in the situation in which Providence had placed him, and who could give his daughter at present but a small part of the share of ten thousand pounds which must be hers hereafter.

Sir Walter indeed, though he had no affection for Anne, and no vanity flattered, to make him really happy on the occasion, was very far from thinking it a bad match for her. On the contrary, when he saw more of Captain Wentworth, saw him repeatedly by daylight and eyed him well, he was very much struck by his personal claims, and felt that his superiority of appearance might be not unfairly balanced against her superiority of rank; and all this, assisted by his well-sounding name, enabled Sir Walter at last to prepare his pen with a very good grace for the insertion of the marriage in the volume of honour.

The only one among them, whose opposition of feeling could

excite any serious anxiety, was Lady Russell. Anne knew that Lady Russell must be suffering some pain in understanding and relinquishing Mr Elliot, and be making some struggles to become truly acquainted with, and do justice to Captain Wentworth. This however was what Lady Russell had now to do. She must learn to feel that she had been mistaken with regard to both; that she had been unfairly influenced by appearances in each; that because Captain Wentworth's manners had not suited her own ideas, she had been too quick in suspecting them to indicate a character of dangerous impetuosity; and that because Mr Elliot's manners had precisely pleased her in their propriety and correctness, their general politeness and suavity, she had been too quick in receiving them as the certain result of the most correct opinions and well regulated mind. There was nothing less for Lady Russell to do, than to admit that she had been pretty completely wrong, and to take up a new set of opinions and of hopes.

There is a quickness of perception in some, a nicety in the discernment of character, a natural penetration, in short, which no experience in others can equal, and Lady Russell had been less gifted in this part of understanding than her young friend. But she was a very good woman, and if her second object was to be sensible and well-judging, her first was to see Anne happy. She loved Anne better than she loved her own abilities; and when the awkwardness of the beginning was over, found little hardship in attaching herself as a mother to the man who was securing the happiness of her other child.

Of all the family, Mary was probably the one most immediately gratified by the circumstance. It was creditable to have a sister married, and she might flatter herself with having been greatly instrumental to the connexion, by keeping Anne with her in the autumn; and as her own sister must be better than her husband's sisters, it was very agreeable that Captain Wentworth should be a richer man than either Captain Benwick or Charles Hayter. – She had something to suffer perhaps when they came into contact again, in seeing Anne restored to the rights of seniority, and the mistress of a very pretty landaulette; but she had a future to look forward to, of powerful consolation. Anne had no Uppercross-hall before her, no landed estate, no head-ship of a family; and if they could but keep Captain Wentworth from being made a baronet, she would not change situations with Anne.

It would be well for the eldest sister if she were equally satis-fied with her situation, for a change is not very probable there. She had soon the mortification of seeing Mr Elliot withdraw; and no one of proper condition has since presented himself to raise even the unfounded hopes which sunk with him.

The news of his cousin Anne's engagement burst on Mr Elliot most unexpectedly. It deranged his best plan of domestic happi-ness, his best hope of keeping Sir Walter single by the watchful-ness which a son-in-law's rights would have given. But, though discomfited and disappointed, he could still do something for his own interest and his own enjoyment. He soon quitted Bath; and on Mrs Clay's quitting it likewise soon afterwards, and being next heard of as established under his protection in London, it was evident how double a game he had been playing, and how determined he was to save himself from being cut out by one artful woman, at least.

Mrs Clay's affections had overpowered her interest, and she had sacrificed, for the young man's sake, the possibility of schem-ing longer for Sir Walter. She has abilities, however, as well as affections; and it is now a doubtful point whether his cunning, or hers, may finally carry the day; whether, after pre-venting her from being the wife of Sir Walter, he may not be wheedled and caressed at last into making her the wife of Sir William.

It cannot be doubted that Sir Walter and Elizabeth were shocked and mortified by the loss of their companion, and the dis-covery of their deception in her. They had their great cousins, to be sure, to resort to for comfort; but they must long feel that to flatter and follow others, without being flattered and followed in turn, is but a state of half enjoyment.

Anne, satisfied at a very early period of Lady Russell's meaning to love Captain Wentworth as she ought, had no other alloy to the happiness of her prospects than what arose from the con-sciousness of having no relations to bestow on him which a man of sense could value. There she felt her own inferiority keenly. The disproportion in their fortune was nothing; it did not give her a moment's regret; but to have no family to receive and estimate him properly; nothing of respectability, of harmony, of good-will to offer in return for all the worth and all the prompt welcome which met her in his brothers and sisters,[17] was a source of as lively pain as her mind could well be sensible of, under circumstances of otherwise strong felicity. She had but two friends in the world to add to his list, Lady Russell and Mrs Smith. To those, however, he was very well disposed to attach himself. Lady Russell, in spite of all her former transgressions, he could now value from his heart. While he was not obliged to say that he believed her to have been right in originally dividing them, he was ready to say almost every thing else in her favour; and as for Mrs Smith, she had claims of various kinds to recommend her quickly and permanently.

Her recent good offices by Anne had been enough in themselves; and their marriage, instead of depriving her of one friend, secured her two. She was their earliest visitor in their settled life; and Captain Wentworth, by putting her in the way of recovering her husband's property in the West Indies; by writing for her, acting for her, and seeing her through all the petty difficulties of the case, with the activity and exertion of a fearless man and a determined friend, fully requited the services which she had rendered, or ever meant to render, to his wife.

Mrs Smith's enjoyments were not spoiled by this improvement of income, with some improvement of health, and the acquisition of such friends to be often with, for her cheerfulness and mental alacrity did not fail her; and while these prime supplies of good remained, she might have bid defiance even to greater accessions of worldly prosperity. She might have been absolutely rich and perfectly healthy, and yet be happy. Her spring of felicity was in the glow of her spirits, as her friend Anne's was in the warmth of her heart. Anne was tenderness itself, and she had the full worth of it in Captain Wentworth's affection. His profession was all that could ever make her friends wish that tenderness less; the dread of a future war all that could dim her sunshine. She gloried in being a sailor's wife, but she must pay the tax of quick alarm for belonging to that profession which is, if possible, more distinguished in its domestic virtues than in its national importance.

THE END

The cancelled Chapter of Persuasion
(for which Chapters 22 and 23 were substituted)

WITH all this knowledge of Mr Elliot and this authority to impart it, Anne left Westgate Buildings, her mind deeply busy in revolving what she had heard, feeling, thinking, recalling, and foreseeing everything, shocked at Mr Elliot, sighing over future Kellynch, and pained for Lady Russell, whose confidence in him had been entire. The embarrassment which must be felt from this hour in his presence! How to behave to him? How to get rid of him? What to do by any of the party at home? Where to be blind? Where to be active? It was altogether a confusion of images and doubts – a perplexity, an agitation which she could not see the end of. And she was in Gay Street, and still so much engrossed that she started on being addressed by Admiral Croft, as if he were a person unlikely to be met there. It was within a few steps of his own door.

'You are going to call upon my wife,' said he. 'She will be very glad to see you.'

Anne denied it.

'No! she really had not time, she was in her way home;' but while she spoke the Admiral had stepped back and knocked at the door, calling out,

'Yes, yes; do go in; she is all alone; go in and rest yourself.'

Anne felt so little disposed at this time to be in company of any sort, that it vexed her to be thus constrained, but she was obliged to stop.

'Since you are so very kind,' said she, 'I will just ask Mrs Croft how she does, but I really cannot stay five minutes. You are sure she is quite alone?'

The possibility of Captain Wentworth had occurred; and most fearfully anxious was she to be assured – either that he was within, or that he was not – *which* might have been a question.

'Oh yes! quite alone, nobody but her mantuamaker with her,

and they have been shut up together this half-hour, so it must be over soon.'

'Her mantuamaker! Then I am sure my calling now would be most inconvenient. Indeed you must allow me to leave my card and be so good as to explain it afterwards to Mrs Croft.'

'No, no, not at all – not at all – she will be very happy to see you. Mind, I will not swear that she has not something particular to say to you, but *that* will all come out in the right place. I give no hints. Why, Miss Elliot, we begin to hear strange things of you (smiling in her face). But you have not much the look of it, as grave as a little judge!'

Anne blushed.

'Aye, aye, that will do. Now, it is right. I thought we were not mistaken.'

She was left to guess at the direction of his suspicions; the first wild idea had been of some disclosure from his brother-in-law, but she was ashamed the next moment, and felt how far more probable that he should be meaning Mr Elliot. The door was opened, and the man evidently beginning to *deny* his mistress, when the sight of his master stopped him. The Admiral enjoyed the joke exceedingly. Anne thought his triumph over Stephen rather too long. At last, however, he was able to invite her up stairs, and stepping before her said, 'I will just go up with you myself and show you in. I cannot stay because I must go to the Post-Office, but if you will only sit down for five minutes I am sure Sophy will come, and you will find nobody to disturb you – there is nobody but Frederick here,' opening the door as he spoke. Such a person to be passed over as a nobody to *her*! After being allowed to feel quite secure, indifferent, at her ease, to have it burst on her that she was to be the next moment in the same room with him! No time for recollection! for planning behaviour or regulating manners! There was time only to turn pale before she had passed through the door, and met the astonished eyes of Captain Wentworth, who was sitting by the fire, pretending to read, and prepared for no greater surprise than the Admiral's hasty return.

Equally unexpected was the meeting on each side. There was nothing to be done, however, but to stifle feelings, and be quietly polite, and the Admiral was too much on the alert to leave any troublesome pause. He repeated again what he had said before about his wife and everybody, insisted on Anne's sitting down and being perfectly comfortable – was sorry he must leave her himself, but was sure Mrs Croft would be down very soon, and would go upstairs and give her notice directly. Anne *was* sitting down, but now she arose again – to entreat him not to interrupt Mrs Croft and re-urge the wish of going away and calling another time. But the Admiral would not hear of it; and if she did not return to the charge with unconquerable perseverance, or did not with a more passive determination walk quietly out of the room (as certainly she might have done), may she not be pardoned? If she *had* no horror of a few minutes' tête-à-tête with Captain Wentworth, may she not be pardoned for not wishing to give him the idea that she had? She reseated herself, and the Admiral took leave, but on reaching the door, said –

'Frederick, a word with *you* if you please.'

Captain Wentworth went to him, and instantly, before they were well out of the room, the Admiral continued –

'As I am going to leave you together, it is but fair I should give you something to talk of; and so, if you please –'

Here the door was very firmly closed, she could guess by which of the two – and she lost entirely what immediately followed, but it was impossible for her not to distinguish parts of the rest, for the Admiral, on the strength of the door's being shut, was speaking without any management of voice, though she could hear his companion trying to check him. She could not doubt their being speaking of her. She heard her own name and Kellynch repeatedly. She was very much distressed. She knew not what to do, or what to expect, and among other agonies felt the possibility of Captain Wentworth's not returning into the room at all, which, after her consenting to stay, would have been – too bad for language. They seemed to be talking of the Admiral's lease of Kellynch. She heard him say something of the lease being signed – or not signed – *that* was not likely to be a very agitating subject, but then followed –

'I hate to be at an uncertainty. I must know at once. Sophy thinks the same.'

Then in a lower tone Captain Wentworth seemed remonstrating, wanting to be excused, wanting to put something off.

'Phoo, phoo,' answered the Admiral, 'now is the time; if you will not speak, I will stop and speak myself.'

'Very well, sir, very well, sir,' followed with some impatience from his companion, opening the door as he spoke –

'You will then, you promise you will?' replied the Admiral in all the power of his natural voice, unbroken even by one thin door.

'Yes, sir, yes.' And the Admiral was hastily left, the door was closed, and the moment arrived in which Anne was alone with Captain Wentworth.

She could not attempt to see how he looked, but he walked immediately to a window as if irresolute and embarrassed, and for about the space of five seconds she repented what she had done – censured it as unwise, blushed over it as indelicate. She longed to be able to speak of the weather or the concert, but could only compass the relief of taking a newspaper in her hand. The distressing pause was over, however; he turned round in half a minute, and coming towards the table where she sat, said in a voice of effort and constraint –

'You must have heard too much already, Madam, to be in any doubt of my having promised Admiral Croft to speak to you on some particular subject, and this conviction determines me to do it, however repugnant to my – to all my sense of propriety to be taking so great a liberty! You will acquit me of impertinence I trust, by considering me as speaking only for another, and speaking by necessity; and the Admiral is a man who can never be thought impertinent by one who knows him as you do. His intentions are always the kindest and the best, and you will perceive that he is actuated by none other in the application which I am now, with – with very peculiar feelings – obliged to make.' He stopped, but merely to recover breath, not seeming to expect any answer. Anne listened as if her life depended on the issue of his speech. He proceeded with a forced alacrity :–

'The Admiral, Madam, was this morning confidently informed that you were – upon my word, I am quite at a loss, ashamed (breathing and speaking quick) – the awkwardness of *giving* information of this sort to one of the parties – you can be at no loss to understand me. It was very confidently said that Mr Elliot – that everything was settled in the family for a union between Mr Elliot and yourself. It was added that you were to live at Kellynch – that Kellynch was to be given up. This the Admiral knew could not be correct. But it occurred to him that it might be the *wish* of the parties. And my commission from him, Madam, is to say, that if the family wish is such, his lease of Kellynch shall be cancelled, and he and my sister will provide themselves with another home, without imagining themselves to be doing any-thing which under similar circumstances would not be done for *them*. This is all, Madam. A very few words in reply from you will be sufficient. That I should be the person commissioned on this subject is extraordinary ! and believe me, Madam, it is no less painful. A very few words, however, will put an end to the awkwardness and distress we may *both* be feeling.'

Anne spoke a word or two, but they were unintelligible; and before she could command herself, he added, 'If you will only tell me that the Admiral may address a line to Sir Walter, it will be enough. Pronounce only the words, *he may*. I shall immediately follow him with your message.' This was spoken, as with a forti-tude which seemed to meet the message.

'No, Sir,' said Anne; 'there is no message. You are misin – the Admiral is misinformed. I do justice to the kindness of his inten-tions, but he is quite mistaken. There is no truth in any such report.'

He was a moment silent. She turned her eyes towards him for the first time since his re-entering the room. His colour was vary-ing, and he was looking at her with all the power and keenness which she believed no other eyes than his possessed.

'No truth in any such report?' he repeated. 'No truth in any *part* of it?' 'None.'

He had been standing by a chair, enjoying the relief of leaning on it, or of playing with it. He now sat down, drew it a little nearer to her, and looked with an expression which had some-thing more than penetration in it – something softer. Her countenance did not discourage. It was a silent but a very power-ful dialogue; on his side supplication, on hers acceptance. Still a little nearer, and a hand taken and pressed; and 'Anne, my own dear Anne!' bursting forth in the fulness of exquisite feeling, – and all suspense and indecision were over. They were re-united. They were restored to all that had been lost. They were carried back to the past with only an increase of attachment and confidence, and only such a flutter of present delight as made them little fit for the interruption of Mrs Croft when she joined them not long afterwards. *She*, probably, in the observations of the next ten minutes saw something to suspect; and though it was hardly possible for a woman of her description to wish the mantuamaker had imprisoned her longer, she might be very likely wishing for some excuse to run about the house, some storm to break the windows above, or a summons to the Admiral's shoemaker below. Fortune favoured them all, however, in another way, in a gentle, steady rain, just happily set in as the Admiral returned and Anne rose to go. She was earnestly invited to stay dinner. A note was despatched to Camden Place, and she staid – staid till ten at night; and during that time the husband and wife, either by the wife's contrivance, or by simply going on in their usual way, were frequently out of the room together – gone upstairs to hear a noise, or downstairs to settle their accounts, or upon the landing place to trim the lamp. And these precious moments were turned to so good an account that all the most anxious feelings of the past were gone through. Before they parted at night, Anne had the felicity of being assured that in the first place (so far from being altered for the worse), she had gained inexpressibly in personal loveliness; and that as to character, hers was now fixed on his mind as *perfection* itself, maintaining the just medium of fortitude and gentleness – that he had never ceased to love and prefer her, though it had been only at Uppercross that he had learnt to do her justice, and only at Lyme that he had begun to understand his own sensations; that at Lyme he had received lessons of more than one kind – the passing admiration of Mr Elliot had at least *roused* him, and the scene on the Cobb, and at Captain Harville's, had fixed her superiority. In his preceding *attempts* to attach himself to Louisa Musgrove (the attempts of anger and pique), he protested that he had continually felt the impossibility of really caring for Louisa, though till *that day*, till the leisure for reflection which followed it, he had not under-stood the perfect excellence of the mind with which Louisa's could so ill bear a comparison; or the perfect, the unrivalled hold it possessed over his own. There he had learnt to distinguish between the steadiness of principle and the obstinacy of self-will, between the darings of heedlessness and the resolution of a col-lected mind; there he had seen everything to exalt in his estima-tion the woman he had lost, and there begun to deplore the pride, the folly, the madness of resentment, which had kept him from trying to regain her when thrown in his way. From that period to the present had his penance been the most severe. He had no sooner been free from the horror and remorse attending the first few days of Louisa's accident, no sooner begun to feel himself alive again, than he had begun to feel himself, though alive, not at liberty.

He found that he was considered by his friend Harville as an engaged man. The Harvilles entertained not a doubt of a mutual attachment between him and Louisa; and though this to a degree was contradicted instantly, it yet made him feel that perhaps by *her* family, by everybody, by *herself* even, the same idea might be held, and that he was not *free* in honour, though if such were to be the conclusion, too free alas! in heart. He had never thought justly on this subject before, he had not sufficiently considered that his excessive intimacy at Uppercross must have its danger of ill consequence in many ways; and that while trying whether he could attach himself to either of the girls, he might be exciting unpleasant reports if not raising unrequited regard.

He found too late that he had entangled himself, and that pre-cisely as he became thoroughly satisfied of his not *caring* for Louisa at all, he must regard himself as bound to her if her feel-ings for him were what the Harvilles supposed. It determined him to leave Lyme, and await her perfect recovery elsewhere. He would gladly weaken by any *fair* means whatever sentiments or speculations concerning him might exist; and he went therefore into Shropshire, meaning after a while to return to the Crofts at Kellynch, and act as he found requisite.

He had remained in Shropshire, lamenting the blindness of

his own pride and the blunders of his own calculations, till at once released from Louisa by the astonishing felicity of her engagement with Benwick.

Bath – Bath had instantly followed in *thought*, and not long after in *fact*. To Bath – to arrive with hope, to be torn by jealousy at the first sight of Mr Elliot; to experience all the changes of each at the concert; to be miserable by this morning's circumstantial report, to be now more happy than language could express, or any heart but his own be capable of.

He was very eager and very delightful in the description of what he had felt at the concert; the evening seemed to have been made up of exquisite moments. The moment of her stepping forward in the octagon room to speak to him, the moment of Mr Elliot's appearing and tearing her away, and one or two subsequent moments, marked by returning hope or increasing despondency, were all dwelt on with energy.

'To see you,' cried he, 'in the midst of those who could not be *my* well-wishers; to see your cousin close by you, conversing and smiling, and feel all the horrible eligibilities and proprieties of the match! To consider it as the certain wish of every being who could hope to influence you! Even if your own feelings were reluctant or indifferent, to consider what powerful support would be his! Was it not enough to make the fool of me which I appeared? How could I look on without agony? Was not the very sight of the friend who sat behind you; was not the recollection of what had been, the knowledge of her influence, the indelible, immovable impression of what persuasion had once done – was it not all against me?'

'You should have distinguished,' replied Anne. 'You should not have suspected me now; the case so different, and my age so different. If I was wrong in yielding to persuasion once, remember it was to persuasion exerted on the side of safety, not of risk. When I yielded, I thought it was to duty; but no duty could be called in aid here. In marrying a man indifferent to me, all risk would have been incurred, and all duty violated.'

'Perhaps I ought to have reasoned thus,' he replied; 'but I could not. I could not derive benefit from the late knowledge I had acquired of your character. I could not bring it into play; it was overwhelmed, buried, lost in those earlier feelings which I had been smarting under year after year. I could think of you only as one who had yielded, who had given me up, who had been influenced by anyone rather than by me. I saw you with the very person who had guided you in that year of misery. I had no reason to believe her of less authority now. The force of habit was to be added.'

'I should have thought,' said Anne, 'that my manner to yourself might have spared you much or all of this.'

'No, no! Your manner might be only the ease which your engagement to another man would give. I left you with this belief; and yet – I was determined to see you again. My spirits rallied with the morning, and I felt that I had still a motive for remaining here. The Admiral's news, indeed, was a revulsion; since that moment I have been decided what to do, and had it been confirmed, this would have been my last day in Bath.'

There was time for all this to pass, with such interruptions only as enhanced the charm of the communication, and Bath could hardly contain any other two beings at once so rationally and so rapturously happy as during that evening occupied the sofa of Mrs Croft's drawing-room in Gay Street.

Captain Wentworth had taken care to meet the Admiral as he returned into the house, to satisfy him as to Mr Elliot and Kellynch; and the delicacy of the Admiral's good-nature kept him from saying another word on the subject to Anne. He was quite concerned lest he might have been giving her pain by touching on a tender part – who could say? She might be liking her cousin better than he liked her; and indeed, upon recollection, if they had been to marry at all, why should they have waited so long? When the evening closed, it is probable that the Admiral received some new ideas from his wife, whose particularly friendly manner in parting with her gave Anne the gratifying persuasion of her seeing and approving. It had been such a day to Anne; the hours which had passed since her leaving Camden Place had done so much! She was almost bewildered – almost too happy in looking back. It was necessary to sit up half the night, and lie awake the remainder, to comprehend with composure her present state, and pay for the overplus of bliss by headache and fatigue.

[*Then followed Chapter 24 of the present edition.*]

A Memoir of Jane Austen

BY HER NEPHEW
J. E. AUSTEN-LEIGH,
VICAR OF BRAY,
BERKS

INTRODUCTION

A GENERATION removed far enough from the Victorians to feel less of the dislike they engendered in their immediate successors can read J. E. Austen-Leigh's *Memoir* of his aunt with the discrimination it deserves and recognize in it, despite limitations of frankness and understanding, one of those pioneering biographies to which the meticulous search of later scholarship has added only a little. It forms a bridge between her time and the late Victorians and Edwardians, whose view of her and her work it helped to shape. When it was written, just over fifty years after her death, Regency society had gone and with it had gone to a great extent the sense (especially evident in *Mansfield Park* but present in most of Jane Austen's novels) that moral values had to be sustained against the threat of influential example. Society near the Court had turned its official back on vice, and that now belonged to the lower orders whose example had no dangerous gilding. In spite of a personal humility that seems genuine, Austen-Leigh writes with staggering complacency of the material and moral advances his generation had achieved; he tends to assimilate his aunt's work to his contemporaries' outlook rather than point the contrast, and he thus contributed to the idea that her works were all charm and urbane comment on a society in which she felt at ease.

He also offers an idealized view of her life within her family and immediate circle of friends. When he wrote the *Memoir* he was 71 and under strong persuasion from other members of the family towards reticence and discretion. He followed the family practice of completely ignoring the existence of her defective or handicapped brother and he played down her love affairs. Her sister Cassandra had done much to the same end by her ruthless destructions and excisions amongst the letters. But the chief responsibility for this polite conspiracy to idealize her situation must rest with Jane Austen herself; Cassandra's censorship was in the spirit of her sister's own tact and gratitude as a poor relation and adored spinster aunt and the patient daughter of a mother who was constantly unwell (and lived to be 88). No one who reads the *Memoir* can doubt that she followed this programme naturally and well and that it reflected part of her personality. It is equally evident that the novels would not have been what they are unless she had at the same time been a very different person.

The slight pieces of evidence for supplementing Austen-Leigh's account have been scrupulously assembled and sifted by R. W. Chapman (*Jane Austen: Facts and Problems,* Oxford, 1948). But there is not a lot to add to the *Memoir* factually. It is possible to make out that the developing attachment between her and Tom Lefroy was more serious and that its breaking in 1796 hurt her more than Austen-Leigh suggests. In 1798 she evidently attracted, but apparently was not attracted by, a Mr Blackall of Emmanuel, who later got a college living and married someone else. In the summer of 1802, during a visit to Teignmouth, there occurred the meeting, described briefly in the *Memoir*, with a man who was so much attracted by her, and she by him, that Cassandra thought it would lead to marriage. They were expecting to see him again but heard from his brother – how soon is uncertain – that he had died. In the autumn of the same year she received a proposal. Austen-Leigh's brief reference to the gentleman whose addressses she declined conceals the more agitated incident of her visit in 1802 to Manydown, an estate near Steventon, where Harris Bigg Wither, the twenty-one-year-old heir, proposed to her (she being about six years older) and was accepted. But the next morning she withdrew her consent, and she and Cassandra returned at once to Steventon, upset but giving no explanation and insisting that their brother, with whom they were staying, should drive them home to Bath next day. In spite of the uncertainties, and the determination of the family to make out that Jane Austen was never seriously unhappy, there is every reason to conclude that in her early and middle twenties she went through the agitations that those years commonly bring, that she experienced disappointment in love and that she refused marriage without it.

Jane Austen's serious creative work emerged gradually from the playful exercises in fiction that she offered for the entertainment of her family. Early versions of *Sense and Sensibility*, *Pride and Prejudice* and *Northanger Abbey* were written between 1796 and 1799. Since even in its final form the last of these is the least mature of her finished novels we can be sure that the other two were very different in their early form from what they became on publication many years later. The story that *Sense and Sensibility* existed first in the form of letters is improbable; it derives solely from a note made at the age of 64 by a niece who was not born until 1805. But she may have heard this said of *Pride and Prejudice*, in which an original letter form can much more plausibly be traced. Jane Austen's father did try in 1797 to get *Pride and Prejudice* (then called *First Impressions*) published, but with no success. There is no record of her writing during the next four years. They included the move to Bath in 1801 (which is thought to have been very unwelcome to her), the abortive romance at Teignmouth and the proposal from Bigg Wither. But in 1803 she put her Bath novel (then called *Susan*, now *Northanger Abbey*) into more finished form and managed with her brother Henry's help to sell it to a publisher – who, however, failed to bring it out in spite of having advertised it. In 1803 or 1804, probably, she was also writing *The Watsons*, a novel that was left unfinished. Her discouraging attempts at publication were followed by her father's death in January 1805; and for the next four years Mrs Austen and her two daughters, with a small income, were living first in lodgings and then in a shared house in Southampton.

Soon after the move to Chawton Cottage was decided on she turned again, and more seriously, to the idea of publication, first trying in 1809 (and without success) to get the purchaser of *Northanger Abbey* to publish it. By 1811, putting aside money to meet the expected loss, she published *Sense and Sensibility* at her own expense, evidently after revision. In the same year she began writing *Mansfield Park*. In 1812 she largely reconstructed *Pride and Prejudice*, which was published in 1813. In the summer of 1813 she finished *Mansfield Park*. *Emma* was written between January 1814 and March 1815, and *Persuasion* between August 1815 and August 1816. In 1816 she also bought back *Northanger Abbey* and revised it for immediate publication (though she shelved it again and had some doubts about its ever appearing).

And finally in the early months of 1817 she was at work on *Sanditon*, unfinished when she died.

The usual view, that she had two creative periods – her early twenties and her late thirties – divided by a largely barren interval, seems misleading. The novels as we know them were all produced in the later period. If the early versions, *Elinor and Marianne*, *First Impressions* and *Susan*, had been published, Jane Austen's standing would be lower. Her creative work went through the stages first of a practice period which grew out of a childhood pursuit and provided entertainment for her family and friends (with easily discouraged attempts at publication); second, of a period in which she wrote little but in which new standards may well have been forming; finally of the period from 1809 to her death, when she committed herself with much more determination to authorship for the public, thoroughly reshaped the early family productions and produced new work with remarkable fertility and freshness.

D.W.H.

PREFACE

THE Memoir of my Aunt, Jane Austen, has been received with more favour than I had ventured to expect. The notices taken of it in the periodical press, as well as letters addressed to me by many with whom I am not personally acquainted, show that an unabated interest is still taken in every particular that can be told about her. I am thus encouraged not only to offer a Second Edition of the Memoir, but also to enlarge it with some additional matter which I might have scrupled to intrude on the public if they had not thus seemed to call for it. In the present Edition, the narrative is somewhat enlarged, and a few more letters are added; with a short specimen of her childish stories. The cancelled chapter of 'Persuasion' is given, in compliance with wishes both publicly and privately expressed. A fragment of a story entitled 'The Watsons' is printed; and extracts are given from a novel which she had begun a few months before her death; but the chief addition is a short tale never before published, called 'Lady Susan.' I regret that the little which I have been able to add could not appear in my First Edition; as much of it was either unknown to me, or not at my command, when I first published; and I hope that I may claim some indulgent allowance for the difficulty of recovering little facts and feelings which had been merged half a century deep in oblivion.

November 17, 1870.

[The cancelled chapter of *Persuasion* is here printed with the novel. *The Watsons, Sanditon, and Lady Susan* are omitted. See Note on Text.]

'He knew of no one but himself who was inclined to the work. This is no uncommon motive. A man sees something to be done, knows of no one who will do it but himself, and so is driven to the enterprise.'

HELPS' *Life of Columbus*, ch. i.

CHAPTER 1

Introductory Remarks – Birth of Jane Austen – Her Family Connections – Their Influence on her Writings.

MORE than half a century has passed away since I, the youngest of the mourners,* attended the funeral of my dear aunt Jane in Winchester Cathedral; and now, in my old age, I am asked whether my memory will serve to rescue from oblivion any events of her life or any traits of her character to satisfy the enquiries of a generation of readers who have been born since she died. Of events her life was singularly barren : few changes and no great crisis ever broke the smooth current of its course. Even her fame may be said to have been posthumous : it did not attain to any vigorous life till she had ceased to exist. Her talents did not introduce her to the notice of other writers, or connect her with the literary world, or in any degree pierce through the obscurity of her domestic retirement. I have therefore scarcely any materials for a detailed life of my aunt; but I have a distinct recollection of her person and character; and perhaps many may take an interest in a delineation, if any such can be drawn, of that prolific mind whence sprung the Dashwoods and Bennets, the Bertrams and Woodhouses, the Thorpes and Musgroves, who have been admitted as familiar guests to the firesides of so many families, and are known there as individually and intimately as if they were living neighbours. Many may care to know whether the moral rectitude, the correct taste, and the warm affections with which she invested her ideal characters, were really existing in the native source whence those ideas flowed, and were actually exhibited by her in the various relations of life. I can indeed bear witness that there was scarcely a charm in her most delightful characters that was not a true reflection of her own sweet temper and loving heart. I was young when we lost her; but the impressions made on the young are deep, and though in the course of

---

* I went to represent my father, who was too unwell to attend himself, and thus I was the only one of my generation present.

fifty years I have forgotten much, I have not forgotten that 'Aunt Jane' was the delight of all her nephews and nieces. We did not think of her as being clever, still less as being famous; but we valued her as one always kind, sympathising, and amusing. To all this I am a living witness, but whether I can sketch out such a faint outline of this excellence as shall be perceptible to others may be reasonably doubted. Aided, however, by a few survivors * who knew her, I will not refuse to make the attempt. I am the more inclined to undertake the task from a conviction that, however little I may have to tell, no one else is left who could tell so much of her.

Jane Austen was born on December 16, 1775, at the Parsonage House of Steventon in Hampshire. Her father, the Rev. George Austen, was of a family long established in the neighbourhood of Tenterden and Sevenoaks in Kent. I believe that early in the seventeenth century they were clothiers. Hasted, in his history of Kent, says: 'The clothing business was exercised by persons who possessed most of the landed property in the Weald, insomuch that almost all the ancient families of these parts, now of large estates and genteel rank in life, and some of them ennobled by titles, are sprung from ancestors who have used this great staple manufacture, now almost unknown here.' In his list of these families Hasted places the Austens, and he adds that these clothiers 'were usually called the Gray Coats of Kent; and were a body so numerous and united that at county elections whoever had their vote and interest was almost certain of being elected.' The family still retains a badge of this origin; for their livery is of that peculiar mixture of light blue and white called Kentish gray, which forms the facings of the Kentish militia.

---

* My chief assistants have been my sisters, Mrs B. Lefroy and Miss Austen, whose recollections of our aunt are, on some points, more vivid than my own. I have not only been indebted to their memory for facts, but have sometimes used their words. Indeed some passages towards the end of the work were entirely written by the latter.

I have also to thank some of my cousins, and especially the daughters of Admiral Charles Austen, for the use of letters and papers which had passed into their hands, without which this Memoir could not have been written.

Mr George Austen had lost both his parents before he was nine years old. He inherited no property from them; but was happy in having a kind uncle, Mr Francis Austen, a successful lawyer at Tunbridge, the ancestor of the Austens of Kippington, who, though he had children of his own, yet made liberal provision for his orphan nephew. The boy received a good education at Tunbridge School, whence he obtained a scholarship, and subsequently a fellowship, at St John's College, Oxford. In 1764 he came into possession of the two adjoining Rectories of Deane and Steventon in Hampshire; the former purchased for him by his generous uncle Francis, the latter given by his cousin Mr Knight. This was no very gross case of plurality, according to the ideas of that time, for the two villages were little more than a mile apart, and their united populations scarcely amounted to three hundred. In the same year he married Cassandra, youngest daughter of the Rev. Thomas Leigh, of the family of Leighs of Warwickshire, who, having been a fellow of All Souls, held the College living of Harpsden, near Henley-upon-Thames. Mr Thomas Leigh was a younger brother of Dr Theophilus Leigh, a personage well known at Oxford in his day, and his day was not a short one, for he lived to be ninety, and held the Mastership of Balliol College for above half a century. He was a man more famous for his sayings than his doings, overflowing with puns and witticisms and sharp retorts; but his most serious joke was his practical one of living much longer than had been expected or intended. He was a fellow of Corpus, and the story is that the Balliol men, unable to agree in electing one of their own number to the Mastership, chose him, partly under the idea that he was in weak health and likely soon to cause another vacancy. It was afterwards said that his long incumbency had been a judgment on the Society for having elected an *Out-College Man.** I imagine that the front of Balliol towards Broad Street which has recently been pulled down must have been built, or at least restored, while he was Master, for the Leigh arms were placed under the cornice at the corner nearest to

---

* There seems to have been some doubt as to the validity of this election; for Hearne says that it was referred to the Visitor, who confirmed it. (Hearne's *Diaries*, v. 2.)

Trinity gates. The beautiful building lately erected has destroyed this record, and thus 'monuments themselves memorials need.'

His fame for witty and agreeable conversation extended beyond the bounds of the University. Mrs Thrale, in a letter to Dr Johnson, writes thus: 'Are you acquainted with Dr Leigh,* the Master of Balliol College, and are you not delighted with his gaiety of manners and youthful vivacity, now that he is eighty-six years of age? I never heard a more perfect or excellent pun than his, when some one told him how, in a late dispute among the Privy Councillors, the Lord Chancellor struck the table with such violence that he split it. "No, no, no," replied the Master; "I can hardly persuade myself that he *split* the *table*, though I believe he *divided* the *Board.*" '

Some of his sayings of course survive in family tradition. He was once calling on a gentleman notorious for never opening a book, who took him into a room overlooking the Bath Road, which was then a great thoroughfare for travellers of every class, saying rather pompously, 'This, Doctor, I call my study.' The Doctor, glancing his eye round the room, in which no books were to be seen, replied, 'And very well named too, sir, for you know Pope tells us, "The proper *study* of mankind is *Man.*" ' When my father went to Oxford he was honoured with an invitation to dine with this dignified cousin. Being a raw undergraduate, unaccustomed to the habits of the University, he was about to take off his gown, as if it were a great coat, when the old man, then considerably turned eighty, said, with a grim smile, 'Young man, you need not strip: we are not going to fight.' This humour remained in him so strongly to the last that he might almost have supplied Pope with another instance of 'the ruling passion strong in death,' for only three days before he expired, being told that an old acquaintance was lately married, having recovered from a long illness by eating eggs, and that the wits said that he had been egged on to matrimony, he immediately trumped the joke, saying, 'Then may the yoke sit easy on him.' I do not know from what common ancestor the Master of Balliol and his great-niece

---

* Mrs Thrale writes Dr *Lee*, but there can be no doubt of the identity of person.

Jane Austen, with some others of the family, may have derived the keen sense of humour which they certainly possessed.

Mr and Mrs George Austen resided first at Deane, but removed in 1771 to Steventon, which was their residence for about thirty years. They commenced their married life with the charge of a little child, a son of the celebrated Warren Hastings,[1] who had been committed to the care of Mr Austen before his marriage, probably through the influence of his sister, Mrs Hancock, whose husband at that time held some office under Hastings in India. Mr Gleig, in his 'Life of Hastings,' says that his son George, the offspring of his first marriage, was sent to England in 1761 for his education, but that he had never been able to ascertain to whom this precious charge was entrusted, nor what became of him. I am able to state, from family tradition, that he died young, of what was then called putrid sore throat; and that Mrs Austen had become so much attached to him that she always declared that his death had been as great a grief to her as if he had been a child of her own.

About this time, the grandfather of Mary Russell Mitford, Dr Russell, was Rector of the adjoining parish of Ashe; so that the parents of two popular female writers must have been intimately acquainted with each other.

As my subject carries me back about a hundred years, it will afford occasions for observing many changes gradually effected in the manners and habits of society, which I may think it worth while to mention. They may be little things, but time gives a certain importance even to trifles, as it imparts a peculiar flavour to wine. The most ordinary articles of domestic life are looked on with some interest, if they are brought to light after being long buried; and we feel a natural curiosity to know what was done and said by our forefathers, even though it may be nothing wiser or better than what we are daily doing or saying ourselves. Some of this generation may be little aware how many conveniences, now considered to be necessaries and matters of course, were unknown to their grandfathers and grandmothers. The lane between Deane and Steventon has long been as smooth as the best turnpike road; but when the family removed from the one residence to the other in 1771, it was a mere cart track, so cut up by deep

ruts as to be impassable for a light carriage. Mrs Austen, who was
not then in strong health, performed the short journey on a
feather-bed, placed upon some soft articles of furniture in the
waggon which held their household goods. In those days it was
not unusual to set men to work with shovel and pickaxe to fill up
ruts and holes in roads seldom used by carriages, on such special
occasions as a funeral or a wedding. Ignorance and coarseness of
language also were still lingering even upon higher levels of
society than might have been expected to retain such mists.
About this time, a neighbouring squire, a man of many acres,
referred the following difficulty to Mr Austen's decision: 'You
know all about these sort of things. Do tell us. Is Paris in France,
or France in Paris? for my wife has been disputing with me about
it.' The same gentleman, narrating some conversation which he
had heard between the rector and his wife, represented the latter
as beginning her reply to her husband with a round oath; and
when his daughter called him to task, reminding him that Mrs
Austen never swore, he replied, 'Now, Betty, why do you pull me
up for nothing? that's neither here nor there; you know very
well that's only *my way of telling the story.*' Attention has lately
been called by a celebrated writer to the inferiority of the clergy
to the laity of England two centuries ago. The charge no doubt is
true, if the rural clergy are to be compared with that higher
section of country gentlemen who went into parliament, and
mixed in London society, and took the lead in their several
counties; but it might be found less true if they were to be compared, as in all fairness they ought to be, with that lower section
with whom they usually associated. The smaller landed proprietors, who seldom went farther from home than their county
town, from the squire with his thousand acres to the yeoman
who cultivated his hereditary property of one or two hundred,
then formed a numerous class – each the aristocrat of his own
parish; and there was probably a greater difference in manners
and refinement between this class and that immediately above
them than could now be found between any two persons who
rank as gentlemen. For in the progress of civilisation, though all
orders may make some progress, yet it is most perceptible in the
lower. It is a process of 'levelling up;' the rear rank 'dressing up,'

as it were, close to the front rank. When Hamlet mentions, as something which he had 'for *three years taken* note of,' that 'the toe of the peasant comes so near the heel of the courtier,' it was probably intended by Shakespeare as a satire on his own times; but it expressed a principle which is working at all times in which society makes any progress. I believe that a century ago the improvement in most country parishes began with the clergy; and that in those days a rector who chanced to be a gentleman and a scholar found himself superior to his chief parishioners in information and manners, and became a sort of centre of refinement and politeness.

Mr Austen was a remarkably good-looking man, both in his youth and his old age. During his year of office at Oxford he had been called 'the handsome Proctor;' and at Bath, when more than seventy years old, he attracted observation by his fine features and abundance of snow-white hair. Being a good scholar he was able to prepare two of his sons for the University, and to direct the studies of his other children, whether sons or daughters, as well as to increase his income by taking pupils.

In Mrs Austen also was to be found the germ of much of the ability which was concentrated in Jane, but of which others of her children had a share. She united strong common sense with a lively imagination, and often expressed herself, both in writing and in conversation, with epigrammatic force and point. She lived, like many of her family, to an advanced age. During the last years of her life she endured continual pain, not only patiently but with characteristic cheerfulness. She once said to me, 'Ah, my dear, you find me just where you left me – on the sofa. I sometimes think that God Almighty must have forgotten me; but I dare say He will come for me in His own good time.' She died and was buried at Chawton, January 1827, aged eighty-eight.

Her own family were so much, and the rest of the world so little, to Jane Austen, that some brief mention of her brothers and sister is necessary in order to give any idea of the objects which principally occupied her thoughts and filled her heart, especially as some of them, from their characters or professions in life, may be supposed to have had more or less influence on her writings: though I feel some reluctance in bringing before public notice persons and circumstances essentially private.

Her eldest brother James, my own father, had, when a very young man, at St John's College, Oxford, been the originator and chief supporter of a periodical paper called 'The Loiterer,' written somewhat on the plan of the 'Spectator' and its successors, but nearly confined to subjects connected with the University. In after life he used to speak very slightingly of this early work, which he had the better right to do, as, whatever may have been the degree of their merits, the best papers had certainly been written by himself. He was well read in English literature, had a correct taste, and wrote readily and happily, both in prose and verse. He was more than ten years older than Jane, and had, I believe, a large share in directing her reading and forming her taste.

Her second brother, Edward,[2] had been a good deal separated from the rest of the family, as he was early adopted by his cousin, Mr Knight, of Godmersham Park in Kent and Chawton House in Hampshire; and finally came into possession both of the property and the name. But though a good deal separated in childhood, they were much together in after life, and Jane gave a large share of her affections to him and his children. Mr Knight was not only a very amiable man, kind and indulgent to all connected with him, but possessed also a spirit of fun and liveliness, which made him especially delightful to all young people.

Her third brother, Henry, had great conversational powers, and inherited from his father an eager and sanguine disposition. He was a very entertaining companion, but had perhaps less steadiness of purpose, certainly less success in life,[3] than his brothers. He became a clergyman when middle-aged; and an allusion to his sermons will be found in one of Jane's letters. At one time he resided in London, and was useful in transacting his sister's business with her publishers.

Her two youngest brothers, Francis and Charles, were sailors during that glorious period of the British navy which comprises the close of the last and the beginning of the present century, when it was impossible for an officer to be almost always afloat, as these brothers were, without seeing service which, in these days, would be considered distinguished. Accordingly, they were continually engaged in actions of more or less importance, and sometimes gained promotion by their success. Both rose to the rank of Admiral, and carried out their flags to distant stations.

Francis lived to attain the very summit of his profession, having died, in his ninety-third year, G.C.B. and Senior Admiral of the Fleet, in 1865. He possessed great firmness of character, with a strong sense of duty, whether due from himself to others, or from others to himself. He was consequently a strict disciplinarian; but, as he was a very religious man, it was remarked of him (for in those days, at least, it was remarkable) that he maintained this discipline without ever uttering an oath or permitting one in his presence. On one occasion, when ashore in a seaside town, he was spoken of as 'the officer who kneeled at church;' a custom which now happily would not be thought peculiar.

Charles was generally serving in frigates or sloops; blockading harbours, driving the ships of the enemy ashore, boarding gun-boats, and frequently making small prizes. At one time he was absent from England on such services for seven years together. In later life he commanded the Bellerophon, at the bombardment of St Jean d'Acre in 1840. In 1850 he went out in the Hastings, in command of the East India and China station, but on the break-ing out of the Burmese war he transferred his flag to a steam sloop, for the purpose of getting up the shallow waters of the Irrawaddy, on board of which he died of cholera in 1852, in the seventy-fourth year of his age. His sweet temper and affectionate disposition, in which he resembled his sister Jane, had secured to him an unusual portion of attachment, not only from his own family, but from all the officers and common sailors who served under him. One who was with him at his death has left this record of him: 'Our good Admiral won the hearts of all by his gentleness and kindness while he was struggling with disease, and endeavouring to do his duty as Commander-in-chief of the British naval forces in these waters. His death was a great grief to the whole fleet. I know that I cried bitterly when I found he was dead.' The Order in Council of the Governor-General of India, Lord Dalhousie, expresses 'admiration of the staunch high spirit which, notwithstanding his age and previous sufferings, had led the Admiral to take his part in the trying service which has closed his career.'

These two brothers have been dwelt on longer than the others because their honourable career accounts for Jane Austen's partiality for the Navy, as well as for the readiness and accuracy with which she wrote about it. She was always very careful not to meddle with matters which she did not thoroughly understand. She never touched upon politics, law, or medicine, subjects which some novel writers have ventured on rather too boldly, and have treated, perhaps, with more brilliancy than accuracy. But with ships and sailors she felt herself at home, or at least could always trust to a brotherly critic to keep her right. I believe that no flaw has ever been found in her seamanship either in 'Mansfield Park' or in 'Persuasion.'

But dearest of all to the heart of Jane was her sister Cassandra, about three years her senior. Their sisterly affection for each other could scarcely be exceeded. Perhaps it began on Jane's side with the feeling of deference natural to a loving child towards a kind elder sister. Something of this feeling always remained; and even in the maturity of her powers, and in the enjoyment of increasing success, she would still speak of Cassandra as of one wiser and better than herself. In childhood, when the elder was sent to the school of a Mrs Latournelle, in the Forbury at Reading, the younger went with her, not because she was thought old enough to profit much by the instruction there imparted, but because she would have been miserable without her sister; her mother observing that 'if Cassandra were going to have her head cut off, Jane would insist on sharing her fate.' This attachment was never interrupted or weakened. They lived in the same home, and shared the same bed-room, till separated by death. They were not exactly alike. Cassandra's was the colder and calmer disposition; she was always prudent and well judging, but with less outward demonstration of feeling and less sunniness of temper than Jane possessed. It was remarked in her family that 'Cassandra had the *merit* of having her temper always under command, but that Jane had the *happiness* of a temper that never required to be commanded.' When 'Sense and Sensibility' came out, some persons, who knew the family slightly, surmised that the two elder Miss Dashwoods were intended by the author for her sister and herself; but this could not be the case. Cassandra's character might indeed represent the 'sense' of Elinor, but Jane's had little in common with the 'sensibility' of Marianne. The young woman who, before the age of twenty, could so clearly discern the failings of Marianne Dashwood, could hardly have been subject to them herself.

This was the small circle, continually enlarged, however, by the increasing families of four of her brothers, within which Jane Austen found her wholesome pleasures, duties, and interests, and beyond which she went very little into society during the last ten years of her life. There was so much that was agreeable and attractive in this family party that its members may be excused if they were inclined to live somewhat too exclusively within it. They might see in each other much to love and esteem, and something to admire. The family talk had abundance of spirit and vivacity, and was never troubled by disagreements even in little matters, for it was not their habit to dispute or argue with each other: above all, there was strong family affection and firm union, never to be broken but by death. It cannot be doubted that all this had its influence on the author in the construction of her stories, in which a family party usually supplies the narrow stage, while the interest is made to revolve round a few actors.

It will be seen also that though her circle of society was small, yet she found in her neighbourhood persons of good taste and cultivated minds. Her acquaintance, in fact, constituted the very class from which she took her imaginary characters, ranging from the member of parliament, or large landed proprietor, to the young curate or younger midshipman of equally good family; and I think that the influence of these early associations may be traced in her writings, especially in two particulars. First, that she is entirely free from the vulgarity, which is so offensive in some novels, of dwelling on the outward appendages of wealth or rank, as if they were things to which the writer was unaccustomed; and, secondly, that she deals as little with very low as with very high stations in life. She does not go lower than the Miss Steeles, Mrs

Elton, and John Thorpe, people of bad taste and underbred manners, such as are actually found sometimes mingling with better
society. She has nothing resembling the Brangtons, or Mr
Dubster and his friend Tom Hicks, with whom Madame
D'Arblay [4] loved to season her stories, and to produce striking
contrasts to her well bred characters.

CHAPTER 2

Description of Steventon – Life at Steventon – Changes of Habits and Customs in the last Century

As the first twenty-five years, more than half of the brief life of Jane Austen, were spent in the parsonage of Steventon, some description of that place ought to be given. Steventon is a small rural village upon the chalk hills of north Hants, situated in a winding valley about seven miles from Basingstoke. The South-Western railway crosses it by a short embankment, and, as it curves round, presents a good view of it on the left hand to those who are travelling down the line, about three miles before entering the tunnel under Popham Beacon. It may be known to some sportsmen, as lying in one of the best portions of the Vine Hunt. It is certainly not a picturesque country; it presents no grand or extensive views; but the features are small rather than plain. The surface continually swells and sinks, but the hills are not bold, nor the valleys deep; and though it is sufficiently well clothed with woods and hedgerows, yet the poverty of the soil in most places prevents the timber from attaining a large size. Still it has its beauties. The lanes wind along in a natural curve, continually fringed with irregular borders of native turf, and lead to pleasant nooks and corners. One who knew and loved it well [5] very happily expressed its quiet charms, when he wrote

> True taste is not fastidious, nor rejects,
> Because they may not come within the rule
> Of composition pure and picturesque,
> Unnumbered simple scenes which fill the leaves
> Of Nature's sketch book.

Of this somewhat tame country, Steventon, from the fall of the ground, and the abundance of its timber, is certainly one of the prettiest spots; yet one cannot be surprised that, when Jane's mother, a little before her marriage, was shown the scenery of her future home, she should have thought it unattractive, com-

pared with the broad river, the rich valley, and the noble hills
which she had been accustomed to behold at her native home near
Henley-on-Thames.

The house itself stood in a shallow valley, surrounded by
sloping meadows, well sprinkled with elm trees, at the end of a
small village of cottages, each well provided with a garden,
scattered about prettily on either side of the road. It was sufficiently commodious to hold pupils in addition to a growing
family, and was in those times considered to be above the average
of parsonages; but the rooms were finished with less elegance than
would now be found in the most ordinary dwellings. No cornice
marked the junction of wall and ceiling; while the beams which
supported the upper floors projected into the rooms below in all
their naked simplicity, covered only by a coat of paint or white-
wash: accordingly it has since been considered unworthy of
being the Rectory house of a family living, and about forty-five
years ago it was pulled down for the purpose of erecting a new
house in a far better situation on the opposite side of the valley.

North of the house, the road from Deane to Popham Lane ran
at a sufficient distance from the front to allow a carriage drive,
through turf and trees. On the south side the ground rose gently,
and was occupied by one of those old-fashioned gardens in which
vegetables and flowers are combined, flanked and protected on
the east by one of the thatched mud walls common in that
country, and overshadowed by fine elms. Along the upper or
southern side of this garden, ran a terrace of the finest turf, which
must have been in the writer's thoughts when she described
Catherine Morland's childish delight in 'rolling down the green
slope at the back of the house.'

But the chief beauty of Steventon consisted in its hedgerows. A
hedgerow, in that country, does not mean a thin formal line of
quickset, but an irregular border of copse-wood and timber, often
wide enough to contain within it a winding footpath, or a rough
cart track. Under its shelter the earliest primroses, anemones, and
wild hyacinths were to be found; sometimes, the first bird's-nest;
and, now and then, the unwelcome adder. Two such hedgerows
radiated, as it were, from the parsonage garden. One, a continua-
tion of the turf terrace, proceeded westward, forming the southern

boundary of the home meadows; and was formed into a rustic shrubbery, with occasional seats, entitled 'The Wood Walk.' The other ran straight up the hill, under the name of 'The Church Walk,' because it led to the parish church, as well as to a fine old manor-house, of Henry VIII.'s time, occupied by a family named Digweed, who have for more than a century rented it, together with the chief farm in the parish. The church itself – I speak of it as it then was, before the improvements made by the present rector –

> A little spireless fane,
> Just seen above the woody lane,

might have appeared mean and uninteresting to an ordinary observer; but the adept in church architecture would have known that it must have stood there some seven centuries, and would have found beauty in the very narrow early English windows, as well as in the general proportions of its little chancel; while its solitary position, far from the hum of the village, and within sight of no habitation, except a glimpse of the gray manor-house through its circling screen of sycamores, has in it something solemn and appropriate to the last resting-place of the silent dead. Sweet violets, both purple and white, grow in abundance beneath its south wall. One may imagine for how many centuries the ancestors of those little flowers have occupied that undisturbed, sunny nook, and may think how few living families can boast of as ancient a tenure of their land. Large elms protrude their rough branches; old hawthorns shed their annual blossoms over the graves; and the hollow yew-tree must be at least coeval with the church.

But whatever may be the beauties or defects of the surrounding scenery, this was the residence of Jane Austen for twenty-five years. This was the cradle of her genius. These were the first objects which inspired her young heart with a sense of the beauties of nature. In strolls along those wood-walks, thick-coming fancies rose in her mind, and gradually assumed the forms in which they came forth to the world. In that simple church she brought them all into subjection to the piety which ruled her in life, and supported her in death.

The home at Steventon must have been, for many years, a pleasant and prosperous one. The family was unbroken by death, and seldom visited by sorrow. Their situation had some peculiar advantages beyond those of ordinary rectories. Steventon was a family living. Mr Knight, the patron, was also proprietor of nearly the whole parish. He never resided there, and consequently the rector and his children came to be regarded in the neighbourhood as a kind of representatives of the family. They shared with the principal tenant the command of an excellent manor, and enjoyed, in this reflected way, some of the consideration usually awarded to landed proprietors. They were not rich, but, aided by Mr Austen's powers of teaching, they had enough to afford a good education to their sons and daughters, to mix in the best society of the neighbourhood, and to exercise a liberal hospitality to their own relations and friends. A carriage and a pair of horses were kept. This might imply a higher style of living in our days than it did in theirs. There were then no assessed taxes. The carriage, once bought, entailed little further expense; and the horses probably, like Mr Bennet's, were often employed on farm work. Moreover, it should be remembered that a pair of horses in those days were almost necessary, if ladies were to move about at all; for neither the condition of the roads nor the style of carriage-building admitted of any comfortable vehicle being drawn by a single horse. When one looks at the few specimens still remaining of coach-building in the last century, it strikes one that the chief object of the builders must have been to combine the greatest possible weight with the least possible amount of accommodation.

The family lived in close intimacy with two cousins, Edward and Jane Cooper, the children of Mrs Austen's eldest sister, and Dr Cooper, the vicar of Sonning, near Reading. The Coopers lived for some years at Bath, which seems to have been much frequented in those days by clergymen retiring from work. I believe that Cassandra and Jane sometimes visited them there, and that Jane thus acquired the intimate knowledge of the topography and customs of Bath, which enabled her to write 'Northanger Abbey' long before she resided there herself. After the death of their own parents, the two young Coopers paid long visits at

Steventon. Edward Cooper did not live undistinguished. When an undergraduate at Oxford, he gained the prize for Latin hexameters on 'Hortus Anglicus' in 1791; and in later life he was known by a work on prophecy, called 'The Crisis,' and other religious publications, especially for several volumes of Sermons,[6] much preached in many pulpits in my youth. Jane Cooper was married from her uncle's house at Steventon, to Captain, afterwards Sir Thomas Williams, under whom Charles Austen served in several ships. She was a dear friend of her namesake, but was fated to become a cause of great sorrow to her, for a few years after the marriage she was suddenly killed by an accident to her carriage.

There was another cousin closely associated with them at Steventon, who must have introduced greater variety into the family circle. This was the daughter of Mr Austen's only sister, Mrs Hancock. This cousin had been educated in Paris, and married to a Count de Feuillade,[7] of whom I know little more than that he perished by the guillotine during the French Revolution. Perhaps his chief offence was his rank; but it was said that the charge of 'incivism,' under which he suffered, rested on the fact of his having laid down some arable land into pasture – a sure sign of his intention to embarrass the Republican Government by producing a famine! His wife escaped through dangers and difficulties to England, was received for some time into her uncle's family, and finally married her cousin Henry Austen. During the short peace of Amiens, she and her second husband went to France, in the hope of recovering some of the Count's property, and there narrowly escaped being included amongst the *détenus*. Orders had been given by Buonaparte's government to detain all English travellers, but at the post-houses Mrs Henry Austen gave the necessary orders herself, and her French was so perfect that she passed everywhere for a native, and her husband escaped under this protection.

She was a clever woman, and highly accomplished, after the French rather than the English mode; and in those days, when intercourse with the Continent was long interrupted by war, such an element in the society of a country parsonage must have been a rare acquisition. The sisters may have been more indebted to this cousin than to Mrs Latournelle's teaching for the considerable knowledge of French which they possessed. She also took the principal parts in the private theatricals in which the family several times indulged, having their summer theatre in the barn, and their winter one within the narrow limits of the dining-room, where the number of the audience must have been very limited. On these occasions, the prologues and epilogues were written by Jane's eldest brother, and some of them are very vigorous and amusing. Jane was only twelve years old at the time of the earliest of these representations, and not more than fifteen when the last took place. She was, however, an early observer, and it may be reasonably supposed that some of the incidents and feelings which are so vividly painted in the Mansfield Park theatricals are due to her recollections of these entertainments.

Some time before they left Steventon, one great affliction came upon the family. Cassandra was engaged to be married to a young clergyman. He had not sufficient private fortune to permit an immediate union; but the engagement was not likely to be a hopeless or a protracted one, for he had a prospect of early preferment from a nobleman with whom he was connected both by birth and by personal friendship. He accompanied this friend to the West Indies, as chaplain to his regiment, and there died of yellow fever, to the great concern of his friend and patron, who afterwards declared that, if he had known of the engagement, he would not have permitted him to go out to such a climate. This little domestic tragedy caused great and lasting grief to the principal sufferer, and could not but cast a gloom over the whole party. The sympathy of Jane was probably, from her age, and her peculiar attachment to her sister, the deepest of all.

Of Jane herself I know of no such definite tale of love to relate. Her reviewer[8] in the 'Quarterly' of January 1821 observes, concerning the attachment of Fanny Price to Edmund Bertram: 'The silence in which this passion is cherished, the slender hopes and enjoyments by which it is fed, the restlessness and jealousy with which it fills a mind naturally active, contented, and unsuspicious, the manner in which it tinges every event, and every reflection, are painted with a vividness and a detail of which we can scarcely conceive any one but a female, and we should almost add, a female writing from recollection, capable.' This conjecture, however probable, was wide of the mark. The picture was drawn from the intuitive perceptions of genius, not from personal experience. In no circumstance of her life was there any similarity between herself and her heroine in 'Mansfield Park.' She did not indeed pass through life without being the object of warm affection. In her youth she had declined the addresses of a gentleman who had the recommendations of good character, and connections, and position in life, of everything, in fact, except the subtle power of touching her heart. There is, however, one passage of romance in her history with which I am imperfectly acquainted, and to which I am unable to assign name, or date, or place, though I have it on sufficient authority. Many years after her death, some circumstances induced her sister Cassandra to break through her habitual reticence, and to speak of it. She said that, while staying at some seaside place, they became acquainted with a gentleman, whose charm of person, mind, and manners was such that Cassandra thought him worthy to possess and likely to win her sister's love. When they parted, he expressed his intention of soon seeing them again; and Cassandra felt no doubt as to his motives. But they never again met. Within a short time they heard of his sudden death. I believe that, if Jane ever loved, it was this unnamed gentleman; but the acquaintance had been short, and I am unable to say whether her feelings were of such a nature as to affect her happiness.

Any description that I might attempt of the family life at Steventon, which closed soon after I was born, could be little better than a fancy-piece. There is no doubt that if we could look into the households of the clergy and the small gentry of that period, we should see some things which would seem strange to us, and should miss many more to which we are accustomed. Every hundred years, and especially a century like the last, marked by an extraordinary advance in wealth, luxury, and refinement of taste, as well as in the mechanical arts which embellish our houses, must produce a great change in their aspect. These changes are always at work; they are going on now, but so silently that we take no note of them. Men soon forget the small objects which they leave behind them as they drift down the stream of life. As Pope says –

> Nor does life's stream for observation stay;
> It hurries all too fast to mark their way.

Important inventions, such as the applications of steam, gas, and electricity, may find their places in history; but not so the alterations, great as they may be, which have taken place in the appearance of our dining and drawing-rooms. Who can now record the degrees by which the custom prevalent in my youth of asking each other to take wine together at dinner became obsolete? Who will be able to fix, twenty years hence, the date when our dinners began to be carved and handed round by servants, instead of smoking before our eyes and noses on the table? To record such little matters would indeed be 'to chronicle small beer.' But, in a slight memoir like this, I may be allowed to note some of those changes in social habits which give a colour to history, but which the historian has the greatest difficulty in recovering.

At that time the dinner-table presented a far less splendid appearance than it does now. It was appropriated to solid food, rather than to flowers, fruits, and decorations. Nor was there much glitter of plate upon it; for the early dinner hour rendered candlesticks unnecessary, and silver forks had not come into general use : while the broad rounded end of the knives indicated the substitute generally used instead of them.*

The dinners too were more homely, though not less plentiful and savoury; and the bill of fare in one house would not be so

---

* The celebrated Beau Brummel, who was so intimate with George IV. as to be able to quarrel with him, was born in 1771. It is reported that when he was questioned about his parents, he replied that it was long since he had heard of them, but that he imagined the worthy couple must have cut their own throats by that time, because when he last saw them they were eating peas with their knives. Yet Brummel's father had probably lived in good society; and was certainly able to put his son into a fashionable regiment, and to leave him 30,000l. (Raikes Memoirs, vol. ii, p. 207.) Raikes believes that he had been Secretary to Lord North. Thackeray's idea that he had been a footman cannot stand against the authority of Raikes, who was intimate with the son.

like that in another as it is now, for family receipts were held in high estimation. A grandmother of culinary talent could bequeath to her descendant fame for some particular dish, and might influence the family dinner for many generations.

Dos est magna parentium
Virtus.

One house would pride itself on its ham, another on its game-pie, and a third on its superior furmity, or tansey-pudding. Beer and home-made wines, especially mead, were more largely consumed. Vegetables were less plentiful and less various. Potatoes were used, but not so abundantly as now; and there was an idea that they were to be eaten only with roast meat. They were novelties to a tenant's wife who was entertained at Steventon Parsonage, certainly less than a hundred years ago; and when Mrs Austen advised her to plant them in her own garden, she replied, 'No, no; they are very well for you gentry, but they must be terribly costly to rear.'

But a still greater difference would be found in the furniture of the rooms, which would appear to us lamentably scanty. There was a general deficiency of carpeting in sitting-rooms, bed-rooms, and passages. A pianoforte, or rather a spinnet or harpsichord, was by no means a necessary appendage. It was to be found only where there was a decided taste for music, not so common then as now, or in such great houses as would probably contain a billiard-table. There would often be but one sofa in the house, and that a stiff, angular, uncomfortable article. There were no deep easy-chairs, nor other appliances for lounging; for to lie down, or even to lean back, was a luxury permitted only to old persons or invalids. It was said of a nobleman, a personal friend of George III. and a model gentleman of his day, that he would have made the tour of Europe without ever touching the back of his travelling carriage. But perhaps we should be most struck with the total absence of those elegant little articles which now embellish and encumber our drawing-room tables. We should miss the sliding bookcases and picture-stands, the letter-weighing machines and envelope cases, the periodicals and illustrated newspapers – above all, the countless swarm of photograph books which now threaten to swallow up all space. A small writing-desk, with a smaller work-box, or netting-case, was all that each young lady contributed to occupy the table; for the large family work-basket, though often produced in the parlour, lived in the closet.

There must have been more dancing throughout the country in those days than there is now: and it seems to have sprung up more spontaneously, as if it were a natural production, with less fastidiousness as to the quality of music, lights, and floor. Many country towns had a monthly ball throughout the winter, in some of which the same apartment served for dancing and tea-room. Dinner parties more frequently ended with an extempore dance on the carpet, to the music of a harpsichord in the house, or a fiddle from the village. This was always supposed to be for the entertainment of the young people, but many, who had little pretension to youth, were very ready to join in it. There can be no doubt that Jane herself enjoyed dancing, for she attributes this taste to her favourite heroines; in most of her works, a ball or a private dance is mentioned, and made of importance.

Many things connected with the ball-rooms of those days have now passed into oblivion. The barbarous law which confined the lady to one partner throughout the evening must indeed have been abolished before Jane went to balls. It must be observed, however, that this custom was in one respect advantageous to the gentleman, inasmuch as it rendered his duties more practicable. He was bound to call upon his partner the next morning, and it must have been convenient to have only one lady for whom he was obliged

> To gallop all the country over,
> The last night's partner to behold,
> And humbly hope she caught no cold.

But the stately minuet still reigned supreme; and every regular ball commenced with it. It was a slow and solemn movement, expressive of grace and dignity, rather than of merriment. It abounded in formal bows and courtesies, with measured paces, forwards, backwards and sideways, and many complicated gyrations. It was executed by one lady and gentleman, amidst the admiration, or the criticism, of surrounding spectators. In its earlier and most palmy days, as when Sir Charles and Lady Grandison delighted the company by dancing it at their own wedding, the gentleman wore a dress sword, and the lady was armed with a fan of nearly equal dimensions. Addison observes that 'women are armed with fans, as men with swords, and sometimes do more execution with them.' The graceful carriage of each weapon was considered a test of high breeding. The clownish man was in danger of being tripped up by his sword getting between his legs: the fan held clumsily looked more of a burden than an ornament; while in the hands of an adept it could be made to speak a language of its own.* It was not everyone who felt qualified to make this public exhibition, and I have been told that those ladies who intended to dance minuets, used to distinguish themselves from others by wearing a particular kind of lappet on their head-dress. I have heard also of another curious proof of the respect in which this dance was held. Gloves immaculately clean were considered requisite for its due performance, while gloves a little soiled were thought good enough for a country dance; and accordingly some prudent ladies provided themselves with two pairs for their several purposes. The minuet expired with the last century: but long after it had ceased to be danced publicly it was taught to boys and girls, in order to give them a graceful carriage.

Hornpipes, cotillons, and reels, were occasionally danced; but the chief occupation of the evening was the interminable country dance, in which all could join. This dance presented a great show of enjoyment, but it was not without its peculiar troubles. The ladies and gentlemen were ranged apart from each other in opposite rows, so that the facilities for flirtation, of interesting intercourse, were not so great as might have been desired by both

---

* See 'Spectator,' No. 102, on the Fan Exercise. Old gentlemen who had survived the fashion of wearing swords were known to regret the disuse of that custom, because it put an end to one way of distinguishing those who had, from those who had not, been used to good society. To wear the sword easily was an art which, like swimming and skating, required to be learned in youth. Children could practise it early with their toy swords adapted to their size.

parties. Much heart-burning and discontent sometimes arose as to *who* should stand above *whom*, and especially as to who was entitled to the high privilege of calling and leading off the first dance: and no little indignation was felt at the lower end of the room when any of the leading couples retired prematurely from their duties, and did not condescend to dance up and down the whole set. We may rejoice that these causes of irritation no longer exist; and that if such feelings as jealousy, rivalry, and discontent ever touch celestial bosoms in the modern ball-room they must arise from different and more recondite sources.

I am tempted to add a little about the difference of personal habits. It may be asserted as a general truth, that less was left to the charge and discretion of servants, and more was done, or superintended, by the masters and mistresses. With regard to the mistresses, it is, I believe, generally understood, that at the time to which I refer, a hundred years ago, they took a personal part in the higher branches of cookery, as well as in the concoction of home-made wines, and distilling of herbs for domestic medicines, which are nearly allied to the same art. Ladies did not disdain to spin the thread of which the household linen was woven. Some ladies liked to wash with their own hands their choice china after breakfast or tea. In one of my earliest child's books, a little girl, the daughter of a gentleman, is taught by her mother to make her own bed before leaving her chamber. It was not so much that they had not servants to do all these things for them, as that they took an interest in such occupations. And it must be borne in mind how many sources of interest enjoyed by this generation were then closed, or very scantily opened to ladies. A very small minority of them cared much for literature or science. Music was not a very common, and drawing was a still rarer, accomplishment; needle-work, in some form or other, was their chief sedentary employment.

But I doubt whether the rising generation are equally aware how much gentlemen also did for themselves in those times, and whether some things that I can mention will not be a surprise to them. Two homely proverbs were held in higher estimation in my early days than they are now – 'The master's eye makes the horse fat;' and, 'If you would be well served, serve yourself.' Some gentlemen took pleasure in being their own gardeners, performing all the scientific, and some of the manual, work themselves. Well-dressed young men of my acquaintance, who had their coat from a London tailor, would always brush their evening suit themselves, rather than entrust it to the carelessness of a rough servant, and to the risks of dirt and grease in the kitchen; for in those days servants' halls were not common in the houses of the clergy and the smaller country gentry. It was quite natural that Catherine Morland should have contrasted the magnificence of the offices at Northanger Abbey with the few shapeless pantries in her father's parsonage. A young man who expected to have his things packed or unpacked for him by a servant, when he travelled, would have been thought exceptionally fine, or exceptionally lazy. When my uncle undertook to teach me to shoot, his first lesson was how to clean my own gun. It was thought meritorious on the evening of a hunting day, to turn out after dinner, lanthorn in hand, and visit the stable, to ascertain that the horse had been well cared for. This was of the more importance, because, previous to the introduction of clipping, about the year 1820, it was a difficult and tedious work to make a long-coated hunter dry and comfortable, and was often very imperfectly done. Of course, such things were not practised by those who had gamekeepers, and stud-grooms, and plenty of well-trained servants; but they were practised by many who were unequivocally gentlemen, and whose grandsons, occupying the same position in life, may perhaps be astonished at being told that 'such things were.'

I have drawn pictures for which my own experience, or what I heard from others in my youth, have supplied the materials. Of course, they cannot be universally applicable. Such details varied in various circles, and were changed very gradually; nor can I pretend to tell how much of what I have said is descriptive of the family life at Steventon in Jane Austen's youth. I am sure the ladies there had nothing to do with the mysteries of the stew-pot or the preserving-pan; but it is probable that their way of life differed a little from ours, and would have appeared to us more homely. It may be that useful articles, which would not now be produced in drawing-rooms, were hemmed, and marked, and

darned in the old-fashioned parlour. But all this concerned only
the outer life; there was as much cultivation and refinement of
mind as now, with probably more studied courtesy and ceremony
of manner to visitors; whilst certainly in that family literary
pursuits were not neglected.

I remember to have heard of only two little things different
from modern customs. One was, that on hunting mornings the
young men usually took their hasty breakfast in the kitchen. The
early hour at which hounds then met may account for this; and
probably the custom began, if it did not end, when they were
boys; for they hunted at an early age, in a scrambling sort of
way, upon any pony or donkey that they could procure, or, in
default of such luxuries, on foot. I have been told that Sir Francis
Austen, when seven years old, bought on his own account, it
must be supposed with his father's permission, a pony for a
guinea and a half; and after riding him with great success for two
seasons, sold him for a guinea more. One may wonder how the
child could have so much money, and how the animal could have
been obtained for so little. The same authority informs me that
his first cloth suit was made from a scarlet habit, which, according to the fashion of the times, had been his mother's usual
morning dress. If all this is true, the future admiral of the British
Fleet must have cut a conspicuous figure in the hunting-field.
The other peculiarity was that, when the roads were dirty, the
sisters took long walks in pattens. This defence against wet and
dirt is now seldom seen. The few that remain are banished from
good society, and employed only in menial work; but a hundred
and fifty years ago they were celebrated in poetry, and considered
so clever a contrivance that Gay, in his 'Trivia,' ascribes the invention to a god stimulated by his passion for a mortal damsel,
and derives the name 'Patten' from 'Patty.'

> The patten now supports each frugal dame,
> Which from the blue-eyed Patty takes the name.

But mortal damsels have long ago discarded the clumsy implement. First it dropped its iron ring [9] and became a clog; afterwards it was fined down into the pliant galoshe – lighter to wear
and more effectual to protect – a no less manifest instance of

gradual improvement than Cowper indicates when he traces through eighty lines of poetry his 'accomplished sofa' back to the original three-legged stool.

As an illustration of the purposes which a patten was intended to serve, I add the following epigram, written by Jane Austen's uncle, Mr Leigh Perrot, on reading in a newspaper the marriage of Captain Foote to Miss Patten:—

> Through the rough paths of life, with a patten your guard
>   May you safely and pleasantly jog;
> May the knot never slip, nor the ring press too hard,
>   Nor the Foot find the Patten a clog.

At the time when Jane Austen lived at Steventon, a work was carried on in the neighbouring cottages which ought to be recorded, because it has long ceased to exist.

Up to the beginning of the present century, poor women found profitable employment in spinning flax or wool. This was a better occupation for them than straw plaiting, inasmuch as it was carried on at the family hearth, and did not admit of gadding and gossiping about the village. The implement used was a long narrow machine of wood, raised on legs, furnished at one end with a large wheel, and at the other with a spindle on which the flax or wool was loosely wrapped, connected together by a loop of string. One hand turned the wheel, while the other formed the thread. The outstretched arms, the advanced foot, the sway of the whole figure backwards and forwards, produced picturesque attitudes, and displayed whatever of grace or beauty the work-woman might possess.* Some ladies were fond of spinning, but they worked in a quieter manner, sitting at a neat little machine of varnished wood, like Tunbridge ware, generally turned by the foot, with a basin of water at hand to supply the moisture required for forming the thread, which the cottager took by a more direct and natural process from her own mouth. I remember two such elegant little wheels in our own family.

It may be observed that this hand-spinning is the most primi-

---

* Mrs Gaskell, in her tale of 'Sylvia's Lovers,' declares that this hand-spinning rivalled harp-playing in its gracefulness.

tive of female accomplishments, and can be traced back to the earliest times. Ballad poetry and fairy tales are full of allusions to it. The term 'spinster' still testifies to its having been the ordinary employment of the English young woman. It was the labour assigned to the ejected nuns by the rough earl who said, 'Go spin, ye jades, go spin.' It was the employment at which Roman matrons and Grecian princesses presided amongst their handmaids. Heathen mythology celebrated it in the three Fates spinning and measuring out the thread of human life. Holy Scripture honours it in those 'wise-hearted women' who 'did spin with their hands, and brought that which they had spun' for the construction of the Tabernacle in the wilderness : and an old English proverb carries it still farther back to the time 'when Adam delved and Eve span.' But, at last, this time-honoured domestic manufacture is quite extinct amongst us – crushed by the power of steam, overborne by a countless host of spinning jennies, and I can only just remember some of its last struggles for existence in the Steventon cottages.

CHAPTER 3

Early Compositions – Friends at Ashe – A very old Letter – Lines on the Death of Mrs Lefroy – Observations on Jane Austen's Letter-writing

I KNOW little of Jane Austen's childhood. Her mother followed a custom, not unusual in those days, though it seems strange to us, of putting out her babies to be nursed in a cottage in the village. The infant was daily visited by one or both of its parents, and frequently brought to them at the parsonage, but the cottage was its home, and must have remained so till it was old enough to run about and talk; for I know that one of them, in after life, used to speak of his foster mother as 'Movie,' the name by which he had called her in his infancy. It may be that the contrast between the parsonage house and the best class of cottages was not quite so extreme then as it would be now, that the one was somewhat less luxurious, and the other less squalid. It would certainly seem from the results that it was a wholesome and invigorating system, for the children were all strong and healthy. Jane was probably treated like the rest in this respect. In childhood every available opportunity of instruction was made use of. According to the ideas of the time, she was well educated, though not highly accomplished, and she certainly enjoyed that important element of mental training, associating at home with persons of cultivated intellect. It cannot be doubted that her early years were bright and happy, living, as she did, with indulgent parents, in a cheerful home, not without agreeable variety of society. To these sources of enjoyment must be added the first stirrings of talent within her, and the absorbing interest of original composition. It is impossible to say at how early an age she began to write. There are copy books extant containing tales some of which must have been composed while she was a young girl, as they had amounted to a considerable number by the time she was sixteen. Her earliest stories are of a slight and flimsy texture, and are generally intended to be nonsensical, but the nonsense has much spirit in it.

They are usually preceded by a dedication of mock solemnity to some one of her family. It would seem that the grandiloquent dedications prevalent in those days had not escaped her youthful penetration. Perhaps the most characteristic feature in these early productions is that, however puerile the matter, they are always composed in pure simple English, quite free from the over-ornamented style which might be expected from so young a writer. One of her juvenile effusions is given, as a specimen of the kind of transitory amusement which Jane was continually supplying to the family party.

THE MYSTERY.

AN UNFINISHED COMEDY.

—

DEDICATION.

To the Rev. George Austen.

SIR, — I humbly solicit your patronage to the following Comedy, which, though an unfinished one, is, I flatter myself, as complete a *Mystery* as any of its kind.

I am, Sir, your most humble Servant,

THE AUTHOR.

THE MYSTERY, A COMEDY.

Dramatis Personæ.

Men.	*Women.*
COL. ELLIOTT.	FANNY ELLIOTT.
OLD HUMBUG.	MRS HUMBUG
YOUNG HUMBUG.	*and*
SIR EDWARD SPANGLE	DAPHNE.
and	
CORYDON.	

ACT I.

SCENE I. – A *Garden.*

Enter CORYDON.

Corydon. But hush : I am interrupted. [*Exit* CORYDON.
Enter OLD HUMBUG *and his* SON, *talking.*

Old Hum. It is for that reason that I wish you to follow my advice. Are you convinced of its propriety?

Young Hum. I am, sir, and will certainly act in the manner you have pointed out to me.

Old Hum. Then let us return to the house. [*Exeunt.*

SCENE II. – *A parlour in* HUMBUG'S *house.* MRS HUMBUG *and* FANNY *discovered at work.*

Mrs Hum. You understand me, my love?

Fanny. Perfectly, ma'am: pray continue your narration.

Mrs Hum. Alas! it is nearly concluded; for I have nothing more to say on the subject.

Fanny. Ah! here is Daphne.

Enter DAPHNE.

Daphne. My dear Mrs Humbug, how d'ye do? Oh! Fanny, it is all over.

Fanny. Is it indeed!

Mrs Hum. I'm very sorry to hear it.

Fanny. Then 'twas to no purpose that I –

Daphne. None upon earth.

Mrs Hum. And what is to become of – ?

Daphne. Oh! 'tis all settled. (*Whispers* MRS HUMBUG.)

Fanny. And how is it determined?

Daphne. I'll tell you. (*Whispers* FANNY.)

Mrs Hum. And is he to – ?

Daphne. I'll tell you all I know of the matter. (*Whispers* MRS HUMBUG *and* FANNY.)

Fanny. Well, now I know everything about it, I'll go away.

Mrs Hum.
Daphne. } And so will I. [*Exeunt.*

SCENE III. – *The curtain rises, and discovers* SIR EDWARD SPANGLE *reclined in an elegant attitude on a sofa fast asleep.*

Enter COL. ELLIOTT.

Col. E. My daughter is not here, I see. There lies Sir Edward. Shall I tell him the secret? No, he'll certainly blab it. But he's asleep, and won't hear me; – so I'll e'en venture. (*Goes up to* SIR EDWARD, *whispers him, and exit.*)

END OF THE FIRST ACT.

FINIS.

Her own mature opinion of the desirableness of such an early habit of composition is given in the following words of a niece [10] : –

'As I grew older, my aunt would talk to me more seriously of my reading and my amusements. I had taken early to writing verses and stories, and I am sorry to think how I troubled her with reading them. She was very kind about it, and always had some praise to bestow, but at last she warned me against spending too much time upon them. She said – how well I recollect it ! – that she knew writing stories was a great amusement, and *she* thought a harmless one, though many people, she was aware, thought otherwise; but that at my age it would be bad for me to be much taken up with my own compositions. Later still – it was after she had gone to Winchester – she sent me a message to this effect, that if I would take her advice I should cease writing till I was sixteen; that she had herself often wished she had read more, and written less in the corresponding years of her own life.' As this niece was only twelve years old at the time of her aunt's death, these words seem to imply that the juvenile tales to which I have referred had, some of them at least, been written in her childhood.

But between these childish effusions, and the composition of her living works, there intervened another stage of her progress, during which she produced some stories, not without merit, but which she never considered worthy of publication. During this preparatory period her mind seems to have been working in a very different direction from that into which it ultimately settled. Instead of presenting faithful copies of nature, these tales were generally burlesques, ridiculing the improbable events and exaggerated sentiments which she had met with in sundry silly romances. Something of this fancy is to be found in 'Northanger Abbey,' but she soon left it far behind in her subsequent course. It would seem as if she were first taking note of all the faults to be avoided, and curiously considering how she ought *not* to write before she attempted to put forth her strength in the right direction. The family have, rightly, I think, declined to let these early works be published. Mr Shortreed observed very pithily of Walter Scott's early rambles on the borders, 'He was makin' himsell a' the time; but he didna ken, may be, what he was about till years had passed. At first he thought of little, I dare say, but the queerness and the fun.' And so, in a humbler way, Jane Austen was 'makin' hersell,' little thinking of future fame, but caring only for 'the queerness and the fun;' and it would be as unfair to expose this preliminary process to the world, as it would be to display all that goes on behind the curtain of the theatre before it is drawn up.

It was, however, at Steventon that the real foundations of her fame were laid. There some of her most successful writing was composed at such an early age as to make it surprising that so young a woman could have acquired the insight into character, and the nice observation of manners which they display. 'Pride and Prejudice,' which some consider the most brilliant of her novels, was the first finished, if not the first begun. She began it in October 1796, before she was twenty-one years old, and completed it in about ten months, in August 1797. The title then intended for it was 'First Impressions.' 'Sense and Sensibility' was begun, in its present form, immediately after the completion of the former, in November 1797; but something similar in story and character had been written earlier under the title of 'Elinor and Marianne;' and if, as is probable, a good deal of this earlier production was retained, it must form the earliest specimen of her writing that has been given to the world. 'Northanger Abbey,' though not prepared for the press till 1803, was certainly first composed in 1798.

Amongst the most valuable neighbours of the Austens were Mr and Mrs Lefroy and their family. He was rector of the adjoining parish of Ashe; she was sister to Sir Egerton Brydges, to whom we are indebted for the earliest notice of Jane Austen that exists. In his autobiography, speaking of his visits at Ashe, he writes thus: 'The nearest neighbours of the Lefroys were the Austens of Steventon. I remember Jane Austen, the novelist, as a

little child. She was very intimate with Mrs Lefroy, and much
encouraged by her. Her mother was a Miss Leigh, whose paternal
grandmother was sister to the first Duke of Chandos. Mr Austen
was of a Kentish family, of which several branches have been
settled in the Weald of Kent, and some are still remaining there.
When I knew Jane Austen, I never suspected that she was an
authoress; but my eyes told me that she was fair and handsome,
slight and elegant, but with cheeks a little too full.' One may
wish that Sir Egerton had dwelt rather longer on the subject of
these memoirs, instead of being drawn away by his extreme
love for genealogies to her great-grandmother and ancestors. That
great-grandmother however lives in the family records as Mary
Brydges, a daughter of Lord Chandos, married in Westminster
Abbey to Theophilus Leigh of Addlestrop in 1698. When a girl
she had received a curious letter of advice and reproof, written by
her mother from Constantinople. Mary, or 'Poll,' was remaining
in England with her grandmother, Lady Bernard, who seems to
have been wealthy and inclined to be too indulgent to her grand-
daughter. This letter is given. Any such authentic document,
two hundred years old, dealing with domestic details, must
possess some interest. This is remarkable, not only as a specimen
of the homely language in which ladies of rank then expressed
themselves, but from the sound sense which it contains. Forms
of expression vary, but good sense and right principles are the
same in the nineteenth that they were in the seventeenth
century.

'My Deares Poll,

'Yr letters by Cousin Robbert Serle arrived here not before the
27th of Aprill, yett were they hartily wellcome to us, bringing ye
joyful news which a great while we had longed for of my most
dear Mother & all other relations & friends good health which I
beseech God continue to you all, & as I observe in yrs to yr Sister
Betty ye extraordinary kindness of (as I may truly say) the best
Mothr & Gnd Mothr in the world in pinching herself to make you
fine, so I cannot but admire her great good Housewifry in afford-
ing you so very plentifull an allowance, & yett to increase her
Stock at the rate I find she hath done; & think I can never suffi-

ciently mind you how very much it is y^r duty on all occasions to pay her y^r gratitude in all humble submission & obedience to all her commands soe long as you live. I must tell you 'tis to her bounty & care in ye greatest measure you are like to owe y^r well living in this world, & as you cannot but be very sensible you are an extra-ordinary charge to her so it behoves you to take particular heed th^t in ye whole course of y^r life, you render her a proportionable comfort, especially since 'tis ye best way you can ever hope to make her such amends as God requires of y^r hands. but Poll! it grieves me a little & y^t I am forced to take notice of & reprove you for some vaine expressions in y^r lett^{rs} to y^r Sister – you say concerning y^r allowance "you aime to bring y^r bread & cheese even" in this I do not discommend you, for a foule shame indeed it would be should you out run the Constable having soe liberall a provision made you for y^r maintenance – but ye reason you give for y^r resolution I cannot at all approve for you say "to spend more you can't" thats because you have it not to spend, otherwise it seems you would. So y^t 'tis y^r Grandmoth^{rs} discretion & not yours th^t keeps you from extravagancy, which plainly appears in ye close of y^r sentence, saying y^t you think it simple covetousness to save out of y^{rs} but 'tis my opinion if you lay all on y^r back 'tis ten tymes a greater sin & shame th^n to save some what out of soe large an allowance in y^r purse to help you at a dead lift. Child, we all know our beginning, but who knows his end? Y^e best use th^t can be made of fair weath^r is to provide against foule & 'tis great discretion & of noe small commendations for a young woman betymes to shew herself housewifly & frugal. Y^r Mother neither Maide nor wife ever yett bestowed forty pounds a yeare on herself & yett if you never fall und^r a worse reputation in ye world th^n she (I thank God for it) hath hitherto done, you need not repine at it, & you cannot be ignorant of ye difference th^t was between my fortune & what you are to expect. You ought likewise to consider th^t you have seven brothers & sisters & you are all one man's children & therefore it is very unreasonable that one should expect to be preferred in finery soe much above all ye rest for 'tis impossible you should soe much mistake y^r ffather's condition as to fancy he is able to allow every one of you forty pounds a yeare a piece, for such an allow-

ance with the charge of their diett over and above will amount
to at least five hundred pounds a yeare, a sum y^r poor ffather can
ill spare, besides doe but bethink y^{r}self what a ridiculous sight it
will be when y^r grandmoth^r & you come to us to have noe less
th^n seven waiting gentlewomen in one house, for what reason
can you give why every one of y^r Sist^{rs} should not have every one
of y^m a Maide as well as you, & though you may spare to pay y^r
maide's wages out of y^r allowance yett you take no care of y^e
unnecessary charge you put y^r ffath^r to in y^r increase of his
family, whereas if it were not a piece of pride to have ye name of
keeping y^r maide she y^t waits on y^r good Grandmother might
easily doe as formerly you know she hath done, all ye business
you have for a maide unless as you grow old^r you grow a veryer
Foole which God forbid !

'Poll, you live in a place where you see great plenty & splendour
but let not ye allurements of earthly pleasures tempt you to forget
or neglect ye duty of a good Christian in dressing y^r bett^r part
which is y^r soule, as will best please God. I am not against y^r
going decent & neate as becomes y^r ffathers daughter but to
clothe y^{r}self rich & be running into every gaudy fashion can
never become y^r circumstances & instead of doing you creditt &
getting you a good prefer^{nt} it is ye readiest way you can take to
fright all sober men from ever thinking of matching th^{m}selves
with women that live above thy^r fortune, & if this be a wise way
of spending money judge you ! & besides, doe but reflect what an
od sight it will be to a stranger that comes to our house to see y^r
Grandmother^r y^r Moth^r & all y^r Sisters in a plane dress & you
only trick^d up like a bartlemew-babby – you know what sort of
people those are th^t can't faire well but they must cry rost meate
now what effect could you imagine y^r writing in such a high
straine to y^r Sisters could have but eithe^r to provoke th^m to envy
you or murmur against us. I must tell you neith^r of y^r Sisters
have ever had twenty pounds a yeare allowance from us yett, &
yett they^r dress hath not disparaged neith^r th^m nor us & without
incurring ye censure of simple covetousness they will have some
what to shew out of their saving that will doe th^m creditt & I
expect y^t you th^t are theyr elder Sister sh^d rather sett th^m
examples of ye like nature th^n tempt th^m from treading in y^e

steps of their good Grandmoth^r & poor Moth^r. This is not half
what might be saide on this occasion but believing thee to be a
very good natured dutyfull child I sh^d have thought it a great
deal too much but y^t having in my coming hither past through
many most desperate dangers I cannot forbear thinking & preparing myself for all events, & therefore not knowing how it may
please God to dispose of us I conclude it my duty to God & thee
my d^r child to lay this matter as home to thee as I could, assuring
you my daily prayers are not nor shall not be wanting that God
may give you grace always to remember to make a right use of
this truly affectionate counsell of y^r poor Moth^r. & though I
speak very plaine down-right english to you yett I would not have
you doubt but that I love you as hartily as any child I have & if
you serve God and take good courses I promise you my kindness
to you shall be according to y^r own hart's desire, for you may be
certain I can aime at nothing in what I have now writ but y^r real
good which to promote shall be ye study & care day & night

      'Of my dear Poll

          'thy truly affectionate Moth^r.

            'Eliza Chandos.

'Pera of Galata, May ye 6th 1686.

'P.S. – Thy ffath^r & I send thee our blessing, & all thy broth^{rs}
& sist^{rs} they^r service. Our harty & affectionate service to my
broth^r & sist^r Childe & all my dear cozens. When you see my
Lady Worster & cozen Howlands pray present th^m my most
humble service.'

This letter shows that the wealth acquired by trade was already
manifesting itself in contrast with the straitened circumstances
of some of the nobility. Mary Brydges's 'poor ffather,' in whose
household economy was necessary, was the King of England's
ambassador at Constantinople; the grandmother, who lived in
'great plenty and splendour,' was the widow of a Turkey
merchant. But then, as now, it would seem, rank had the power
of attracting and absorbing wealth.

At Ashe also Jane became acquainted with a member of the
Lefroy family, who was still living when I began these memoirs,

a few months ago; the Right Hon. Thomas Lefroy, late Chief
Justice of Ireland. One must look back more than seventy years
to reach the time when these two bright young persons were, for
a short time, intimately acquainted with each other, and then
separated on their several courses, never to meet again; both
destined to attain some distinction in their different ways, one to
survive the other for more than half a century, yet in his extreme
old age to remember and speak, as he sometimes did, of his former
companion, as one to be much admired, and not easily forgotten
by those who had ever known her.

Mrs Lefroy herself was a remarkable person. Her rare endowments of goodness, talents, graceful person, and engaging manners, were sufficient to secure her a prominent place in any
society into which she was thrown; while her enthusiastic
eagerness of disposition rendered her especially attractive to a
clever and lively girl. She was killed by a fall from her horse on
Jane's birthday, Dec. 16, 1804. The following lines to her memory
were written by Jane four years afterwards, when she was thirty-
three years old. They are given, not for their merits as poetry, but
to show how deep and lasting was the impression made by the
elder friend on the mind of the younger : –

TO THE MEMORY OF MRS LEFROY.

1.

The day returns again, my natal day;
  What mix'd emotions in my mind arise !
Beloved Friend; four years have passed away
  Since thou wert snatched for ever from our eyes.

2.

The day commemorative of my birth,
  Bestowing life, and light, and hope to me,
Brings back the hour which was thy last on earth.
  Oh ! bitter pang of torturing memory !

3.

Angelic woman ! past my power to praise
  In language meet thy talents, temper, mind,
Thy solid worth, thy captivating grace,
  Thou friend and ornament of human kind.

4.

But come, fond Fancy, thou indulgent power;
  Hope is desponding, chill, severe, to thee:
Bless thou this little portion of an hour;
  Let me behold her as she used to be.

5.

I see her here with all her smiles benign,
  Her looks of eager love, her accents sweet,
That voice and countenance almost divine,
  Expression, harmony, alike complete.

6.

Listen ! It is not sound alone, 'tis sense,
  'Tis genius, taste, and tenderness of soul:
'Tis genuine warmth of heart without pretence,
  And purity of mind that crowns the whole.

7.

She speaks ! 'Tis eloquence, that grace of tongue,
  So rare, so lovely, never misapplied
By her, to palliate vice, or deck a wrong:
  She speaks and argues but on virtue's side.

8.

Hers is the energy of soul sincere;
  Her Christian spirit, ignorant to feign,
Seeks but to comfort, heal, enlighten, cheer,
  Confer a pleasure or prevent a pain.

9.

Can aught enhance such goodness? yes, to me
  Her partial favour from my earliest years
Consummates all : ah ! give me but to see
  Her smile of love ! The vision disappears.

10.

'Tis past and gone. We meet no more below.
  Short is the cheat of Fancy o'er the tomb.
Oh ! might I hope to equal bliss to go,
    To meet thee, angel, in thy future home.

11.

> Fain would I feel an union with thy fate:
>   Fain would I seek to draw an omen fair
> From this connection in our earthly date.
>   Indulge the harmless weakness. Reason, spare.

The loss of their first home is generally a great grief to young persons of strong feeling and lively imagination; and Jane was exceedingly unhappy [11] when she was told that her father, now seventy years of age, had determined to resign his duties to his eldest son, who was to be his successor in the Rectory of Steventon, and to remove with his wife and daughters to Bath. Jane had been absent from home when this resolution was taken; and, as her father was always rapid both in forming his resolutions and in acting on them, she had little time to reconcile herself to the change.

A wish has sometimes been expressed that some of Jane Austen's letters should be published. Some entire letters, and many extracts, will be given in this memoir; but the reader must be warned not to expect too much from them. With regard to accuracy of language indeed every word of them might be printed without correction. The style is always clear, and generally animated, while a vein of humour continually gleams through the whole; but the materials may be thought inferior to the execution, for they treat only of the details of domestic life. There is in them no notice of politics or public events; scarcely any discussions on literature, or other subjects of general interest. They may be said to resemble the nest which some little bird builds of the materials nearest at hand, of the twigs and mosses supplied by the tree in which it is placed; curiously constructed out of the simplest matters.

Her letters have very seldom the date of the year, or the signature of her christian name at full length; but it has been easy to ascertain their dates, either from the post-mark, or from their contents.

The two following letters are the earliest that I have seen. They were both written in November 1800; before the family removed from Steventon. Some of the same circumstances are referred to in both.

The first is to her sister Cassandra, who was then staying with their brother Edward at Godmersham Park, Kent:—

'Steventon, Saturday evening, Nov 8th.

'My dear Cassandra,

'I thank you for so speedy a return to my two last, and particularly thank you for your anecdote of Charlotte Graham and her cousin, Harriet Bailey, which has very much amused both my mother and myself. If you can learn anything farther of that interesting affair, I hope you will mention it. I have two messages; let me get rid of them, and then my paper will be my own. Mary fully intended writing to you by Mr Chute's frank, and only happened entirely to forget it, but will write soon; and my father wishes Edward to send him a memorandum of the price of the hops. The tables are come, and give general contentment. I had not expected that they would so perfectly suit the fancy of us all three, or that we should so well agree in the disposition of them; but nothing except their own surface can have been smoother. The two ends put together form one constant table for everything, and the centre piece stands exceedingly well under the glass, and holds a great deal most commodiously, without looking awkwardly. They are both covered with green baize, and send their best love. The Pembroke has got its destination by the sideboard, and my mother has great delight in keeping her money and papers locked up. The little table which used to stand there has most conveniently taken itself off into the best bedroom; and we are now in want only of the chiffonniere, which is neither finished nor come. So much for that subject; I now come to another, of a very different nature, as other subjects are very apt to be. Earle Harwood has been again giving uneasiness to his family and talk to the neighbourhood; in the present instance, however, he is only unfortunate, and not in fault.

'About ten days ago, in cocking a pistol in the guard-room at Marcau,[12] he accidentally shot himself through the thigh. Two young Scotch surgeons in the island were polite enough to propose taking off the thigh at once, but to that he would not consent; and accordingly in his wounded state was put on board a cutter and conveyed to Haslar Hospital, at Gosport, where the bullet was extracted, and where he now is, I hope, in a fair way of doing well. The surgeon of the hospital wrote to the family on the occasion, and John Harwood went down to him immediately, attended by James,* whose object in going was to be the means of bringing back the earliest intelligence to Mr and Mrs Harwood, whose anxious sufferings, particularly those of the latter, have of course been dreadful. They went down on Tuesday, and James came back the next day, bringing such favourable accounts as greatly to lessen the distress of the family at Deane, though it will probably be a long while before Mrs Harwood can be quite at ease. *One* most material comfort, however, they have; the assurance of its being really an accidental wound, which is not only positively declared by Earle himself, but is likewise testified by the particular direction of the bullet. Such a wound could not have been received in a duel. At present he is going on very well, but the surgeon will not declare him to be in no danger.† Mr Heathcote met with a genteel little accident the other day in hunting. He got off to lead his horse over a hedge, or a house, or something, and his horse in his haste trod upon his leg, or rather ancle, I believe, and it is not certain whether the small bone is not broke. Martha has accepted Mary's invitation for Lord Portsmouth's ball. He has not yet sent out his own invitations, but *that* does not signify; Martha comes, and a ball there is to be. I think it will be too early in her mother's absence for me to return with her.

'*Sunday Evening.* – We have had a dreadful storm of wind in the fore part of this day, which has done a great deal of mischief among our trees. I was sitting alone in the dining-room when an odd kind of crash startled me – in a moment afterwards it was repeated. I then went to the window, which I reached just in time to see the last of our two highly valued elms descend into the Sweep ! ! ! ! ! The other, which had fallen, I suppose, in the first crash, and which was the nearest to the pond, taking a more

---

* James, the writer's eldest brother.　　　† The limb was saved.

easterly direction, sunk among our screen of chestnuts and firs, knocking down one spruce-fir, beating off the head of another, and stripping the two corner chestnuts of several branches in its fall. This is not all. One large elm out of the two on the left-hand side as you enter what I call the elm walk, was likewise blown down; the maple [13] bearing the weathercock was broke in two, and what I regret more than all the rest is, that all the three elms which grew in Hall's meadow, and gave such ornament to it, are gone; two were blown down, and the other so much injured that it cannot stand. I am happy to add, however, that no greater evil than the loss of trees has been the consequence of the storm in this place, or in our immediate neighbourhood. We grieve, therefore, in some comfort.

'I am yours ever,

'J.A.'

The next letter, written four days later than the former, was addressed to Miss Lloyd,[14] an intimate friend, whose sister (my mother) was married to Jane's eldest brother : —

'*Steventon, Wednesday evening, Nov. 12th.*

'My dear Martha,

'I did not receive your note yesterday till after Charlotte had left Deane, or I would have sent my answer by her, instead of being the means, as I now must be, of lessening the elegance of your new dress for the Hurstbourne ball by the value of 3*d.* You are very good in wishing to see me at Ibthorp so soon, and I am equally good in wishing to come to you. I believe our merit in that respect is much upon a par, our self-denial mutually strong. Having paid this tribute of praise to the virtue of both, I shall here have done with panegyric, and proceed to plain matter of fact. In about a fortnight's time I hope to be with you. I have two reasons for not being able to come before. I wish so to arrange my visit as to spend some days with you after your mother's return. In the 1st place, that I may have the pleasure of seeing her, and in the 2nd, that I may have a better chance of bringing you back with me. Your promise in my favour was not quite absolute, but if your will is not perverse, you and I will do all in our power to overcome your scruples of conscience. I hope we shall meet next week to talk all this over, till we have tired ourselves with the very idea of my visit before my visit begins. Our invitations for the 19th are arrived, and very curiously they are worded.* Mary mentioned to you yesterday poor Earle's unfortunate accident, I dare say. He does not seem to be going on very well. The two or three last posts have brought less and less favourable accounts of him. John Harwood has gone to Gosport again to-day. We have two families of friends now who are in a most anxious state; for though by a note from Catherine this morning there seems now to be a revival of hope at Manydown, its continuance may be too reasonably doubted. Mr Heathcote,† however, who has broken the small bone of his leg, is so good as to be going on very well. It could be really too much to have three people to care for.

'You distress me cruelly by your request about books. I cannot think of any to bring with me, nor have I any idea of our wanting them. I come to you to be talked to, not to read or hear reading; I can do that at home; and indeed I am now laying in a stock of intelligence to pour out on you as my share of the conversation. I am reading Henry's History of England, which I will repeat to you in any manner you may prefer, either in a loose, desultory, unconnected stream, or dividing my recital, as the historian divides it himself, into seven parts: – The Civil and Military: Religion: Constitution: Learning and Learned Men: Arts and Sciences: Commerce, Coins, and Shipping: and Manners. So that for every evening in the week there will be a different subject. The Friday's lot – Commerce, Coins, and Shipping – you will find the least entertaining; but the next even-

---

* The invitation, the ball dress, and some other things in this and the preceding letter refer to a ball annually given at Hurstbourne Park, on the anniversary of the Earl of Portsmouth's marriage with his first wife. He was the Lord Portsmouth whose eccentricities afterwards became notorious, and the invitations, as well as other arrangements about these balls, were of a peculiar character.

† The father of Sir William Heathcote, of Hursley, who was married to a daughter of Mr Bigge Wither, of Manydown, and lived in the neighbourhood.

ing's portion will make amends. With such a provision on my part, if you will do yours by repeating the French Grammar, and Mrs Stent * will now and then ejaculate some wonder about the cocks and hens, what can we want? Farewell for a short time. We all unite in best love, and I am your very affectionate

'J.A.'

The two next letters must have been written early in 1801, after the removal from Steventon had been decided on, but before it had taken place. They refer to the two brothers who were at sea, and give some idea of a kind of anxieties and uncertainties to which sisters are seldom subject in these days of peace, steamers, and electric telegraphs. At that time ships were often windbound or becalmed, or driven wide of their destination; and sometimes they had orders to alter their course for some secret service; not to mention the chance of conflict with a vessel of superior power – no improbable occurrence before the battle of Trafalgar. Information about relatives on board men-of-war was scarce and scanty, and often picked up by hearsay or chance means; and every scrap of intelligence was proportionably valuable: –

'My dear Cassandra,

'I should not have thought it necessary to write to you so soon, but for the arrival of a letter from Charles to myself. It was written last Saturday from off the Start, and conveyed to Popham Lane by Captain Boyle, on his way to Midgham. He came from Lisbon in the "Endymion." I will copy Charles's account of his conjectures about Frank: "He has not seen my brother lately, nor does he expect to find him arrived, as he met Captain Inglis at Rhodes, going up to take command of the 'Petrel,' as he was coming down; but supposes he will arrive in less than a fortnight from this time, in some ship which is expected to reach England about that time with dispatches from Sir Ralph Abercrombie." The event must show what sort of a conjuror Captain Boyle is. The "Endymion" has not been plagued with any more prizes. Charles spent three pleasant days in Lisbon.

* A very dull old lady, then residing with Mrs Lloyd.

'They were very well satisfied with their royal passenger,* whom they found jolly and affable, who talks of Lady Augusta as his wife, and seems much attached to her.

'When this letter was written, the "Endymion" was becalmed, but Charles hoped to reach Portsmouth by Monday or Tuesday. He received my letter, communicating our plans, before he left England; was much surprised, of course, but is quite reconciled to them, and means to come to Steventon once more while Steventon is ours.'

From a letter written later in the same year : –

'Charles has received 30l. for his share of the privateer, and expects 10l. more; but of what avail is it to take prizes if he lays out the produce in presents to his sisters? He has been buying gold chains and topaze crosses for us. He must be well scolded. The "Endymion" has already received orders for taking troops to Egypt, which I should not like at all if I did not trust to Charles being removed from her somehow or other before she sails. He knows nothing of his own destination, he says, but desires me to write directly, as the "Endymion" will probably sail in three or four days. He will receive my yesterday's letter, and I shall write again by this post to thank and reproach him. We shall be unbearably fine.'

---

* The Duke of Sussex, son of George III, married, without royal consent, to the Lady Augusta Murray.

CHAPTER 4

Removal from Steventon – Residences at Bath and at Southampton –
Settling at Chawton.

THE family removed to Bath in the spring of 1801, where they
resided first at No. 4 Sydney Terrace, and afterwards in Green
Park Buildings. I do not know whether they were at all attracted
to Bath by the circumstance that Mrs Austen's only brother, Mr
Leigh Perrot, spent part of every year there. The name Perrot,
together with a small estate at Northleigh in Oxfordshire, had
been bequeathed to him by a great uncle. I must devote a few
sentences to this very old and now extinct branch of the Perrot
family; for one of the last survivors, Jane Perrot, married to a
Walker, was Jane Austen's great grandmother, from whom she
derived her Christian name. The Perrots were settled in Pem-
brokeshire at least as early as the thirteenth century. They were
probably some of the settlers whom the policy of our Plantagenet
kings placed in that county, which thence acquired the name of
'England beyond Wales,' for the double purpose of keeping open
a communication with Ireland from Milford Haven, and of over-
awing the Welsh. One of the family seems to have carried out
this latter purpose very vigorously; for it is recorded of him that
he slew *twenty-six men* of Kemaes, a district of Wales, and *one*
wolf. The manner in which the two kinds of game are classed
together, and the disproportion of numbers, are remarkable; but
probably at that time the wolves had been so closely killed down,
that *lupicide* was become a more rare and distinguished exploit
than *homicide*. The last of this family died about 1778, and their
property was divided between Leighs and Musgraves, the larger
portion going to the latter. Mr Leigh Perrot pulled down the
mansion, and sold the estate to the Duke of Marlborough, and the
name of these Perrots is now to be found only on some monuments in the church of Northleigh.

Mr Leigh Perrot was also one of several cousins to whom a
life interest in the Stoneleigh property in Warwickshire was left,

after the extinction of the earlier Leigh peerage, but he compromised his claim to the succession in his lifetime. He married a niece of Sir Montague Cholmeley of Lincolnshire. He was a man of considerable natural power, with much of the wit of his uncle, the Master of Balliol, and wrote clever epigrams and riddles, some of which, though without his name, found their way into print; but he lived a very retired life, dividing his time between Bath and his place in Berkshire called Scarlets. Jane's letters from Bath make frequent mention of this uncle and aunt.

The unfinished story, now published under the title of 'The Watsons,' must have been written during the author's residence in Bath. In the autumn of 1804 she spent some weeks at Lyme, and became acquainted with the Cobb, which she afterwards made memorable for the fall of Louisa Musgrove. In February 1805, her father died at Bath, and was buried at Walcot Church. The widow and daughters went into lodgings for a few months,[15] and then moved to Southampton. The only records that I can find about her during those four years are the three following letters to her sister; one from Lyme, the others from Bath. They shew that she went a good deal into society, in a quiet way, chiefly with ladies; and that her eyes were always open to minute traits of character in those with whom she associated.

EXTRACT FROM A LETTER FROM JANE AUSTEN
TO HER SISTER

'Lyme, Friday, Sept. 14 (1804).

'My dear Cassandra, – I take the first sheet of fine striped paper to thank you for your letter from Weymouth, and express my hopes of your being at Ibthorp before this time. I expect to hear that you reached it yesterday evening, being able to get as far as Blandford on Wednesday. Your account of Weymouth contains nothing which strikes me so forcibly as there being no ice in the town. For every other vexation I was in some measure prepared, and particularly for your disappointment in not seeing the Royal Family go on board on Tuesday, having already heard from Mr Crawford that he had seen you in the very act of being too late.

But for there being no ice, what could prepare me! You found my letter at Andover, I hope, yesterday, and have now for many hours been satisfied that your kind anxiety on my behalf was as much thrown away as kind anxiety usually is. I continue quite well; in proof of which I have bathed again this morning. It was absolutely necessary that I should have the little fever and indisposition which I had: it has been all the fashion this week in Lyme. We are quite settled in our lodgings by this time, as you may suppose, and everything goes on in the usual order. The servants behave very well, and make no difficulties, though nothing certainly can exceed the inconvenience of the offices, except the general dirtiness of the house and furniture, and all its inhabitants. I endeavour, as far as I can, to supply your place, and be useful, and keep things in order. I detect dirt in the water decanters, as fast as I can, and keep everything as it was under your administration. ... The ball last night was pleasant, but not full for Thursday. My father staid contentedly till half-past nine (we went a little after eight), and then walked home with James and a lanthorn, though I believe the lanthorn was not lit, as the moon was up; but sometimes this lanthorn may be a great convenience to him. My mother and I staid about an hour later. Nobody asked me the two first dances; the next two I danced with Mr Crawford, and had I chosen to stay longer might have danced with Mr Granville, Mrs Granville's son, whom my dear friend Miss A. introduced to me, or with a new odd-looking man who had been eyeing me for some time, and at last, without any introduction, asked me if I meant to dance again. I think he must be Irish by his ease, and because I imagine him to belong to the hon^bl B.'s, who are son, and son's wife of an Irish viscount, bold queer-looking people, just fit to be quality at Lyme. I called yesterday morning (ought it not in strict propriety to be termed yester-morning?) on Miss A. and was introduced to her father and mother. Like other young ladies she is considerably genteeler than her parents. Mrs A. sat darning a pair of stockings the whole of my visit. But do not mention this at home, lest a warning should act as an example. We afterwards walked together for an hour on the Cobb; she is very converseable in a common way; I do not perceive wit or genius, but she has sense and some degree of taste, and her manners are very engaging. She seems to like people rather too easily.

'Your's affect^ly,

'J.A.'

Letter from Jane Austen to her sister Cassandra at Ibthorp, alluding to the sudden death of Mrs Lloyd at that place: –

'*25 Gay Street (Bath), Monday, April 8, 1805.*

'My dear Cassandra, – Here is a day for you. Did Bath or Ibthorp ever see such an 8th of April? It is March and April together; the glare of the one and the warmth of the other. We do nothing but walk about. As far as your means will admit, I hope you profit by such weather too. I dare say you are already the better for change of place. We were out again last night. Miss Irvine invited us, when I met her in the Crescent, to drink tea with them, but I rather declined it, having no idea that my mother would be disposed for another evening visit there so soon; but when I gave her the message, I found her very well inclined to go; and accordingly, on leaving Chapel, we walked to Lansdown. This morning we have been to see Miss Chamberlaine look hot on horseback. Seven years and four months ago we went to the same riding-house to see Miss Lefroy's performance! * What a different set are we now moving in! But seven years, I suppose, are enough to change every pore of one's skin and every feeling of one's mind. We did not walk long in the Crescent yesterday. It was hot and not crowded enough; so we went into the field, and passed close by S. T. and Miss S.† again. I have not yet seen her face, but neither her dress nor air have anything of the dash or stylishness which the Browns talked of; quite the contrary; indeed, her dress is not even smart, and her appearance very quiet. Miss Irvine says she is never speaking a word. Poor wretch; I am afraid she is *en pénitence*. Here has been that excellent Mrs Coulthart calling, while my mother was out, and I was believed to be so. I always respected her, as a good-

---

* Here is evidence that Jane Austen was acquainted with Bath before it became her residence in 1801. See p. 288.

† A gentleman and lady lately engaged to be married.

hearted friendly woman. And the Browns have been here; I find their affidavits on the table. The "Ambuscade" reached Gibraltar on the 9th of March, and found all well; so say the papers. We have had no letters from anybody, but we expect to hear from Edward to-morrow, and from you soon afterwards. How happy they are at Godmersham now! I shall be very glad of a letter from Ibthorp, that I may know how you all are, but particularly yourself. This is nice weather for Mrs J. Austen's going to Speen, and I hope she will have a pleasant visit there. I expect a prodigious account of the christening dinner; perhaps it brought you at last into the company of Miss Dundas again.

'*Tuesday.* – I received your letter last night, and wish it may be soon followed by another to say that all is over; but I cannot help thinking that nature will struggle again, and produce a revival. Poor woman! May her end be peaceful and easy as the exit we have witnessed! And I dare say it will. If there is no revival, suffering must be all over; even the consciousness of existence, I suppose, was gone when you wrote. The nonsense I have been writing in this and in my last letter seems out of place at such a time, but I will not mind it; it will do you no harm, and nobody else will be attacked by it. I am heartily glad that you can speak so comfortably of your own health and looks, though I can scarcely comprehend the latter being really approved. Could travelling fifty miles produce such an immediate change? You were looking very poorly here, and everybody seemed sensible of it. Is there a charm in a hack postchaise? But if there were, Mrs Craven's carriage might have undone it all. I am much obliged to you for the time and trouble you have bestowed on Mary's cap, and am glad it pleases her; but it will prove a useless gift at present, I suppose. Will not she leave Ibthorp on her mother's death? As a companion you are all that Martha can be supposed to want, and in that light, under these circumstances, your visit will indeed have been well timed.

'*Thursday.* – I was not able to go on yesterday; all my wit and leisure were bestowed on letters to Charles and Henry. To the former I wrote in consequence of my mother's having seen in the papers that the "Urania" was waiting at Portsmouth for the convoy for Halifax. This is nice, as it is only three weeks ago that you wrote by the "Camilla." I wrote to Henry because I had a letter from him in which he desired to hear from me very soon. His to me was most affectionate and kind, as well as entertaining; there is no merit to him in *that*; he cannot help being amusing. He offers to meet us on the sea coast, if the plan of which Edward gave him some hint takes place. Will not this be making the execution of such a plan more desirable and delightful than ever? He talks of the rambles we took together last summer with pleasing affection.

'Yours ever,

'J.A.'

FROM THE SAME TO THE SAME

'*Gay St. Sunday Evening, April 21 (1805).*

'My dear Cassandra, – I am much obliged to you for writing to me again so soon; your letter yesterday was quite an unexpected pleasure. Poor Mrs Stent! it has been her lot to be always in the way; but we must be merciful, for perhaps in time we may come to be Mrs Stents ourselves, unequal to anything, and unwelcome to everybody. . . . My morning engagement was with the Cookes, and our party consisted of George and Mary, a Mr L., Miss B., who had been with us at the concert, and the youngest Miss W. Not Julia; we have done with her; she is very ill; but Mary. Mary W.'s turn is actually come to be grown up, and have a fine complexion, and wear great square muslin shawls. I have not expressly enumerated myself among the party, but there I was, and my cousin George was very kind, and talked sense to me every now and then, in the intervals of his more animated fooleries with Miss B., who is very young, and rather handsome, and whose gracious manners, ready wit, and solid remarks, put me somewhat in mind of my old acquaintance L. L. There was a monstrous deal of stupid quizzing and common-place nonsense talked, but scarcely any wit; all that bordered on it or on sense came from my cousin George, whom altogether I like very well. Mr B. seems nothing more than a tall young man. My evening engagement and walk was with Miss A., who had called on me the day before, and gently upbraided me in her turn with a change of manners to her since she had been in Bath, or at least of late. Unlucky me! that my notice should be of such consequence, and my manners so bad! She was so well disposed, and so reasonable, that I soon forgave her, and made this engagement with her in proof of it. She is really an agreeable girl, so I think I may like her; and her great want of a companion at home, which may well make any tolerable acquaintance important to her, gives her another claim on my attention. I shall endeavour as much as possible to keep my intimacies in their proper place, and prevent their clashing. Among so many friends, it will be well if I do not get into a scrape; and now here is Miss Blashford come. I should have gone distracted if the Bullers had staid. . . . When I tell you I have been visiting a countess this morning, you will immediately, with great justice, but no truth, guess it to be Lady Roden. No: it is Lady Leven, the mother of Lord Balgonie. On receiving a message from Lord and Lady Leven through the Mackays, declaring their intention of waiting on us, we thought it right to go to them. I hope we have not done too much, but the friends and admirers of Charles must be attended to. They seem very reasonable, good sort of people, very civil, and full of his praise.* We were shewn at first into an empty drawing-room, and presently in came his lordship, not knowing who we were, to apologise for the servant's mistake, and to say himself what was untrue,[16] that Lady Leven was not within. He is a tall gentlemanlike looking man, with spectacles, and rather deaf. After sitting with him ten minutes we walked away; but Lady Leven coming out of the dining parlour as we passed the door, we were obliged to attend her back to it, and pay our visit over again. She is a stout woman, with a very handsome face. By this means we had the pleasure of hearing Charles's praises twice over. They think themselves excessively obliged to him, and estimate him so highly as to wish Lord Balgonie, when he is quite recovered, to go out to him. There is a pretty little Lady Marianne of the party, to be shaken hands with, and asked if she remembered Mr Austen. . . .

---

* It seems that Charles Austen, then first lieutenant of the 'Endymion', had had an opportunity of shewing attention and kindness to some of Lord Leven's family.

'I shall write to Charles by the next packet, unless you tell me in the meantime of your intending to do it.

'Believe me, if you chuse,

'Yʳ affᵗᵉ Sister.'

Jane did not estimate too highly the 'Cousin George' mentioned in the foregoing letter; who might easily have been superior in sense and wit to the rest of the party. He was the Rev. George Leigh Cooke, long known and respected at Oxford, where he held important offices, and had the privilege of helping to form the minds of men more eminent than himself. As Tutor in Corpus Christi College, he became instructor to some of the most distinguished undergraduates of that time: amongst others to Dr Arnold, the Rev. John Keble, and Sir John Coleridge. The latter has mentioned him in terms of affectionate regard, both in his Memoir of Keble, and in a letter which appears in Dean Stanley's 'Life of Arnold.' Mr Cooke was also an impressive preacher of earnest awakening sermons. I remember to have heard it observed by some of my undergraduate friends that, after all, there was more good to be got from George Cooke's plain sermons than from much of the more laboured oratory of the university pulpit. He was frequently Examiner in the schools, and occupied the chair of the Sedleian Professor of Natural Philosophy, from 1810 to 1853.

Before the end of 1805, the little family party removed to Southampton. They resided in a commodious old-fashioned house in a corner of Castle Square.

I have no letters of my aunt, nor any other record of her, during her four years' residence [17] at Southampton; and though I now began to know, and, what was the same thing, to love her myself, yet my observations were only those of a young boy, and were not capable of penetrating her character, or estimating her powers. I have, however, a lively recollection of some local circumstances at Southampton, and as they refer chiefly to things which have been long ago swept away, I will record them. My grandmother's house had a pleasant garden, bounded on one side by the old city walls; the top of this wall was sufficiently wide to afford a pleasant walk, with an extensive view, easily accessible to ladies by steps. This must have been a part of the identical walls which witnessed the embarkation of Henry V. before the battle of Agincourt, and the detection of the conspiracy of Cambridge, Scroop, and Grey, which Shakspeare has made so picturesque; when, according to the chorus in Henry V., the citizens saw

> The well-appointed King at Hampton Pier
> Embark his royalty.

Among the records of the town of Southampton, they have a minute and authentic account, drawn up at that time, of the encampment of Henry V. near the town, before his embarkment for France. It is remarkable that the place where the army was encamped, then a low level plain, is now entirely covered by the sea, and is called Westport.* At that time Castle Square was occupied by a fantastic edifice, too large for the space in which it stood, though too small to accord well with its castellated style, erected by the second Marquis of Lansdowne, half-brother to the well-known statesman, who succeeded him in the title. The Marchioness had a light phaeton, drawn by six, and sometimes by eight little ponies, each pair decreasing in size, and becoming lighter in colour, through all the grades of dark brown, light brown, bay, and chestnut, as it was placed farther away from the carriage. The two leading pairs were managed by two boyish postilions, the two pairs nearest to the carriage were driven in hand. It was a delight to me to look down from the window and see this fairy equipage put together; for the premises of this castle were so contracted that the whole process went on in the little space that remained of the open square. Like other fairy works, however, it all proved evanescent. Not only carriage and ponies, but castle itself, soon vanished away, 'like the baseless fabric of a vision.' On the death of the Marquis in 1809, the castle was pulled down. Few probably remember its existence; and any one who might visit the place now would wonder how it ever could have stood there.

In 1809 Mr Knight was able to offer his mother the choice of two houses on his property; one near his usual residence at God-

---

* See Wharton's note to Johnson and Steevens' Shakspeare.

mersham Park in Kent; the other near Chawton House, his occasional residence in Hampshire. The latter was chosen; and in that year the mother and daughters, together with Miss Lloyd, a near connection who lived with them, settled themselves at Chawton Cottage.

Chawton may be called the *second*, as well as the *last* home of Jane Austen; for during the temporary residences of the party at Bath and Southampton she was only a sojourner in a strange land; but here she found a real home amongst her own people. It so happened that during her residence at Chawton circumstances brought several of her brothers and their families within easy distance of the house. Chawton must also be considered the place most closely connected with her career as a writer; for there it was that, in the maturity of her mind, she either wrote or rearranged, and prepared for publication the books by which she has become known to the world. This was the home where, after a few years, while still in the prime of life, she began to droop and wither away, and which she left only in the last stage of her illness, yielding to the persuasion of friends hoping against hope.

This house stood in the village of Chawton, about a mile from Alton, on the right hand side, just where the road to Winchester branches off from that to Gosport. It was so close to the road that the front door opened upon it; while a very narrow enclosure, paled in on each side, protected the building from danger of collision with any runaway vehicle. I believe it had been originally built for an inn, for which purpose it was certainly well situated. Afterwards it had been occupied by Mr Knight's steward; but by some additions to the house, and some judicious planting and skreening, it was made a pleasant and commodious abode. Mr Knight was experienced and adroit at such arrangements, and this was a labour of love to him. A good-sized entrance and two sitting-rooms made the length of the house, all intended originally to look upon the road, but the large drawing-room window was blocked up and turned into a book-case, and another opened at the side which gave to view only turf and trees, as a high wooden fence and hornbeam hedge shut out the Winchester road, which skirted the whole length of the little domain. Trees were planted each side to form a shrubbery walk, carried round the enclosure, which gave a sufficient space for ladies' exercise. There was a pleasant irregular mixture of hedgerow, and gravel walk, and orchard, and long grass for mowing, arising from two or three little enclosures having been thrown together. The house itself was quite as good as the generality of parsonage-houses then were, and much in the same style; and was capable of receiving other members of the family as frequent visitors. It was sufficiently well furnished; everything inside and out was kept in good repair, and it was altogether a comfortable and ladylike establishment, though the means which supported it were not large.

I give this description because some interest is generally taken in the residence of a popular writer. Cowper's unattractive house in the street of Olney has been pointed out to visitors, and has even attained the honour of an engraving in Southey's edition of his works: but I cannot recommend any admirer of Jane Austen to undertake a pilgrimage to this spot. The building indeed still stands, but it has lost all that gave it its character.[18] After the death of Mrs Cassandra Austen, in 1845, it was divided into tenements for labourers, and the grounds reverted to ordinary uses.

CHAPTER 5

Description of Jane Austen's person, character, and tastes.

As my memoir has now reached the period when I saw a great deal of my aunt, and was old enough to understand something of her value, I will here attempt a description of her person, mind, and habits. In person she was very attractive; her figure was rather tall and slender, her step light and firm, and her whole appearance expressive of health and animation. In complexion she was a clear brunette with a rich colour; she had full round cheeks, with mouth and nose small and well formed, bright hazel eyes, and brown hair forming natural curls close round her face. If not so regularly handsome as her sister, yet her countenance had a peculiar charm of its own to the eyes of most beholders. At the time of which I am now writing, she never was seen, either morning or evening, without a cap; I believe that she and her sister were generally thought to have taken to the garb of middle age earlier than their years or their looks required; and that, though remarkably neat in their dress as in all their ways, they were scarcely sufficiently regardful of the fashionable, or the becoming.

She was not highly accomplished according to the present standard. Her sister drew well, and it is from a drawing of hers that the likeness prefixed to this volume has been taken. Jane herself was fond of music, and had a sweet voice, both in singing and in conversation; in her youth she had received some instruction on the pianoforte; and at Chawton she practised daily, chiefly before breakfast. I believe she did so partly that she might not disturb the rest of the party who were less fond of music. In the evening she would sometimes sing, to her own accompaniment, some simple old songs, the words and airs of which, now never heard, still linger in my memory.

She read French with facility, and knew something of Italian. In those days German was no more thought of than Hindostanee, as part of a lady's education. In history she followed the old

330

guides – Goldsmith, Hume, and Robertson. Critical enquiry into the usually received statements of the old historians was scarcely begun. The history of the early kings of Rome had not yet been dissolved into legend. Historic characters lay before the reader's eyes in broad light or shade, not much broken up by details. The virtues of King Henry VIII. were yet undiscovered, nor had much light been thrown on the inconsistencies of Queen Elizabeth; the one was held to be an unmitigated tyrant, and an embodied Blue Beard; the other a perfect model of wisdom and policy. Jane, when a girl, had strong political opinions, especially about the affairs of the sixteenth and seventeenth centuries. She was a vehement defender of Charles I. and his grandmother Mary; but I think it was rather from an impulse of feeling than from any enquiry into the evidences by which they must be condemned or acquitted. As she grew up, the politics of the day occupied very little of her attention, but she probably shared the feeling of moderate Toryism which prevailed in her family. She was well acquainted with the old periodicals from the 'Spectator' downwards. Her knowledge of Richardson's works was such as no one is likely again to acquire, now that the multitude and the merits of our light literature have called off the attention of readers from that great master. Every circumstance narrated in Sir Charles Grandison, all that was ever said or done in the cedar parlour, was familiar to her; and the wedding days of Lady L. and Lady G. were as well remembered as if they had been living friends. Amongst her favourite writers, Johnson in prose, Crabbe in verse, and Cowper in both, stood high. It is well that the native good taste of herself and of those with whom she lived, saved her from the snare into which a sister novelist [19] had fallen, of imitating the grandiloquent style of Johnson. She thoroughly enjoyed Crabbe; perhaps on account of a certain resemblance to herself in minute and highly finished detail; and would sometimes say, in jest, that, if she ever married at all, she could fancy being Mrs Crabbe; looking on the author quite as an abstract idea, and ignorant and regardless what manner of man he might be. Scott's poetry gave her great pleasure; she did not live to make much acquaintance with his novels. Only three of them were published before her death; but it will be seen by the following extract from one of her letters, that she was quite prepared to admit the merits of 'Waverley'; and it is remarkable that, living, as she did, far apart from the gossip of the literary world, she should even then have spoken so confidently of his being the author of it : —

'Walter Scott has no business to write novels; especially good ones. It is not fair. He has fame and profit enough as a poet, and ought not to be taking the bread out of other people's mouths. I do not mean to like "Waverley," if I can help it, but I fear I must. I am quite determined, however, not to be pleased with Mrs —'s, should I ever meet with it, which I hope I may not. I think I can be stout against anything written by her. I have made up my mind to like no novels really, but Miss Edgeworth's, E's, and my own.' [20]

It was not, however, what she *knew*, but what she *was*, that distinguished her from others. I cannot better describe the fascination which she exercised over children than by quoting the words of two of her nieces. One says : —

'As a very little girl I was always creeping up to aunt Jane, and following her whenever I could, in the house and out of it. I might not have remembered this but for the recollection of my mother's telling me privately, that I must not be troublesome to my aunt. Her first charm to children was great sweetness of manner. She seemed to love you, and you loved her in return. This, as well as I can now recollect, was what I felt in my early days, before I was old enough to be amused by her cleverness. But soon came the delight of her playful talk. She could make everything amusing to a child. Then, as I got older, when cousins came to share the entertainment, she would tell us the most delightful stories, chiefly of Fairyland, and her fairies had all characters of their own. The tale was invented, I am sure, at the moment, and was continued for two or three days, if occasion served.'

Again : 'When staying at Chawton, with two of her other nieces, we often had amusements in which my aunt was very helpful. She was the one to whom we always looked for help. She would furnish us with what we wanted from her wardrobe; and she would be the entertaining visitor in our make-believe house. She amused us in various ways. Once, I remember, in giving a conversation as between myself and my two cousins, supposing we were all grown up, the day after a ball.'

Very similar is the testimony of another niece: – 'Aunt Jane was the general favourite with children; her ways with them being so playful, and her long circumstantial stories so delightful. These were continued from time to time, and were begged for on all possible and impossible occasions; woven, as she proceeded, out of nothing but her own happy talent for invention. Ah! if but one of them could be recovered! And again, as I grew older, when the original seventeen years between our ages seemed to shrink to seven, or to nothing, it comes back to me now how strangely I missed her. It had become so much a habit with me to put by things in my mind with a reference to her, and to say to myself, I shall keep this for aunt Jane.'

A nephew of hers used to observe that his visits to Chawton, after the death of his aunt Jane, were always a disappointment to him. From old associations he could not help expecting to be particularly happy in that house; and never till he got there could he realise to himself how all its peculiar charm was gone. It was not only that the chief light in the house was quenched, but that the loss of it had cast a shade over the spirits of the survivors. Enough has been said to show her love for children, and her wonderful power of entertaining them; but her friends of all ages felt her enlivening influence. Her unusually quick sense of the ridiculous led her to play with all the common-places of everyday life, whether as regarded persons or things; but she never played with its serious duties or responsibilities, nor did she ever turn individuals into ridicule. With all her neighbours in the village she was on friendly, though not on intimate, terms. She took a kindly interest in all their proceedings, and liked to hear about them. They often served for her amusement; but it was her own nonsense that gave zest to the gossip. She was as far as possible from being censorious or satirical. She never abused them or *quizzed* them – *that* was the word of the day; an ugly word, now obsolete; and the ugly practice which it expressed is much less prevalent now than it was then. The laugh which she occasionally raised was by imagining for her neighbours, as she was equally ready to imagine for her friends or herself, impossible contingencies, or by relating in prose or verse some trifling anecdote coloured to her own fancy, or in writing a fictitious history of what they were supposed to have said or done, which could deceive nobody.

The following specimens may be given of the liveliness of mind which imparted an agreeable flavour both to her correspondence and her conversation: –

ON READING IN THE NEWSPAPERS THE MARRIAGE OF MR GELL TO MISS GILL, OF EASTBOURNE

At Eastbourne Mr Gell, From being perfectly well,
Became dreadfully ill, For love of Miss Gill.
So he said, with some sighs, I'm the slave of your *iis*;
Oh, restore, if you please, By accepting my *ees*.[21]

ON THE MARRIAGE OF A MIDDLE-AGED FLIRT WITH A MR WAKE, WHOM, IT WAS SUPPOSED SHE WOULD SCARCELY HAVE ACCEPTED IN HER YOUTH.

Maria, good-humoured, and handsome, and tall,
For a husband was at her last stake;
And having in vain danced at many a ball,
Is now happy to *jump at a Wake*.

'We were all at the play last night to see Miss O'Neil in Isabella. I do not think she was quite equal to my expectation. I fancy I want something more than can be. Acting seldom satisfies me. I took two pockethandkerchiefs, but had very little occasion for either. She is an elegant creature, however, and hugs Mr Young delightfully.'

'So, Miss B. is actually married, but I have never seen it in the papers; and one may as well be single if the wedding is not to be in print.'

Once, too, she took it into her head to write the following mock panegyric on a young friend, who really was clever and handsome: –

1.

In measured verse I'll now rehearse
The charms of lovely Anna:
And, first, her mind is unconfined
Like any vast savannah.

2.

Ontario's lake may fitly speak
    Her fancy's ample bound:
Its circuit may, on strict survey
    Five hundred miles be found.

3.

Her wit descends on foes and friends
    Like famed Niagara's Fall;
And travellers gaze in wild amaze,
    And listen, one and all.

4.

Her judgment sound, thick, black, profound,
    Like transatlantic groves,
Dispenses aid, and friendly shade
    To all that in it roves.

5.

If thus her mind to be defined
    America exhausts,
And all that's grand in that great land
    In similes it costs –

6.

Oh how can I her person try
    To image and portray?
How paint the face, the form how trace
    In which those virtues lay?

7.

Another world must be unfurled,
    Another language known,
Ere tongue or sound can publish round
    Her charms of flesh and bone.

I believe that all this nonsense was nearly extempore, and that the fancy of drawing the images from America arose at the moment from the obvious rhyme which presented itself in the first stanza.

The following extracts are from letters addressed to a niece [22] who was at that time amusing herself by attempting a novel, probably never finished, certainly never published, and of which I know nothing but what these extracts tell. They show the good-natured sympathy and encouragement which the aunt, then herself occupied in writing 'Emma,' could give to the less matured powers of the niece. They bring out incidentally some of her opinions concerning compositions of that kind : –

EXTRACTS.

'*Chawton, Aug.* 10, 1814.

'Your aunt C. does not like desultory novels, and is rather fearful that yours will be too much so; that there will be too frequent a change from one set of people to another, and that circumstances will be sometimes introduced, of apparent consequence, which will lead to nothing. It will not be so great an objection to me. I allow much more latitude than she does, and think nature and spirit cover many sins of a wandering story. And people in general do not care much about it, for your comfort. . . .'

'*Sept.* 9.

'You are now collecting your people delightfully, getting them exactly into such a spot as is the delight of my life. Three or four families in a country village is the very thing to work on; and I hope you will write a great deal more, and make full use of them while they are so very favourably arranged.'

'*Sept.* 28.

'Devereux Forrester being ruined by his vanity is very good : but I wish you would not let him plunge into a "vortex of dissipation." I do not object to the thing, but I cannot bear the expression : it is such thorough novel slang; and so old that I dare say Adam met with it in the first novel that he opened.'

'*Hans Place* (*Nov.* 1814).

'I have been very far from finding your book an evil, I assure you. I read it immediately, and with great pleasure. Indeed, I do think you get on very fast. I wish other people of my acquaintance could compose as rapidly. Julian's history was quite a surprise to me. You had not very long known it yourself, I suspect; but I have no objection to make to the circumstance; it is very well told, and his having been in love with the aunt gives Cecilia an additional interest with him. I like the idea; a very proper compliment to an aunt! I rather imagine, indeed, that nieces are seldom chosen but in compliment to some aunt or other. I dare say your husband was in love with me once, and would never have thought of you if he had not supposed me dead of a scarlet fever.'

Jane Austen was successful in everything that she attempted with her fingers. None of us could throw spilikins [23] in so perfect a circle, or take them off with so steady a hand. Her performances with cup and ball [24] were marvellous. The one used at Chawton was an easy one, and she has been known to catch it on the point above an hundred times in succession, till her hand was weary. She sometimes found a resource in that simple game, when unable, from weakness in her eyes, to read or write long together. A specimen of her clear strong handwriting [25] is here given. Happy would the compositors for the press be if they had always so legible a manuscript to work from. But the writing was not the only part of her letters which showed superior handiwork. In those days there was an art in folding and sealing. No adhesive envelopes made all easy. Some people's letters always looked loose and untidy; but her paper was sure to take the right folds, and her sealing-wax to drop into the right place. Her needlework both plain and ornamental was excellent, and might almost have put a sewing machine to shame. She was considered especially great in satin stitch. She spent much time in these occupations, and some of her merriest talk was over clothes which she and her companions were making, sometimes for themselves, and sometimes for the poor. There still remains a curious specimen of her needlework made for a sister-in-law, my mother. In a very small bag is deposited a little rolled up housewife, furnished with minikin needles and fine thread. In the housewife is a tiny pocket, and in the pocket is enclosed a slip of paper, on which, written as with a crow quill, are these lines : —

This little bag, I hope, will prove
  To be not vainly made;
For should you thread and needles want,
  It will afford you aid.

And, as we are about to part,
  'T will serve another end:
For, when you look upon this bag,
  You'll recollect your friend.

It is the kind of article that some benevolent fairy might be supposed to give as a reward to a diligent little girl. The whole is of flowered silk, and having been never used and carefully preserved, it is as fresh and bright as when it was first made seventy years ago; and shows that the same hand which painted so exquisitely with the pen could work as delicately with the needle.

I have collected some of the bright qualities which shone, as it were, on the surface of Jane Austen's character, and attracted most notice; but underneath them there lay the strong foundations of sound sense and judgment, rectitude of principle, and delicacy of feeling, qualifying her equally to advise, assist, or amuse. She was, in fact, as ready to comfort the unhappy, or to nurse the sick, as she was to laugh and jest with the light-hearted. Two of her nieces were grown up, and one of them was married, before she was taken away from them. As their minds became more matured, they were admitted into closer intimacy with her, and learned more of her graver thoughts; they know what a sympathising friend and judicious adviser they found her to be in many little difficulties and doubts of early womanhood.

I do not venture to speak of her religious principles: that is a subject on which she herself was more inclined to *think* and *act* than to *talk*, and I shall imitate her reserve; satisfied to have shown how much of Christian love and humility abounded in her heart, without presuming to lay bare the roots whence those graces grew. Some little insight, however, into these deeper recesses of the heart must be given, when we come to speak of her death.

CHAPTER 6

Habits of Composition resumed after a long interval – First publication – The interest taken by the Author in the success of her Works.

It may seem extraordinary that Jane Austen should have written so little during the years that elapsed between leaving Steventon and settling at Chawton; especially when this cessation from work is contrasted with her literary activity both before and after that period. It might rather have been expected that fresh scenes and new acquaintance would have called forth her powers; while the quiet life which the family led both at Bath and Southampton must have afforded abundant leisure for composition; but so it was that nothing which I know of, certainly nothing which the public have seen, was completed in either of those places. I can only state the fact, without assigning any cause for it; but as soon as she was fixed in her second home, she resumed the habits of composition which had been formed in her first, and continued them to the end of her life. The first year of her residence at Chawton seems to have been devoted to revising and preparing for the press 'Sense and Sensibility,' and 'Pride and Prejudice'; but between February 1811 and August 1816, she began and completed 'Mansfield Park,' 'Emma,' and 'Persuasion,' so that the last five years of her life produced the same number of novels with those which had been written in her early youth. How she was able to effect all this is surprising, for she had no separate study to retire to, and most of the work must have been done in the general sitting-room, subject to all kinds of casual interruptions. She was careful that her occupation should not be suspected by servants, or visitors, or any persons beyond her own family party. She wrote upon small sheets of paper which could easily be put away, or covered with a piece of blotting paper. There was, between the front door and the offices, a swing door which creaked when it was opened; but she objected to having this little inconvenience remedied, because it gave her notice when anyone was coming. She was not, however, troubled with companions like her own Mrs Allen in 'Northanger Abbey,' whose 'vacancy of mind and incapacity for thinking were such that, as she never talked a great deal, so she could never be entirely silent; and therefore, while she sat at work, if she lost her needle, or broke her thread, or saw a speck of dirt on her gown, she must observe it, whether there were any one at leisure to answer her or not.' In that well occupied female party there must have been many precious hours of silence during which the pen was busy at the little mahogany writing-desk,* while Fanny Price, or Emma Woodhouse, or Anne Elliot was growing into beauty and interest. I have no doubt that I and my sisters and cousins, in our visits to Chawton, frequently disturbed this mystic process, without having any idea of the mischief that we were doing; certainly we never should have guessed it by any signs of impatience or irritability in the writer.

As so much had been previously prepared, when once she began to publish, her works came out in quick succession. 'Sense and Sensibility' was published in 1811, 'Pride and Prejudice' at the beginning of 1813, 'Mansfield Park' in 1814, 'Emma' early in 1816; 'Northanger Abbey' and 'Persuasion' did not appear till after her death, in 1818. It will be shown farther on why 'Northanger Abbey,' though amongst the first written, was one of the last published. Her first three novels were published by Egerton, her last three by Murray. The profits of the four which had been printed before her death had not at that time amounted to seven hundred pounds.

I have no record of the publication of 'Sense and Sensibility,' nor of the author's feelings at this her first appearance before the public; but the following extracts from three letters to her sister give a lively picture of the interest with which she watched the reception of 'Pride and Prejudice,' and show the carefulness with which she corrected her compositions, and rejected much that had been written : –

---

* This mahogany desk, which has done good service to the public, is now in the possession of my sister, Miss Austen.

'*Chawton, Friday, January 29 (1813).*

'I hope you received my little parcel by J. Bond on Wednesday evening, my dear Cassandra, and that you will be ready to hear from me again on Sunday, for I feel that I must write to you to-day. I want to tell you that I have got my own darling child from London. On Wednesday I received one copy sent down by Falkener, with three lines from Henry to say that he had given another to Charles and sent a third by the coach to Godmersham. ... The advertisement is in our paper to-day for the first time: 18s. He shall ask 1*l*. 1s. for my two next, and 1*l*. 8s. for my stupidest of all. Miss B. dined with us on the very day of the book's coming, and in the evening we fairly set at it, and read half the first vol. to her, prefacing that, having intelligence from Henry that such a work would soon appear, we had desired him to send it whenever it came out, and I believe it passed with her unsuspected. She was amused, poor soul ! *That* she could not help, you know, with two such people to lead the way, but she really does seem to admire Elizabeth. I must confess that I think her as delightful a creature as ever appeared in print, and how I shall be able to tolerate those who do not like *her* at least I do not know. There are a few typical [26] errors; and a "said he," or a "said she," would sometimes make the dialogue more immediately clear; but "I do not write for such dull elves" as have not a great deal of ingenuity themselves.[27] The second volume is shorter than I could wish, but the difference is not so much in reality as in look, there being a larger proportion of narrative in that part. I have lop't and crop't so successfully, however, that I imagine it must be rather shorter than "Sense and Sensibility" altogether. Now I will try and write of something else.'

'*Chawton, Thursday, February 4 (1813).*

'My dear Cassandra, – Your letter was truly welcome, and I am much obliged to you for all your praise; it came at a right time, for I had had some fits of disgust. Our second evening's reading to Miss B. had not pleased me so well, but I believe something must be attributed to my mother's too rapid way of getting on : though she perfectly understands the characters herself, she cannot speak as they ought. Upon the whole, however, I am quite vain enough and well satisfied enough. The work is rather too light, and bright, and sparkling; it wants shade; it wants to be stretched out here and there with a long chapter of sense, if it could be had; if not, of solemn specious nonsense, about something unconnected with the story; an essay on writing, a critique on Walter Scott, or the history of Buonaparté, or something that would form a contrast, and bring the reader with increased delight to the playfulness and epigrammatism of the general style. ... The greatest blunder in the printing that I have met with is in page 220, v. 3, where two speeches are made into one. There might as well be no suppers at Longbourn; but I suppose it was the remains of Mrs Bennett's old Meryton habits.'

The following letter seems to have been written soon after the last two: in February 1813: –

'This will be a quick return for yours, my dear Cassandra; I doubt its having much else to recommend it; but there is no saying; it may turn out to be a very long and delightful letter. I am exceedingly pleased that you can say what you do, after having gone through the whole work, and Fanny's praise is very gratifying. My hopes were tolerably strong of *her*, but nothing like a certainty. Her liking Darcy and Elizabeth is enough. She might hate all the others, if she would. I have her opinion under her own hand this morning, but your transcript of it, which I read first, was not, and is not, the less acceptable. To *me* it is of course all praise, but the more exact truth which she sends *you* is good enough. ... Our party on Wednesday was not unagreeable, though we wanted a master of the house less anxious and fidgety, and more conversible. Upon Mrs —'s mentioning that she had sent the rejected addresses [28] to Mrs H., I began talking to her a little about them, and expressed my hope of their having amused her. Her answer was, "Oh dear yes, very much, very droll indeed, the opening of the house, and the striking up of the fiddles !" What she meant, poor woman, who shall say? I sought no farther. As soon as a whist party was formed, and a round table threatened, I made my mother an excuse and came away, leaving just as many for *their* round table as there were at Mrs Grant's.*

---

* At this time, February 1813, 'Mansfield Park' was nearly finished.

I wish they might be as agreeable a set. My mother is very well, and finds great amusement in glove-knitting, and at present wants no other work. We quite run over with books. She has got Sir John Carr's "Travels in Spain," and I am reading a Society [29] octavo, an "Essay on the Military Police [30] and Institutions of the British Empire," by Capt. Pasley of the Engineers, a book which I protested against at first, but which upon trial I find delightfully written and highly entertaining. I am as much in love with the author as I ever was with Clarkson or Buchanan, or even the two Mr Smiths of the city. The first soldier I ever sighed for; but he does write with extraordinary force and spirit. Yesterday, moreover, brought us "Mrs Grant's Letters," with Mr White's compliments; but I have disposed of them, compliments and all, to Miss P., and amongst so many readers or retainers of books as we have in Chawton, I dare say there will be no difficulty in getting rid of them for another fortnight, if necessary. I have disposed of Mrs Grant for the second fortnight to Mrs —. It can make no difference to *her* which of the twenty-six fortnights in the year the 3 vols. lie on her table. I have been applied to for information as to the oath taken in former times of Bell, Book, and Candle, but have none to give. Perhaps you may be able to learn something of its origin where you now are. Ladies who read those enormous great stupid thick quarto volumes which one always sees in the breakfast parlour there must be acquainted with everything in the world. I detest a quarto. Capt. Pasley's book is too good for their society. They will not understand a man who condenses his thoughts into an octavo. I have learned from Sir J. Carr that there is no Government House at Gibraltar. I must alter it [31] to the Commissioner's.'

The following letter belongs to the same year, but treats of a different subject. It describes a journey from Chawton to London, in her brother's curricle, and shows how much could be seen and enjoyed in course of a long summer's day by leisurely travelling amongst scenery which the traveller in an express train now rushes through in little more than an hour, but scarcely sees at all : –

'*Sloane Street, Thursday, May 20 (1813).*

'My dear Cassandra,

'Before I say anything else, I claim a paper full of halfpence on the drawing-room mantel-piece; I put them there myself, and forgot to bring them with me. I cannot say that I have yet been in any distress for money, but I chuse to have my due, as well as the Devil. How lucky we were in our weather yesterday! This wet morning makes one more sensible of it. We had no rain of any consequence. The head of the curricle was put half up three or four times, but our share of the showers was very trifling, though they seemed to be heavy all round us, when we were on the Hog's-back, and I fancied it might then be raining so hard at Chawton as to make you feel for us much more than we deserved. Three hours and a quarter took us to Guildford, where we staid barely two hours, and had only just time enough for all we had to do there; that is, eating a long and comfortable breakfast, watching the carriages, paying Mr Harrington, and taking a little stroll afterwards. From some views which that stroll gave us, I think most highly of the situation of Guildford. We wanted all our brothers and sisters to be standing with us in the bowling-green, and looking towards Horsham. I was very lucky in my gloves – got them at the first shop I went to, though I went into it rather because it was near than because it looked at all like a glove shop, and gave only four shillings for them; after which everybody at Chawton will be hoping and predicting that they cannot be good for anything, and their worth certainly remains to be proved; but I think they look very well. We left Guildford at twenty minutes before twelve (I hope somebody cares for these minutiæ), and were at Esher in about two hours more. I was very much pleased with the country in general. Between Guildford and Ripley I thought it particularly pretty, also about Painshill; and from a Mr Spicer's grounds at Esher, which we walked into before dinner, the views were beautiful. I cannot say what we did *not* see, but I should think there could not be a wood, or a meadow, or palace, or remarkable spot in England that was not spread out before us on one side or other. Claremont is going to be sold : a Mr Ellis has it now. It is a house that seems never to have prospered. After dinner we walked forward to be overtaken at the coachman's time, and before he did overtake us we were very near Kingston. I fancy it was about half-past six when we reached this house – a twelve hours' business, and the horses did not appear more than reasonably tired. I was very tired too, and glad to get to bed early, but am quite well to-day. I am very snug in the front drawing-room all to myself, and would not say "thank you" for any company but you. The quietness of it does me good. I have contrived to pay my two visits, though the weather made me a great while about it, and left me only a few minutes to sit with Charlotte Craven.* She looks very well, and her hair is done up with an elegance to do credit to any education. Her manners are as unaffected and pleasing as ever. She had heard from her mother to-day. Mrs Craven spends another fortnight at Chilton. I saw nobody but Charlotte, which pleased me best. I was shewn upstairs into a drawing-room, where she came to me, and the appearance of the room, so totally unschool-like, amused me very much; it was full of modern elegancies.

'Yours very affec^{tly.},

J.A.'

The next letter, written in the following year, contains an account of another journey to London, with her brother Henry, and reading with him the manuscript of 'Mansfield Park' : –

'Henrietta Street, Wednesday, March 2 (1814).

'My dear Cassandra,

'You were wrong in thinking of us at Guildford last night: we were at Cobham. On reaching G. we found that John and the horses were gone on. We therefore did no more than we had done at Farnham – sit in the carriage while fresh horses were put in, and proceeded directly to Cobham, which we reached by seven, and about eight were sitting down to a very nice roast fowl, &c. We had altogether a very good journey, and everything at Cobham was comfortable. I could not pay Mr Harrington ! That was the only alas ! of the business. I shall therefore return his bill, and

---

* The present Lady Pollen, of Redenham, near Andover, then at a school in London.

my mother's 2*l*., that you may try your luck. We did not begin reading till Bentley Green. Henry's approbation is hitherto even equal to my wishes. He says it is different from the other two, but does not appear to think it at all inferior. He has only married Mrs R. I am afraid he has gone through the most entertaining part. He took to Lady B. and Mrs N. most kindly, and gives great praise to the drawing of the characters. He understands them all, likes Fanny, and, I think, foresees how it will all be. I finished the "Heroine" last night, and was very much amused by it. I wonder James did not like it better. It diverted me exceedingly. We went to bed at ten. I was very tired, but slept to a miracle, and am lovely to-day, and at present Henry seems to have no complaint. We left Cobham at half-past eight, stopped to bait and breakfast at Kingston, and were in this house considerably before two. Nice smiling Mr Barlowe met us at the door and, in reply to enquiries after news, said that peace was generally expected. I have taken possession of my bedroom, unpacked my bandbox, sent Miss P.'s two letters to the twopenny post,[32] been visited by M^d. B., and am now writing by myself at the new table in the front room. It is snowing. We had some snowstorms yesterday, and a smart frost at night, which gave us a hard road from Cobham to Kingston; but as it was then getting dirty and heavy, Henry had a pair of leaders put on to the bottom of Sloane St. His own horses, therefore, cannot have had hard work. I watched for *veils* as we drove through the streets, and had the pleasure of seeing several upon vulgar heads. And now, how do you all do? – you in particular, after the worry of yesterday and the day before. I hope Martha had a pleasant visit again, and that you and my mother could eat your beef-pudding. Depend upon my thinking of the chimney-sweeper as soon as I wake to-morrow. Places are secured at Drury Lane for Saturday, but so great is the rage for seeing Kean that only a third and fourth row could be got; as it is in a front box, however, I hope we shall do pretty well – Shylock, a good play for Fanny – she cannot be much affected, I think. Mrs Perigord has just been here. She tells me that we owe her master for the silk-dyeing. My poor old muslin has never been dyed yet. It has been promised to be done several times. What wicked people dyers are. They begin with dipping their own souls in scarlet sin. It is evening. We have drank tea, and I have torn through the third vol. of the "Heroine." I do not think it falls off. It is a delightful burlesque, particularly on the Radcliffe style. Henry is going on with "Mansfield Park." He admires H. Crawford : I mean properly, as a clever, pleasant man. I tell you all the good I can, as I know how much you will enjoy it. We hear that Mr Kean is more admired than ever. There are no good places to be got in Drury Lane for the next fortnight, but Henry means to secure some for Saturday fortnight, when you are reckoned upon. Give my love to little Cass. I hope she found my bed comfortable last night.[33] I have seen nobody in London yet with such a long chin as Dr Syntax, nor anybody quite so large as Gogmagolicus.

'Yours aff^{ly.},

'J. Austen.'

CHAPTER 7

*Seclusion from the literary world – Notice from the Prince Regent –
Correspondence with Mr Clarke – Suggestions to alter
her style of writing.*

JANE AUSTEN lived in entire seclusion from the literary world :
neither by correspondence, nor by personal intercourse was she
known to any contemporary authors. It is probable that she never
was in company with any person whose talents or whose celebrity
equalled her own; so that her powers never could have been
sharpened by collision with superior intellects, nor her imagination aided by their casual suggestions. Whatever she produced
was a genuine home-made article. Even during the last two or
three years of her life, when her works were rising in the estimation of the public, they did not enlarge the circle of her acquaintance. Few of her readers knew even her name, and none knew
more of her than her name. I doubt whether it would be possible
to mention any other author of note, whose personal obscurity
was so complete. I can think of none like her, but of many to
contrast with her in that respect. Fanny Burney, afterwards
Madame D'Arblay, was at an early age petted by Dr Johnson, and
introduced to the wits and scholars of the day at the tables of Mrs
Thrale and Sir Joshua Reynolds. Anna Seward, in her self-consti-
tuted shrine at Lichfield, would have been miserable, had she not
trusted that the eyes of all lovers of poetry were devoutly fixed
on her. Joanna Baillie and Maria Edgeworth were indeed far from
courting publicity; they loved the privacy of their own families,
one with her brother and sister in their Hampstead villa, the other
in her more distant retreat in Ireland; but fame pursued them,
and they were the favourite correspondents of Sir Walter Scott.
Crabbe, who was usually buried in a country parish, yet sometimes visited London, and dined at Holland House, and was received as a fellow-poet by Campbell, Moore, and Rogers; and on
one memorable occasion he was Scott's guest at Edinburgh, and

gazed with wondering eyes on the incongruous pageantry with which George IV. was entertained in that city. Even those great writers who hid themselves amongst lakes and mountains associated with each other; and though little seen by the world were so much in its thoughts that a new term, 'Lakers,' was coined to designate them. The chief part of Charlotte Brontë's life was spent in a wild solitude compared with which Steventon and Chawton might be considered to be in the gay world; and yet she attained to personal distinction which never fell to Jane's lot. When she visited her kind publisher in London, literary men and women were invited purposely to meet her : Thackeray bestowed upon her the honour of his notice; and once in Willis's Rooms,* she had to walk shy and trembling through an avenue of lords and ladies, drawn up for the purpose of gazing at the author of 'Jane Eyre.' Miss Mitford, too, lived quietly in 'Our Village,' devoting her time and talents to the benefit of a father scarcely worthy of her; but she did not live there unknown. Her tragedies gave her a name in London. She numbered Milman and Talfourd amongst her correspondents; and her works were a passport to the society of many who would not otherwise have sought her. Hundreds admired Miss Mitford on account of her writings for one who ever connected the idea of Miss Austen with the press. A few years ago, a gentleman visiting Winchester Cathedral desired to be shown Miss Austen's grave. The verger, as he pointed it out, asked, 'Pray, sir, can you tell me whether there was anything particular about that lady; so many people want to know where she was buried?' During her life the ignorance of the verger was shared by most people; few knew that 'there was anything particular about that lady.'

It was not till towards the close of her life, when the last of the works that she saw published was in the press, that she received the only mark of distinction ever bestowed upon her; and that was remarkable for the high quarter whence it emanated rather than for any actual increase of fame that it conferred. It happened thus. In the autumn of 1815 she nursed her brother Henry

---

* See Mrs Gaskell's 'Life of Miss Brontë,' vol. ii. p. 215.

through a dangerous fever and slow convalescence at his house in Hans Place. He was attended by one of the Prince Regent's physicians. All attempts to keep her name secret had at this time ceased, and though it had never appeared on a title-page, all who cared to know might easily learn it: and the friendly physician was aware that his patient's nurse was the author of 'Pride and Prejudice.' Accordingly he informed her one day that the Prince was a great admirer of her novels; that he read them often, and kept a set in every one of his residences; that he himself therefore had thought it right to inform his Royal Highness that Miss Austen was staying in London, and that the Prince had desired Mr Clarke, the librarian of Carlton House, to wait upon her. The next day Mr Clarke made his appearance, and invited her to Carlton House, saying that he had the Prince's instructions to show her the library and other apartments, and to pay her every possible attention. The invitation was of course accepted, and during the visit to Carlton House Mr Clarke declared himself commissioned to say that if Miss Austen had any other novel forthcoming she was at liberty to dedicate it to the Prince. Accordingly such a dedication was immediately prefixed to 'Emma,' which was at that time in the press.

Mr Clarke was the brother of Dr Clarke, the traveller and mineralogist, whose life has been written by Bishop Otter. Jane found in him not only a very courteous gentleman, but also a warm admirer of her talents; though it will be seen by his letters that he did not clearly apprehend the limits of her powers, or the proper field for their exercise. The following correspondence took place between them.

Feeling some apprehension lest she should make a mistake in acting on the verbal permission which she had received from the Prince, Jane addressed the following letter to Mr Clarke:—

'Nov. 15, 1815.

'Sir, – I must take the liberty of asking you a question. Among the many flattering attentions which I received from you at Carlton House on Monday last was the information of my being at liberty to dedicate any future work to His Royal Highness the Prince Regent, without the necessity of any solicitation on my part. Such, at least, I believed to be your words; but as I am very anxious to be quite certain of what was intended, I entreat you to have the goodness to inform me how such a permission is to be understood, and whether it is incumbent on me to show my sense of the honour, by inscribing the work now in the press to His Royal Highness; I should be equally concerned to appear either presumptuous or ungrateful.'

The following gracious answer was returned by Mr Clarke, together with a suggestion which must have been received with some surprise:—

'Carlton House, Nov. 16, 1815.

'Dear Madam, — It is certainly not *incumbent* on you to dedicate your work now in the press to His Royal Highness; but if you wish to do the Regent that honour either now or at any future period I am happy to send you that permission, which need not require any more trouble or solicitation on your part.

'Your late works, Madam, and in particular "Mansfield Park," reflect the highest honour on your genius and your principles. In every new work your mind seems to increase its energy and power of discrimination. The Regent has read and admired all your publications.

'Accept my best thanks for the pleasure your volumes have given me. In the perusal of them I felt a great inclination to write and say so. And I also, dear Madam, wished to be allowed to ask you to delineate in some future work the habits of life, and character, and enthusiasm of a clergyman, who should pass his time between the metropolis and the country, who should be something like Beattie's Minstrel —

> Silent when glad, affectionate tho' shy,
>   And in his looks was most demurely sad;
>   And now he laughed aloud, yet none knew why.

Neither Goldsmith, nor La Fontaine in his "Tableau de Famille," have in my mind quite delineated an English clergyman, at least of the present day, fond of and entirely engaged in literature, no man's enemy but his own. Pray, dear Madam, think of these things.

> 'Believe me at all times with sincerity and
> respect, your faithful and obliged servant,
> 'J. S. Clarke, Librarian.'

The following letter, written in reply, will show how unequal the author of 'Pride and Prejudice' felt herself to delineating an enthusiastic clergyman of the present day, who should resemble Beattie's Minstrel :—

'Dec. 11.

'Dear Sir, — My "Emma" is now so near publication that I feel it right to assure you of my not having forgotten your kind recommendation of an early copy for Carlton House, and that I have Mr Murray's promise of its being sent to His Royal Highness, under cover to you, three days previous to the work being really out. I must make use of this opportunity to thank you, dear Sir, for the very high praise you bestow on my other novels. I am too vain to wish to convince you that you have praised them beyond their merits. My greatest anxiety at present is that this fourth work should not disgrace what was good in the others. But on this point I will do myself the justice to declare that, whatever may be my wishes for its success, I am strongly haunted with the idea that to those readers who have preferred "Pride and Prejudice" it will appear inferior in wit, and to those who have preferred "Mansfield Park" inferior in good sense. Such as it is, however, I hope you will do me the favour of accepting a copy. Mr Murray will have directions for sending one. I am quite honoured by your thinking me capable of drawing such a clergyman as you gave the sketch of in your note of Nov. 16th. But I assure you I am *not*. The comic part of the character I might be equal to, but not the good, the enthusiastic, the literary. Such a man's conversation must at times be on subjects of science and philosophy, of which I know nothing; or at least be occasionally abundant in quotations and allusions which a woman who, like me, knows only her own mother tongue, and has read little in that, would be totally without the power of giving. A classical education, or at any rate a very extensive acquaintance with

English literature, ancient and modern, appears to me quite indispensable for the person who would do any justice to your clergyman; and I think I may boast myself to be, with all possible vanity, the most unlearned and uninformed female who ever dared to be an authoress.

'Believe me, dear Sir,

'Your obliged and faithful hum^bl Ser^t.

'Jane Austen.' *

Mr Clarke, however, was not to be discouraged from proposing another subject. He had recently been appointed chaplain and private English secretary to Prince Leopold, who was then about to be united to the Princess Charlotte; and when he again wrote to express the gracious thanks of the Prince Regent for the copy of 'Emma' which had been presented, he suggests that 'an historical romance illustrative of the august House of Cobourg would just now be very interesting,' and might very properly be dedicated to Prince Leopold. This was much as if Sir William Ross had been set to paint a great battle-piece; and it is amusing to see with what grave civility she declined a proposal which must have struck her as ludicrous, in the following letter :–

'My dear Sir, – I am honoured by the Prince's thanks and very much obliged to yourself for the kind manner in which you mention the work. I have also to acknowledge a former letter forwarded to me from Hans Place. I assure you I felt very grateful for the friendly tenor of it, and hope my silence will have been considered, as it was truly meant, to proceed only from an unwillingness to tax your time with idle thanks. Under every interesting circumstance which your own talents and literary labours have placed you in, or the favour of the Regent bestowed, you have my best wishes. Your recent appointments I hope are a step to something still better. In my opinion, the service of a court can hardly be too well paid, for immense must be the sacrifice of time and feeling required by it.

---

* It was her pleasure to boast of greater ignorance than she had any just claim to. She knew more than her mother tongue, for she knew a good deal of French and a little of Italian.

'You are very kind in your hints as to the sort of composition which might recommend me at present, and I am fully sensible that an historical romance, founded on the House of Saxe Cobourg, might be much more to the purpose of profit or popularity than such pictures of domestic life in country villages as I deal in. But I could no more write a romance than an epic poem. I could not sit seriously down to write a serious romance under any other motive than to save my life; and if it were indispensable for me to keep it up and never relax into laughing at myself or at other people, I am sure I should be hung before I had finished the first chapter. No, I must keep to my own style and go on in my own way; and though I may never succeed again in that, I am convinced that I should totally fail in any other.

'I remain, my dear Sir,

'Your very much obliged, and sincere friend,

'J. Austen.'

'Chawton, near Alton, April 1, 1816.'

Mr Clarke should have recollected the warning of the wise man, 'Force not the course of the river.' If you divert it from the channel in which nature taught it to flow, and force it into one arbitrarily cut by yourself, you will lose its grace and beauty.

> But when his free course is not hindered,
> He makes sweet music with the enamelled stones,
> Giving a gentle kiss to every sedge
> He overtaketh in his pilgrimage:
> And so by many winding nooks he strays
> With willing sport.

All writers of fiction, who have genius strong enough to work out a course of their own, resist every attempt to interfere with its direction. No two writers could be more unlike each other than Jane Austen and Charlotte Brontë; so much so that the latter was unable to understand why the former was admired, and confessed that she herself 'should hardly like to live with her ladies and gentlemen, in their elegant but confined houses;' but each writer equally resisted interference with her own natural style of composition. Miss Brontë, in reply to a friendly critic, who had

354

warned her against being too melodramatic, and had ventured to
propose Miss Austen's works to her as a study, writes thus:—

'Whenever I *do* write another book, I think I will have nothing
of what you call "melodrama." I *think* so, but I am not sure. I
think, too, I will endeavour to follow the counsel which shines
out of Miss Austen's "mild eyes," to finish more, and be more
subdued; but neither am I sure of that. When authors write best,
or, at least, when they write most fluently, an influence seems to
waken in them which becomes their master — which will have its
way — putting out of view all behests but its own, dictating certain words, and insisting on their being used, whether vehement
or measured in their nature, new moulding characters, giving
unthought of turns to incidents, rejecting carefully elaborated
old ideas, and suddenly creating and adopting new ones. Is it not
so? And should we try to counteract this influence? Can we
indeed counteract it?' *

The playful raillery with which the one parries an attack on
her liberty, and the vehement eloquence of the other in pleading
the same cause and maintaining the independence of genius, are
very characteristic of the minds of the respective writers.

The suggestions which Jane received as to the sort of story that
she ought to write were, however, an amusement to her, though
they were not likely to prove useful; and she has left amongst
her papers one entitled, 'Plan of a novel according to hints from
various quarters.' The names of some of those advisers are written
on the margin of the manuscript opposite to their respective
suggestions.

'Heroine to be the daughter of a clergyman, who after having
lived much in the world had retired from it, and settled on a
curacy with a very small fortune of his own. The most excellent
man that can be imagined, perfect in character, temper, and
manner, without the smallest drawback or peculiarity to prevent
his being the most delightful companion to his daughter from one
year's end to the other. Heroine faultless in character, beautiful
in person, and possessing every possible accomplishment. Book
to open with father and daughter conversing in long speeches,

* Mrs Gaskell's 'Life of Miss Brontë,' vol. ii. p. 53.

elegant language, and a tone of high serious sentiment. The father induced, at his daughter's earnest request, to relate to her the past events of his life. Narrative to reach through the greater part of the first volume; as besides all the circumstances of his attachment to her mother, and their marriage, it will comprehend his going to sea as chaplain to a distinguished naval character about the court; and his going afterwards to court himself, which involved him in many interesting situations, concluding with his opinion of the benefits of tithes[34] being done away with. ... From this outset the story will proceed, and contain a striking variety of adventures. Father an exemplary parish priest, and devoted to literature; but heroine and father never above a fortnight in one place: he being driven from his curacy by the vile arts of some totally unprincipled and heartless young man desperately in love with the heroine, and pursuing her with unrelenting passion. No sooner settled in one country of Europe, than they are compelled to quit it, and retire to another, always making new acquaintance, and always obliged to leave them. This will of course exhibit a wide variety of character. The scene will be for ever shifting from one set of people to another, but there will be no mixture, all the good will be unexceptionable in every respect. There will be no foibles or weaknesses but with the wicked, who will be completely depraved and infamous, hardly a resemblance of humanity left in them. Early in her career, the heroine must meet with the hero: all perfection, of course, and only prevented from paying his addresses to her by some excess of refinement. Wherever she goes, somebody falls in love with her, and she receives repeated offers of marriage, which she refers wholly to her father, exceedingly angry that *he* should not be the first applied to. Often carried away by the anti-hero, but rescued either by her father or the hero. Often reduced to support herself and her father by her talents, and work for her bread; continually cheated, and defrauded of her hire; worn down to a skeleton, and now and then starved to death. At last, hunted out of civilised society, denied the poor shelter of the humblest cottage, they are compelled to retreat into Kamtschatka, where the poor father quite worn down, finding his end approaching, throws himself on the ground, and after four or five hours of tender advice and parental admonition to his miserable child, expires in a fine burst of literary enthusiasm, intermingled with invectives against the holders of tithes. Heroine inconsolable for some time, but afterwards crawls back towards her former country, having at least twenty narrow escapes of falling into the hands of anti-hero; and at last, in the very nick of time, turning a corner to avoid him, runs into the arms of the hero himself, who, having just shaken off the scruples which fettered him before, was at the very moment setting off in pursuit of her. The tenderest and completest *éclaircissement* takes place, and they are happily united. Throughout the whole work heroine to be in the most elegant society, and living in high style.'

Since the first publication of this memoir, Mr Murray of Albemarle Street has very kindly sent to me copies of the following letters, which his father received from Jane Austen, when engaged in the publication of 'Emma.' The increasing cordiality of the letters shows that the author felt that her interests were duly cared for, and was glad to find herself in the hands of a publisher whom she could consider as a friend.

Her brother had addressed to Mr Murray a strong complaint of the tardiness of a printer :–

'*23 Hans Place, Thursday, November 23 (1815).*

'Sir, – My brother's note last Monday has been so fruitless, that I am afraid there can be but little chance of my writing to any good effect; but yet I am so very much disappointed and vexed by the delays of the printers, that I cannot help begging to know whether there is no hope of their being quickened. Instead of the work being ready by the end of the present month, it will hardly, at the rate we now proceed, be finished by the end of the next; and as I expect to leave London early in December, it is of consequence that no more time should be lost. Is it likely that the printers will be influenced to greater dispatch and punctuality by knowing that the work is to be dedicated, by permission, to the Prince Regent? If you can make that circumstance operate, I shall be very glad. My brother returns 'Waterloo' with many thanks for the loan of it. We have heard much

of Scott's account of Paris.* If it be not incompatible with other arrangements, would you favour us with it, supposing you have any set already opened? You may depend upon its being in careful hands.
'I remain, Sir, your ob$^{t.}$ humble Se$^{t.}$

'J. Austen.'

'*Hans Place, December 11 (1815).*

'Dear Sir. – As I find that "Emma" is advertised for publication as early as Saturday next, I think it best to lose no time in settling all that remains to be settled on the subject, and adopt this method as involving the smallest tax on your time.

In the first place, I beg you to understand that I leave the terms on which the trade should be supplied with the work entirely to your judgment, entreating you to be guided in every such arrangement by your own experience of what is most likely to clear off the edition rapidly. I shall be satisfied with whatever you feel to be best. The title-page must be "Emma, dedicated by permission to H.R.H. the Prince Regent." And it is my particular wish that one set should be completed and sent to H.R.H. two or three days before the work is generally public. It should be sent under cover to the Rev. J. S. Clarke, Librarian, Carlton House. I shall subjoin a list of those persons to whom I must trouble you to forward also a set each, when the work is out; all unbound, with "From the Authoress" in the first page.

'I return you, with very many thanks, the books you have so obligingly supplied me with. I am very sensible, I assure you, of the attention you have paid to my convenience and amusement. I return also "Mansfield Park," as ready for a second edition, I believe, as I can make it. I am in Hans Place till the 16th. From that day inclusive, my direction will be Chawton, Alton, Hants.
'I remain, dear Sir,

'Y^r faithful humb. Serv$^t.$

'J. Austen.

'I wish you would have the goodness to send a line by the bearer, stating *the day* on which the set will be ready for the Prince Regent.'

---

* This must have been 'Paul's Letters to his Kinsfolk.'

'Hans Place, December 11 (1815)

'Dear Sir, – I am much obliged by yours, and very happy to feel everything arranged to our mutual satisfaction. As to my direction about the title-page, it was arising from my ignorance only, and from my having never noticed the proper place for a dedication. I thank you for putting me right. Any deviation from what is usually done in such cases is the last thing I should wish for. I feel happy in having a friend to save me from the ill effect of my own blunder.

'Yours, dear Sir, &c.

'J. Austen.'

'Chawton, April 1, 1816.

'Dear Sir, – I return you the "Quarterly Review" with many thanks. The Authoress of "Emma" has no reason, I think, to complain of her treatment in it, except in the total omission of "Mansfield Park." I cannot but be sorry that so clever a man as the Reviewer [35] of "Emma" should consider it as unworthy of being noticed. You will be pleased to hear that I have received the Prince's thanks for the *handsome* copy I sent him of "Emma." Whatever he may think of *my* share of the work, yours seems to have been quite right.

'In consequence of the late event [36] in Henrietta Street. I must request that if you should at any time have anything to communicate by letter, you will be so good as to write by the post, directing to me (Miss J. Austen), Chawton, near Alton; and that for anything of a larger bulk, you will add to the same direction, by *Collier's Southampton coach.*

'I remain, dear Sir,

'Yours very faithfully,

'J. Austen.'

About the same time the following letters passed between the Countess of Morley and the writer of 'Emma.' I do not know whether they were personally acquainted with each other, nor in what this interchange of civilities originated :–

THE COUNTESS OF MORLEY TO MISS J. AUSTEN.

'Saltram, December 27 (1815).

'Madam, – I have been most anxiously waiting for an introduction to "Emma," and am infinitely obliged to you for your kind recollection of me, which will procure me the pleasure of her acquaintance some days sooner than I should otherwise have had it. I am already become intimate with the Woodhouse family, and feel that they will not amuse and interest me less than the Bennetts, Bertrams, Norrises, and all their admirable predecessors. I can give them no higher praise.

'I am, Madam, your much obliged
'F. Morley.'

MISS J. AUSTEN TO THE COUNTESS OF MORLEY.

'Madam, – Accept my thanks for the honour of your note, and for your kind disposition in favour of "Emma." In my present state of doubt as to her reception in the world, it is particularly gratifying to me to receive so early an assurance of your Ladyship's approbation. It encourages me to depend on the same share of general good opinion which "Emma's" predecessors have experienced, and to believe that I have not yet, as almost every writer of fancy does sooner or later, overwritten myself.

'I am, Madam,
'Your obliged and faithful Servt.
'J. Austen.

'December 31, 1815.'

CHAPTER 8

*Slow growth of her fame – Ill success of first attempts at publication –
Two Reviews of her works contrasted.*

SELDOM has any literary reputation been of such slow growth
as that of Jane Austen. Readers of the present day know the rank
that is generally assigned to her. They have been told by Archbishop Whately, in his review of her works, and by Lord
Macaulay, in his review of Madame D'Arblay's, the reason why
the highest place is to be awarded to Jane Austen, as a truthful
drawer of character, and why she is to be classed with those who
have approached nearest, in that respect, to the great master
Shakspeare. They see her safely placed, by such authorities, in
her niche, not indeed amongst the highest orders of genius, but
in one confessedly her own, in our British temple of literary
fame; and it may be difficult to make them believe how coldly
her works were at first received, and how few readers had any
appreciation of their peculiar merits. Sometimes a friend or neighbour, who chanced to know of our connection with the author,
would condescend to speak with moderate approbation of 'Sense
and Sensibility,' or 'Pride and Prejudice'; but if they had known
that we, in our secret thoughts, classed her with Madame
D'Arblay or Miss Edgeworth, or even with some other novel
writers of the day whose names are now scarcely remembered,
they would have considered it an amusing instance of family
conceit. To the multitude her works appeared tame and common-
place,* poor in colouring, and sadly deficient in incident and

* A greater genius than my aunt shared with her the imputation
of being *commonplace.* Lockhart, speaking of the low estimation in
which Scott's conversational powers were held in the literary and
scientific society of Edinburgh, says: 'I think the epithet most in
vogue concerning it was "commonplace."' He adds, however, that one
of the most eminent of that society was of a different opinion, 'who,
when some glib youth chanced to echo in his hearing the consolatory
tenet of local mediocrity, answered quietly, "I have the misfortune to

interest. It is true that we were sometimes cheered by hearing that a different verdict had been pronounced by more competent judges: we were told how some great statesman or distinguished poet held these works in high estimation; we had the satisfaction of believing that they were most admired by the best judges, and comforted ourselves with Horace's 'satis est Equitem mihi plaudere.' So much was this the case, that one of the ablest men of my acquaintance * said, in that kind of jest which has much earnest in it, that he had established it in his own mind, as a new test of ability, whether people *could* or *could not* appreciate Miss Austen's merits.

But though such golden opinions were now and then gathered in, yet the wide field of public taste yielded no adequate return either in praise or profit. Her reward was not to be the quick return of the cornfield, but the slow growth of the tree which is to endure to another generation. Her first attempts at publication were very discouraging. In November, 1797, her father wrote the following letter to Mr Cadell:—

'Sir, — I have in my possession a manuscript novel, comprising 3 vols., about the length of Miss Burney's "Evelina." As I am well aware of what consequence it is that a work of this sort sh^d make its first appearance under a respectable name, I apply to you. I shall be much obliged therefore if you will inform me whether you choose to be concerned in it, what will be the expense of publishing it at the author's risk, and what you will venture to advance for the property of it, if on perusal it is approved of. Should you give any encouragement, I will send you the work.

'I am, Sir, your humble Servant,
'George Austen.'

'Steventon, near Overton, Hants,
'1st Nov. 1797.'

think differently from you — in my humble opinion Walter Scott's *sense* is a still more wonderful thing than his genius." ' — Lockhart's *Life of Scott*, vol. iv. chap. v.
* The late Mr R. H. Cheney.

This proposal was declined by return of post! The work thus summarily rejected must have been 'Pride and Prejudice.'

The fate of 'Northanger Abbey' was still more humiliating. It was sold, in 1803, to a publisher in Bath,[37] for ten pounds, but it found so little favour in his eyes, that he chose to abide by his first loss rather than risk farther expense by publishing such a work. It seems to have lain for many years unnoticed in his drawers; somewhat as the first chapters of 'Waverley' lurked forgotten amongst the old fishing-tackle in Scott's cabinet. Tilneys, Thorpes, and Morlands consigned apparently to eternal oblivion! But when four novels of steadily increasing success had given the writer some confidence in herself, she wished to recover the copyright of this early work. One of her brothers [38] undertook the negotiation. He found the purchaser very willing to receive back his money, and to resign all claim to the copyright. When the bargain was concluded and the money paid, but not till then, the negotiator had the satisfaction of informing him that the work which had been so lightly esteemed was by the author of 'Pride and Prejudice.' I do not think that she was herself much mortified by the want of early success. She wrote for her own amusement. Money, though acceptable, was not necessary for the moderate expenses of her quiet home. Above all, she was blessed with a cheerful contented disposition, and an humble mind; and so lowly did she esteem her own claims, that when she received 150l. from the sale of 'Sense and Sensibility,' she considered it a prodigious recompense for that which had cost her nothing. It cannot be supposed, however, that she was altogether insensible to the superiority of her own workmanship over that of some contemporaries who were then enjoying a brief popularity. Indeed a few touches in the following extracts from two of her letters show that she was as quicksighted to absurdities in composition as to those in living persons.

'Mr C.'s opinion is gone down in my list; but as my paper relates only to "Mansfield Park," I may fortunately excuse myself from entering Mr D's. I will redeem my credit with him by writing a close imitation of "Self-Control," as soon as I can. I will improve upon it. My heroine shall not only be wafted down an American river in a boat by herself. She shall cross the

Atlantic in the same way; and never stop till she reaches Gravesend.'

'We have got "Rosanne" in our Society, and find it much as you describe it; very good and clever, but tedious. Mrs Hawkins' great excellence is on serious subjects. There are some very delightful conversations and reflections on religion : but on lighter topics I think she falls into many absurdities; and, as to love, her heroine has very comical feelings. There are a thousand improbabilities in the story. Do you remember the two Miss Ormsdens introduced just at last? Very flat and unnatural. Mad^elle. Cossart is rather my passion.'

Two notices of her works appeared in the 'Quarterly Review.' One in October 1815, and another, more than three years after her death, in January 1821. The latter article is known to have been from the pen of Whately, afterwards Archbishop of Dublin.* They differ much from each other in the degree of praise which they award, and I think also it may be said, in the ability with which they are written. The first bestows some approval, but the other expresses the warmest admiration. One can scarcely be satisfied with the critical acumen of the former writer, who, in treating of 'Sense and Sensibility,' takes no notice whatever of the vigour with which many of the characters are drawn, but declares that 'the interest and *merit* of the piece depends *altogether* upon the behaviour of the elder sister !' Nor is he fair when, in 'Pride and Prejudice,' he represents Elizabeth's change of sentiments towards Darcy as caused by the sight of his house and grounds. But the chief discrepancy between the two reviewers is to be found in their appreciation of the commonplace and silly characters to be found in these novels. On this point the differ-

---

* Lockhart had supposed that this article had been written by Scott, because it exactly accorded with the opinions which Scott had often been heard to express, but he learned afterwards that it had been written by Whately; and Lockhart, who became the Editor of the Quarterly, must have had the means of knowing the truth. (See Lockhart's *Life of Sir Walter Scott*, vol. v. p. 158.) I remember that, at the time when the review came out, it was reported in Oxford that Whately had written the article at the request of the lady whom he afterwards married.

ence almost amounts to a contradiction, such as one sometimes
sees drawn up in parallel columns, when it is desired to convict
some writer or some statesman of inconsistency. The Reviewer,
in 1815, says: 'The faults of these works arise from the minute
detail which the author's plan comprehends. Characters of folly
or simplicity, such as those of old Woodhouse and Miss Bates, are
ridiculous when first presented, but if too often brought forward,
or too long dwelt on, their prosing is apt to become as tiresome
in fiction as in real society.' The Reviewer, in 1821, on the contrary, singles out the fools as especial instances of the writer's
abilities, and declares that in this respect she shows a regard to
character hardly exceeded by Shakspeare himself. These are his
words: 'Like him (Shakspeare) she shows as admirable a discrimination in the character of fools as of people of sense; a merit
which is far from common. To invent indeed a conversation full
of wisdom or of wit requires that the writer should himself
possess ability; but the converse does not hold good, it is no fool
that can describe fools well; and many who have succeeded pretty
well in painting superior characters have failed in giving individuality to those weaker ones which it is necessary to introduce
in order to give a faithful representation of real life : they exhibit
to us mere folly in the abstract, forgetting that to the eye of the
skilful naturalist the insects on a leaf present as wide differences
as exist between the lion and the elephant. Slender, and Shallow,
and Aguecheek, as Shakspeare has painted them, though equally
fools, resemble one another no more than Richard, and Macbeth,
and Julius Cæsar; and Miss Austen's * Mrs Bennet, Mr Rush-
worth, and Miss Bates are no more alike than her Darcy, Knightley, and Edmund Bertram. Some have complained indeed of finding her fools too much like nature, and consequently tiresome.
There is no disputing about tastes; all we can say is, that such
critics must (whatever deference they may outwardly pay to
received opinions) find the "Merry Wives of Windsor" and
"Twelfth Night" very tiresome; and that those who look with
pleasure at Wilkie's pictures, or those of the Dutch school, must

* In transcribing this passage I have taken the liberty so far to
correct it as to spell her name properly with an 'e.'

admit that excellence of imitation may confer attraction on that which would be insipid or disagreeable in the reality. Her minuteness of detail has also been found fault with; but even where it produces, at the time, a degree of tediousness, we know not whether that can justly be reckoned a blemish, which is absolutely essential to a very high excellence. Now it is absolutely impossible, without this, to produce that thorough acquaintance with the characters which is necessary to make the reader ;eartily interested in them. Let any one cut out from the "Iliad" or from Shakspeare's plays everything (we are far from saying that either might not lose some parts with advantage, but let him reject everything) which is absolutely devoid of importance and interest *in itself*; and he will find that what is left will have lost more than half its charms. We are convinced that some writers have diminished the effect of their works by being scrupulous to admit nothing into them which had not some absolute and independent merit. They have acted like those who strip off the leaves of a fruit tree, as being of themselves good for nothing, with the view of securing more nourishment to the fruit, which in fact cannot attain its full maturity and flavour without them.'

The world, I think, has endorsed the opinion of the later writer; but it would not be fair to set down the discrepancy between the two entirely to the discredit of the former. The fact is that, in the course of the intervening five years, these works had been read and reread by many leaders in the literary world. The public taste was forming itself all this time, and 'grew by what it fed on.' These novels belong to a class which gain rather than lose by frequent perusals, and it is probable that each Reviewer represented fairly enough the prevailing opinions of readers in the year when each wrote.

Since that time, the testimonies in favour of Jane Austen's works have been continual and almost unanimous. They are frequently referred to as models; nor have they lost their first distinction of being especially acceptable to minds of the highest order. I shall indulge myself by collecting into the next chapter instances of the homage paid to her by such persons.

CHAPTER 9

Opinions expressed by eminent persons – Opinions of others of less eminence – Opinion of American readers.

INTO this list of the admirers of my Aunt's works, I admit those only whose eminence will be universally acknowledged. No doubt the number might have been increased.

Southey, in a letter to Sir Egerton Brydges, says: 'You mention Miss Austen. Her novels are more true to nature, and have, for my sympathies, passages of finer feeling than any others of this age. She was a person of whom I have heard so well and think so highly, that I regret not having had an opportunity of testifying to her the respect which I felt for her.'

It may be observed that Southey had probably heard from his own family connections of the charm of her private character. A friend of hers, the daughter of Mr Bigge Wither, of Manydown Park near Basingstoke, was married to Southey's uncle, the Rev. Herbert Hill, who had been useful to his nephew in many ways, and especially in supplying him with the means of attaining his extensive knowledge of Spanish and Portuguese literature. Mr Hill had been Chaplain to the British Factory at Lisbon, where Southey visited him and had the use of a library in those languages which his uncle had collected. Southey himself continually mentions his uncle Hill in terms of respect and gratitude.

S. T. Coleridge would sometimes burst out into high encomiums of Miss Austen's novels as being, 'in their way, perfectly genuine and individual productions.'

I remember Miss Mitford's saying to me: 'I would almost cut off one of my hands, if it would enable me to write like your aunt with the other.'

The biographer of Sir J. Mackintosh says: 'Something recalled to his mind the traits of character which are so delicately touched in Miss Austen's novels. . . He said that there was genius in sketching out that new kind of novel. . . He was vexed for the

A MEMOIR

credit of the "Edinburgh Review" that it had left her unnoticed.*
.. The "Quarterly" had done her more justice... It was impossible for a foreigner to understand fully the merit of her works.
Madame de Staël, to whom he had recommended one of her
novels, found no interest in it; and in her note to him in reply
said it was "vulgaire": and yet, he said, nothing could be more
true than what he wrote in answer: "There is no book which
that word would so little suit." ... Every village could furnish
matter for a novel to Miss Austen. She did not need the common
materials for a novel, strong emotions, or strong incidents.†

It was not, however, quite impossible for a foreigner to appreciate these works; for Mons. Guizot writes thus: 'I am a great
novel reader, but I seldom read German or French novels. The
characters are too artificial. My delight is to read English novels,
particularly those written by women. "C'est toute une école de
morale." Miss Austen, Miss Ferrier, &c., form a school which in
the excellence and profusion of its productions resembles the
cloud of dramatic poets of the great Athenian age.'

In the 'Keepsake' of 1825 [39] the following lines appeared,
written by Lord Morpeth, afterwards seventh Earl of Carlisle,
and Lord-Lieutenant of Ireland, accompanying an illustration of a
lady reading a novel.

> Beats thy quick pulse o'er Inchbald's thrilling leaf,
> Brunton's high moral, Opie's deep wrought grief?
> Has the mild chaperon claimed thy yielding heart,
> Carroll's dark page, Trevelyan's gentle art?
> Or is it thou, all perfect Austen? Here
> Let one poor wreath adorn thy early bier,
> That scarce allowed thy modest youth to claim
> Its living portion of thy certain fame!
> Oh! Mrs Bennet! Mrs Norris too!
> While memory survives we'll dream of you.
> And Mr Woodhouse, whose abstemious lip
> Must thin, but not too thin, his gruel sip.

* Incidentally she had received high praise in Lord Macaulay's
Review of Madame D'Arblay's Works in the 'Edinburgh'.
† Life of Sir J. Mackintosh, vol. ii. p. 472.

Miss Bates, our idol, though the village bore;
And Mrs Elton, ardent to explore.
While the clear style flows on without pretence,
With unstained purity, and unmatched sense:
Or, if a sister e'er approached the throne,
She called the rich 'inheritance' her own.

The admiration felt by Lord Macaulay would probably have taken a very practical form, if his life had been prolonged. I have the authority of his sister, Lady Trevelyan, for stating that he had intended to undertake the task upon which I have ventured. He purposed to write a memoir of Miss Austen, with criticisms on her works, to prefix it to a new edition of her novels, and from the proceeds of the sale to erect a monument to her memory in Winchester Cathedral. Oh! that such an idea had been realised! That portion of the plan in which Lord Macaulay's success would have been most certain might have been almost sufficient for his object. A memoir written by him would have been a monument.

I am kindly permitted by Sir Henry Holland to give the following quotation from his printed but unpublished recollections of his past life: –

'I have the picture still before me of Lord Holland lying on his bed, when attacked with gout, his admirable sister, Miss Fox, beside him reading aloud, as she always did on these occasions, some one of Miss Austen's novels, of which he was never wearied. I well recollect the time when these charming novels, almost unique in their style of humour, burst suddenly on the world. It was sad that their writer did not live to witness the growth of her fame.'

My brother-in-law, Sir Denis Le Marchant, has supplied me with the following anecdotes from his own recollections: –

'When I was a student at Trinity College, Cambridge, Mr Whewell, then a Fellow and afterwards Master of the College, often spoke to me with admiration of Miss Austen's novels. On one occasion I said that I had found "Persuasion" rather dull. He quite fired up in defence of it, insisting that it was the most beautiful of her works. This accomplished philosopher was deeply versed in works of fiction. I recollect his writing to me from Caernarvon, where he had the charge of some pupils, that he was weary of *his* stay, for he had read the circulating library twice through.

'During a visit I paid to Lord Lansdowne, at Bowood, in 1846, one of Miss Austen's novels became the subject of conversation and of praise, especially from Lord Lansdowne, who observed that one of the circumstances of his life which he looked back upon with vexation was that Miss Austen should once have been living some weeks in his neighbourhood without his knowing it.

'I have heard Sydney Smith, more than once, dwell with eloquence on the merits of Miss Austen's novels. He told me he should have enjoyed giving her the pleasure of reading her praises in the "Edinburgh Review." "Fanny Price" was one of his prime favourites.'

I close this list of testimonies, this long 'Catena Patrum,' with the remarkable words of Sir Walter Scott, taken from his diary for March 14, 1826 : * 'Read again, for the third time at least, Miss Austen's finely written novel of "Pride and Prejudice." The young lady had a talent for describing the involvements and feelings and characters of ordinary life, which is to me the most wonderful I ever met with. The big Bow-Wow strain I can do myself like any now going; but the exquisite touch which renders ordinary common-place things and characters interesting from the truth of the description and the sentiment is denied to me. What a pity such a gifted creature died so early !' The well-worn condition of Scott's own copy of these works attests that they were much read in his family. When I visited Abbotsford, a few years after Scott's death, I was permitted, as an unusual favour, to take one of these volumes in my hands. One cannot suppress the wish that she had lived to know what such men thought of her powers, and how gladly they would have cultivated a personal acquaintance with her. I do not think that it would at all have impaired the modest simplicity of her character; or that we should have lost our own dear 'Aunt Jane' in the blaze of literary fame.

It may be amusing to contrast with these testimonies from the great, the opinions expressed by other readers of more ordinary

---

* Lockhart's *Life of Scott*, vol. vi. chap. vii.

intellect. The author herself has left a list of criticisms which it had been her amusement to collect, through means of her friends. This list contains much of warm-hearted sympathising praise, interspersed with some opinions which may be considered surprising.

One lady could say nothing better of 'Mansfield Park,' than that it was 'a mere novel.'

Another owned that she thought 'Sense and Sensibility' and 'Pride and Prejudice' downright nonsense; but expected to like 'Mansfield Park' better, and having finished the first volume, hoped that she had got through the worst.

Another did not like 'Mansfield Park.' Nothing interesting in the characters. Language poor.

One gentleman read the first and last chapters of 'Emma,' but did not look at the rest because he had been told that it was not interesting.

The opinions of another gentleman about 'Emma' were so bad that they could not be reported to the author.

'Quot homines, tot sententiæ.'

Thirty-five years after her death there came also a voice of praise from across the Atlantic. In 1852 the following letter was received by her brother Sir Francis Austen: –

'*Boston, Massachusetts, U.S.A. 6th Jan. 1852.*

'Since high critical authority has pronounced the delineations of character in the works of Jane Austen second only to those of Shakspeare, transatlantic admiration appears superfluous; yet it may not be uninteresting to her family to receive an assurance that the influence of her genius is extensively recognised in the American Republic, even by the highest judicial authorities. The late Mr Chief Justice Marshall, of the supreme Court of the United States, and his associate Mr Justice Story, highly estimated and admired Miss Austen, and to them we owe our introduction to her society. For many years her talents have brightened our daily path, and her name and those of her characters are familiar to us as "household words." We have long wished to express to some of her family the sentiments of gratitude and affection she has inspired, and request more information relative to her life than is given in the brief memoir prefixed to her works.

'Having accidentally heard that a brother of Jane Austen held a high rank in the British Navy, we have obtained his address from our friend Admiral Wormley, now resident in Boston, and we trust this expression of our feelings will be received by her relations with the kindness and urbanity characteristic of Admirals of *her creation*. Sir Francis Austen, or one of his family, would confer a great favour by complying with our request. The autograph of his sister, or a few lines in her handwriting, would be placed among our chief treasures.

'The family who delight in the companionship of Jane Austen, and who present this petition, are of English origin. Their ancestor held a high rank among the first emigrants to New England, and his name and character have been ably represented by his descendants in various public stations of trust and responsibility to the present time in the colony and state of Massachusetts. A letter addressed to Miss Quincey, care of the Honble Josiah Quincey, Boston, Massachusetts, would reach its destination.'

Sir Francis Austen returned a suitable reply to this application; and sent a long letter of his sister's which, no doubt, still occupies the place of honour promised by the Quincey family.

CHAPTER 10

Observations on the Novels.

It is not the object of these memoirs to attempt a criticism on Jane Austen's novels. Those particulars only have been noticed which could be illustrated by the circumstances of her own life; but I now desire to offer a few observations on them, and especially on one point, on which my age renders me a competent witness – the fidelity with which they represent the opinions and manners of the class of society in which the author lived early in this century. They do this the more faithfully on account of the very deficiency with which they have been sometimes charged – namely, that they make no attempt to raise the standard of human life, but merely represent it as it was. They certainly were not written to support any theory or inculcate any particular moral, except indeed the great moral which is to be equally gathered from an observation of the course of actual life – namely, the superiority of high over low principles, and of greatness over littleness of mind. These writings are like photographs, in which no feature is softened; no ideal expression is introduced, all is the unadorned reflection of the natural object; and the value of such a faithful likeness must increase as time gradually works more and more changes in the face of society itself. A remarkable instance of this is to be found in her portraiture of the clergy. She was the daughter and the sister of clergymen, who certainly were not low specimens of their order: and she has chosen three of her heroes from that profession; but no one in these days can think that either Edmund Bertram or Henry Tilney had adequate ideas of the duties of a parish minister. Such, however, were the opinions and practice then prevalent among respectable and conscientious clergymen before their minds had been stirred, first by the Evangelical, and afterwards by the High Church movement which this century has witnessed. The country may be congratulated which, on looking back to such a fixed landmark, can find that it has been advancing instead of receding from it.

The long interval that elapsed between the completion of 'Northanger Abbey' in 1798,[40] and the commencement of 'Mansfield Park' in 1811, may sufficiently account for any difference of style which may be perceived between her three earlier and her three later productions. If the former showed quite as much originality and genius, they may perhaps be thought to have less of the faultless finish and high polish which distinguish the latter. The characters of the John Dashwoods, Mr Collins, and the Thorpes stand out from the canvas with a vigour and originality which cannot be surpassed; but I think that in her last three works are to be found a greater refinement of taste, a more nice sense of propriety, and a deeper insight into the delicate anatomy of the human heart, marking the difference between the brilliant girl and the mature woman. Far from being one of those who have over-written themselves, it may be affirmed that her fame would have stood on a narrower and less firm basis, if she had not lived to resume her pen at Chawton.

Some persons have surmised that she took her characters from individuals with whom she had been acquainted. They were so life-like that it was assumed that they must once have lived, and have been transferred bodily, as it were, into her pages. But surely such a supposition betrays an ignorance of the high prerogative of genius to create out of its own resources imaginary characters, who shall be true to nature and consistent in themselves. Perhaps, however, the distinction between keeping true to nature and servilely copying any one specimen of it is not always clearly apprehended. It is indeed true, both of the writer and of the painter, that he can use only such lineaments as exist, and as he has observed to exist, in living objects; otherwise he would produce monsters instead of human beings; but in both it is the office of high art to mould these features into new combinations, and to place them in the attitudes, and impart to them the expressions which may suit the purposes of the artist; so that they are nature, but not exactly the same nature which had come before his eyes; just as honey can be obtained only from the natural flowers which the bee has sucked; yet it is not a reproduction of the odour or flavour of any particular flower, but becomes something different when it has gone through the process of transformation which that little insect is able to effect. Hence, in the case of painters, arises the superiority of original compositions over portrait painting. Reynolds was exercising a higher faculty when he designed Comedy and Tragedy contending for Garrick, than when he merely took a likeness of that actor. The same difference exists in writings between the original conceptions of Shakspeare and some other creative geniuses, and such full-length likenesses of individual persons, 'The Talking Gentleman' for instance, as are admirably drawn by Miss Mitford. Jane Austen's powers, whatever may be the degree in which she possessed them, were certainly of that higher order. She did not copy individuals, but she invested her own creations with individuality of character. A reviewer in the 'Quarterly' speaks of an acquaintance who, ever since the publication of 'Pride and Prejudice,' had been called by his friends Mr Bennet, but the author did not know him. Her own relations never recognised any individual in her characters; and I can call to mind several of her acquaintance whose peculiarities were very tempting and easy to be caricatured of whom there are no traces in her pages. She herself, when questioned on the subject by a friend, expressed a dread of what she called such an 'invasion of social proprieties.' She said that she thought it quite fair to note peculiarities and weaknesses, but that it was her desire to create, not to reproduce; 'besides,' she added, 'I am too proud of my gentlemen to admit that they were only Mr A. or Colonel B.' She did not, however, suppose that her imaginary characters were of a higher order than are to be found in nature; for she said, when speaking of two of her great favourites, Edmund Bertram and Mr Knightley : 'They are very far from being what I know English gentlemen often are.'

She certainly took a kind of parental interest in the beings whom she had created, and did not dismiss them from her thoughts when she had finished her last chapter. We have seen, in one of her letters, her personal affection for Darcy and Elizabeth; and when sending a copy of 'Emma' to a friend whose daughter had been lately born, she wrote thus : 'I trust you will be as glad to see my "Emma," as I shall be to see your Jemima.' She was very fond of Emma, but did not reckon on her being a general favourite; for, when commencing that work, she said, 'I am going to take a heroine whom no one but myself will much like.' She would, if asked, tell us many little particulars about the subsequent career of some of her people. In this traditionary way we learned that Miss Steele never succeeded in catching the Doctor; that Kitty Bennet was satisfactorily married to a clergyman near Pemberley, while Mary obtained nothing higher than one of her uncle Philips' clerks, and was content to be considered a star in the society of Meriton; that the 'considerable sum' given by Mrs Norris to William Price was one pound; that Mr Woodhouse survived his daughter's marriage, and kept her and Mr Knightley from settling at Donwell, about two years; and that the letters placed by Frank Churchill before Jane Fairfax, which she swept away unread, contained the word 'pardon.' Of the good people in 'Northanger Abbey' and 'Persuasion' we know nothing more than what is written: for before those works were published their author had been taken away from us, and all such amusing communications had ceased for ever.

CHAPTER 11

Declining health of Jane Austen – Elasticity of her spirits – Her resignation and humility – Her death.

EARLY in the year 1816 some family troubles[41] disturbed the usually tranquil course of Jane Austen's life; and it is probable that the inward malady, which was to prove ultimately fatal, was already felt by her; for some distant friends,* whom she visited in the spring of that year, thought that her health was somewhat impaired, and observed that she went about her old haunts, and recalled old recollections connected with them in a particular manner, as if she did not expect ever to see them again. It is not surprising that, under these circumstances, some of her letters were of a graver tone than had been customary with her, and expressed resignation rather than cheerfulness. In reference to these troubles in a letter to her brother Charles, after mentioning that she had been laid up with an attack of bilious fever, she says: 'I live up stairs for the present and am coddled. I am the only one of the party who has been so silly, but a weak body must excuse weak nerves.' And again, to another correspondent: 'But I am getting too near complaint; it has been the appointment of God, however secondary causes may have operated.' But the elasticity of her spirits soon recovered their tone. It was in the latter half of that year that she addressed the following lively letters to a nephew,[42] one while he was at Winchester School, the other soon after he had left it : –

'Chawton, July 9, 1816.

'My Dear E. – Many thanks. A thank for every line, and as many to Mr W. Digweed for coming. We have been wanting very much to hear of your mother, and are happy to find she continues to mend, but her illness must have been a very serious one indeed. When she is really recovered, she ought to try change of air, and

---

* The Fowles, of Kintbury, in Berkshire.

come over to us. Tell your father that I am very much obliged to
him for his share of your letter, and most sincerely join in the
hope of her being eventually much the better for her present discipline. She has the comfort moreover of being confined in such
weather as gives one little temptation to be out. It is really too
bad, and has been too bad for a long time, much worse than any
one *can* bear, and I begin to think it will never be fine again. This
is a *finesse* of mine, for I have often observed that if one writes
about the weather, it is generally completely changed before the
letter is read. I wish it may prove so now, and that when Mr W.
Digweed reaches Steventon to-morrow, he may find you have
had a long series of hot dry weather. We are a small party at
present, only grandmamma, Mary Jane, and myself. Yalden's
coach cleared off the rest yesterday. I am glad you recollected to
mention your being come home.* My heart began to sink within
me when I had got so far through your letter without its being
mentioned. I was dreadfully afraid that you might be detained at
Winchester by severe illness, confined to your bed perhaps, and
quite unable to hold a pen, and only dating from Steventon in
order, with a mistaken sort of tenderness, to deceive me. But now
I have no doubt of your being at home. I am sure you would not
say it so seriously unless it actually were so. We saw a countless
number of post-chaises full of boys pass by yesterday morning †
– full of future heroes, legislators, fools, and villains. You have
never thanked me for my last letter, which went by the cheese. I
cannot bear not to be thanked. You will not pay us a visit yet of
course; we must not think of it. Your mother must get well first,
and you must go to Oxford and *not* be elected; after that a little
change of scene may be good for you, and your physicians I hope
will order you to the sea, or to a house by the side of a very considerable pond.‡ Oh! it rains again. It beats against the window.

* It seems that her young correspondent, after dating from his
home, had been so superfluous as to state in his letter that he was
returned home, and thus to have drawn on himself this banter.

† The road by which many Winchester boys returned home ran
close to Chawton Cottage.

‡ There was, though it exists no longer, a pond close to Chawton
Cottage, at the junction of the Winchester and Gosport roads.

Mary Jane and I have been wet through once already to-day; we set off in the donkey-carriage for Farringdon, as I wanted to see the improvement Mr Woolls is making, but we were obliged to turn back before we got there, but not soon enough to avoid a pelter all the way home. We met Mr Woolls. I talked of its being bad weather for the hay, and he returned me the comfort of its being much worse for the wheat. We hear that Mrs S. does not quit Tangier: why and wherefore? Do you know that our Browning is gone? You must prepare for a William when you come, a good-looking lad, civil and quiet, and seeming likely to do. Good bye. I am sure Mr W. D.* will be astonished at my writing so much, for the paper is so thin that he will be able to count the lines if not to read them.

'Yours affec^{ly},

'Jane Austen.'

In the next letter will be found her description of her own style of composition, which has already appeared in the notice prefixed to 'Northanger Abbey' and 'Persuasion': –

'Chawton, Monday, Dec. 16th (1816).

'My Dear E., – One reason for my writing to you now is, that I may have the pleasure of directing to you Esqre. I give you joy of having left Winchester. Now you may own how miserable you were there; now it will gradually all come out, your crimes and your miseries – how often you went up by the Mail to London and threw away fifty guineas at a tavern, and how often you were on the point of hanging yourself, restrained only, as some ill-natured aspersion upon poor old Winton has it, by the want of a tree within some miles of the city. Charles Knight and his companions passed through Chawton about 9 this morning; later than it used to be. Uncle Henry and I had a glimpse of his handsome face, looking all health and good humour. I wonder when you will come and see us. I know what I rather speculate upon,

---

* Mr Digweed, who conveyed the letters to and from Chawton, was the gentleman named in page 287, as renting the old manor-house and the large farm at Steventon.

but shall say nothing. We think uncle Henry in excellent looks. Look at him this moment, and think so too, if you have not done it before; and we have the great comfort of seeing decided improvement in uncle Charles, both as to health, spirits, and appearance. And they are each of them so agreeable in their different way, and harmonise so well, that their visit is thorough enjoyment. Uncle Henry writes very superior sermons. You and I must try to get hold of one or two, and put them into our novels: it would be a fine help to a volume; and we could make our heroine read it aloud on a Sunday evening, just as well as Isabella Wardour, in the "Antiquary," is made to read the "History of the Hartz Demon" in the ruins of St Ruth, though I believe, on recollection, Lovell is the reader. By the bye, my dear E., I am quite concerned for the loss your mother mentions in her letter. Two chapters and a half to be missing is monstrous! It is well that I have not been at Steventon lately, and therefore cannot be suspected of purloining them: two strong twigs and a half towards a nest of my own would have been something. I do not think, however, that any theft of that sort would be really very useful to me. What should I do with your strong, manly, vigorous sketches, full of variety and glow? How could I possibly join them on to the little bit (two inches wide) of ivory on which I work with so fine a brush, as produces little effect after much labour?

'You will hear from uncle Henry how well Anna is. She seems perfectly recovered. Ben was here on Saturday, to ask uncle Charles and me to dine with them, as to-morrow, but I was forced to decline it, the walk is beyond my strength (though I am otherwise very well), and this is not a season for donkey-carriages; and as we do not like to spare uncle Charles, he has declined it too. *Tuesday.* Ah, ah! Mr E. I doubt your seeing uncle Henry at Steventon to-day. The weather will prevent your expecting him, I think. Tell your father, with aunt Cass's love and mine, that the pickled cucumbers are extremely good, and tell him also – "tell him what you will." No, don't tell him what you will, but tell him that grandmamma begs him to make Joseph Hall pay his rent, if he can.

'You must not be tired of reading the word *uncle*, for I have not done with it. Uncle Charles thanks your mother for her letter; it was a great pleasure to him to know that the parcel was received and gave so much satisfaction, and he begs her to be so good as to give three shillings for him to Dame Staples, which shall be allowed for in the payment of her debt here.

'Adieu, Amiable! I hope Caroline behaves well to you.

'Yours affec^{ly},

'J. Austen.'

I cannot tell how soon she was aware of the serious nature of her malady. By God's mercy it was not attended with much suffering; so that she was able to tell her friends as in the foregoing letter, and perhaps sometimes to persuade herself that, excepting want of strength, she was 'otherwise very well;' but the progress of the disease became more and more manifest as the year advanced. The usual walk was at first shortened, and then discontinued; and air was sought in a donkey-carriage. Gradually, too, her habits of activity within the house ceased, and she was obliged to lie down much. The sitting-room contained only one sofa, which was frequently occupied by her mother, who was more than seventy years old. Jane would never use it, even in her mother's absence; but she contrived a sort of couch for herself with two or three chairs, and was pleased to say that this arrangement was more comfortable to her than a real sofa. Her reasons for this might have been left to be guessed, but for the importunities of a little niece, which obliged her to explain that if she herself had shown any inclination to use the sofa, her mother might have scrupled being on it so much as was good for her.

It is certain, however, that the mind did not share in this decay of the bodily strength. 'Persuasion' was not finished before the middle of August in that year; and the manner in which it was then completed affords proof that neither the critical nor the creative powers of the author were at all impaired. The book had been brought to an end in July; and the re-engagement of the hero and heroine effected in a totally different manner in a scene laid at Admiral Croft's lodgings. But her performance did not satisfy her. She thought it tame and flat, and was desirous of producing something better. This weighed upon her mind, the more so probably on account of the weak state of her health; so that one night she retired to rest in very low spirits. But such depression was little in accordance with her nature, and was soon shaken off. The next morning she awoke to more cheerful views and brighter inspirations: the sense of power revived; and imagination resumed its course. She cancelled the condemned chapter, and wrote two others, entirely different, in its stead. The result is that we possess the visit of the Musgrove party to Bath; the crowded and animated scenes at the White Hart Hotel; and the charming conversation between Capt. Harville and Anne Elliot, overheard by Capt. Wentworth, by which the two faithful lovers were at last led to understand each other's feelings. The tenth and eleventh chapters of 'Persuasion' then, rather than the actual winding-up of the story, contain the latest of her printed compositions, her last contribution to the entertainment of the public. Perhaps it may be thought that she has seldom written anything more brilliant; and that, independent of the original manner in which the *dénouement* is brought about, the pictures of Charles Musgrove's goodnatured boyishness and of his wife's jealous selfishness would have been incomplete without these finishing strokes. The cancelled chapter exists in manuscript. It is certainly inferior to the two which were substituted for it: but it was such as some writers and some readers might have been contented with; and it contained touches which scarcely any other hand could have given, the suppression of which may be almost a matter of regret.*

The following letter was addressed to her friend Miss Bigg, then staying at Streatham with her sister, the wife of the Reverend Herbert Hill, uncle of Robert Southey. It appears to have been written three days before she began her last work, which will be noticed in another chapter; and shows that she was not at that time aware of the serious nature of her malady: —

'Chawton, January 24, 1817.

'My dear Alethea, — I think it is time there should be a little writing between us, though I believe the epistolary debt is on

---

* This cancelled chapter is now printed, in compliance with the requests addressed to me from several quarters.

your side, and I hope this will find all the Streatham party well, neither carried away by the flood, nor rheumatic through the damps. Such mild weather is, you know, delightful to *us*, and though we have a great many ponds, and a fine running stream through the meadows on the other side of the road, it is nothing but what beautifies us and does to talk of. *I* have certainly gained strength through the winter and am not far from being well; and I think I understand my own case now so much better than I did, as to be able by care to keep off any serious return of illness. I am convinced that *bile* is at the bottom of all I have suffered, which makes it easy to know how to treat myself. You will be glad to hear thus much of me, I am sure. We have just had a few days' visit from Edward, who brought us a good account of his father, and the very circumstance of his coming at all, of his father's being able to spare him, is itself a good account. He grows still, and still improves in appearance, at least in the estimation of his aunts, who love him better and better, as they see the sweet temper and warm affections of the boy confirmed in the young man : I tried hard to persuade him that he must have some message for William,* but in vain. . . . This is not a time of year for donkey-carriages, and our donkeys are necessarily having so long a run of luxurious idleness that I suppose we shall find they have forgotten much of their education when we use them again. We do not use two at once however; don't imagine such excesses . . . Our own new clergyman †￼ is expected here very soon, perhaps in time to assist Mr Papillon on Sunday. I shall be very glad when the first hearing is over. It will be a nervous hour for our pew, though we hear that he acquits himself with as much ease and collectedness, as if he had been used to it all his life. We have no chance we know of seeing you between Streatham and Winchester : you go the other road and are engaged to two or three houses; if there should be any change, however, you know how welcome you would be. . . . We have been reading the "Poet's Pilgrimage to Waterloo," and generally with much approbation. Nothing will please all the

---

* Miss Bigg's nephew, the present Sir William Heathcote, of Hursley.

† Her brother Henry, who had been ordained late in life.

world, you know; but parts of it suit me better than much that he has written before. The opening – *the proem* I believe he calls it – is very beautiful. Poor man! one cannot but grieve for the loss of the son so fondly described. Has he at all recovered it? What do Mr and Mrs Hill know about his present state?

'Yours aff^ly,

'J. Austen.

'The real object of this letter is to ask you for a receipt, but I thought it genteel not to let it appear early. We remember some excellent orange wine at Manydown, made from Seville oranges, entirely or chiefly. I should be very much obliged to you for the receipt, if you can command it within a few weeks.'

On the day before, January 23rd, she had written to her niece in the same hopeful tone: 'I feel myself getting stronger than I was, and can so perfectly walk to Alton, or back again without fatigue, that I hope to be able to do *both* when summer comes.'

Alas! summer came to her only on her deathbed. March 17th is the last date to be found in the manuscript on which she was engaged; and as the watch of the drowned man indicates the time of his death, so does this final date seem to fix the period when her mind could no longer pursue its accustomed course.

And here I cannot do better than quote the words of the niece to whose private records of her aunt's life and character I have been so often indebted:—

'I do not know how early the alarming symptoms of her malady came on. It was in the following March that I had the first idea of her being seriously ill. It had been settled that about the end of that month, or the beginning of April, I should spend a few days at Chawton, in the absence of my father and mother, who were just then engaged with Mrs Leigh Perrot in arranging her late husband's affairs; but Aunt Jane became too ill to have me in the house, and so I went instead to my sister Mrs Lefroy at Wyards'. The next day we walked over to Chawton to make enquiries after our aunt. She was then keeping her room, but said she would see us, and we went up to her. She was in her dressing gown, and was sitting quite like an invalid in an arm-chair, but she got up and kindly greeted us, and then, pointing to seats which had been arranged for us by the fire, she said, "There is a chair for the married lady, and a little stool for you, Caroline." * It is strange, but those trifling words were the last of hers that I can remember, for I retain no recollection of what was said by anyone in the conversation that ensued. I was struck by the alteration in herself. She was very pale, her voice was weak and low, and there was about her a general appearance of debility and suffering; but I have been told that she never had much acute pain. She was not equal to the exertion of talking to us, and our visit to the sick room was a very short one, Aunt Cassandra soon taking us away. I do not suppose we stayed a quarter of an hour; and I never saw Aunt Jane again.'

In May 1817 she was persuaded to remove to Winchester, for the sake of medical advice from Mr Lyford. The Lyfords have, for some generations, maintained a high character in Winchester for medical skill, and the Mr Lyford of that day was a man of more than provincial reputation, in whom great London practitioners expressed confidence. Mr Lyford spoke encouragingly. It was not, of course, his business to extinguish hope in his patient, but I believe that he had, from the first, very little expectation of a permanent cure. All that was gained by the removal from home was the satisfaction of having done the best that could be done, together with such alleviations of suffering as superior medical skill could afford.

Jane and her sister Cassandra took lodgings in College Street. They had two kind friends living in the Close, Mrs Heathcote and Miss Bigg, the mother and aunt of the present Sir Wm Heathcote of Hursley, between whose family and ours a close friendship has existed for several generations. These friends did all that they could to promote the comfort of the sisters, during that sad sojourn in Winchester, both by their society, and by supplying those little conveniences in which a lodging-house was likely to be deficient. It was shortly after settling in these lodgings that she wrote to a nephew the following characteristic letter, no longer, alas! in her former strong, clear hand.

---

* The writer was at that time under twelve years old.

'Mrs David's, College St., Winton,
Tuesday, May 27th.

'There is no better way, my dearest E., of thanking you for your affectionate concern for me during my illness than by telling you myself, as soon as possible, that I continue to get better. I will not boast of my handwriting; neither that nor my face have yet recovered their proper beauty, but in other respects I gain strength very fast. I am now out of bed from 9 in the morning to 10 at night: upon the sofa, it is true, but I eat my meals with aunt Cassandra in a rational way, and can employ myself, and walk from one room to another. Mr Lyford says he will cure me, and if he fails, I shall draw up a memorial and lay it before the Dean and Chapter, and have no doubt of redress from that pious, learned, and disinterested body. Our lodgings are very comfortable. We have a neat little drawing-room with a bow window overlooking Dr Gabell's garden.* Thanks to the kindness of your father and mother in sending me their carriage, my journey hither on Saturday was performed with very little fatigue, and had it been a fine day, I think I should have felt none; but it distressed me to see uncle Henry and Wm Knight, who kindly attended us on horseback, riding in the rain almost the whole way. We expect a visit from them to-morrow, and hope they will stay the night; and on Thursday, which is a confirmation and a holiday, we are to get Charles out to breakfast. We have had but one visit from *him*, poor fellow, as he is in sick-room, but he hopes to be out to-night. We see Mrs Heathcote every day, and William is to call upon us soon. God bless you, my dear E. If ever you are ill, may you be as tenderly nursed as I have been. May the same blessed alleviations of anxious, sympathising friends be yours: and may you possess, as I dare say you will, the greatest blessing of all in the consciousness of not being unworthy of their love. I could not feel this.

'Your very affecte Aunt,
'J. A.'

The following extract from a letter which has been before printed,

---

* It was the corner house in College Street, at the entrance to Commoners.

written soon after the former, breathes the same spirit of humility and thankfulness :—

'I will only say further that my dearest sister, my tender, watchful, indefatigable nurse, has not been made ill by her exertions. As to what I owe her, and the anxious affection of all my beloved family on this occasion, I can only cry over it, and pray God to bless them more and more.'

Throughout her illness she was nursed by her sister, often assisted by her sister-in-law, my mother. Both were with her when she died. Two of her brothers, who were clergymen, lived near enough to Winchester to be in frequent attendance, and to administer the services suitable for a Christian's death-bed. While she used the language of hope to her correspondents, she was fully aware of her danger, though not appalled by it. It is true that there was much to attach her to life. She was happy in her family; she was just beginning to feel confidence in her own success; and, no doubt, the exercise of her great talents was an enjoyment in itself. We may well believe that she would gladly have lived longer; but she was enabled without dismay or complaint to prepare for death. She was a humble, believing Christian. Her life had been passed in the performance of home duties, and the cultivation of domestic affections, without any self-seeking or craving after applause. She had always sought, as it were by instinct, to promote the happiness of all who came within her influence, and doubtless she had her reward in the peace of mind which was granted her in her last days. Her sweetness of temper never failed. She was ever considerate and grateful to those who attended on her. At times, when she felt rather better, her playfulness of spirit revived, and she amused them even in their sadness. Once, when she thought herself near her end, she said what she imagined might be her last words to those around her, and particularly thanked her sister-in-law for being with her, saying: 'You have always been a kind sister to me, Mary,' [43] When the end at last came, she sank rapidly, and on being asked by her attendants whether there was anything that she wanted, her reply was, 'Nothing but death.' These were her last words. In quietness and peace she breathed her last on the morning of July 18, 1817.

On the 24th of that month she was buried in Winchester Cathedral, near the centre of the north aisle, almost opposite to the beautiful chantry tomb of William of Wykeham. A large slab of black marble in the pavement marks the place. Her own family only attended the funeral. Her sister returned to her desolated home, there to devote herself, for ten years, to the care of her aged mother; and to live much on the memory of her lost sister, till called many years later to rejoin her. Her brothers went back sorrowing to their several homes. They were very fond and very proud of her. They were attached to her by her talents, her virtues, and her engaging manners; and each loved afterwards to fancy a resemblance in some niece or daughter of his own to the dear sister Jane, whose perfect equal they yet never expected to see.

CHAPTER 12

Postscript

WHEN first I was asked to put together a memoir of my aunt, I saw reasons for declining the attempt. It was not only that, having passed the three score years and ten usually allotted to man's strength, and being unaccustomed to write for publication, I might well distrust my ability to complete the work, but that I also knew the extreme scantiness of the materials out of which it must be constructed. The grave closed over my aunt fifty-two years ago; and during that long period no idea of writing her life had been entertained by any of her family. Her nearest relatives, far from making provision for such a purpose, had actually destroyed many of the letters and papers by which it might have been facilitated. They were influenced, I believe, partly by an extreme dislike to publishing private details, and partly by never having assumed that the world would take so strong and abiding an interest in her works as to claim her name as public property. It was therefore necessary for me to draw upon recollections rather than on written documents for my materials; while the subject itself supplied me with nothing striking or prominent with which to arrest the attention of the reader. It has been said that the happiest individuals, like nations during their happiest periods, have no history. In the case of my aunt, it was not only that her course of life was unvaried, but that her own disposition was remarkably calm and even. There was in her nothing eccentric or angular; no ruggedness of temper; no singularity of manner; none of the morbid sensibility or exaggeration of feeling, which not unfrequently accompanies great talents, to be worked up into a picture. Hers was a mind well balanced on a basis of good sense, sweetened by an affectionate heart, and regulated by fixed principles; so that she was to be distinguished from many other amiable and sensible women only by that peculiar genius which shines out clearly enough in her works, but of which a biographer can make little use. The motive which at last induced me to make the attempt is exactly expressed in the passage prefixed to these pages. I thought that I saw something to be done: knew of no one who could do it but myself, and so was driven to the enterprise. I am glad that I have been able to finish my work. As a family record it can scarcely fail to be interesting to those relatives who must ever set a high value on their connection with Jane Austen, and to them I especially dedicate it; but as I have been asked to do so, I also submit it to the censure of the public, with all its faults both of deficiency and redundancy. I know that its value in their eyes must depend, not on any merits of its own, but on the degree of estimation in which my aunt's works may still be held; and indeed I shall esteem it one of the strongest testimonies ever borne to her talents, if for her sake an interest can be taken in so poor a sketch as I have been able to draw.

Bray Vicarage: Sept. 7, 1869.

[*The following note appeared at the end of the first edition but was omitted from the second.*]

Since these pages were in type, I have read with astonishment the strange misrepresentation of my aunt's manners given by Miss Mitford in a letter which appears in her lately-published Life, vol. i. p. 305. Miss Mitford does not profess to have known Jane Austen herself, but to report what had been told her by her mother. Having stated that her mother '*before her marriage*' was well acquainted with Jane Austen and her family, she writes a thus :— 'Mamma says that she was *then* the prettiest, silliest, most affected, husband-hunting butterfly she ever remembers.' The editor of Miss Mitford's Life very properly observes in a note how different this description is from 'every other account of Jane Austen from whatever quarter.' Certainly it is so totally at variance with the modest simplicity of character which I have attributed to my aunt, that if it could be supposed to have a semblance of truth, it must be equally injurious to her memory and to my trustworthiness as her biographer. Fortunately I am not driven to put my authority in competition with that of Miss Mitford, nor to ask which ought to be considered the better witness in this case; because I am able to prove by a reference to dates that Miss Mitford must have been under a mistake, and that her mother could not possibly have known what she was supposed to have reported; inasmuch as Jane Austen, at the time referred to, was a little girl.

Mrs Mitford was the daughter of Dr Russell, Rector of Ashe, a parish adjoining Steventon, so that the families of Austen and Russell must at that time have been known to each other. But the date assigned by Miss Mitford for the termination of the acquaintance is the time of her mother's marriage. This took place in October 1785, when Jane, who had been born in December 1775, was not quite ten years old. In point of fact, however, Miss Russell's opportunities of observing Jane Austen must have come to an end still earlier: for upon Dr Russell's death, in January 1783, his widow and daughter removed from the neighbourhood, so that all intercourse between the families ceased when Jane was little more than seven years old.

All persons who undertake to narrate from hearsay things which are supposed to have taken place before they were born are liable to error, and are apt to call in imagination to the aid of memory: and hence it arises that many a fancy piece has been substituted for genuine history.

I do not care to correct the inaccurate account of Jane Austen's manners in after life: because Miss Mitford candidly expresses a doubt whether she had not been misinformed on that point.

Nov. 17, 1869.

NOTES TO PERSUASION

The Text. Persuasion was published posthumously, with *Northanger Abbey*, in 1818, and the text has given rise to few difficulties beyond fairly obvious misprints which have been corrected by various commentators and editors. R. W. Chapman's edition (1923) brought together both these corrections and a few more speculative emendations, together with helpful notes; every subsequent edition must be indebted to it, though on one or two readings and interpretations I differ from him. I have omitted the catchwords from page to page and have numbered the chapters continuously instead of making a break after Volume I.

1. [p. 37] *daughters' sake*. 1st ed. has *daughter's* but Chapman's suggested change seems necessary if the next sentence is to tell.
2. [p. 51] *rear admiral of the white*. The navy was divided into three squadrons, the Red, the White and the Blue, in that order of seniority. (It was not until 1864 that these colours were given instead to broader divisions of the nation's seamen: the Merchant Service, the Royal Navy and the Royal Naval Reserve.) Within each squadron were the three ranks of Rear Admiral, Vice Admiral and Admiral; the flag officer's ladder of status therefore had nine rungs (with Admiral of the Fleet as a tenth), starting with Rear Admiral of the Blue and working up, by seniority, through the colours as well as the ranks. At the end of the Napoleonic wars there were seventy-six Rear Admirals. (Cf. Michael Lewis, *England's Sea-Officers: the Story of the Naval Profession*, London, 1939.)
3. [p. 51] *the deputation*. Originally the necessary commission by which the lord of the manor appointed a gamekeeper, the deputation became the means of giving others the privilege of shooting game in the manor.
4. [p. 58] *by successive captures*. Prize money provided rich rewards for officers and was an important recruiting incentive. P. K. Kemp (*Prize Money*, Aldershot, 1946) records that Captain William Parker, who went to sea at the age of eleven and was commanding the *Amazon* frigate at eighteen, kept a detailed journal of his prize money. When in 1812, at the age of thirty, he paid off the *Amazon*, he had made £40,000 in prize money. Every member of the crew of

ships within signalling distance at the time of a capture received a share, as did the Admiral commanding the station, whether he was present or not. Early in the 1760s the *Hermione*, a Spanish ship captured by two British vessels, was condemned in the Prize Court for £519,705. 10s. The Commander-in-Chief of the Mediterranean received £64,963, his one-eighth share. Each captain received the same (and would have had twice the sum had he been alone), and the seamen and marines £485 each. When two Spanish frigates were captured in 1799 by four British frigates the share of each sailor was £182.8.9½d., and of each midshipman and petty officer £791.8.0½d.

5. [p. 78] *the school-master*. Although a schoolmaster (to teach writing, arithmetic and the study of navigation) was officially required in every ship he was seldom a capable man or given adequate backing by his commander. The passage implies Captain Wentworth's unusual concern for the proper theoretical training of his midshipmen.

6. [p. 109] *hedge-row*. For a description of the broad hedge-row referred to here, with a path down the middle, see A *Memoir of Jane Austen* by J. E. Austen-Leigh, Chapter 2.

7. [p. 123] *dispensation*. It has been estimated that over half the incumbents of English parishes in the eighteenth century were absentees.

8. [p. 135] *the feelings of Emma towards her Henry*. The reference is to Matthew Prior, *Henry and Emma*, in which Emma expresses abject willingness to serve the non-existent rival with whom her Henry pretends to be in love in order to test her.

9. [p. 158] *Gowland*. Gowland's lotion was evidently an established treatment by then, since Chapman quotes an advertisement in the Bath Chronicle of the period for 'Mrs Vincent's Gowland's lotion'.

10. [p. 180] *a three shilling piece*. From 1811 to 1816 the Bank of England issued one-and-sixpenny and three-shilling pieces. These were token coins of a lower silver content than the regal coins and relieved the shortage of silver caused by the wars. The three-shilling piece was slightly larger than the present half-crown.

11. [p. 184] *Molland's*. Chapman quotes the Bath Directory for 1812 as saying that Mrs Molland was 'Cook and confectioner' at 2 Milsom-street.

12. [p. 189] *pity and disdain*. Chapman's odd suggestion that this implies Anne's belief that Lady Russell had really seen Wentworth and was prevaricating seems baseless. The deliberately excessive phrase is a comment on the disproportionate significance that

NOTES

Anne, in love, has momentarily attached to the incident; it exemplifies the sympathetic irony with which Jane Austen can treat her heroine.

13. [p. 198] *Miss Larolles*. In Fanny Burney's *Cecilia*, Miss Larolles, who was the head of the Voluble sect in fashionable society, 'talking faster than she thinks', vainly tried to attract the attention of Mr Meadows, the languid head of the Insensiblists, by sitting on the outside of the benches: 'It's the shockingest thing you can conceive, to be made sit in the middle of those forms; one might as well be at home, for nobody can speak to one.'

14. [p. 243] *prepare it for all the immortality*. Chapman changes this to *prepare for it . . .*, accepting for the sake of its elegance a conjecture by A. C. Bradley. But this is more like Bradley's elegance than Jane Austen's. It would imply that the lovers were preparing for the future recall of the moment; and this would be too much deliberated. Jane Austen's phrase means that they spontaneously made it so perfect as to be worthy of the long remembrance which she knows it was destined to have.

15. [p. 248] *posted into the Laconia*. Chapman is mistaken in thinking this implies promotion to the rank of 'post-captain'. There was no such rank, though the term was commonly used of a Captain who commanded a vessel large enough to have a Master for navigation and a separate commissioned 'post' of Captain. (As a Commander, his rank when he first met Anne, Wentworth's full description would have been 'Master and commander'.) In rank he remained Captain. For a lucid account of these intricacies of of organization and title, in a navy which only gradually substituted the principle of 'rank' for that of 'post' (or office), see Michael Lewis, *op. cit.*

16. [p. 250] *as high in his profession as merit and activity could place him*. Further promotion depended upon seniority.

17. [p. 253] *his brothers and sisters*. This, as is usual in Jane Austen, includes the brother- and sister-in-law.

NOTES TO A MEMOIR OF
JANE AUSTEN

The Text. The text follows the second, enlarged edition (1871), with minor misprints corrected, but omits the cancelled chapter of *Persuasion* (here included with the novel), *Lady Susan*, and the unfinished novels *The Watsons* and *Sanditon* (the last of which Austen-Leigh partly paraphrased). Austen-Leigh was not as scrupulous as a modern editor would be about following exactly the text of the letters he quotes (and in one instance he fuses two letters) but I have not included notes of minor changes, nor of the identity of acquaintances mentioned in the letters. What is known of them can be found conveniently in Chapman's indispensable edition of the *Letters* (Oxford, 1959). The postscript that Austen-Leigh added to his first edition (1870) and omitted from the second, dealing with Mary Russell Mitford's curious account of Jane Austen, is included here because the story she started is one of those that the truth finds difficult to overtake.

1. [p. 277] *a son of the celebrated Warren Hastings.* This is questioned in the other main source of biographical information, *Life and Letters of Jane Austen* by William Austen-Leigh and Richard Arthur Austen-Leigh (London, 1913). Their only argument against it is that a three-year-old is a curious charge for a bachelor, but although George Austen would obviously have employed help in caring for him he might have taken responsibility for the boy (who was also named George). George Austen's only sister, Philadelphia, had married Tysoe Saul Hancock, a surgeon in India whom Hastings befriended. Hastings spoke of being under great obligation to Philadelphia and made generous financial provision for her and her daughter Elizabeth, to whom he was godfather. The association between Hastings and the Austen family continued; Jane's brother Henry wrote to congratulate Hastings on his acquittal in 1792.
2. [p. 280] *Her second brother, Edward.* Austen-Leigh thus conceals the existence of the actual second brother, George, who was in some way defective and is scarcely mentioned in surviving family letters, although according to Chapman he lived from 1766 to 1838.

3. [p. 280] *less success in life.* Austen-Leigh avoids mentioning that Henry was partner in a firm of London bankers, went bankrupt in 1816, and at once took Orders (as he had earlier contemplated) and settled down as a country clergyman for the rest of his life (dying in 1850). The authors of the *Life and Letters* say that he was Jane Austen's favourite brother.

4. [p. 284] *Madame D'Arblay.* Usually referred to by her maiden name of Fanny Burney.

5. [p. 285] *One who knew and loved it well.* Chapman gives reasons for guessing that this was Austen-Leigh's father, James Austen.

6. [p. 289] *volumes of Sermons.* Writing to Cassandra in 1816, Jane Austen says 'We do not much like Mr Cooper's new Sermons; – they are fuller of Regeneration & Conversion than ever –'.

7. [p. 289] *de Feuillade.* This should be de Feuillide, a French army officer who had an estate in Guyenne. They were married in 1781; their son, Hastings, was born in England in 1786 and died in 1801. The Comte de Feuillide was guillotined in 1794, having attempted to bribe an official to favour the Marquise de Marbœuf who was on trial. It was she who was accused of trying to produce famine by laying down arable land to animal feeding crops. Henry Austen married Eliza de Feuillide in 1797.

8. [p. 290] *Her reviewer.* Whately (cf. Chapter 8).

9. [p. 298] *iron ring.* Pattens were raised by an oval ring of iron under the wooden sole.

10. [p. 304] *a niece.* Caroline Austen, Austen-Leigh's sister.

11. [p. 312] *exceedingly unhappy.* The authors of the *Life and Letters* say that she fainted when she was told without warning that they were to leave Steventon, and that Cassandra's destruction of her sister's letters for the next two months 'was a proof of their emotional interest'.

12. [p. 313] *Marcau.* A misreading of Marcou, the islands of Saint-Marcouf off the French coast, then occupied by British forces.

13. [p. 315] *maple.* Jane Austen wrote Maypole, which makes more sense for a weathercock.

14. [p. 315] *Miss Lloyd.* Mrs Lloyd (whose mother Mrs Craven has been suggested as the 'original' of Lady Susan) was a widow who lived for a time with her two unmarried daughters in the parsonage at Deane, the living that Jane Austen's father held with Steventon. Mary Lloyd married James Austen as his second wife in 1797. Martha Lloyd made her home with Mrs Austen, Cassandra and Jane after Mr Austen's death and lived in the house they shared with Frank Austen and his first wife in Southampton. She then

moved with them to Chawton, and in 1828 married Frank Austen as his second wife.

15. [p. 320] *went into lodgings for a few months.* Actually for sixteen months.

16. [p. 325] *say himself what was untrue.* Bowdlerized from Jane Austen's 'tell a lie himself'.

17. [p. 326] *four years' residence.* In fact only from late 1806 to early 1809.

18. [p. 329] *has lost all that gave it its character.* It has now been restored as a memorial to Jane Austen and is open to the public.

19. [p. 331] *a sister novelist.* Fanny Burney.

20. [p. 332] *Miss Edgeworth's, E's, and my own.* The passage comes from a letter to Anna Austen, who was Austen-Leigh's half-sister and, like him, tried writing novels. Jane Austen actually wrote 'Miss Edgeworth's, Yours & my own. –' Austen-Leigh, who was called Edward, would hardly have altered it to flatter himself, but Anna may have thought it a tactful alteration in sending him a copy.

21. [p. 334] *your iis . . . my ees.* Jane Austen actually wrote 'your *eyes*' and '*my ease*'.

22. [p. 335] *a niece.* Anna Austen, who became Mrs B. Lefroy.

23. [p. 337] *spilikins.* Slips or rods of wood etc. were piled in a heap and the player had to pull them off with a hook one at a time without disturbing the rest.

24. [p. 337] *cup and ball.* The ball was attached to a stick having a cup at one end and a spike at the other; the ball was tossed in the air and caught either in the cup or on the spike.

25. [p. 337] *A specimen of her . . . handwriting.* Austen-Leigh included a facsimile of the verse on Mr Gell and Miss Gill.

26. [p. 341] *typical.* The word has now been ousted by 'typographical' but was then current in the same sense.

27. [p. 341] *I do not write . . .* Based on a couplet from *Marmion*, this is apparently the first of clerihews, spoilt by Austen-Leigh's setting out. Jane Austen wrote it in the familiar form:

> I do not write for such dull elves
>
> As have not a great deal of ingenuity themselves.

28. [p. 342] *the rejected addresses.* James and Horace Smith, *Rejected Addresses*, 1812.

29. [p. 343] *Society.* This was the Chawton Reading Society. In one of the two letters from which Austen-Leigh here combines extracts Jane Austen writes: 'The Miss Sibleys want to establish a Book Society in their side of the country, like ours. What can be a

stronger proof of that superiority in ours over the Steventon &
Manydown society . . .?'

30. [p. 343] *Military Police.* Though in the title it was Military Policy,
the O.E.D. shows that 'police' was current in the sense of administration, and notes that the earlier pronunciation commonly
put the accent on the first syllable.

31. [p. 343] *I must alter it.* In *Mansfield Park* which she was then
writing.

32. [p. 346] *the twopenny post.* This was the local London letter post
which existed from 1801 to 1839. In *Sense and Sensibility* Marianne
uses it to send her letter to Willoughby.

33. [p. 347] *found my bed comfortable last night.* The sentence in
fact went on 'and has not filled it with fleas.'

34. [p. 356] *tithes.* The value of abolishing tithes was part of the
theme proposed to her by J. S. Clarke in a letter not quoted here.
Austen-Leigh has not shown the full relation between the Plan and
Clarke's letters, which are even funnier than they appear in this
account (cf. Chapman's edition of the *Letters*).

35. [p. 359] *Reviewer.* The rather poor review was by Sir Walter
Scott.

36. [p. 359] *the late event.* Henry Austen's bankruptcy.

37. [p. 363] *in Bath.* Though the family were then in Bath the publisher was Crosby, of London.

38. [p. 363] *One of her brothers.* Henry, who helped her in all her
later dealings with publishers.

39. [p. 368] *of 1825.* Chapman notes that this should be 1835.

40. [p. 374] *in 1798.* According to Cassandra's memorandum this
should be 1799.

41. [p. 377] *some family troubles.* Henry's bankruptcy occurred in
March 1816, but the letters that Austen-Leigh goes on to quote date
from 1817 and refer to the disappointment the family felt at the
will of James Leigh Perrot, Mrs Austen's brother. Although he
made large bequests to members of the family, all were subject to
his widow's life interest. They were none of them well off, except
Edward, and had hoped for immediate benefit. Where Austen-Leigh
quotes her as saying 'I am the only one of the party who has been
so silly' she actually wrote 'I am the only one of the legatees
who . . .'

42. [p. 377] *a nephew.* Austen-Leigh, the author of the *Memoir*.

43. [p. 387] *Mary.* James's second wife, formerly Mary Lloyd.